DRY BONES

Richard Beard studied at Cambridge, the Open University, and the University of East Anglia. He is the author of three other highly-praised novels, *X20*, *Damascus*, and *The Cartoonist*.

Richard Beard

DRY BONES

VINTAGE

Contents

HVMANI COR-   PORIS OSSIVM
SIMVL COMPACTO-   RVM ANTERIORI
EX FACIE EXPRES-   SIO.

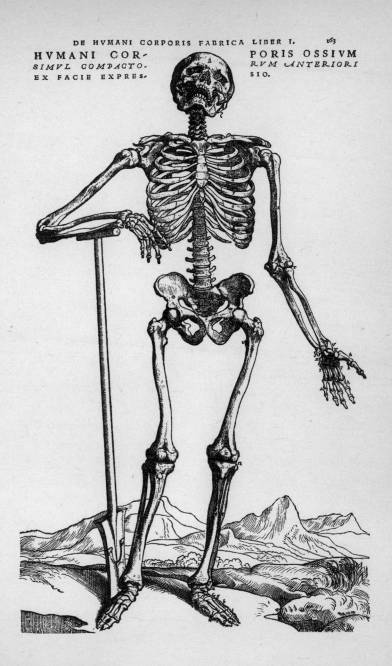

To Mum and Dad

Becket's Toe

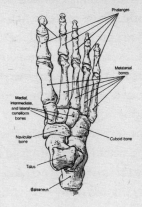

'Run away: you're a dead man.'

Reginald fitzUrse, murderer of Becket

Thomas à Becket's toe-bone did exactly what a holy relic was fabled to do. It made its own wishes clear. It didn't want to spend one moment longer on the restaurant terrace of the Hôtel Beau Rivage.

I stood up. In the middle of the Chaplain's farewell lunch, I left the table. And even though we had a four o'clock flight to Heathrow, I walked back through the streets of Geneva to the English Church of All Saints, a ring of keys in one hand, Thomas à Becket's toe-bone in the other.

At the church, a workman in blue overalls was up on the tower, checking a pulley, then fixing a rope to the cockerel weathervane. All Saints had a tower not a spire, in the Norman style, an English parish church which history had dropped into the middle of a busy street in the Swiss city of

Geneva. It was squeezed between banks and hotels, and glinting shops selling watches and clocks.

On the pavement outside the church, in the spring sunshine, the church furnishings looked out of their element, or from another world. Plain-ended bench-pews were stacked unevenly beside broad choir-stalls and the brass eagle lectern. In a patient queue, awaiting collection, folded altar-cloths and boxes of stained baptism pamphlets; hymnals ancient and modern; the slotted wooden hymn-rack, numbers still in place, white on black.

The pair of Swiss removal men were now in the church doorway, wondering what I wanted. I told them to stop what they were doing. Go home. They nodded, shuffling a little, but they didn't object or meet my eye: churches made everyone nervous.

Inside, I pulled the door shut into its arch of solid stone, and Geneva's traffic immediately damped to a more distant rumble of tractors on the brown ploughed fields of England. I locked the door from the inside, then turned to see the altar skewed half-way down the church, and the tiled aisle in black and white a pathway between two emptied halves. Dust rose from where the pews had once been, making rays to the coloured glass in the windows.

The font had gone, as had the ragged banners commemorating England's famous dead, at Inkermann and the Somme, at Waterloo. The crucifix had gone, and the sanctuary lamp, the chalice and flagons, all gavelled off by the auctioneers, leaving behind only the famous godspace. It was the sense of something absent, a god-shaped hole.

Apart from the altar, they'd left behind two bin-bags of unsold jumble, and a tight package of choir-robes back from the laundry. The organ was still there, and the wooden

2

canopy over the octagonal pulpit, but only because Joseph Moholy had reserved them both. He'd also reserved Becket's toe-bone.

Which was in my pocket, wrapped in a circular hand-kerchief of embroidered purple silk, very soft and agreeable to touch. I put it on the altar, unwrapping the silk and smoothing it into a circle. The toe-bone of Thomas à Becket, English saint and martyr, was small and pointed and delicate. It looked like a marker, or a counter for some intricate game.

I bent my head very close to it, closing my eyes, first my ear and then my nose almost touching it. I was smelling Becket's toe, my eyebrows arching, twitching. I coughed into my hand, then reset myself, and smelled again.

Hard to tell. I licked my index finger, and nakedly touched it. I rolled it over, and back again. And then I ran my finger against the grain, which made my own toes curl inside my shoes, scrunching back into my feet, feeling for the pulse of my own living blood and the stretch of my skin and the crack of my joints.

I shivered.

Of course I did. Since always, though most actively among Catholics and Buddhists, relics had been used as aids to meditation and prayer. Unfeigned concentration on a sacred relic allowed the true believer an insight into the character and virtue of that elected saint.

However small the relic, from whatever part of the body, the grace remained intact. A toe-bone amassed as much saintly residue as a skull, preserving on earth in a distinct object some essential remnant of blessedness, of a chosen soul.

Elbows on the altar, leaning forward, I concentrated hard on the stopper of Becket's toe.

3

Some believers were more susceptible than others. There were recorded instances of trance, and pilgrims knocked senseless by the proximity of a favourite saint. Through their stubborn human remains, godly spirits could be seen to intercede in this world now, a direct influence on everyday conduct.

At Canterbury, Becket's shrine had once been the most popular in all Europe: virtually as if Becket were there. He was the saint to whom pilgrims appealed in the crisis of their lives, his relics satisfying a common desire for self-improvement, and for change. His bones encouraged reflection and reassessment, and certain gifted pilgrims, those sincerest in their veneration, would begin to think and act like Becket the saint. That's how relics work.

If at all. The Reformation had insisted on a more earthly logic, and Protestants took against the idea, damming the transmigration of souls. John Calvin himself wrote an angry and definitive pamphlet, *An Admonition Concerning Relics*, and in 1538 Becket's four jewelled shrines at Canterbury were smashed in all honesty by the commissioners of Henry VIII. From now on, Protestants and the English Church would be believing that enlightenment came from within.

For the errors of the past, Becket took much of the blame, and his shrine was overturned, his bones punted and bounced down the nave at Canterbury. The newly enlightened English grabbed him by the handful and hurled him outside, bones spinning through the trees of the cathedral orchard. Then the reformed sinners looked each other in the eye, suddenly shamed, before making amends by collecting the unsainted Becket into an unmarked grave.

A hundred years later, guided to the spot by nervous vergers, Cromwell's New Model Army grimly dug Becket up again. As a sign of their utter Puritan contempt, and fresh from felling the sacred ancient thorn of Glastonbury, they loaded all that remained of Becket into the barrel of a republican cannon.

They didn't even take aim. They lit the fuse and walked away, brushing the saltpetre from their hands. Boom.

That night, the Calvinist roundheads slept deeply the sleep of the just. Meanwhile, dogged local opportunists ran hunched through the windfalls, like spaniels, scavenging fragments of bone into greasy leather aprons. For weeks afterwards, they skulked the inns at the cathedral gates, watchful for long-haired Catholics in secret flight to the coast. A modest, yeomanly approach would be attempted, eyes averted, gradually growing in confidence. Then, with a painful show of reluctance, miming a wail and lament for the cruel second end of Becket the greatest of saints, the Canterbury scavengers would suggest a vast and inflated price for the last-known bones of the martyr.

Their customers seldom lasted the night. Before dawn, the city's visiting idolaters and vile purchasers of relics were denounced to Cromwell's soldiers. Becket's remains were then stolen back by local crones, who'd lurk toothless and cackling for next week's wave of the faithful.

Various fragments did escape to Europe, joining the detached fingers known to have reached Belgium with Becket's family. In the centuries which followed, Becket relics were occasionally bartered between Roman churches, an English saint of fluctuating value in a market complacent with saints of its own. After the first modern war, to distance himself from the ancient cult of relics, Pius XI presented Becket's toe to the Anglican Bishop of Gibraltar, as a gift of reconciliation between Christians. From there, despite protests from a sub-committee of cardinals, Becket was transferred to the Church of All Saints, in Geneva. As a quiet embarrassment, an unknown quantity, his toe-bone had been almost forgotten for nearly a century.

In despair, less than a week ago, I'd turned to Becket for help.

The Bishop of Gibraltar, responsible for the entire Anglican diocese of Europe, had just refused the Chaplain permission for a farewell service of deconsecration.

It would be purely ceremonial, the Bishop explained in his e-mail, *and besides, we can't afford it*.

Churches abroad were expensive, and, unlike churches at home, they were seldom remembered in the legacies of English dead. The Swiss property taxes were ruinous, and progressive voices in the Synod had been murmuring for some time now about the embarrassment of an exclusively Anglican presence in the cities of a united Europe. There was the questionable taint of imperialism, and an isolationist variety of pride, each Anglican church an outdated and perhaps even offensive anomaly.

Don't blame me, the Bishop wrote, *our Church is in crisis. Not to worry, though. It's always in crisis. Just do the best you can!*

The departing Chaplain had already done the best he could, in several years of failed jumble-sales and cake-bakes. Among other ingenious plans for raising money to save the church, he'd asked his loyal flock to put something aside every time it rained, in memory of England. But there were quibbles (*please, Vicar, one moment of your time*) about how much rain counted as rain, and anyway that week was unseasonably fine, and the Chaplain found himself out among the banks and the watch shops, alone and palms upward, waiting.

Eventually, after exhausting all Anglican methods of fundraising, he tried the charismatic ploy of standing the congregation in a circle, holding hands, and pleading directly with God to save the church. God hadn't answered. Or he had, but the answer was no.

That was when I'd made my own contribution, turning to Becket for help. The results had been immediate, if unexpected, and ever since I'd felt unusually proud of being a deacon, as if it wasn't, after all, the biggest mistake of my life.

Thomas à Becket had also started out as a deacon. A forceful man, confident in his plated destiny, he'd helped Archbishop Theobald protect the status of the Church in a difficult period. Within ten years, in 1155, at the age of thirty-six, he'd been appointed Royal Chancellor to King Henry II.

I felt good about myself for deserting the Chaplain's lunch, even though I now had less than two hours before our plane was scheduled to leave. It had been the right thing to do, and I was as sure of it as a raving madman, a man possessed. I'd reappraised my capabilities, and I was stronger than I'd realised. At the age of thirty-four, only two years from the Chancellorship of all England, I could single-handedly save the Church of All Saints from closure.

Shutting my eyes, breathing deeply, I allowed myself to feel untouchable, aloof from human frailty. All Saints had always been an unusual posting, but I now suspected I'd been sent here in recognition that *I wasn't like everyone else*. God was asking something special of me in the city of Geneva, and Becket's pride rubbed off as a kind of dangerous audacity. It made all virtue seem possible, and all ambition, and I foresaw a glowing future of heroic service and sacrifice, a glorious dying of the self. Arduous though my mission promised to be, and unfashionable, there was no other way to live.

Beside the altar, on the cold floor, I knelt and prayed for God's pity on the Chaplain, for his doubts and his weakness, and his waste of a God-given opportunity to stand alone, defy secular pressure, and personally reinvent the Church. At the same time, I moved Becket's toe loosely between my fingers. It felt both rough and tongueish, and I turned it like a one-bone rosary, just as I had earlier in the day on my way to the restaurant.

The lunch had started badly. When I arrived, the minister from the American church and some of our regulars were already chatting. Everybody was well wrapped in coats and scarves, and they'd chosen the terrace for its view of the lake, glittering green and hard from the melt of glaciers.

They were already on to the winds, Switzerland's favourite weather. The Bise was a cold wind which froze the head. The Föhn was warm and enervating, and drove even staid professionals in horror from the streets. Today, everyone agreed, it was the Bise that was blowing, and several people hugged themselves and theatrically chattered their teeth.

I wasn't wearing a coat. I wasn't even wearing a sweater. I had on a short-sleeved cotton shirt and the Bise was blowing and I was freezing, and it felt sublime.

Apart from the American minister, who was now sitting on my left, I recognised Mrs Meier the stiff-lipped church treasurer, Mr Oti the warden, and Stella the attractive Hong Kong girl who worked as an interpreter at the United Nations. They were all staring, and on any other day I'd probably have wanted to check my appearance.

On this particular day, however, my inner idea of what I looked like was unusually secure. I was tall and slender, with a pale complexion and dark hair. Many people found me handsome. My features were straight, though my nose was rather long. My forehead was wide, my eyes bright, and, despite a tendency to stutter, my expression was memorably calm as I prepared to disregard the demands of the secular world.

They were all still looking at me, Mrs Meier wincing a little at the sight of their visiting assistant deacon usurping the head of the table.

'We were saving that place for the Chaplain,' the American minister said. He was an Episcopalian, an intense man with a square beard and a pocket Bible.

'There's an empty seat on my right,' I said. 'He can just as easily sit there.'

It was a pointless quarrel, but I started it anyway. To discourage them further, I opened a menu, and felt disdainful towards the many luxury foods I wasn't going to order. In the early days, as Chancellor, Becket had been famed for lavish extravagance. He kept more than twenty changes of clothing, much of it trimmed with silk and the rarest of furs. He never travelled without hounds and hawks, wild monkeys and wolves, crossing the Channel on diplomatic missions with six boatloads of knights, stewards, lechers, harlots.

The testimony from that time was unanimous. From the moment Thomas assumed control of the Church, his character underwent a spectacular change. In an abrupt conversion, he instantly renounced all the flim and the flam, and put on a new and better man.

The Chaplain, later than expected, arrived in exuberant mood. He happily took the chair to my right. He laughed, and clapped me on the back, this living proof that God called to the ministry those people who already looked like vicars. It saved time. The Chaplain looked vulnerable and undecided and naïve, his beard gappy, his hair in need of a trim. At the same time, in the last few days, I'd noticed his face losing its uncertainty, relaxing into something more civilian.

'Champagne,' he said, clapping his hands for a waiter. 'To celebrate.'

Some of the people giggled, but the Chaplain was already emptying a large envelope, full of print-outs of the latest e-mails to the parish. 'One final duty,' he said, 'and then I'm free.' He handed a decent stack to Mrs Meier, and four or five loose sheets to me.

'From Helena,' he said. 'And they all say the same thing.'

'I asked you not to read them.'

'Still, we'll be home in a couple of hours. Sort it out then, eh? God,' he said, leaning back in his chair and throwing his hands out wide, 'free! For the first time in years, truly free.'

He drained half his champagne before Mrs Meier could propose a toast. He laughed, then drank again to his own good health.

I had one sip, a minor concession, and thankfully didn't enjoy it. As the Chaplain moved round the table, effusively saying his goodbyes, other people came and went in the vacated seat next to mine. At one point, Stella leant towards me and asked how I felt.

'I'm fine. Why?'

'You look unwell.'

I reassured her, but faltered slightly when she stared at my lips, as foreigners sometimes did, and also interpreters trained in lip-reading, and of course women who wanted to sleep with me. She stared at my lips. I stared at hers, and imagined them quashed on my chin, my chest, reminding me of another life, and a little light fornication to add to Becket's publicly renounced vices of venery and hawking, dicing, pride, ostentation, and other confessable but otherwise deadly sins.

As a young man Becket had made errors, like I had, but we'd both been reformed by a touch from the finger of God. I hadn't slept with anyone for nearly three months, and even then it had only been Helena, and at the time I'd loved her.

Exiled in France, Thomas à Becket had taken to wearing a vest and breeches woven from goat's hair, and was scourged three times daily by his loyal attendant Robert of Merton. I was cold, my bare forearms up in gooseflesh, and out beside my plate I had Becket's toe squeezed tight in my fist, tighter, clenching my teeth when the sharp edges of the bone cut redly across the jagged arrow of my life-line.

'You're *sure* you're alright?'

The minister from the American church was now back in his original place, sitting on my left. He must have forgiven me, because in a neighbourly way he asked for the keys to All Saints. He smiled and held out his hand.

'No,' I said.

We'd agreed to leave the keys at the American church, where Joseph Moholy, the new owner, could send someone to pick them up.

'Let's not make this difficult,' the American sighed. He lowered his voice, which I construed as threatening behaviour. I therefore stared back at him without blinking.

'Don't ruin your last day,' he whispered harshly. 'You're in enough trouble as it is.'

'Is that a fact?'

'Everyone knows why they sent you. Now don't be obstructive.'

Becket was generally recognised as the patron saint of problem priests. He'd been martyred for protecting clergy who preferred sex to marriage, robbed their own churches, or devised a personal theology to ease the pain at funerals. He insisted that ordained servants of the Lord, including way-ward deacons, be treated as exceptional cases, descended as they were in a direct line of succession from the Apostles. They were themselves, but they were also of one body with the evangelists, and all the holy saints.

Meaning, quite clearly, that my mistakes were never just my own. None of it was entirely my fault. 'You know nothing about me.'

'I've spoken to the Chaplain,' the American hissed, 'and it seems you have little remaining credit with the Almighty. Now, give me the keys.'

'No.'

'Please.'

'No.'

Exasperated, he looked away, pretending to survey the party along the rest of the table. I knew what he was doing. He was taking the measure of my imperious nature, and mentally recommending a course in humility. He turned back and tried again.

'In a few hours' time you'll be home. Just go quietly.'

Thomas à Becket returned to England from exile on 1 December 1170, with a bodyguard of five knights in full armour. Twenty-nine days later he was dead.

'I'm not going,' I said, hands balled in fists on the table, still the only person at lunch not to have eaten, and not to have moved from my original seat at the head of the table. I felt strong and unassailable, and looking forward to a squabble, which wasn't out of character. Enthusiasm for an argument was a general fault of the twelfth century.

The American fetched the Chaplain. I now had one of them on either side, the American hunched sharply forward, his fingers interlocked on the tablecloth in the first stage of Here's a Church.

12

The Chaplain was laughing again. Out loud and un-restrained.

'Frankly, I don't give a hoot. He can do what he wants. I'm out of here.'

'Look,' the American said, 'you don't understand. Your church was for sale. Joseph Moholy bought it. I have an arrangement with Moholy to deliver the keys.'

'And I have an arrangement to get on a plane,' the Chaplain said. 'It's called a ticket.'

'What about your deacon?'

'Jay was foisted on me. I did what I could. Now I consider myself unfoisted. I simply don't care. I resign. Look.'

He drew his finger gleefully across his throat. 'Read my neck. No collar.'

And with that, he went back to Stella who was looking very neat and pretty and reminding me of the story of Abelard, one of Becket's professors during his studies in Paris. Abelard had a child with his beautiful student Eloise. It was a glorious expression of love, a love-child. Unfortunately, Eloise also had an incorruptible uncle. He took Abelard to one side, and righteously removed his testicles.

I wished the Chaplain better luck, naturally, though clearly the paths of our lives were diverging.

The American stayed beside me, and for the first time I sensed he was pleading. 'I'll have to phone him,' he said. 'If you don't give me the keys, I'll have no choice. I'll have to phone and tell him.'

'You do that.'

'He'll send someone round. Is that what you want?'

In Geneva, everyone knew the stories about Joseph Moholy. Even me, and I'd been in the city less than a month. Moholy had once bought, from an Iraqi antiquities dealer, eleven pages of *The Book of Vestiges of Times Past*. They were supposedly by the master-calligrapher Ibn Al Bawwab. When revealed as fakes, the Iraqi had his fingers amputated under the wheels of an early-morning tram. The exact details of how this came about depended on the version of the story.

My own instinct, when I'd met Joseph Moholy for the first time, had been not to like him. It was a reaction I often had to anyone richer and more successful than me, and still living. At the time, we knew him only as a Swiss–Hungarian entrepreneur and trader in antiquities, who'd visited the church among the first of the prospective buyers. He was elegant, even dapper, and light on his feet for a silver-haired man in his fifties. From a purely professional point of view, I'd thought him sad, and a little lonely, and in need of saving. He seemed to be missing something, but actively, as if the absence could be remedied by the acquisition of one single object, though it wasn't clear what that object actually was.

All Saints was a protected building, and the conditions of sale insisted that Church Commissioners approve its intended use. They'd already turned down a fast-food franchise, a chain of dance and work-out studios, and an heiress who needed more square metres to rehearse her militant theatre. Moholy had proposed an exhibition space for art objects from around the world, which the Church Commissioners found acceptable.

We did wonder how a man with a single, ordinary-looking gallery of antiquities in the Rue de la Croix d'Or could afford to buy a church in central Geneva. Or why he'd even want it. But, apart from that, he seemed normal, a polite non-believer, which in the Church of England didn't count against him.

'Moholy won't be happy,' the minister said, 'especially when he finds himself locked out of his own church.'

This wasn't the American minister's problem, and he resented feeling involved. In the States, Christianity was buoyant with new converts and born-agains, and one out of three US citizens had personally spoken with Jesus. The prospect of a closing church simply didn't arise. 'Stop being so stubborn. Give me the keys.'

'There's good that needs to be done.'

'You're a junior deacon. You were brought in to lend a hand with the heavy lifting.'

'I know what you're trying to say,' I said, using my knuckles to push away my unused plate. I stood up, and prepared to leave. 'You were expecting someone less unswerving.'

An empty church like All Saints offered a limited range of amusements. Turning Becket's toe in my fingers, I looked for dropped collection coins in the open spaces left by the pews. I started to hum, tunelessly. It happened sometimes. I just couldn't find the right note on which to start. I considered putting Becket back in the safe, but was diverted by the disc of purple silk he'd originally been wrapped in. There was a pattern woven by hand into the circle of material. Holding it up to one of the windows, the design struck me as curious. Four straight lines were woven as a square, each corner touching the circumference of the circular piece of silk. It was a square inside a circle, a square peg in a round hole. Inside the square, there was an irregular pattern of small blocked-in rectangles, hand-sewn in uneven rows.

I dropped the toe-bone into my pocket and folded the cloth into a semi-circle, then into slices, and took it to the safe. All Saints dated from 1845, and had been financed by Geneva's bankers. Out of habit, they'd had a safe embedded in one of the walls, neatly concealed behind a memorial tablet. This plaque of white marble remembered an aristocratic second son and member of the Alpine Club who'd died in a fall from the Eiger, and the handle was a genuine Victorian ice-axe. I swung it open, and found a place inside for the folded cloth, between dusty bottles of Sanctifex and an optimistic back-up box of one thousand hosts. I checked again, but we'd definitely run out of candles, which was a shame.

Towards the end of his life, Becket became very fond of excommunication. He'd light a candle, say the name of a rival, and then dash the candle to the ground.

Another day, perhaps.

I checked the church door, making sure it was locked, and then dragged the bin-bags of jumble further down the aisle. At the top of one was a pair of driving-gloves, and a blue plastic sports-bag. Underneath, it was mostly clothes, dresses and sweaters and a large grey suit. I was still cold in my flimsy short-sleeved shirt, so I rummaged through and laid out all the sweaters. There were four in all, including a striped tank-top, a Guernsey, and a red stretch turtleneck. I unbuttoned my shirt as I made my choice; not of the warmest, but the harshest.

The winner, by some margin, was a round-necked sweater in electric-blue imitation mohair. It scratched at my naked skin everywhere it touched, which was pretty much everywhere, and not that surprising since it was meant for a teenage girl. It was simple homespun, short in the sleeve and body, tight at the neck and under the arms, and all across the back. And the front. I flinched and wriggled. The bodily irritation was unbearable, exquisite.

In parishes back in England, this was the clergy's last week in white before the long summer drone of Sundays after Pentecost (green), stretching right through from now until

16

October. But this wasn't a parish in England. It was Geneva, where I'd consulted Becket in the crisis of my life, and Thomas à Becket advised tight and bright-blue mohair.

I ended up on the floor in the corner furthest from the door, clutching Becket's toe, my shoulders itching and hunched and itching, listening for the quarter-hours from the chiming clock in the tower. Each additional bell made it harder to imagine rushing for the airport, and easier to keep a close hold on the toe-bone, waiting for nothing much but the next fifteen minutes.

This wasn't despair, or even depression. I convinced myself it was contrition, hoping to be excused all the bad things I'd ever done, as recently as lunch-time. It wasn't cracking up. It was the first step in a personal reformation which started with penance for the liberty I'd enjoyed in my former life.

Although possibly, from another point of view, I could see that curling up in the corner of an empty church, wearing a teenager's electric-blue sweater, relying on a lucky bone, I could see that this might look like despair, like depression and cracking up.

Thomas à Becket had a mother, who was very special and nothing like the other mothers. She had visionary dreams of her son's resplendence, and his future as a distinguished man. She encouraged him to make the most of himself, to renounce the pleasures of skating on the shin-bones of animals across the Smithfield ice in favour of floggings and book-work at school. At his daily lessons by six, often without breakfast, Thomas studied until dusk, his over-education gradually making him useless for the common work of the world.

The Church was uncommon work, and now as then it was due a revival. All it needed was individual men and women of heroic quality. Someone had to stand up. To get it started, perhaps just the one special person, and all my life I'd been looking for a life's work. I was physically strong, and could live on gruel. I was unmarried and childless. If I sacrificed what little I had, even if it was my own self, I'd somehow get what I wanted, the proof I was priestly material, dean of chapter, bishop.

From now on, I'd therefore faithfully put others before self, and reinvigorate the good works of St Thomas. All Saints had a long history of helping the distressed, and in Geneva there were Filipinas trapped in prostitution, and homeless drug-addicts from the Balkans. Stranded in camps outside the city were penniless refugees from Kabul, or Baghdad, who'd somehow arrived in Geneva and were hoping to reach London by Christmas. In fact there were any number of victims of the American West, here like everywhere in need of help.

Another quarter-hour. If I hurried, and was lucky with a taxi, I could still make it to the airport.

But there again, of his eight years as Archbishop, Becket had spent six in exile, far from the chafing restraint of convention and petty deanery synods. The time to return to England would come, of course it would, but by then the ordinary people would have understood my long absence, some prostrating themselves before me, others tearing off their clothes and strewing them in my path, kindly ensuring that my feet need never touch the vulgar dirt of the road.

There was a thud at the door, echoing through the church. I hugged the horrible, scratchy sweater close round my prickled skin. Another thud. My heart lurched, and as my clenched hand reached to still it Becket was hard against my breast. Waiting for hatchets, the grunt of men making effort and the splinter of wood, I grew the Archbishop from the bone of his big toe, in sandals, feet splayed as he stopped, stood, listened for the flow and rush of approaching chain-mail. In the afternoon light dusting through the coloured windows, Becket was upright and without fear, shining with self-belief. I had in mind a tall, white-haired, beak-faced man; the person I intended to become. Noble, stubborn, waiting unmoved for death.

I stood up and strode fearlessly down the hard tiled aisle of the church, as the door thudded once again. From the closed inside, on the safe side, I forcefully asked who it was, and there was something unlike me about my voice, the empty church playing new acoustic tricks. 'Who is it?'

'I've been sent by Joseph Moholy.'

Not in armour, nor wielding a broadsword, nor with several armed companions. It wasn't even a man. It was a woman's voice.

'You don't scare me.'

'Open the door. I think I can help you.'

'What do you want?'

'You're frightened, aren't you?'

Becket was never frightened. I stored his toe-bone safely in my pocket, took out the keys, and unlocked the door. It was definitely a woman.

'Hi,' she said breezily, 'my name's Rifka.'

She held out her hand, and I looked at it.

'And you must be the deacon, James Mason. Great sweater.' She gave up on the handshake. 'Can I come in?'

'Rifka what?'

She was already past me, a crop-haired blonde woman about half a head shorter than I was. She was wearing a corduroy coat, and carrying a canvas bag across her shoulder. Her face was round, or wide, and she had a nose in two goes like a boxer, something I'd always found immensely attractive.

I locked her in, but she didn't seem bothered as she contemplated the empty spaces of the church, the skewed altar and the crumbling walls in cream and powdery white, like relief maps of territory in the clouds.

She was in her late thirties, and her full name was Rifka 'Who-works-for-Joseph-Moholy', and she was in good shape without being thin. She went over to the altar, turned, and using her arms she sprang herself up to sit on its edge. She looked around some more, her overbite tight over very fine teeth, making it seem she was always about to smile, or find something amusing.

'I won't mess about,' she said, and I couldn't immediately place her accent. It was Australian German, or Austrian New Zealand. 'Moholy had a call from the American church. He sent me down to investigate. Now. I have carrots, and I have sticks. Your call.'

Whenever she swung her legs, the heels of her boots collided with the front of the altar. 'Are you alright? You don't look too great.'

'I haven't eaten.'

'You should eat.'

Her grey eyes were scuffed round the pupil with brown, and I was secretly gratified by her concern with my health. As a reformed man, in 1164, Becket had contracted mystery pains in his face and stomach. He was advised by doctors with twenty years' experience to indulge, for therapeutic reasons, in sexual congress. For his own well-being. Presumably with the beautiful and willing Avice of Stafford, a discarded mistress of the king.

Becket held up his hands in horror, pushing the world away. (Avice backed against a trembling arras, hands crossed shoulder to shoulder, flashing bright glances from beneath teasing and darkened eyelashes.) Thomas à Becket turned on his heel and fled the room. He went outside, and climbed some way up a steep hill, to a place where flat rocks stood either side of an icy stream. He looked down on the monastery at Pontigny, his home in exile, and then further off to the distant mountains. He hitched up his robes, took his weight on his elbows, and lowered himself up to the waist in the freezing water of the stream, where he held himself, teeth clenched, until his arms and legs shuddered with the effort and the cold.

'What's the stick?'

'Let's start with the carrot. Is it money you want?'

It felt like a temptation, money for nothing. I stubbornly crossed my arms, which made me itch from elbow to elbow, and also across my shoulders and neck. Rifka looked at her watch.

'Your Chaplain is already at the airport. He's about to take off. He couldn't tell us why you're still here, and nor could the pastor from the American church. Luckily for you, Moholy knows more than the both of them put together.'

She opened her canvas bag and pulled out a sheet of paper in a plastic wallet. 'This is the inventory of the fixtures and fittings of the church, as agreed before purchase. You may remember that Moholy reserved the organ, which I see is still here, tick, the wooden canopy on the pulpit, tick, and also Thomas à Becket's toe-bone. In which case,' Rifka said brightly, looking up from the page, 'the toe-bone must still be here. Somewhere.'

I stood without moving, trusting in silence, in my own private exile. Archbishop of Canterbury by the age of forty-four, I'd been expecting my next ten years of steady advancement to begin more smoothly. Rifka hopped off the altar and went to search the safe, which I'd left unlocked. She turned back, eyebrows raised.

'Own up,' she said. 'You've taken it, haven't you?'

'No.' But I couldn't lie. I could resist, and defy, and argue, but I found no special talent for deceit. 'Yes.'

I took Becket from my pocket, and held him up between my fingers.

'Oh damn,' Rifka said, her face closing in. 'You really oughtn't to have touched that.' She chewed on the side of her mouth, keeping her distance. 'Moholy guessed you probably had. Though he also presumed you were an educated man, and thought you'd probably survive.'

She rummaged through her bag for some water, then reached into the top pocket of her shirt for a small glass bottle. She pressed down and round on the child-proof cap, shook out some white pills, tipped them into her mouth, and washed them down. As she put everything back again, she said, 'Relics do have a certain addictive power, don't they?'

'Do they?'

'They connect us to the whole stretch of eternity. Now. Can I have Thomas à Becket. I'm asking nicely.'

'It belongs to the church.'

'And the church belongs to Joseph Moholy. Look, there's nothing sinister about it. Relics have always changed ownership. It's what used to be called translation, the translation of relics.'

'I think they often used to be stolen,' I said, frowning. 'Didn't they?'

'Or purchased,' Rifka countered. 'To save them from neglect. Your own Protestant Church considers Becket's toe-bone an object without value. That's right, isn't it? It therefore seems unlikely they'd oppose the removal of a holy relic in which no one actually believes.'

'I have a duty to history.'

'In a blue mohair jumper? I can see your belly-button.'

She was misjudging me. My appearance was unimportant, as irrelevant as the money she'd offered earlier. I had no intention of giving up Becket.

Rifka sighed, and for inspiration, instead of heaven, she looked closely at her fingernails. 'Moholy warned me you might be like this, but take care, because I've only one more carrot. We're prepared to be reasonable. You've been living in the church apartment, which, as you're aware, Moholy has also bought. He says there's no rush, you can go on staying there. Not a problem. However, he did ask me to find out if you'd any ambition.'

She looked into my eyes, first the left, then the right.

'Well, James, are you ambitious?'

A Becket cult, glamorous with sapphires and rubies, had flourished at Canterbury for 300 years. A million pilgrims travelled to touch the spot where Becket had fallen, to pray not for his soul, but for his intercession, and to buy tiny lead ampoules of his infinitely diluted blood which healed the deaf and the dumb, cured dropsy and the King's Evil, brought cows and horses back to life, and exorcised demons in possession of hopeless souls.

'Yes,' I said. 'In my own small way, I suppose I am.'

Rifka threw up her arms. 'At last, something we can agree on. Moholy might be able to help. He's on the track of something special, and thinks you may be interested.'

'Me?'

'You're a vicar.'

'I'm a deacon. I don't see how he can help me.'

'Remember, James, last of the carrots. Moholy proposes the two of you should meet. You can go to his villa, have a look around. And personally, I recommend you use your head and bite this carrot. Avoid the stick. That's my personal recommendation.'

She was now behind the altar, leaning forward on her elbows, and all her movements had been easy and athletic, suggesting great reserves of strength, or speed. She moved about the church with an owner's sense of assurance.

'Opt for the carrot, not the stick. Really. Moholy can be very strange, unpredictable, but he thinks he may have work for you. And now I've seen you, I think he may be right.'

With Becket a sharp reminder in my soft clerical palm, I considered it for at least a second. 'The church needs Becket. This is where he belongs.'

'You think Becket's the only one?'

Rifka was growing irritable now, impatient. She searched inside her bag, didn't find what she was looking for, so held it open and looked again. She slid a plastic box on to the altar, and then a white disc tightly wrapped in clingfilm. 'There's more to relics than Becket, you know. Becket's just the start. Just the margins.'

'But Moholy wants Thomas à Becket.'

She laughed, letting a brief explosion of air escape through her nose. 'It's not Becket, that I know for sure. Whatever's keeping him awake at night is more important than Becket. *Someone* far more important.'

Only Thomas à Becket, alone in the world, knew that there was no one more important than Thomas à Becket. Could that be right? This was no time for humility, or self-doubt. Swallowing hard, I could see that inside the plastic box on the altar there was a solid-looking section of bone, like an uneven marble, and the flat disc in clingfilm was also bone. Becket needed to assert his own pre-eminence, to find thirteen poor folk daily between matins and dawn, to feed them and clothe them and wash their wretched feet.

'Trust Moholy,' Rifka said. 'Humour him. That or the stick.'

If I clutched the bone hard enough, until it impressed my flesh, I could convince myself there was nothing to fear. Thomas à Becket had publicly humbled the king himself, Henry II, an all-powerful descendant of Fulk the Black and William the Conqueror. At the West Gate of the Cathedral Close, Henry had felt compelled to remove his boots. In the rain and sleet he'd undressed to his underwear, a hair-shirt from neck to knees, in feeble imitation of Thomas. Reaching the shrine, Henry had creaked to his knees, then prostrated himself, his face flat to the jewelled floor, the inner skin of his royal cheek mashed fleshily between his teeth. As further penance, he went on to claim a vigorous whipping from the bishops, the abbot, and all eighty of the privileged Canterbury monks.

Yes, Mr Joseph Moholy, you be very careful.

I had an idea of what a saint ought to do, so I tried to do it. With Becket in my hand, I stumbled outside to help people, the door in its old arch like an ear opening to the city-noise of Geneva. The sun was lower now, but the vicious Bise was still blowing, freezing my head and slicing through the open weave of the sweater.

The banks and shops had closed, but the exchange booths were still changing money. People passed by in cars, or hanging to the straps of trams. In every direction I saw prosperity, everyone well and warmly dressed for business, in banking and pharmaceuticals, luxury goods or peace. I was in religion, and in my black clerical trousers and boil-washed blue sweater I was zealously cold. I was shivering and goose-fleshed and pure and virtuous and very fervently cold. And though I ran one way, and then the other, slapping my arms for warmth, I failed to catch any poor beggars in immediate need of feeding or humble and tender foot-washing.

I stumbled in front of a car, and there was some panicked horn and screech. Pedestrians accelerated and veered away. The poor and needy were elsewhere, which I knew didn't make it any better, but for me, here and now in Geneva, what was the good I'd been called upon to do?

There was a girl, some distance up the street beyond the central Post Office, but coming my way. She looked different from the others, in lace-up boots and ripped jeans. I didn't want to frighten her, so I waited until her white sweatshirt was close enough to read. Up near the neckline, in bold black letters, it said *Intellectual Property*.

And below her breasts, the letters jagged by the material pleating into her belt, *Is Theft*.

I lurched towards her, my tight sweater riding high above my belly-button, but she saw me coming and held both hands straight out, palms flat towards me. And continued to stay well clear by turning a semi-circle to pass me by, keeping me in view at all times, showing no sign whatsoever of welcoming salvation.

Which was when it occurred to me, at last, that this wasn't a time or a place in which a man like Becket could prosper. I felt a weariness, a sudden relaxation in the tension of my will. I'd never be able to sustain it. I couldn't possibly keep myself lowered in the freezing river, because good intentions weren't enough. I was lonely for Helena, and Stella, and even Rifka. I wanted to embrace them all, and most warmly. A vow of chastity was too hard, especially when these days by their own free-will most people were already excommunicated. It made my only remaining pleasure of dashing the candles seem a little redundant. Everyone was already excommunicated from the spiritual, by choice, and I saw no joy in my future as a blissful martyr. I wasn't strong enough to die for the Church of England, not like Thomas à Becket, not like my dad.

People who suffered believed in God. For a long time, I'd been jealous of that sincere, serious place, only I didn't want to suffer. I was therefore hardly the type of person to sustain this Becket-like imitation of Christ. It just wasn't me.

I scurried back inside the church, and startled Rifka, who was making a close inspection of the silk cloth which had once wrapped Becket. I slapped his toe-bone on the altar, and stumbled backwards and away from it.

And felt alone, and abruptly abandoned, and for the first time genuinely cold, so cold it made me weak. Should have worn another sweater, and at least one coat. And a scarf and a hat. Should have flown back to England, while I had the chance. I blew into my hands, and slapped at my shoulders, trying to rub some comfort into the itch of my feeble arms.

I'd got my life all wrong. Unlike Becket, who knew exactly what was required. He'd left home at twenty-two, and sensibly gone to learn the basics of financial management from Osbert Eightpenny, in the City. After three assiduous years, he'd been head-hunted into the retinue of the Archbishop of Canterbury. It was a very prudent start. Impeccable. He grew up in London, of course. That had to help. And his father Gilbert Becket was a prosperous merchant, a former sheriff, with contacts and connections already in place. Thomas also had the motivational edge of his mother dying young, and, like all boys' mothers, Becket's mother was very special.

27

I shared none of these advantages. My mother wasn't dead, we didn't come from London. I was not destined to be a conspicuous and gifted servant of the Lord our God. I threw the church keys on to the altar beside the toe-bone.

'Actually,' Rifka said. 'Moholy's less bothered about the keys. He said you could hold on to them. For a while, anyway.'

Under the influence of Becket, this would have been a triumph. But instead, I now saw the church for what it was, old and cold and empty.

'Come on, chicken,' Rifka said. She had an arm round my shoulder, and I was grateful for the human warmth. 'I know it's bad. I know it is. You'll be feeling cold, and weak, and a little lost. It happens to us all. That's why I brought you this.'

She held out the plastic box with a transparent lid she'd shown me earlier. Inside, on a bed of cotton wool, was the uneven marble of greyish bone.

'That should help you through the worst of it,' she said. 'It's a bone from Sir Humphry Davy. With Joseph Moholy's compliments.'

Davy's Foot

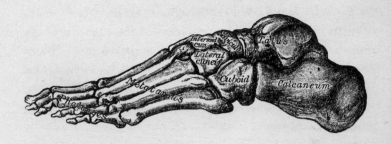

'If matter cannot be destroy'd
The living mind can never die
If e'en creative when alloy'd
How sure its immortality.'

Humphry Davy, *Untitled Poem*

Sir Humphry Davy was knighted in 1813, at the age of thirty-five, one year from now. Sir Jay Mason, Knight of the British Empire. Imagine that.

From humble and distant beginnings, in Penzance at the furthest edge of England, Davy achieved public eminence in the Age of Personality (the first one) as President of the Royal Society, and the first knight of science since Newton. He was a self-made man and friend to Coleridge and Wordsworth, an aspiring poet who discovered the mind-altering qualities of nitrous oxide, later known as laughing gas. Davy's mentor Thomas Beddoes, in his *Medicinal Uses of Factitious Airs*, had classified the gas an instant killer. Davy inhaled it. It made him laugh.

His reputation enhanced, he repeated the experiment with carbon monoxide, and barely survived.

Davy specialised in *substances the nature of which is not yet perfectly known*. He made significant discoveries, many of them invaluable, like his isolation of the elements potassium and chlorine. His papers on matter and electricity provided the foundation for modern physics, and with his lab assistant Michael Faraday he was among the first freethinkers fully to appreciate the excitement of electricity as the mood of the future.

Davy was a split personality, a romantic scientist. He was also a social climber of some skill and, towards the end of his life, a professional curmudgeon and bully.

On Saturday morning, recovering in bed, I tried to make sense of what had happened to me the day before. I found myself alone in Geneva, in Joseph Moholy's flat, the day after the closure of the church and the date on my ticket home. I also had older problems of my own making that I was choosing to ignore, but which one day, surely one day, I'd be happy to face. As soon as I became better than or at least different from the person who'd caused the problems.

Fortunately, on this particular morning, I felt exceptionally clear-headed, reflecting that abroad and far from home it was acceptable to be anxious, and to compensate by acting out roles. Some early mistakes were inevitable, and, looking back now, I was glad to be rid of the influence of Becket. He was so self-willed, so ostentatious and stubborn. It was feasible to become a saintly man, at least I hoped so, but not in a single day.

Better to keep an open mind, and in a spirit of sceptical

enquiry to question everything. There was usually a perfectly rational explanation, even for behaviour as changeable as mine.

I therefore dressed warmly and sensibly (coat, scarf, cap), and arrived at Geneva's oldest cemetery with the last of the morning's rose-coloured clouds, gilled pink and fresh from the lake. It was nine o'clock, and the gates were already open at the Cimetière des Rois, a square plot of land between a multi-storey retirement home and the fire-station. Set back from the road behind a waist-high wall, it had no church attached, but was put to use by the various Protestant cults squeezed for space in the centre of the city, including (until very recently) All Saints.

On the right of the cemetery gate, on the way in, there was an open-sided pavilion sheltering drawer over drawer of named and dated ashes, like an oversized chemical cabinet. Behind and above this loomed the stacked windows with closed orange curtains on the less coveted side of the retirement home. At the back and along its left-hand edge, the cemetery of kings was closed off by high walls, ivy veining the stonework.

It would soon be a bright morning. The low sun was full in my face, and as I closed the cemetery gate it felt like the most splendid of times to be alive. The possibility of making original and unexpected discoveries was like being born anew, every day of the week.

Even at nine o'clock, even on a Saturday, there was a funeral. A clustered family in black made a silent semi-circle, backs turned to a one-man mechanical digger, in yellow, parked just behind them. I didn't let this gloomy scene affect my mood. As long ago as the boy Davy, as far back as the French Revolution, natural philosophers had already rejected

Priestley's concept of the resurrection of the body. Some part of us might live on, but it wasn't the body, and in this cemetery like every other all that remained was the body; not even that, the bones.

Sir Humphry Davy's final resting place was clearly marked on the indexed map at the cemetery entrance, and I could reach it while maintaining a respectable distance from the mourners. The way I saw it, I was an unremarkable if dark little man, with fine and curious eyes, about five foot seven but often stooped and seeming shorter. They wouldn't look at me twice. Though perhaps they might have done, on another day, if they'd known that I held in my fist a bone, a mere fragment, but allegedly from the skeleton of Sir Humphry Davy.

On my discreet and roundabout route towards Davy, I noticed that about a third of the graves in the Cimetière des Rois were amateur shrines, with wilting flowers and letters of devotion trapped beneath glass jars containing candles. It was a high proportion, but for 300 years Geneva had been a favourite place for the famous to avoid taxes and criticism, to wallow and die.

I stopped briefly at John Calvin. His was not a grave overflown by trumpet-blowing angels. The headstone was about the size of a shoebox, rounded at the top and marked J.C. No epitaph, no dates. There were no flowers, or snuffed candles in old sauerkraut jars, no smudged letters of homage in transparent plastic envelopes. Calvin hadn't wanted to be buried here at all, or even have a headstone, horrified as he was by the idea of his gravesite as a shrine. It was only several years after his death that the city surrendered to public pressure, and provided this token memorial.

It was sometimes suggested that Calvin's body wasn't

actually here. His more literal disciples, at Calvin's apparent request, had secretly buried the body elsewhere. This was just a stone, a sentimental scrap for the weaker brethren, although personally I found this story hard to believe. Everyone wants to be remembered, whatever they might say.

At Davy's graveside, I clasped my hands respectfully below my belt, his fragment of bone secure inside two layers of flesh and fingers. I rocked forward on my toes. Even with the fading lettering, and the ageing stonework liver-spotted with lichen, I was delighted by the solid, immodest memorial to the English scientist Sir Humphry Davy. He had a very large rectangular stone, with breadth as well as width, whereas the nearby Calvin had barely a shoebox.

Despite the bone between my fingers, I could see no evidence that the grave had been disturbed or damaged.

Intrigued, I decided to extend my investigation, and my second line of rational enquiry took me to the Basilique de Notre Dame, up by the station. It was Geneva's largest Catholic church, and clearly thriving on the unashamed hoodoo of virgin births and a bleeding Jesus and the hell of fire without end. Blurred by candle-light and incense, I made my circuit in a clockwise direction, looking out for relics. First, though, I bought some candles from a rack, and lit one to Dad. Then I lit one for Davy, and although the candles were a cream colour, the wax they burnt was black. I wasn't superstitious, but I didn't like it. I shouldn't imagine the Catholics liked it, either.

The Basilica's proudest relic was the leg-bone of St Clothilde, wife to Clovis, King of the Franks, and with her sister Chrona the foundress of Christian Geneva. Unfortunately, she was out on loan, to an exhibition making a tour of southern Italy. In St Clothilde's place, as a temporary exhibit,

I found the bones of St Ursula, a British queen from the third century who'd promised to marry a routinely tyrannical German. On two conditions. He had to convert to Christianity. And as an escort across the North Sea, Ursula would require eleven virginal companions, each in her own ship with a thousand attendant virgins. After several convivial years in Cologne, Ursula announced that she and her female attendants would be walking to Rome to meet the Pope. On their way back, all 11,012 of them were savagely massacred, by Huns. The bones were gathered up, and venerated ever after as relics.

However, these bones on temporary display in Geneva's Basilica were fakes. It was a progressive exhibit, demonstrating the irrepressible potency of the human urge to believe. The bones were well-documented frauds from the sixteenth century, no earlier, and probably about 1520.

At the cemetery, and then the Basilica, I'd been hoping to make sense of the unexpected Becketness which had come over me yesterday. I didn't seem to have made much progress. I tossed Davy's foot-bone in the air, and caught it two-handed, over St Ursula. There must be some way I could approach this predicament objectively, even scientifically, as a conundrum with a practical solution. Good science would always conquer superstition, as in the case of Davy's famous safety-lamp. In that instance, prior to Davy's fool-proof lamp, underground mining explosions caused by firedamp had often been blamed on a foul-tempered god, called Gwillam.

Since yesterday's intercession by Becket, I had some serious questions to ask about relics. What were they, exactly, and what could they do? Did they offer a channel through which supernatural power was made available for the needs of everyday life? Had I at last found an infallible means of changing for the better, and correcting my many failings?

Humphry Davy had been comfortable with the idea that substances change, according to different electrical states, or chemical arrangements, or temperatures. Matter was constantly modifying and adapting in character. Perhaps bones, after death, could also generate some imperfectly known power. The possibility couldn't be excluded from any unprejudiced scientific enquiry.

I therefore vowed to establish, using approved scientific methods, whether the essence of a human life could somehow implode, at the moment of death, into the physical remains left behind.

The lab conditions I had available to me were primitive. The church apartment was on the third floor of a sixties block, opposite a cosmetics packing-plant. There was coloured glass in the upper panels of the interior doors, mostly amber but also random red and green, and the woodblock flooring was yellow. The Chaplain had wilfully left behind everything he disliked about the Church of England, including a set of table-mats with etchings of county-town castles, and the pastoral answer-machine always blinking with many messages.

I skipped through the first nine, none of which was new. Message 10 was Stella, asking me if I was feeling any better. Message 11 was Rifka, who wanted me to phone her mobile, something about the church. And message 12 was Rifka again. But women weren't interesting to me, not today. Today was the investigation of bones, and for that I'd be needing the best possible light.

The living-room and adjoining bedroom both had windows over the street. However, for the purposes of my experiment, and despite cupboards packed with the Chaplain's cheap sherry, his instant cake-mixes and other false economies, I selected the kitchen.

It was 11.43 a.m. Wearing the cleanest of my blue-black cardigans, at the kitchen table beneath the scientific flicker of the striplight, I began my objective examination of the bone allegedly a relic of the English scientist Sir Humphry Davy. There was nothing ghoulish about it, just a bit of man with the meat off, about an inch across and an inch thick, like an uneven dice, and according to a diagram in the apartment's *Illustrated Oxford Dictionary*, a possible match for several of the small bones in the puzzle of the human foot. A visual examination was inconclusive: it was a grey colour, white moving to grey via yellow and brown, like a bad tooth, or a Sunday lamb-bone on a Monday. It also had that same rough tongueish texture I'd noticed in Becket's toe.

Stop. Concentrate. Was it in any way out of the ordinary? Was there any special power which lingered, at first obscurely but then growing, some sense of inverted magnitude radiating from this tiny and compact bone? I wanted to know if this relic of Sir Humphry Davy could act like Becket had, like a relic known to be holy. Could the character of Humphry Davy, like sanctity, be expected to rub off?

I rubbed the foot-bone in a particular way against the outside sleeve of my cardigan, like a polishing of Newton's apple. Closing my eyes, I was then almost persuaded by the illusion that there emanated, very faintly, a perfumed smell which lifted my spirits, like a sweet remembered pleasure. I blinked my eyes open, and stared amazed at the fragment of bone.

I rubbed it again, more fiercely this time, against my chest and then my stomach, like a nylon block I was making electric.

There it was again, that smell of pearl and pink, the odour of sanctity. I frowned, then crossed the hallway to the bedroom, where the window was open over the stutter of cars across tram-lines. On the other side of the street, beyond a stretched grid of second-storey tram-cables, white-coated women in the windows of the packing-plant were assembling gloss-finish boxes, their fingers repetitive and delicate.

The mid-air cables crackled like crisp-packets, and an orange Geneva tram scattered blue sparks as it rattled beneath the window.

Before now, during deliveries to the cosmetics plant, I'd been able to smell the candied arrival of nail-varnish.

I latched the window. Back in the kitchen, I put some water into a saucepan to boil, and from the maximum gas I lit a cream-coloured candle I'd bought at a bargain price from the votive stocks of Geneva's Basilica. Holding the foot-bone at the very ends of my fingers, I steadied the candle beneath it, and observed its reaction to naked flame. In the heyday of saintly relics, the Middle Ages, authentic remains were thought immune to fire. The immediate consequence of this received wisdom, in the ingenious 1300s, was the vigorous production of fake relics made from asbestos.

In my own controlled experiment, Davy's foot was slowly staining black, though I wasn't sure whether scientifically this counted as damage. I kept it in the flame, remembering my first chemistry set, aged about ten. All through Boxing Day, and well into the night, I tried to make things go bang while my brother Tom was allowed to fail at alchemy, because he was older. This memory, appearing from nowhere, made me suspect I'd always been interested in science, though I hadn't fully acknowledged it until now.

The Catholic flame scorched my fingers and I yelped,

jumping up and dropping both bone and candle. I stamped out the flame, shaking off my fingers then sucking at the burn. This was science at the frontier of the nineteenth century, approximate and unsterilised, and in bursts of rapid experimental progress injury was an occupational hazard. The water reached boiling-point, hissing on to the gas. I flipped it down to simmer, then crawled under the table, looking for Davy's foot-bone. It had skittered beneath the fridge. I hooked it out, wiped it off, and popped it into the boiling water, setting the timer for twenty minutes.

Twenty minutes later, in the simmering saucepan, I had an elixir. It was easy, if you knew how. The water which had boiled the bone was now an infusion of Sir Humphry Davy. I poured a small taster into an ecumenical mug, and swilled it round, to cool it. I sniffed it, blew on it, took a last look into it. And then I drank it.

It tasted faintly like chicken. Anyway, it was inoffensive, so I poured the rest of the elixir out of the saucepan and into the mug. After drying off the bone, I swallowed the lot. The taste of eternity needed more salt. Otherwise, nearly all my original questions remained unanswered.

Fortunately, Sir Humphry Davy had never been scared of the difficult questions. Such as: are hydrogen and nitrogen, at the usual temperatures of the atmosphere, bodies of the same character in the aeroform state as zinc and quicksilver in the heat of ignition? Back then, it was like asking about angels. The answer, as it happened, was $2K + 2NH_3 = 2KNH_3 + H_2$, which would always be unsatisfactory, even if it was right and God was a very clever chemist and this was the answer to everything.

Davy was soon conceding that the human condition could never be entirely explained by the emerging laws of chemistry, and my own recent experiments inclined me to agree. Davy coped with this disappointment by teaching himself to fish. He became an expert angler, but only after conscientiously fulfilling his many obligations to the Royal Society.

He was with me in my pocket as I dutifully checked for recent e-mails. Among the Chaplain's newsgroups, and a circular from Lambeth Palace, there were two new messages. The first was a reminder from the Rassemblement des Eglises Chrétiennes de Genève (subject: 'Today's Meeting'). I left that one alone while I moved my things into the Chaplain's emptied closets. Everything I owned fitted inside a military parson's kit-bag I'd inherited from Dad, and along with my own stuff I also had Dad's unsafe razor, and in case of emergency his favourite red chasuble (of no obvious use to Mum or Tom).

Then I went back to the computer and the second new message, meant for me personally but sent via the parish address. It was from Helena (subject: 'you two-faced bastard').

Davy's marriage, only last year at the age of thirty-three, was in those days considered late. He wrote at the time that his life began on the night his proposal was accepted. But it wasn't a success. He and Mrs Apreece remained childless, and, as Lady Davy, Jane Apreece refused to stay inert at home as the domestic base-element Davy had hoped for. She insisted on *doing* things. Whenever they were apart, Davy could summon a romantic wistfulness for the ideal of love. More often, when they were together, he thought of her as a distraction, a restless inconvenience who coerced him into busy and often wasteful trips to Bath. As the years went by, the unhappiness of their marriage became notorious, and the bad temper of both parties was often remarked upon. In fact, most observers judged their union a rationalised compromise from the start: they'd been growing older, with no one close to offer comfort.

I opened Helena's message.

No relationships were perfect, and because absence had softened my heart, I was ready to be persuaded by any improvement on celibacy. Helena wanted to fly over. She wanted to know if I was still alive. Was it true that I'd been ill?

I was still alive, yes. But I was not two-faced, of all things. Admittedly I'd changed in the last few years, as everyone had. I wasn't the same person: my skin had entirely replaced itself, and practically none of my atoms had survived that summer we'd fallen in love.

I shut down the machine. As founder of London Zoo, Davy's interest in natural history had introduced him to the reproductive charm of the ragworm. The female chases the male until she gets hold of him. She then eats him, and he explodes inside her, fertilising her eggs. And then she, too, dies. The baby ragworms grow, or live on, or triumph. Anyway, they're the only survivors.

If I was going to escape that fate in Geneva, and continue my scientific research into bones, I'd need to find a job. Davy was a Theist, recognising that theology and science have much in common, partners in a common quest for understanding. He saw no necessary contradiction. Both proceeded as if there was a truth out there to be discovered, a system of organisation worthy of praise, a purpose as a ground of hope. I could therefore continue my scientific research *and* work as a churchman, the only job for which I was even half qualified.

I consulted the Chaplain's folder of wealthy institutions, his wish-list of benefactors, and, feeling confident they'd want to support my life of genuine enquiry, I made a call to the Centre for European Nuclear Research. CERN, a twenty-minute bus-ride from Geneva's city-centre, is an isolated campus of 10,000 scientists, and beneath the surrounding mountains they've constructed a twenty-seven-kilometre atom-velodrome, whizzing quarks and gluons in opposite directions and hoping for spectacular collisions. The invisible particles collide. The scientists watch.

It was at CERN that the Higgs-Boson particle was first identified. Until very recently, this particle represented the holy grail of nuclear physics, explaining why the universe has mass and how everything holds together. Before they found it, it was known to nuclear physicists as God's particle, and they pursued it with the same fervour once reserved for saints and angels. Then they found it, they have it. We have it. But now they're looking for something else.

That morning I couldn't interest the Director of Human Resources in the forgiveness of sins. He said it didn't seem important. The Press Office showed no curiosity in eternal life, not even hypothetically. They weren't even prepared to experiment.

Undeterred, I was accompanied by Davy's foot to the regular Saturday lunch-time meeting of the Rassemblement des Eglises Chrétiennes de Genève. The minister from the American church smiled horribly at me, wishing I were dead, asking me how long I was planning to stay. 'And what about your church?'

'I still have the key.'

'But no furniture. And no congregation. Buddy.'

He was undoubtedly an American, but he was also formerly a Germanic Dutch Nordic Scandinavian, with unbreakable ice in his soul. I didn't argue, but my leg closest to Davy cramped for the whole hour as God's Protestant intermediaries discussed greenhouse gases and genetically modified crops, and our moral responsibility to the planet, or the people, or even both. The Lutherans disagreed with the American Episcopalians who disagreed with the Southern Baptists and the Dutch Reform Church.

As the Anglican representative, I agreed with everybody.

Over our sandwich lunch, watching God's most junior deputies grin and pick their teeth, it occurred to me that I moved far too infrequently among superior people. I felt a nagging sense of underachievement, suspecting that in another life, in Geneva, instead of this I'd almost certainly have been roistering in gravy with Byron and Scrope Davis at the Villa Diodati. Church-folk these days had no class, and whatever her other failings, mostly of a personal nature, Mrs Apreece was at least the widow of Shuckburgh Apreece (the baronet's son). She was also a cousin of Sir Walter Scott, actually.

I remembered Rifka's suggestion from yesterday of a possible visit to Moholy's villa. Today, unlike yesterday, I was tempted. Men like me, with talent but no family, had only a limited number of opportunities in life, and Davy was barely forty-nine years old when crippled with palsy. In only fifteen years' time, I could be paralysed and wracked with regret for the many things I'd never done.

For the sake of scientific investigation, I therefore put my personal difficulties to one side, and surrendered myself to the delayed effect of elixir of Sir Humphry Davy. With a social boldness that was otherwise unlike me, I phoned the number Rifka had left on the answering machine, and between us we deftly arranged a visit to Moholy's villa, five miles out along the more fashionable southern bank of the lake.

'A word of warning,' Rifka said. 'He has mood swings. He can be a monster, so be careful. And don't say anything stupid.'

I decided to walk. I had my walking-boots, confident they'd come in useful in mountainous Switzerland, and also some knee-length walking-shorts. I topped these with a tartan shirt and a green tie, because, despite being small and unexceptional, I still knew how to show myself off to advantage.

The pedestrian route to the villa was bordered by the magnificence of Lake Geneva. On one side. And on the other by a dual carriageway. I gazed out over the glass-calm water, and the reflected mountains of the French Jura looked sublime, like spilt religion. *Oh most magnificent and noble Nature!*, but the rest of the verse escaped me, and then I tripped over my own feet.

But I didn't fall over. An Italian lorry sounded its horn, and then a higher-pitched builder's van, but I ignored the speeding traffic. Instead, I felt myself seduced by reality observed, at least to the left of me, and a sense of the breathing seam that sustains all life. It was a religion of lakeside grass and flowers, placid water, mountains, and nature as an experience of the holy.

Over an hour later, just beyond a lay-by and a bus-stop, the path stopped abruptly at a wall marked Private Property. The dual carriageway kinked inland to the right of a strand of houses, like scale models of French châteaux, each now with private lakeside frontage. Three or four properties along, I found the high iron gates to Moholy's villa. They were open, and at the end of a white gravel drive there was a silver Mercedes, a Jeep, and a pair of ornamental trees in slatted pots either side of the villa's open double-doors. A small bird clung upside down to a first-floor window-frame, pattering the glass with its beak, aiming at dead flies trapped in the webs of spiders.

I put my head inside the entrance hall, and called out. No reply. I stepped inside. Nobody. Selecting a door at random, I found a room so long, and so wide, it had an eleven-piece suite. There was a fireplace at each end, and over each fireplace a mirror reflecting telescopically for miles, or ages. On other walls there were chivalric crests and more mirrors, too high to reflect anything but themselves, and I was abruptly a provincial Englishman, from as far away as Penzance, too easily impressed by all that was universally impressive: money, power, the proof that not all men are equal.

I stepped back from the doorway when I heard feet on the stone staircase. I'd been expecting Rifka, but it was Moholy himself, though not the hard and acquisitive businessman I remembered from his visits to the church. He saw me and clapped his hands. I didn't move, but he was already turning and skipping back up the stairs.

'Come on up,' he said, and waved me to join him. I decided to pretend I was used to it. This was my kind of house, after all, though perhaps a little unambitious, at least when compared to the estate I was always planning to buy at Stowey, with its own private woodcocks.

Moholy was wearing jeans and a tucked-in business shirt buttoned to the wrists, no tie. As in the church, I had the impression of neatness, dapperness. Tasselled loafers, yellow socks, and nothing like the monster of Rifka's warning.

'I've heard all about yesterday,' he said, as I followed him up the staircase. It forked at about half-way. We turned left. 'You have quite a gift, by the sounds of it.'

The stairs led to a landing, and up a few more steps into a long narrow room. Tall windows overlooked a terrace, and a lawn sloping down to the lake, where a bobbing rowing-boat was tied to a jetty.

'We should go out one day,' I said, admiring the view, hands clasped behind my back, having a go at some upwardly mobile chat.

'Sorry?'

'Fishing.'

'Oh. Do you fish?'

And I thought no, never, of course I didn't. I was out of my depth and didn't know what I was saying. 'Whenever I can. Mostly salmon and trout.'

It soon became clear that this room was Moholy's storage for his gallery's ever changing stock of historical material things. Floating in white polystyrene chips, in steel trunks and tea-chests, he had the global range of gods and demons. There was no space left for furniture except in the gaps between the windows, occupied by carvings of life-sized pot-bellied black boys, with red and gold fruit at their feet.

Moholy was weaving between the crates to the end of the room, expecting me to follow. He had the brightness of eye of the true enthusiast, and nothing to hold him back. 'Come on. Come and say hello to Becket. I gather you're already acquainted.'

He spoke English with the classic Geneva accent. There was sometimes a trace of French, like flour on a bread roll, but the dough was pre-baked somewhere in the United States. In Switzerland, like the rest of Europe, English with an English accent was increasingly rare: it betrayed second-rate language learning, or a lack of ambition.

The second and smaller room had a lower ceiling, and heavily closed curtains. A single switch operated all the spots at once, trained on sloping glass-topped tables, and round all four walls display cabinets mounted on cupboards with closed wicker doors.

'Voilà,' he said, stepping aside, and just for a moment I hesitated. Where was Rifka? Why was Moholy so eager?

But, despite his reputation, I was openly intrigued by the plinth.

The centre of this second room was dominated not by one, but in fact by three black plinths, of different heights, pushed together like a rostrum. On the lowest level, on a burnished bronze plate, was a blackened walnut: *Van Gogh's Ear*. A little higher, in second place, floating in liquid in a polished glass jar, was something which looked like a sun-dried tomato: *Van Gogh's Ear*. On the highest level, supreme, there was a closed golden pill-box: *The Holy Prepuce*.

'Becket's over here,' Moholy said, skipping to one of the cabinets, and there he was, *Becket's Toe, 1170*, labelled on velvet beside *The Arm of Leonardo da Vinci, 1519*.

'How does he look?'

'Smaller,' I said.

'Take your time. It's a little cramped, I know, but the tour starts to the left of the door, goes round the room, and finishes at the central podium.'

With Davy in my pocket, I was curious and couldn't resist, although at first, close to the door, the collection seemed surprisingly tame. Moholy had started with lockets, open on their forgetful remnants of love, ancient curls in discoloured ribbon. After that, he progressed to several extracts from the poet Byron's anthology of pubic hair, which Byron had systematically collected from the women he slept with, each clump filed neatly in a separate, named envelope. I winced, but in a nice revenge, in a cabinet about a third of the way round the room, Moholy also had

46

Byron's bleakly crippled foot, embalmed in tattered bandages.

'Why are you showing me this?'

'Rifka thinks you have a special talent.'

He was leaning back against a display cabinet on the other side of the exhibition, his feet daintily crossed at the ankles. 'You've felt it, haven't you, James? Can I call you James?'

'Jay.'

'And besides, you're exactly the kind of adaptable chap I need.'

The self-made Davy, half his mind forever trapped in Penzance with his poor widowed mother, had little defence against flattery. It was everything he wanted to hear, a justification of his evasion of the grind of paying his father's debts, and a blessing on his absence from his mother's pitiful milliner's shop at the far edge of England, Europe, the world and everywhere.

'I could really believe in someone like you,' Moholy said. 'And even better, you're a vicar.'

'I'm not a vicar.'

'You have the hardness of heart of the educated. I can use that.'

'How?'

'All in good time. Have a look at what I've got.'

The Jaw of Suleiman the Magnificent, 1566.

The Finger of Michelangelo Buonarotti, 1564.

Oliver Cromwell's Skull, 1658.

This continuing fascination, even after death, was the genuine measure of any one person's greatness. I felt a little unsteady, and if I hadn't known that I too was also destined for greatness, I might briefly have been overwhelmed by my own insignificance.

'What's a prepuce?' I asked, swallowing and turning all my attention to the podium at the centre of the room. Moholy's eyes sparkled.

'This is my favourite. It's a triumph of the collectors' logic.'

'But what exactly is it?'

'It's the *carne vera sancta*. It's the foreskin of Jesus Christ, the son of God.'

I was appalled, and felt a little sick. What a horrible idea. How fascinating. 'I never heard of that before.'

'Want to see it?'

'I don't know. Do I?'

'Up to you.'

'It's not real, is it?'

'Why not?'

'Well, if it was, I'd have heard about it. Everyone would.'

'It is what it is, that much I know. It is a detached and dried human foreskin. Whether it was ever attached to Jesus is admittedly less easy to authenticate.' Moholy reached for the pill-box, his elegant fingers trembling slightly as he opened it up. 'Even the Vatican disapproves,' he said, approvingly. 'Since 1900 they've threatened excommunication to anyone writing about it, or even talking about it.'

'Is that a fact?'

'That's a fact.'

I peeked inside the box. After twenty centuries, the foreskin of Jesus Christ was dry and hard like a discard of rusty glue.

Moholy proudly explained that all other relics of Christ were secondary: splinters of the True Cross, the fateful nails, the chalice used to collect his blood, the shroud. There could be no actual primary relic from the body of Christ the incarnate son of God, no physical proof of his existence, because the New Testament swore on the Holy Bible that his mortal body ascended whole into heaven. It stood to reason: there was none of the physical body left behind, only belongings.

'What about fingernails?' I asked, detached and scientific as I was.

'Five have been recorded,' Moholy said confidently, holding up his own fingers, 'all, strangely enough, from the left hand.'

'Haircuts,' I suggested, exploring the possibilities, thinking through the logic. 'He must occasionally have had his hair trimmed. What about his hair?'

'The milk teeth of Jesus, the spilt blood of the son of God, the sweat and tears of Christ our Lord. Anything he might have left behind, however small and seemingly insignificant, somebody, somewhere, has tried to collect.'

'Placenta?'

'Good thinking. Haven't come across that one. Though there's a school of thought which contests that the Holy Grail is the womb of Mary, the literal container of Christ's blood.'

'Umbilical cord?'

'Collectors call it the Holy Navel. But how likely is that? How likely are milk teeth, or individual drops of sweat? The holy prepuce is different.'

Moholy pinched it out of its little box, and held it clamped between two fingers and a thumb, narrowing his eyes. 'Circumcision was a major event. Of all the primary relics of Jesus, it seems most likely that the prepuce could have been saved, and venerated. They say it was a great comfort to Mary, after the crucifixion.'

I nodded sympathetically, sure it would have been, and who could deny a grieving mother comfort, of any kind? There was something fantastically logical about it, impossibly believable.

'So it really is his? Is it really His?'

Moholy sighed, and carefully replaced the prepuce. He restored the pill-box to its place of honour, leaving open the lid.

'Nothing,' he said, his disappointment unmistakable. 'I feel no particular divine urge.'

'As if you would.'

'You're not convinced, are you, James?'

'Jay. Call me Jay.'

'You're still not a believer, are you?'

'I'm a deacon.'

'In the Church of England. I mean a real believer. In the passion. In the power of relics.'

'I think it's highly unlikely.'

'Oh come now. Examples are widely documented, from St Augustine all the way through to the venerable Matt Talbot, who cures alcoholics in Dublin to this very day. It's an ancient knowledge, another we're in danger of losing. My personal breakthrough, though, my own small contribution, has been the discovery that it also works with secular remains.'

'What does?'

'The influence. The power.'

Moholy reached into one of the wicker cupboards beneath the display cabinets, and pulled out something flat wrapped in a paint-stained sheet. He clamped it under his arm as we went back to the stock-room, where I had to raise my hand against the bright surprise daylight. He threw the sheet aside, and propped two painted canvases in the angle between floor and wall, directly across from the first tall window.

'Self-portraits,' Moholy said. 'That's how I've been trying to get to the bottom of this.'

He separated the paintings, and balanced them side by side.

'Before I acquired Vincent's ears, I'd never picked up a paintbrush in my life.'

We took a step back and looked solemnly at the two paintings, self-portraits by Moholy in the approximate style of Van Gogh; expressionist, instinctive, the brushwork swirled and broken.

'In the other room you have two distinct ears,' I said, remaining patient. In the process of scientific investigation, I'd discovered, it was essential to keep returning to first principles. 'I seem to remember that Van Gogh only lost the one. He only cut off one of his ears.'

'You're right, and only one of them is the true relic. How can I tell? Because only one of them works. That's how I know which of the two is authentic.'

In the paintings, Moholy had lengthened his face and reddened his hair, making himself look a little like Vincent Van Gogh. His research into relics was clearly much more advanced than my own.

'Give me an opinion.'

Neither painting looked more obviously like a Van Gogh than the other.

'Yes, I know,' Moholy said, 'I can't decide either.'

He put his chin in his hand, and arched back his upper body. He squinted, then closed one eye. 'I just get frustrated and depressed, and give up trying to tell them apart before I'm tempted to slice my ear off. Or something.'

I took a step away from Moholy, my host, and turned this information one way and then the other with a platinum spatula, staying as neutral as possible while applying different acids and reagents, establishing the true nature of this particular madness. It wasn't immediately evident. I put my hands in my pockets, to make closer contact with Sir Humphry, but it turned out that Davy was a pioneer at the forefront of the failure of science. It had started as organised common sense, but had since developed into something far stranger; quarks and gluons that nobody could see on strings round the huge underground doughnuts of CERN. Life couldn't be explained by science, and in Davy's time, as in ours, there was nothing so fatal to the human mind as to suppose that one view was ultimate, that there were no mysteries in nature, that our triumphs were complete, and we had no new worlds to discover.

Davy accepted early in his career that matter changed under different conditions, as did human character. So why not the attributes and properties of human remains?

I pulled back from the edge, because after all I was not a second Newton. My own ignorance frightened me, made me flinch away from the awful stretching realm of everything I'd never understand.

'I said,' Moholy said, evidently for the second time, 'how's the apartment?'

He was stacking the two Van Goghs back together again, and covering them with the sheet. 'Rather burnt your bridges yesterday, didn't you?'

'I could go back to England any time.'

'Perhaps.'

'Thanks for letting me stay in the apartment.'

It cost me nothing to say it. This was simply my phase of accepting patronage just as one day I'd surely be a patron myself, as Davy was to Faraday.

'You need a job, don't you?'

Moholy carried his paintings back to their cupboard, and while he was bending down he said I could borrow any relic I wanted. 'Just while you're at a loose end,' he added. 'Don't be shy. Take your pick.'

I considered the bones, the labels, the possibilities, and had several rapid fantasies before reason intervened. Not wanting to disappoint him, I took one of the lockets by the door.

'You can do better than that.'

'No, really.'

From another of the wicker cupboards he brought out a large book, bound in red leather. He straightened up and wiped off the cover. 'Take a look at this.'

He handed me the book, and the binding was very soft, like calfskin. I went into the next room and over to the window to read its spine, but the spine was blank. I opened it, and inside was a standard ring-binder, upsidedown. I turned it the right way up.

The folder contained perhaps thirty typed pages, each one in an individual plastic wallet. Each page was headed with a famous name, then dates, followed by a short biography, and a price. The names were in alphabetical order, starting with *Becket, Thomas*. I flipped through to the back, where there was an index, and against the names in the index there was occasionally an adhesive red dot, like in an art catalogue. There was a dot against *Davy, Sir Humphry*, another against *Mann, Thomas*, and also *Niven, David*.

'I know,' Moholy tutted. 'I hold up my hands and admit it. The list is short, and patchy, but we're still quite a small operation and as yet active only in Switzerland. But tell me. Who would *you* pick?'

'I don't think it's any of my business,' I said, closing the folder and handing it back.

'Allow me to make a suggestion.'

Moholy pulled some slim-profile glasses out of his shirt-pocket, perched them on the end of his nose, and turned to the index. He peered at it from top to bottom, his eyebrows bouncing curiously from one name to the next.

Then he licked his finger, and flipped to the page he wanted, propping the open catalogue on a makeshift stand of plastic chips in a tea-chest. As he silently read the biography on the selected page, he reached up to scratch the side of his nose, then tapped his teeth with a fingernail.

'I recommend number 23.' He checked with me over the top of his glasses, as if at a restaurant. '*Joyce, James.* An excellent choice, I think. I have many clients who lack culture. It's a type of insecurity, and often results in a mania for collection. Yes, James Joyce. He'd be perfect, especially when I mention that at the end of his life, to the *cognoscenti* of literary taste who know this sort of thing, and with whom personally my clients would like to be connected, he was known as Joyce, James Jesus. He's a relic I could sell tomorrow.'

I coughed, and Moholy stopped.

'How about it?'

'Well,' I said. 'I don't like to quibble, but isn't James Joyce still buried?'

Moholy looked at me with straight and steely eyes, closed the book, and held it against his chest. He carefully took off his specs. 'James. Jay. This could be the answer to all your problems. What have you got to lose?'

Sir Humphry Davy collapsed in a Geneva hotel-room at the age of fifty, only sixteen years from now, depressed and lonely, childless, estranged from his wife, not carrying a Davy-lamp to ensure his own safety. I was losing my way, too easily distracted from the discipline of a scientific approach, and I had to sit down.

There was no furniture, so I sat on the floor, in the corner where we'd propped the Van Goghs. I didn't want to think this through, because logic and reason were not infallible, and in moments of stress I became sentimental, professing undying love to Mrs Apreece, and composing sonnets to my very special mother. At that moment, disarmed by Moholy's proposal, I wanted nothing else but to be back in the safety of Penzance, with Mum, and her home-made marinaded pilchards.

I vaguely remember Moholy making a call on a mobile. And then a little while later Rifka, blonde Rifka with the two-stage nose, kneeling in front of me and offering me a glass of water. The light from the tall window behind her head darkened her features, surrounding her with a luminescent glow.

'He was probably a bit brusque,' Rifka said, 'was he? That's the way he sometimes is.'

Moholy appeared behind Rifka's shoulder, and said that if it made me feel any better he apologised, though he didn't look very sorry. He put his hand flat on his throat, then exercised his jaw. 'I didn't mean to rush you, it must be something I ate. But think about what I said, Jay. Phone me from the apartment. From my apartment.'

'What shall I do with him until then?' Rifka asked, fractionally turning her head. 'He seems to be in shock.'

'Fix a date to show him the ropes. Then get him out of here.'

I tried to wave down a taxi, as befitted my station as a knight of the realm, but my heart wasn't in it. Also, taxis were forbidden by Geneva law from stopping on dual carriage-ways for Alpine walkers in shorts and tartan shirts and skew-whiff ties.

At the bus-stop, I watched the traffic, and then the clouds

turning blue-black in the distance over the city. I was sitting on a plastic flip-down seat, and I had my forearms pressed together between my thighs, and I was rocking forwards and backwards, backwards and forwards, barely holding myself together.

I was waiting for a bus. I was wearing climbing boots and a shirt and tie. I had with me a gold eighteenth-century locket, and a section of bone from Sir Humphry Davy's foot. Events may have passed me by, and I may have seen a world I was never meant to see, and I ought very urgently to have been back in England attending to earlier responsibilities, but I was still recognisably waiting for a bus, which was a great if fragile comfort.

In 1826, Davy had a total nervous breakdown. Numb with opium and acetate of cocaine, escaping his work, he came to a halt in Geneva, banging up hard against the limits of reasonable thinking. Davy the scientist wanted the secret of existence, and found himself a stranded self, without any answers. Science had no more access to certainty than religion, and he'd tried both, looking always beyond the simplistic defeatism of we are born, we live, we die. He couldn't leave well alone, and now he was paying heavily for all that inhaling, combusting, fusing and combining, poking and scrubbing at elements and alloys and crystals, and sundry ethereal substances.

Davy would have resurrected the dead, if necessary. I was fairly sure of that, and it frightened me. He wasted his final years in pursuit of a theory of unification, hoping for a principle of connection like an amalgam of everything he'd ever learnt, and ever known. Science would cohere with theology, with imagination and emotion, with poetry and the absolute everything. Understanding would be all.

56

Relics appealed to the same weakness. They seemed to offer a unique point of contact between man and God. They could join heaven and earth, the immaterial and the material, the living and the dead.

Davy would have dug up James Joyce, as proposed by Moholy, and I craved all Davy's early success. His triumphant discoveries and promotions, his curiously modern career, cut off from early friends and family by his meteoric rise, rootless and free. But I envied him less his lonely death in a Geneva hotel-room, correcting the proofs of *Salmonia*, a series of dialogues told in different voices which were really all his own, confused at the end by the sense that there was so much more to say than he could ever have said by himself.

Perhaps if he and Lady Davy had succeeded in having children. It might have made all the difference. Davy might never have broken down, his reputation cracking and scattering as he shook at the meaning of life in a laboratory, seeking by clinical experiment to establish the existence and wisdom of God.

A horn was sounding. I looked up, and a silver Mercedes was stopped in the lay-by of the bus-stop, engine running, and in the driver's seat was Rifka. The near-side window slid down, by electricity, and she leant over the passenger seat to speak with me.

'Everything alright?'

I needed opium, or acetate of cocaine, but all I had was Davy's impossible foot, and its increasingly familiar influence: investigate, ask questions, receive incomplete answers, despair.

'I'm waiting for the bus.'

'I can see that. Do you want a lift?'

'No.'

The car was gently idling.

'Jay?'

'What.'

'Sir Humphry Davy. You forgot to give him back.'

I opened up my hands, and there he was. I could have kept him, if I'd wanted, but Davy had made so many mistakes. In the very last days, almost at the end, he instructed his travelling companion John Tobin Junior to delay his burial, should he die in Geneva. And he withheld permission for an autopsy, just in case he should merely be sleeping, and presently about to awake.

The Geneva city laws made no allowances for delusions such as these, and anyway, decay was already setting in. There were no miracles, and two centuries later Davy's foot-bone was yet to exhibit unquestionable evidence of Davy's revival. Its influence was purely subjective. In lab tests, the bone had stained in fire, and although conditions were only approximate to the standards of the day, initial results suggested elixir of Davy was limited at best in its effectiveness.

'Where's the box?' Rifka asked, smiling nicely. I didn't have the plastic box.

'Just put it on the seat, then.'

I put Davy's foot on the leather seat of the Mercedes, and the relief was immediate. It was suddenly just a dry piece of old bone, human matter without a soul.

Rifka slipped the car into drive. 'Thanks,' she said. 'And don't forget our appointment tomorrow.'

The Mason Family Ankle

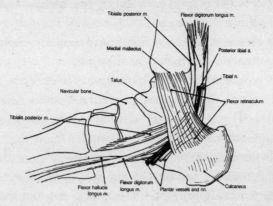

'In any true life you must go and be exposed outside the small circle that encompasses two or three heads in the same history of love. Try and stay, though, inside. See how long you can.'

Saul Bellow, *The Adventures of Augie March*

I woke up the next morning feeling neutral to good. Then I remembered that I'd been under severe pressure, cracking up, falling apart. I'd had a bad couple of days, but I could now put the bones behind me, and pull myself together. Be normal. Remember who you are.

I am deacon Jay James Mason, Mason Minor, younger brother of Tom Mason, second son of the late Timothy Thomas James Mason, MA, and Mrs Angharad Bethany Mason, adventurer and exile, currently of Almuñécar near Granada, on the coast of southern Spain. Submitting to the influence of relics was a dangerous kind of evasion. I had my own identity, my history, my life.

I had a girlfriend, Helena Byczynski, who was three months pregnant. At this stage, no one but us was allowed to know, what with nature being so unpredictably dangerous and corrective. The baby was a secret. And Helena and I were living in separate countries.

It was therefore quite possible that I was not coping well with the situation in which I found myself.

What would Mum and Dad have done? They'd have married and had the baby and started a refreshing new family of Masons. That's what they actually did. I wondered how they'd gone through with it, but already I knew the answer. It was a life's work. Instead of discovering potassium, or saving the English Church, they did the decent thing.

It was Sunday morning in Geneva, a city until recently home to an outpost of the Anglican Church, and a compassionate short-term assignment for a clerical underachiever without other commitments. The Appointments Board didn't know about Helena. But they knew about Dad, were sympathetic, and as one they'd agreed that a short trip abroad might help me reflect on my ongoing stumble between deacon and priest.

I went to the bathroom, stepping barefoot between coloured shapes projected across the parquet by the glass panels in the doors. On a shelf within reach of the toilet was an old edition of *Crockford's Clerical Directory*. These books are annual lists of decent people who in any given year sacrifice themselves for the benefit of the nation. I looked up Dad, Mason Senior, in 1993:

Mason, Timothy Thomas James
b 40 Nottm Univ BA 61 St Jo Coll Dur MA 66 Ridley Hall Cam
66 d 67 p 68 C St Nic w St Jo Newport *Linc* 67–69; Mil Ch

C/Coy Para 3 69–73; V Mydroilyn w Dihewyd *St D* 73–77; V Sewerby cum Merton and Grindale *Ripon* 77–83; V Limber Magna w Somersby *Chich* 83–88; P-in-C Penzance w Stonegrave, Nunnington and Stockly *Truro* 88–90; P-in-C Wallsend St Luke *Newc* from 90

In religious code, this was the geography of my childhood; chopping, changing, learning to adapt, adapting. Fatally for a career in the Anglican Church, Mason Senior had never developed the required comedy of kindness, indignation and mild buffoonery. He had all the right qualities, but in the wrong proportions, and was shunted from one humble parish to another, God's envoy among the schizophrenia of provincial England, watching it lurch without warning from drug-induced ram-raids to asphyxia of the soul by embroidered cushion.

At its worst (V Sewerby cum Merton and Grindale *Ripon* 77–83) it was unstoppable poverty and indignity and death, with mental no-hopers gurning at all hours at an open unlockable door. At its best (V Limber Magna w Somersby *Chich* 83–88) it was a glazed outskirt parish where much golf was played, and unhappiness was mostly gossip. The locals had the courtesy to die on time, and effective or not, underpaid or not, whatever the horror of his handicap, Mason Senior was genuinely esteemed for his unique entitlement to redeem his four-ball from sin.

Dad was in a rut of doing the decent thing. He obstinately stood up for goodness, at whatever cost to himself, and in Dad I saw that the essence of ministerial life was putting others first. At home, he was often on the telephone. It was usually parishioners calling in their cries for help, and when he was out we had our rote-learnt answer off by heart.

'Sorry, I am unable to help you. But my dad will be back in a minute.'

For the first ten years of my life, I assumed there was no problem on earth that Dad couldn't solve. He'll be back in a minute. He'll be able to help.

Dad had been in a war, in Ireland, as chaplain to a parachute battalion (Mil Ch C/Coy Para 3 69–73). He'd patrolled the streets of Crossmaglen, with a Bible and medikit instead of a gun, which was foolhardy and incredibly brave and a great disappointment. He still had the faded red beret and a stencilled khaki kit-bag, and I thought of him not as a vicar, but as a soldier in clerical disguise, undercover on some vitally important mission to save the world as we knew it.

He believed in fresh air. And Snakes and Ladders. Red phoneboxes, and waitresses in white blouses in country-house hotels. It was all part of his undeviating creed of England, and he frequently braced his spirituality with wet weekends under canvas on the Brecon Beacons, and unsupported kayak-trips across the Bristol Channel. By the Sunday, after battling nature and winning, he'd also believe in one holy catholic and apostolic Church. He acknowledged one baptism for the forgiveness of sins, and he looked for the resurrection of the dead.

Dad's dad was also a vicar, but the strongest memory I had of him was his funeral. It had gathered us all together: Grandfather Mason (deceased), Mason Senior, Mother Mason, Thomas Mason Major, and James Mason Minor. Tom, wearing Dad's regimental beret to keep him brave, sat near the end of our row at the front, giggling about Granddad's leg. As part of dying from a lifetime on his feet, and some metal in his thigh from a Stop sign in Normandy, Grandfather Mason had developed a blood-clot in his ankle.

At the hospital, they decided to amputate, thinking the old man's famous reserves of faith would allow him to cope, at the age of eighty, with only one foot.

Dad was standing beside the coffin. Tom giggled, and hunched his head forward and covered his ears with his arms. That week, Dad's chasuble and stole were violet, and that week, like every other, it was my dad who was God's agent on earth. I was crying, and so was Mum. But it was alright, because Dad could help. Dad could always help. He was about to offer explanations, starting with proof of God's existence, and evidence of life after death. He would then justify old age and blood-clots and bereavement, before taking questions on specific conundrums of luck. These were the things I expected him to know. He must do, or why was he always on the phone? And why else was it my dad and not the other dads standing there in black and white and violet, in a direct line of descent from the Apostles, leading the most solemn rituals of England?

There were a few coughs, wondering why Mason Senior hadn't started.

He started.

There are many rooms in my father's house. If there were not, I would have told you.

By the psalm, or at the latest by the New Testament reading, it became evident that Dad wasn't the police. He wasn't going to investigate Granddad's death, or patch together reasons from clues a trained mind would always uncover. He wasn't a rogue cop, incensed but logical, on a fierce personal and professional quest to find out why, and who, and what on earth for.

And how best to take revenge.

Dad was resigned. He lit a candle, and holding it aloft

above the coffin, he ended the service by commending the life of Grandfather Mason to God. I started singing Happy Birthday. Tom lifted his feet from the floor, and squinnied out loud.

It was a difficult time. I was about ten, and had recently learnt at my private boarding school that all men were born equal.

'Except Jesus,' Dad reminded me.

We'd been given several days leave-out for the funeral, and at the end of a very long day Mum was putting us to bed.

'Never mind Jesus,' Mum said, on this occasion in her Yorkshire voice, somewhere between Kes and rugby league. My mum was very special. Like every boy's mother, she wasn't like the other mothers: she could do all the voices. 'Eh oop,' she said, 'never mind 'im upstairs. You lads be whatever you blinking well want.'

That evening, after vigorous teeth-cleaning, Mum read us a story which ended happily. She loved doing the dialogue, trying out different accents as the flickering night-light found the hidden silver grain of her hair. Last thing, before going downstairs, she turned in the half-open doorway and told us she meant it, and we really could be whatever we wanted. And even though Dad was already out again, at Parish Council, or a hospital visit, she sealed our conspiracy by whispering, with no accent at all: 'but not a vicar, I beg of you both, please'.

In the top bunk, Tom was already snoring with his nose squashed to the wall. I was only pretending to sleep, and Mum suddenly came back and whispered in my ear that I was a very special little boy, oh my little baby. I opened my eyes. Mum smiled uncertainly, but I was still worried about Granddad. I asked how long before he changed into a skeleton.

'I don't know,' Mum said, in her kindest, most compassionate voice. Her normal voice. 'Not straight away. It takes a little while.'

'I saw a skeleton once, in a museum.'

'Was it interesting?'

'It was dead.'

Mum kissed me and pressed her cheek against my forehead. She told me how wonderful I was, but even then she ought to have taken more care. I was the last in a long line of cosseted English clerics, of discounts at private choir-schools, and therefore a long history of shelter, in which the craziest ambition can bud and breed.

Choir-school, which was free to the children of vicars, taught me that life was hard and boys have more than one identity. It might be the same for girls, but we were all boys, so I'd no way of knowing. At boarding school, there was no Mum and Dad, so we picked our own alternative influences. As parental substitutes, I had Buck Rogers of the twenty-fifth century, Wonderwoman and Geoffrey Boycott, a random greatest and latest. That was the way to live. Tom had his own heroes, but I always collected more posters and more commemorative stickers, and bought more plastic models with my hoarded birthday postal orders.

Dad couldn't understand it. Most mornings in the holidays we'd ask for ninety-nine pence, for whatever was newest and most improved. Dad would say no, because none of the collectable cards or fetishes did anything reliably useful, like placating fate. They failed to block even the smallest acts of God, like a broken saucer in the washing-up, or how frequently he lost his glasses.

In Geneva, if it wasn't already too late, I was hoping that memories such as these could save me. Dad's bones were in the ground, and I could still hear my mother's voice in anger demanding to know if I actually believed in God (*well, James, do you?*). Trapped, under pressure, I'd been forced to admit that the only thing I'd ever believed unconditionally, was that I believed, yes Mum I did believe, unconditionally in my family's love.

That's where I should look for help. I went to the kitchen, and started tidying up. Mum had never been a great tidier, modelling herself on her own mum, who one summer in Swansea had fallen in love with an acrobat, but failed to run off with the circus. After that, housework was always a defeat. So, like Dad, I put packets back in cupboards, wiped surfaces, and was about to start on the washing-up when I saw Moholy's golden locket on the table. I took it to the swing-bin under the sink, and emptied out the contents. This was how to be sane, and not to fall apart. Remember what holds you together, your roots.

In the bedroom, I meant to tidy away Dad's red chasuble. It was Sunday, and by this time every Sunday Dad would have finished Morning Prayer and be readying himself for Family Communion. Without worrying too hard at the reasons, sensing my father's gentle influence, I folded the chasuble into a carrying bag. Then I dressed, putting on a dark lambswool cardigan of the type modelled by vicars for a hundred years. Then my black zip-up jacket, which I only ever wore to work.

On a Sunday, with the banks closed and so many people not going to church, Geneva was a ghost-town. The city's symbol, the Jet d'Eau, was a high-rise, high-pressure geyser in the harbour, which could push seven tons of water 140 metres into the air. Often, it was turned off, and today, on my way to the Church of All Saints, there was no sign of it. In

Geneva, even the landmarks were ghostly, making the place seem unfixed, just right for its population always coming and going, constantly changing the city's character.

Mum would have defied the Swiss quietness, like a challenge. She'd even have hated the lake, a timid ocean, sedate in its reaction to every dramatic moon. Between the antiques galleries and the shops selling precious stones, she'd have made rude noises and done funny voices, and generally have acted oddly.

As for Dad, he'd have loved Geneva. In the Old Town the dismal Cathedral and bleak alleys made it feel acceptable to be uptight. The 500 banks were like clenched fists, and nobody was openly letting themselves go.

When I reached the church, I was surprised to see a small group waiting in the arched doorway. I recognised the burly figure of Mr Oti, who was something cultural in the Nigerian embassy, and a formerly dependable All Saints warden.

'At last,' he said. 'We thought you weren't coming.'

'I wasn't. I'm not. What do you mean?'

'Mrs Meier told us all about it. You kept the key. You wouldn't give up the church without a fight.'

The weather. I took immediate refuge in the weather. 'Brrr,' I said. 'Not so warm. Let's go inside.'

I unlocked the door, and everyone followed me in. Which wasn't what I had in mind, not exactly, but there were more people than I'd originally thought, with others arriving all the time, expats, Africans, and representatives from all the cricket-playing nations. Helpfully, Mr Oti and Mr Dharmasena, another occasional church-warden, carried the two bin-bags of jumble out of harm's way and down the aisle to the vestry. One man at each end, they then lifted the altar back to its customary position.

I peeked out at all this activity from behind the vestry door. The Geneva faithful were English enough to be filling up the empty space from the back. I didn't know them well, but there was a family of Indians from a flooded village in Madhya Pradesh. There were two sisters from Sierra Leone, whose family owned cows made worthless by European dumping of surplus beef. And there were also the regular Sri Lankans.

Mr Dharmasena owned a bar by the station, and showed cricket on satellite to his many compatriots in Geneva who worked washing pots. He'd chaired the All Saints pledge fund for nearly a decade, ever since he and an earnest gathering of batsmen and bowlers had picked out this particular church for their prayers to the god of cricket. Three rows of Sri Lankans had knelt in mumbled silence, pleading for a miraculous victory in the Cricket World Cup.

In the final that year, Sri Lanka hammered Australia, who were unbeatable.

The Sri Lankans were among those most anguished by the sale of the Anglican church. Others in the congregation could seek spiritual comfort elsewhere, but what did the God of the Episcopalians or the Geneva Reformed Church know about cricket? And why would he even care?

'Peace be with you,' Mr Dharmasena said, rubbing his hands together, looking at me expectantly. Mr Oti joined us in the vestry and punctured the transparent plastic wrapper round the parcel of returned laundry. He pulled out a black server's cassock and a blue choir surplice, so recently ironed and starched he could balance them across his forearms like a tray. He tried to be solemn, then smiled hugely.

'I'm not really allowed,' I said. 'I don't have the authority.'

'God works in mysterious ways.'

'Yes, Mr Dharmasena, I've heard that he does.'

'So.'

'There aren't any chairs or anything.'

'No one minds.'

'The English church won't let us down,' Mr Oti said. 'That's what we were always promised.'

He transferred the robes from his forearms to mine, and winked. 'See you in two shakes, and James Mason?'

'That's my name.'

'Good luck.'

They left me alone, and Dad would have said that feeling trapped was much the same as feeling called. I put the cassock and surplice aside, and sorted through the laundry for a clerical shirt, and a slip-in collar. There was a head-and-shoulders mirror on a chain on the back of the door, and in the black shirt and white collar I looked serious and a little worried and very like my dad. His face was plainly visible in mine, and the clear sight I had of him instantly collapsed my sense of self. I'd always wanted to be an original, resisting my resemblance to Dad, who in turn resembled *his* dad. But dressed in the family way, challenged by a hopeful congregation, nothing in the world seemed so consequent as being what I was most expected to be. My father's son. An Anglican minister. Human blancmange.

I flipped the mirror round to its hardboard backing. It didn't work: I was still my dad, this realisation like the beginning of the end of ambition. I pulled Dad's red chasuble over my head, and settled its cloak on my shoulders. I opened the door, walked out into the church, and stood at the front. Remembering many months of Sundays, I lifted up my hands.

Do you not know that you are God's temple and that God's spirit dwells in you?

I had my doubts. Just for a moment, imitating Dad in front of all these expectant people, I felt like an impostor, with no real idea of what I was doing. And you know (the place and the occasion rousing an old family habit), life's a bit like that.

No, that's wrong. Life *is* that.

I summoned my best impression of my father, just as my dad had always made a stab at his dad, and maybe that's all there was, each new Mason just an updated version of the Masons who'd gone before.

Jesus appeared to his disciples at the sea of Tiberius, after he had risen from the dead (Alleluia!).

It was the building itself which eventually helped me relax. A century and a half of sincere devotion had left a residue, and the vaulted roof still fluttered with prayers snagged between the beams. I settled myself, and concentrated on giving my people what they wanted. It was Sunday, and they were here out of hope and habit, English-speaking people who felt sentimental about trees. Warm weather made them nostalgic, and they had an appetite for words and music with a spiritual heft. Faith, love, forgiveness, the oldest mysteries of humanity. Come and get it, in English, at the English church.

I looked the length of the empty building along its strip of chequered aisle, and through trembling eyelashes I blurred a vision of God and his infinite English ministry. Beyond the coloured glare of the windows was a scorching summer's day, and wicker baskets on the handlebars of heavy hand-held Raleighs, school-bands, and a tombola seasonally fixed on the village green.

I couldn't hold it. Nobody could. For at least a generation, perhaps longer, nobody had been able to hold it. I needed more height. I climbed the stairs to the pulpit, my mind flicking through its Rolodex of sermons (*Have you ever felt that life is pointless?*). I set myself securely, then leant forward on one elbow.

'Has anyone here recently felt that they wanted to be someone else?'

Nobody answered. It was a question I was supposed to answer myself (*I know I have*). But I didn't know what came next, after the answer. I started again, with the glory of God. Heads dropped, disappointed, so I drew strength from the binding example of Mason Senior, and his enduring creed of England. We had a superior sense of justice and fair play. We were more tolerant than the French, and less corruptible than the Italians. We weren't Americans. And standing defiant but ever cheerful, we the English alone had saved all other peoples from the evil of German fascism.

It was what my people wanted. I therefore found a moral in restored Alvis sports cars, and England as a pastoral version of God, of grass meadows and small copses near verdant Melton Mowbray. And this was my serious point, I concluded, wagging my finger for emphasis, *this* is my serious point: Melton Mowbray isn't like that. It isn't. Everyone knows that. But the surviving Anglican congregation in Melton Mowbray, from the ribbon developments to the enterprise parks, is praying this same prayer, to this same vision. That was my serious point.

We even had a communion, of sorts. I shared out a granary loaf which Mrs Meier had meant for a family of swans she'd seen on the lake. I tore off big Protestant mouthfuls, and some of the older Anglicans were still chewing as I thanked them for coming, and shook their hands at the door.

It was all false, of course.

After the disappointment of Granddad's funeral, I couldn't see the use in having a dad as a vicar. For everyone else, the *vicar* was the vicar. It wasn't even a disguise.

At the wake afterwards, I crept up on Dad, circling him, protecting myself from the evil eye with the *mano cornuto* held out rigidly in a line between our eyes. I insisted on knowing if Granddad had gone to heaven.

'Just tell me. Nobody will tell me if he's happy in heaven.'

'Yes, my son, he is.'

'Why?'

'Because he was a good man.'

'Why?'

'Because he helped people and tried not to hurt them.'

'Why?'

'Because he thought that was the right thing to do.'

'Why?'

'You know, James, that's a very good question.'

Which Dad couldn't answer. For Granddad, the Church may have been a regular and even sensible career-choice, priests in that distant past as conformist and socially acceptable as lawyers were now, or accountants. If he'd wanted, he could probably have been anything. A generation later, it was inexcusable, and now Dad was stupidly going the way of his own father, vicaring, being good, dying.

Mum, obliged to move house every few years and work all week to supplement a vicar's stipend, thought it an almighty mistake, a life lost. Tom, too ashamed to invite his first girl-friends back to a vicarage, couldn't agree more. The three of us therefore invented passwords, and a secret handshake. With Mum's encouragement, we gave our word of honour to do everything in our power to distract Mason Senior, the vicar, Dad, from the error of his Anglican ways.

At Christmas, in the first act of our conspiracy, Tom and I feigned astonishment as we unwrapped our present from

Mum, from Mum's own earnings as a temp. It was a chemistry set one down from the best you could get. It was also a weapon in the entrenched war between religion and science. The next day, fingers burnt and raw, with singed eyebrows and stubby eyelashes, we asked Dad to help us with a complicated set-up for transmuting water into wine, and then wine into blood, all in the one smooth sequence. Later, we tried out various corrosive reagents on invincible tins of pilchards, to see if five fish could be transformed by chemical reaction into a meal for all the family.

On this occasion, Dad allowed us our facetiousness. He was patient and good-humoured, but still a vicar who worked all hours and couldn't afford a pair of decent US-spec skateboards. Science couldn't shake him.

We therefore tried unsettling him with superstitions stronger and more potent than his own. Mason Senior would come back from Eucharist or Evensong, and his two sons would be waiting in the darkened lounge to offer him a palm-reading, or a consultation with the Tarot. We learnt the rituals and the occult routines, wrapping our cards in black silk, lighting incense sticks and intoning chants to the ibis-headed Egyptian god Thoth. We invoked the Cabbala, and the Holy Grail, and the Knights of the Rosy Cross, hoping Dad would think that this time we'd really lost it.

We tried everything. Using a T-square and the pointy end of a compass from the now neglected chemistry set, I pricked a tiny hole in the ankle of the skeleton on the Tarot death-card. Whatever dilemma Dad offered the ancient oracle, the reading from now on would always be Death.

He was supposed to ask questions about his career, about relationships, or about money, but he'd usually ruin it for everyone by asking the cards about the day of judgement.

With a flourish I'd deal out Death anyway, to increasingly reduced effect.

Q. Is there a day of judgement?

A. Death

Q. Did Christ die on the cross and on the third day rise again?

A. Death

Q. Anyone see the score in the cricket?

A. Death

I'd get my hair ruffled, as Dad cheerfully adopted his own dad's belief that English middle-class niceness was a manifestation of the divine, possessing a quiet force which had sustained an independent Christian sect for almost 500 years. His only regular excitement was shaving with an old safety-razor, which was never very safe. It was a little daily test of the Lord Our Shepherd. There was rarely any blood.

Most of the time Dad was genial, courteous and tolerant, all the qualities which gave the Church a bad name. He believed in pre-warmed pots of tea and a thriving cricket team as an ideal of living well, the middle-aged cleric crouched at mid-on, bowling some creaky off-spin, batting seven or eight, and serving beyond the call of duty behind the sticky clubhouse bar.

'You should come along,' he said. 'Turn your arm over. You might even enjoy it.'

He had no idea how embarrassing it was, having a dad who was so unfailingly nice to people. It wasn't normal. Once, when the disabled groundsman tried to throw me and Tom and Tom's friend Rob and Rob's dad off the outfield for using the sight-screen as a soccer goal, Rob's dad told the limping old duffer to shut up and fuck off.

And he had.

'How depressing,' Mason Senior said.

We weren't getting through to him. He was stuck in a backwater, pricked with twitchy boatmen and the perfect circles of breathing fish. He was content with his designated viewpoint, and the patient dedicated benches: *In memory of the Reverend T. T. J. Mason, who liked to sit.*

We used to slam our bedroom door and slouch down to the bridge over the motorway, the modern equivalent of the circus. Leaning over the barrier, we'd look down at all those cars and lorries, moving, speeding, heading somewhere, anywhere. We'd envy them all. And then gob on them.

Dad hardly noticed we'd gone. He'd come home at strange hours in the week of the Epiphany, raving about the splendour of the English language in the 1662 Book of Common Prayer. Tom would be in front of the television, flicking through the channels looking for role models: 'That's great, Dad. Fuckadelic.'

'Tom, why do you have to be so provocative all the time?'

'I don't.'

'You could even try to be nice,' Dad suggested, as we sat down to eat, without Mum again who was usually out at work. 'If you dared. Is it because you're frightened?'

'Lo,' Tom said, looking up to heaven, his knife and fork planted squarely in his fists. He started without the Bible on one of the few biblical quotes he thought he actually knew, 'Lo, though I walk through the shadow of the valley of the shadow of the valley of the shadow of death, I will fear no evil.'

'Why is that?' Dad asked, showing genuine interest. 'Why shouldn't either of you boys be afraid? I am. Frequently.'

'Because,' Tom said, pushing his chin forward and trying not to blink, actually not wanting to hear that his own father

75

was frequently afraid, 'because I am the meanest mother-fucker in the valley.'

Mason Senior slowly closed his eyes, put down his knife and fork, and coughed, not forgetting to put his hand politely in front of his mouth.

'I don't think that's quite right, is it?'

'*Everyone* knows that, Dad. It's on T-shirts all over the planet, except maybe the one *you* come from.'

Religion reflected badly on all of us, as if the Masons had something to hide. Dad didn't seem to realise that anyone who consistently launched conversations about God was probably unhinged. It made us seem like a family of extremists, suggesting that many other things must already privately have skewed, the taste for religion a last chance for chronic neurotics before the crystal-readings of Avalon, and the outer wastes of psychic space.

Wrong. All wrong.

Dad was an anchor. He was stable, and level-headed, exactly the influence I needed to keep myself together. I was a deacon and Dad was a priest; I was flaky and he was a rock. It was my own fault: I'd never worked hard enough on being like him, on simply being nice.

But it was never too late to start.

When the congregation finally dispersed, I pulled off Dad's chasuble. In my clerical shirt and collar, I jogged across the street to a Swiss Telecom phonebox. I felt energised, and full of purpose, only too happy to be failing at the miserable task of falling properly apart.

I looked up the UK code on a chart above the phone, then punched in Helena's otherwise familiar number. I waited. It rang. It answered.

She wasn't in. It was the answer-machine, and I put down the phone. I waved through the glass at the last stragglers from the church as they broke up their conversations and strolled away. With a spring in their step, I thought. Under the influence of Dad, and at thirty-four my dad had been a dad twice over, I dismissed any remnant of Davy. There was something indulgent and self-seeking in Davy's voluntary exile and wilful search for difference. The romantic ideal of the solitary hero was limited and self-destructive: if Dad had thought like that, then where would I be now?

Today, it was self-evident to me that everyone should get married and have children.

I pressed redial, and breathed heavily through my nose while Helena's voice worked calmly through to the beep. Like Dad, I intended to be accommodating, professionally sensitive to what people wanted. I therefore invested faith in my clerical training, and kept my voice almost under control as I apologised and explained. It was quite a long message. I hadn't been myself lately, there was some truth in that. But I was on the mend, and now I was feeling, well not fine exactly, but better. I said several other things, in the interests of making peace. I said she should call me.

As I pushed out of the phonebox, I realised it was some time since I'd enjoyed the sensation of virtue. It was an underrated emotion. I checked my watch. In the interests of Anglican niceness and courtesy, I intended to stay rigorously true to my word, and even though I had no intention of digging up the bones of the writer James Joyce, I'd made a promise to meet with Rifka. I started to walk, then jog, in the general direction of the station. It was important to be punctual.

*

There was a midday train which stopped at Céligny, a small and pretty village about half an hour from Geneva. From the age of thirty, Richard Burton had chosen to make the village of Céligny his home. Not the Victorian Richard Burton, who recorded the stories of Mohammed the Shalabi and the Man of Al-Yaman, but Richard Burton the ill-fated actor from Wales.

Rifka had been waiting at Geneva station, eating a bagel beside some Russian buskers playing the balalaika. She had some tools wrapped in a canvas sack, but I liked to think I was fairly unshockable by the difference of other people's lives. In one parish (*Sewerby cum Merton and Grindale*), an abandoned pensioner had been partially eaten by her King Charles spaniel before Dad discovered the body. In another (*Stonegrave, Nunnington and Stockly*), a verger who worked as an engineer on the cross-Channel ferry announced at weekly prayer that he would soon be living as a woman.

I took the tolerant Anglican view: it'd probably be fine. James Joyce was a Catholic, and hardly even that. Body-snatching wasn't necessarily a bad or even wrong thing to do. Yes it was, sometimes; and no it wasn't, at others. One mustn't judge. It all depended; and anyway, we were only going to practise. Whatever that might mean.

In our seats beside the window, I discovered that Rifka's presence was comforting. She had an easy and attractive manner, an inner serenity, and I was tempted to tell her about Dad, a strong fine man who thought deeply about luck, and stood up for goodness. Instead, because bragging wasn't in my nature, I looked out at this year's April from the calendar of beautiful Europe. The sun was chasing away high clouds split like ribs, and frosting the lake with a layer of mist. Far over on the other side, in black and snow above the haze, rose the peaks of huge French mountains.

I interlocked all my fingers, cracked the knuckles, then lifted a latticed double-fist to my mouth, as if boyishly about to blow the sound of a calling owl. Each movement was clearly reflected in the gleam of the speeding window.

'Where are we going, exactly?'

'Like I said yesterday. Practice.'

At Céligny, we walked steeply uphill past the lunch-time Café de la Gare. Behind the bar, photos of Richard Burton with the proprietor were occasionally admired by coachloads of Rhondda tourists who also, it was said, sang out loud at his graveside in Welsh. We passed in front of the house where Burton used to live. It was nothing special. One of his granite elder brothers, drunk, had tripped over by the gate and ended up paralysed. Burton's first wife Sybil had attempted suicide here, with pills, but otherwise it was unpretentious.

I offered to carry Rifka's tools, as Dad would certainly have done, and we carried on uphill as far as the village church, leaving the road at a path which levelled out at the new cemetery. We walked past the cemetery. A grass track brought us to a much prettier, much older cemetery, and the gravestone of Richard Burton (1925–1984). He was buried not far from Alastair Maclean (1922–1987), the *Guns of Navarone* man, and also *Where Eagles Dare*.

'Keep going,' Rifka said, 'we're not there yet.'

The path dropped away into trees, which sheltered and concealed the tributary of a mountain stream, and through the shifting cover of leaves the sunlight glimmered on the flow of water, bubbling and chattering over deadwood and stones. The path, which had once forked both ways, was blocked upstream by brambles and overgrowing branches. Rifka pushed through, and I followed. We heard a dog, but never actually saw it. We kept going.

Behind a matted break of copper beech, flat in an un-expected glade, Rifka stopped at a neat row of several small headstones.

'This is it,' she said, 'let's take a break.'

I laid down the tools, and went to inspect the gravestones. It took me a few moments, after clearing away ivy and dry leaves, to realise with some relief that these weren't people. Rifka had brought me out to Céligny to practise on house-hold pets.

'Not just any pets,' Rifka said, coming up behind me. From between the trees sunshine patterned the gladed stones in strips and spikes. 'They're all dogs. And not just any dogs. These are the former friends and companions of the actress Elizabeth Taylor.'

Mum would have loved this. Dad would have been polite, so as not to offend Rifka's sensibilities. For the same reason, he wouldn't have walked away. Probably, if they'd been together, Mum and Dad would have had a bicker, about how much enthusiasm it was appropriate to show.

Rifka knelt down and unrolled the canvas sack. Inside, there was a trowel, a chisel, a claw-hammer, a two-foot crowbar and a roll of black bin-liners. From her pocket, she added a small plastic pot.

'Very important,' she said, 'In the pot there's a paste, a mix of cement powder and wall-filler. I suggest you always prepare it in advance.'

'Slow down,' I said. 'I'm just looking.'

'In that case, remember it's not as hard as it looks. The easiest are the straight earthworks, when they simply shovel the soil back over the coffin. Then it's just gardening. The hardest are those with stone linings and insets, often made of granite, but we don't have to learn everything at once.

Elizabeth Taylor's dogs are a good place to start. They're similar in design to most celebrity graves, only on a smaller scale. Now. Take a closer look. They have an upright stone, the headstone, and also a recumbent stone which seals the actual grave. Our work is with the recumbent, and occasionally you'll find one covered in soil, or gravel, and sometimes it carries an inscription. Ignore all that. The only thing that matters is a sound technique.'

Rifka cleared the climbing ivy off one of the stones. It was evidently from the period when Liz was wearing furs and hoarding gold and generally going native, and it belonged to Spätzli (1964–1973 *Schreng au em Hemmel witer, Spätzli Bueb*). Rifka started me off with the chisel, demonstrating the best method for chipping away at the mortar seal. It looked fairly harmless.

We took turns, and as I gradually improved my technique, Rifka told me that in the Middle Ages the sale of relics was quite an industry. There was buying, selling, cheating, stealing, just like industry as we know it today. Relics were like land, or silver. They were another asset to be managed, one among many.

'The Medicis did relics,' she said, 'the Rothschilds and the Morgans did them. The Gettys are famous for it, and make larceny a full-time occupation and a virtue. It's still the traditional pursuit of the seriously rich, and you know why?'

No, I said, I didn't know why. I chipped away the last of the mortar and laid down the chisel.

'Because very rich people earn the privilege of not having to want the obvious.'

Money. Money wasn't important to rich people, which meant you could see what they really wanted, and what all people would really want, if they didn't first get stuck on money.

'Relics?'

'Mortal remains which excite immortal longings.'

Once the mortar was gone, we moved on to the correct positioning of the crowbar, and how to work it in beneath the recumbent. It was most important to slide not prise. On my first attempt, with the crowbar well in under the recumbent stone of nine-year-old Spätzli, I heaved and the stone cracked, sounding off through the woods like a gunshot.

'Bugger.'

Fortunately, Elizabeth Taylor was a serial dog-lover, and I could afford to make mistakes. Rifka handed me the chisel again, but this time she didn't help me on Mr Woo (*1968–1974 Small, Dumb, Adored*).

'They start with memorabilia,' Rifka said, sometimes interrupting herself to correct my angles. 'But they soon progress. They want to buy proximity to greatness, and then they're seduced by the exclusivity. Relics are like brands in reverse. Not available in all good shops, nowhere near you. It's exactly the kind of unique commodity the rich will buy when money's no object. Bluntly, there's a demand. And Moholy's the supply.'

'Not exactly,' I said. I straightened up because my back was stiff, and as I stretched out I emphasised my point by waving the chisel. 'Moholy showed me the catalogue. There were very few names in the index with red dots. Out of all those people, only a handful had found buyers.'

'Don't be so sure. The dots are the ones immediately available, as of now. The other ones are *potentially* available.'

'Meaning?'

'We haven't dug them up yet. But the ones we've already got are being bought all the time. They're priced on a sliding scale depending on celebrity and difficulty of extraction, but, once they're out, Moholy doesn't offer the whole skeleton. That wouldn't make commercial sense. He sells them in bits, because however small the fragment, the power of the whole remains intact. With relics, that's the way it is.'

I sat back on my heels, and put the chisel aside. I picked up the crowbar, but Rifka had reminded me what we were actually doing. Or not doing. But practising on animals to do.

'What about the law?'

'It's against the law. But it's a crime without victims.'

'That's what all criminals say.'

'In this case it's true. And if we acquire the relics in a way which is untraceable, and then sell them discreetly to private collectors, it's in everybody's interests to keep it quiet.'

'What about the family?'

'Anyone dead for more than a few years and family outrage is pure sentimentality. This isn't murder. And it's hardly even theft. It's not as if the bones belong to anybody, and we're meticulously discreet. That's the secret. We've never damaged a grave, and the condition of the gravesites remains un-changed, as if untouched. Remember Davy in Geneva. You'd never have noticed. The bones are gone, but nobody ever knows. It's a kind of secret resurrection. And theologically, it's watertight.'

Yes, I knew that. I'd thought exactly the same thing only yesterday in the cemetery of kings, standing over Calvin and Davy. The soul was long gone. All that remained was the body. Not even the body, the bones.

'Jesus, Rifka. How did you ever get involved in something like this?'

'The crowbar, Jay. Have another go with the crowbar.'

'Tell me.'

She shrugged. 'Where I come from everybody gets buried. No choice. It's a religion thing.'

'So how can you be doing this?'

'I know what you're saying. My parents wouldn't approve. But Anglicans aren't the only ones whose God has let them down. Now. The crowbar.'

This time I worked much more slowly, finally sliding open the grave and keeping the recumbent intact. It took much longer than I expected.

'Excellent,' Rifka said, 'now use the trowel. Dig into the goldmine.'

'And why me? Why spend all this time on me?'

'We need an expert. We can't just hire East Germans and hand them discount sledgehammers. We take more care than that. It's a question of courtesy.'

'And good business sense. Yes, I understand all that. But why me?'

'You're the last of the Anglicans. You have nothing left to lose.'

'Why not keep on doing it yourself?'

Rifka came over and squatted on the other side of the open grave of Mr Woo. She took something out of her bag, and palmed it in her hand. It was the white disc, tightly wrapped in clingfilm, which she'd first shown me on the altar at All Saints. This time I looked at it more closely, and it was like a flat sea-shell, a sand dollar. She tossed it over and it landed on the grass between my feet.

'Jung's knee-cap,' she said. 'Yup.'

Against the mud and grass, even inside clingfilm, it was whiter than both Becket's toe and Davy's foot, as if it had been scraped, or chalked. It had definitely not been verified by fire, at least not recently.

'The patella of Carl Gustav Jung, the famous psychotherapist. The clingfilm helps, but it still does my head in.'

She took her pill-bottle from the pocket of her shirt, and threw back two or three of the pills. 'Shot nerves,' she said. 'There's a limit to how long anyone can do this. I've reached mine. It's time to move on.'

'So why would I agree to take over?'

'Look at Jung's knee. In fact, you can keep it.'

'Maybe I don't want it.'

'A memento,' Rifka said, 'but don't worry, I suspect it's worthless. I haven't even shown it to Moholy.'

'Why not?'

'I didn't like the look of the man who brought it into the shop. People come into Moholy's gallery all the time, promising the world. They bring in a statue of the jackal god Anubis, who'll protect your dead. They have oracle bones from the Sheng dynasty, which offer guidance when addressing the spirits. My head's had enough. Whereas you're a deacon. You believe there's something out there.'

'I might do.'

'Who did Moholy ask you to get?'

'Joyce, James. James Joyce. That was the only name he mentioned.'

'Really? Well, I suppose Joyce is a good enough place to start, but Moholy's after someone much more important, even than that. I don't know who. I don't even know if Moholy knows, but lately he's been preoccupied, as if he has something big on his mind, something foolish. The Holy Grail, or the Philosopher's Stone, that scale of foolish. It's because he has no instinct for the spiritual, and he hates that.

He really feels the lack of religious urges, so he's likely to go over the top.'

'Very interesting,' I said, 'but none of my concern.'

'I'd always hoped to be there when he finds it. Unfortunately . . .' She tapped the side of her head with her finger. 'A bone too far.'

Back on her feet, Rifka went over to Een So (*1972–1978 My Darling Precious Sleep Thee Well, Een So*). She patted the top of the headstone, a fine slab of white granite speckled with black crystals, and then decorated the miniature recumbent with sticks and stones to stand in for jam-jars and candles and letters. 'Anyone who can do it discreetly,' she said, staring neutrally at my right shoulder, 'well, it's a licence to print money.'

Like learning languages in retirement, I could appreciate the knowledge even if I never intended to use it. There was a method, which the son of an ex-soldier in me could appreciate. Before setting out, and this made sense to me, check all equipment is clean and in good order. Prepare paste of cement powder and ready-mixed wall-filler, if possible matching colour to original mortar.

Important: attempt in dry conditions *only*. Unwrap tools, and turn canvas sack inside-out. Lay sack beside recumbent stone. If recumbent overlaid with gravel or stones, remove and place on sack. Likewise turf. Chip away mortar securing recumbent to headstone and/or vault. Insert crowbar. Slide recumbent free, then turn topside down. Dig earth on to underside of stone, keeping clean its right-side-up. Locate bones. Transfer bones, still in mud or clay, to bin-liner. When backfilling, replace earth loosely. Turn and replace recumbent stone. Reseal using cement/filler compound, and re-lay all gravel or turf removed earlier.

Collect original mortar-chippings, and disperse at distance.

As the afternoon wore on the temperature dropped, but I began to enjoy the physical challenge, and my own proficiency. It was good to be outside and working with my hands, sucking in lungfuls of fresh mountain air.

After only half a day of practice, I was doing a competent job of work on Elizabeth Taylor's Een So. Sustained physical exertion cleared my head, and I could see there was something of the fanatic about me, a priest half bent on martyrdom. I was also simply curious, to see what the bones would look like.

The remains of Een So, dearly beloved of Elizabeth Taylor, turned out to be a skeleton about as long in bones as a two-litre bottle of water. Apart from a slight flattening of the surrounding grass, which would spring out overnight, no casual observer would ever suspect the disturbed peace of this small celebrity lap-dog. It made me feel very proud.

I applied the final touch of stonedust paste with my fingers, then dabbed with a stick to make it look pitted and weathered. 'There,' I said. I sat back on my heels and surveyed my work. 'What do you think?'

'Not bad. But don't leave the twig.'

All the way back to Geneva, every twenty minutes or so, Rifka swallowed a pill. She reminded me that the stones covering people were larger, and therefore heavier. Extra care was needed. She handed me a car key.

'That's for the van,' she said.

'What van?'

'It's a white Peugeot 305. I'm going to park it outside your apartment. You'll need it for Zurich and James Joyce.'

She stopped me before I could say anything. 'If you don't want to do it, just drive the van back to Moholy's shop. It's not a problem.'

And I believed her, wanting to believe the best of people. I took the key, and dropped it into my pocket next to Jung sealed in clingfilm. My unequivocal intention was to return the van to Moholy first thing in the morning, of course it was. That is, until I reached the flat, where Dad's good influence was cruelly overwhelmed.

The answer-machine, as always, was flashing. There was one new message, making a total of thirteen. Unlucky. I went through all the other messages first. They were the same as before. The thirteenth and newest message was from Helena. She thanked me for calling. She was relieved that I was coming to my senses. And she'd managed to reserve a ticket.

She'd see me tomorrow, then, at the airport. At a quarter past ten.

'In the morning, Jay. Quarter past ten in the morning.'

I couldn't believe it. Had I actually asked her to fly over? She said I had, so I suppose I must have done. I was the good-hearted but forgetful vicar, in a line of ditzy vicars. It must have been instinctive, involuntary, but, now I thought about it, Dad would have done the same. Especially in the haze of virtue after a service on a Sunday. He'd have phoned Helena and nicely proposed a reunion, because that was the decent thing to do, and what Helena would have wanted.

God. Just look where niceness and good manners could get you.

In a bout of self-recrimination I circled the flat, hid Jung at the back of a kitchen cupboard, sat down, circled again. How could I have been so foolish? Where was the famous free-will? In the bedroom I stopped, and found myself staring at the bed. And where was she going to sleep? I appealed to Dad for help, determined if at all possible to follow his example. I'd received a difficult phone-call, and Dad was out of the house. He would not be back in a minute. He was no longer able to help. And I had no replacement answer by heart.

When Tom and I were young, and life was hard in the parish of Sewerby cum Merton and Grindale, Dad would occasionally come home an empty shell, his niceness all caked and desiccated. Mum would cope by stapling his hair to the mattress, before hammering his head to the bed-frame with six-inch nails.

Metaphorically.

Mum had a temper, and a tendency to crack. Dad was falling apart more quietly. He was melting. He tried to keep himself together with prayer and faith, and learning from the lives of the saints, as if every day were just another jump from a plane.

But Mum seldom let up. In a language Dad might one day understand, she'd underboil his eggs, or iron a hole in the shape of an iron in the front of his clerical shirt. She emptied the Hoover-bag into his Repeat Offenders box-file. For nights on end, whatever his prayers, she'd keep him awake, her standard complaint that he was an able and attractive man who ought to be making money. For the sake of the children, for the security and settling-down, or just to know before next Christmas where we'd be living next Christmas, without enough money for Christmas.

I'd hide in cupboards with my fingers in my ears, and pretend it wasn't happening. Each individual argument was a personal assault, because if on another night, thirty-four years and nine months previously, it had been like this, then where and who would I be now?

The next morning, or when I was back at school, I had time to rationalise. Mum and Dad sometimes overreacted to each other. And that, I reasoned, was an acceptable definition of love.

Mum never calmed down. At that time, she couldn't see anything through. During her days as a temp she was encouraged to enrol in courses supposed to advance her career by broadening her experience. She tried circus skills, psychology for beginners, creative writing and amateur dramatics. But she'd quickly give them up, resentful of anything connected to work while her boys were stepping out in other people's shoes, from the charity shops.

Basically, money was the problem. I don't know what happened at home when I was away at school, a poor posh person living a double life, but I'd definitely stopped thinking that everyone was born equal. My revised opinion, encouraged by Mum, was that there were people like Dad, and then there were special and gifted people, like me. I used to fantasise, denying my clerical heritage, that Tom was always Tom but I was my Mum's secret love-child, my secret father someone famously blessed with talent. We often talked about it, but Mum couldn't say exactly who it was: it was a secret.

I was trying to find my way, and, like the most mundane fellows everywhere, I didn't want to be like my dad. I wanted to be a star.

During the holidays, Dad would sometimes catch hold of me and pull me in and wrap his arms around me, squeezing me tightly until I could hardly breathe. Or he'd ask, out of nowhere, if anyone fancied staying in and playing a game of chess.

Yes right, Dad. I went out and had my left ear pierced, seven times. Mum gave me the money. I was determined to fill every Mason vicarage with my own sense of the hopelessness of the human condition, whose true and drastically corrupted nature only adolescents of my age and inclination were fully qualified to recognise.

I told Dad I was trying to find myself.

'Well,' he said. 'That's good.'

Better, I thought, siding with Mum, than choosing an optional poverty so prolonged (compared to everyone else who was sane and able-bodied) it was almost pretentious. It was Dad's only pretension, which I found intensely annoying. To make up for it, I cultivated *all* the pretensions.

I read philosophy and French novels. I noted full moons, and at sixteen made mad dashes on a step-through Honda across the flats and downs of Salisbury Plain, stopping off at Stonehenge to wassail the Apple Tree and bow to the Elder, worshipping at the pagan wonder of old Albion. Mum would follow me down in the car.

'How embarrassing is that?' Tom used to ask. 'Going to festivals with your mum, trying to be someone you're not?'

But in fact it wasn't embarrassing at all. We were peas from the same pod, and, waiting for solstice dawns on the Hergest Ridge, I agreed with Mum and like-minded fellow travellers that organised religion was over. In its place, and in the place of all fear, there would be science, creativity, imagination and sex. But then later, in the shadow of some ancient long-barrow, in the dark scary hours before dawn, I'd secretly make the sign of the cross.

It was a sensible precaution: it kept Satan at a distance.

The next day I'd be wretchedly sick on cider and dope, before biking home in daylight to tell Dad how fantastic it all was.

I was trying very hard to be unlike him, which was fairly standard behaviour. Dad had always wanted so little for us that we'd end up, not ordinary exactly, but Christian and caring and kind. I gave him one last chance. During a long summer holiday, I volunteered to act as sidesperson in his church, along with a girl from the parish called Alice.

Mum refused outright to wash my socks. She said she sometimes wished I'd never been born. She thought I was turning into Dad, but she was wrong. It was exactly the opposite, because for our generation church was seriously weird. It was the most shocking rebellion I could think of, because nothing could be more deviant than giving up a Sunday morning in bed to stand in a white cape holding a precious-metal goblet heavy with the viscous blood of Christ. For Alice, it was like becoming a lesbian. It opened up the world. She suddenly didn't have to be the prettiest girl in the party dress, with the pink-ribbon Alice band. Nor did she have to smoke cigarettes she hated or put the wind up the school bully by asking him in public if he fancied a blow-job.

Standing at the front of the church, either side of Mason Senior the geeky vicar, we put ourselves beyond saving, lost in our religious streaks, praying over and over again that sex, when it happened, would be special. And when it did, between the two of us, it was. Alice said. We were seventeen years old. Not long after, she stopped coming to church.

She became a Goth, and said I was too tame for her. If only I'd been more rebellious, less like Dad, bought a long dark coat and some matt-black hair-paint. I did try. I stopped serving in church, and developed an astounding openness to the credible, the incredible, to anything. The family bucket of religion, passed down in a fire-chain from Mason to Mason, I spilt carelessly some distance from any actual fire. Clothes in alternative fashion became my sacred ju-jus and fetishes. Choosing the right music re-enacted ancient patterns of belonging, and an extra earring assuaged the gods by complying with this month's tribal fad. I was trying to set myself free, fashioning a new personality, applauding my friends' nose-rings and tongue-studs as talismans against the devil, who was always plotting to enter the body at any available orifice. Is that right? Fine, I could believe that. It felt like an essential part of the James Mason Minor I was at the time.

'You're just like Mum,' Tom said, as yet again in my double life I took out all the earrings for another half of term at choir-school. 'But you can't see it, can you?'

Tom was now away at University studying Economics, and on one of his rare visits home he asked Dad why he always wore his collar as often and visibly as possible. In fact, Dad used to buy a new set each year to maintain their astonishing whiteness.

'It concentrates the mind,' Dad said. 'And keeps the problem before the eyes of the people.'

'What problem is that then, Dad?' Tom asked. Within two months of leaving College he had his own car, and his own flat, and everything else that people were generally thought to want. 'What exactly *is* the problem?'

'*The* problem. Life, death, how are we supposed to live? *That* problem.'

'Actually, I don't have a problem with that.'

Tom was immune. For some time now he'd stopped even pretending to be good. Every evening he drove home from the City in his roadster with electric everything to a kitchen with a glass kettle, and by his second year in London, eating Japanese noodles on expenses, he earned five times as much as a vicar after twenty years on apologetics and paste sandwiches. Mason Senior wrestled with the divine secrets of existence. Tom Mason Major bought from the bottom and sold at the top. Thine is the glory, Tom. Our dad still had his uses: an Anglican vicar in the family could be good value, especially at dinner parties with Bachelors of Arts and Sciences, where not one highly paid graduate under the age of forty had progressed much further than not believing in God.

That was Tom. We'd drifted apart, even though we looked very similar and still had our special handshake, which we pushed and pulled before embracing each other. When we met, Tom paid for everything, and if Tom could do all that, so unlike Mum and Dad, then what could *I* do?

It was a long time since Tom had finished with our plot against Dad. For Mum, it was never finished. It was war; it was always war, and I must have inherited the same failing, never knowing when to stop. I often asked Dad how he got to be a priest.

'Stubbornness.'

'Didn't you ever want to be anything else?'

'Of course I did. Lots of things.'

I advised him to let himself go, and stop being so hard on himself. With my multiple earrings and a leather pouch greasy with the resin of soft drugs, impressionable, a lounger-about and a scrounger, I encouraged my father the vicar, the source of aid and comfort to all in need, to regret every pound per square inch of his English uptightness.

'Be *yourself*,' I said.

I'd failed to notice that for Mason Senior uptight meant tightened up, like a nut or a bolt, like a machine. That was how he kept on going, week after week, coping with me and Mum while conforming to European norms of health and safety. That's how he didn't fall apart, or malfunction, or fly off the handle.

'Lighten up,' I'd say, flicking a lit match into the washing-up water, tilting my chair back and blowing a couple of smoke-rings. 'Stop pressing down. See what comes to the surface.'

One yellow summer Sunday, with the local colour washed pale as August, I came home from not working on my A-levels to the news that Mum had packed and gone. I was eighteen, and she should have waited, for the sake of the children.

'This is so *unlike* her,' people said.

The parishioners blamed it on the weather, and BBC drama, and the time of her life. They acted out their different versions of crisis counselling. Some of them even blamed it on me, as if I and my mother were one and the same. 'This isn't like her *at all*. But there again, she hasn't been herself recently.'

'Face it,' Tom said, home for the weekend to help with the fall-out, 'she's a fucking schizo. Always was. Always will be.'

I stayed at home and sulked. A month or so after Mum left, a letter arrived from the French Pyrenees, in which she tried very hard to explain herself. She blamed the length of the long haul, the constant moving, the diocesan indifference, and the hurtful ignorance of the people. The spiritual rewards, she wrote, remained stubbornly spiritual. And in any reasonable analysis, at the end of the day, when you added it all up, her husband the vicar of thine good parish had only himself to blame.

Being helpful, I typed up the letter for the parish magazine. It was the least I could do, sitting at the computer in the middle of the night, and at the last moment pasting it in over a regular feature called 'The Things Children Say'. Mum wrote that Mason Senior was more committed to the Church than he'd ever been to her, or his boys. He'd often been away or unreachable, and had consistently refused to earn anything even close to a decent wage. Ever.

And he was sleeping with another woman. Yours sincerely, Mrs Mason.

Dad had stopped pressing down. He'd untightened, and lightened up, and with his eyes open he'd kissed a recently arrived divorcee. In her front room, standing up. So that the principled neighbours and everyone else could see. He never explained himself, or apologised. He let people dismiss it as a moment of weakness, but even then he never openly asked for strength, only forgiveness.

After Mum's letter, Dad stopped seeing the other woman. He went back almost to normal, and, though the effort was clearly great, he responded to every jibe and sly remark with restraint and tolerance, except during Lent.

That's when we all had to be careful, when he showed us another side of himself. For Lent, every year from then on, Mason Senior gave up the consolation of religion. And as he grew older, every year was more horrifying than the last. It was only during Lent, outside the shelter of divine justice, that he saw the true extent to which evil prospered. He was appalled at the addled mind of the mother country, losing her memory, stumbling, forgetful that unlike most other nations she had her very own God to pull her through. If that's what she wanted. He'd been preaching it for years, but it looked increasingly unlikely that this was what the nation wanted, in thrall as it was to a freshly invented England of devil's-head tattoos, and by-passes, and sharp business practice made pretty much perfect.

During Lent, Dad became a drinker, four weeks wall-eyed every spring-time, working his way through the bottles of dry sherry he was given every Christmas by parishioners. About half-way down the bottle, he'd vow to found a militant wing of the Anglican Church, deciding that God and England deserved better than unpuncturable niceness. His Bishops were constantly asking him if he was strong enough to dismiss the pretence of strength in favour of a constant, honest, perhaps even weakening admission of weakness.

No. Not any more, not always. Not during Lent.

Mason Senior, an ex-military man with a strategic vision of a radical new Church, said no. It was time for good Christians to stop feeling guilty and alienated and feeble for being tolerant and persuadable and understanding. He'd had enough of the platitudes, the declining numbers, the constant bickering and petty disputes: the Anglo-Catholics said candles, the Evangelicals said guitars, and for any public occasion, especially when televised, an archdeacon could be trusted to select with care whichever was the less appropriate.

At the end of the violence of Lent, his face cut to bits by his shaky safety-razor, Dad breathed a sigh of relief and recorked any surviving bottles. Out of the closet came his scarlet chasuble, his seasonal favourite, and he wore it humbly all through Holy Week until, on Easter day itself, he changed in triumph to the white and the gold. He lifted up his hands. He received the consolation of religion. He stood there at the front, and he lifted up his hands, and he tried to make something understood which one day would be universally understood, if it was the truth.

People, he said, you must be good and gentle to each other.

Mum had a bolder approach.

And I was somewhere in the middle, with Helena arriving tomorrow, and an outstanding offer to dig up the dead. To be honest, I was so nervous that I didn't know what to do. I lacked self-confidence in a situation like this. Frankly, I was in a panic – in several minds at once.

If I disappointed Moholy, and he reclaimed the flat, then where else could I go to hide?

But then there was Helena, and how could I possibly be the father of children? One day they'd turn into someone like me, inevitably, and I didn't wish that on anyone.

And if we did have a child, Helena and I, I knew from Mum the horror of bringing up children with not enough money. Moholy was offering a fortune for Joyce. I couldn't remember from the catalogue exactly how much, but a lot. And Rifka had suggested, once I'd proved I could dig discreetly, that Joyce was only the beginning.

Mum was urging me on, hollering from afar in an accent just too distant to identify. Go on, my son. I lifted my hand to my ear. The earrings were long gone, the holes almost closed, but I could still hear Mum's voice and it was getting closer, easier to hear, more insistent. 'Relics mean heroes,' she said, in a professor's voice, a brilliant and enthused professor, pushing pretend half-moon glasses past the delicate kink in her nose. 'They're reminders of human possibility. Dear boy. The burial and disappearance of the great is almost perverse. Dig the old blighters up. Let's have a little look at them. After all, they were the mighty.'

Dad would never have done it, not in a million years.

'You're right. He'd never have risked it, never have *braved* it. But you're not your dad, are you, Jay? Are you?'

God no. This was it, at last, an opportunity to demonstrate clearly to myself that I was escaping Dad's fate, objective evidence of the off-the-scale distance between me and those hapless vicarages. Until now, however far it may have seemed, the distance had never been far enough.

Dad had lived too long surrounded by religious notions of good and evil, endurance and suffering, life after death, heaven. These notions, once common currency, were now an oddity, and he hadn't worked out even the basics of how modern life was best to be lived.

Mum was nearly sixty and somewhere on the sunny Spanish coast in a sarong, where not even her children could pile their troubles on her head. She was the winner. That was the way to live.

The weather held, overcast but dry. It was very dark and late on a Sunday night, and I'd just driven two and a half hours along an empty motorway to the upbeat soundtrack of Mum's many voices. In my black zip-up jacket, Rifka's tools wrapped in my dad's army kit-bag, I stepped out of Moholy's Peugeot van at Fluntern cemetery in Zurich. It was 1 a.m. I turned my shoulder to the sweep of headlights from a solitary car, then squeezed shut the driver's door. A thin haze of cloud was blurring the moon and stars, but in my opinion, and considering Zurich was a major European city, it felt unnaturally quiet and dark.

The Swiss Germans were all in bed, lights off. I could be anybody, do anything. They were letting me do what I liked.

Fluntern cemetery was held back from the pavement by a hip-high wall, flat and inviting on top. Trees bustled on the other side, with the active quiet of a park. I walked as far as the end of the wall, and the next block along, right after the cemetery, was the Zurich City Zoo. All closed up and quiet. Hearing nothing but a distant moped, I turned and swung myself neatly over the cemetery wall, immediately crouching low so I couldn't be seen from the road. I stayed there for a while, hunched over my kit-bag wrap of tools, breathing through my nose, waiting for my eyes to adapt.

It did occur to me, as I squatted there in the shadow of the wall, that I wasn't frightened of getting caught. Maybe I wanted to get caught, like a shoplifter. It was a cry for help. But that wasn't Mum's style. She was more practical than that, and quietly confident that among the famous dead few would be easier to raise than Joyce. The older the stone, the harder it was to shift, but in burial years James Joyce was barely sixty. Nora, buried in with him, was a sprightly fifty, so the stone had been moved once already, and was unlikely to have become fixed and brittle. Nor was it one of the more complicated designs: no headstone, and the inscribed recumbent was free of gravel or turf. It was a simple lift and shift. Just as importantly, from what I knew about Joyce, I didn't think the old tinker would mind. He'd see it as a tribute to his genius: *of course* he was first up. And also he quite fancied some company, a drink or two, and maybe later a spider-dance and a racy but convivial sing-song, *I gave it to Nellie To stick in her belly The leg of the duck The leg of the duck.*

Under cover behind the wall, I rehearsed the siting of the Joyce plot, James and Nora under a single stone up some steps on a raised terrace, in the shade of some fancy bushes and a blustery yew. I ought to get started. Fluntern was twice the size of the cemetery in Geneva, and Joyce was away at the back, and the dark was often impenetrable. Cradling the kit-bag in my arms like a baby, I crouched low. With knees bent, I stalked between the gravestones, my stride long and slow, carefully landing each foot on the grass to avoid the tell-tale gravel of the paths. There was something dark, right in front of me. I stopped. It stopped. I nudged it with my toe, and it was an angel in night-black marble, easy to miss.

I thought I heard something. I heard something. I thought I did. I dropped to one knee. It was a grunting, or sniffing. I stopped breathing, shrinking down, listening more closely. Leaves, an aeroplane at high altitude, a window closing. I was suddenly afraid of dogs. An owl. Then another snuffle, but further off. Then silence again, except for a vehicle, ignorant in the distance.

The noises were coming from the zoo. I kept listening, to make sure that this was where the noise was coming from. Restless warthogs, wild buffalo, that was it. A sound would start up, as the animals in straw turned and groaned, then flopped and settled just as suddenly.

It stopped, it started again, and even though it was definitely the zoo, I had another sensation, very intense, that in the dark of the cemetery, among the irregular rows of squat graves, I was no longer alone. My breathing was shallow, less than silent. In any direction I could see no further than a single headstone, but I was overwhelmed by this sudden acute sense of other people. The cemetery was full of them. They may have been dead, but they were still there, all of them, just below the surface.

More noise from the zoo, mammals shifting and sighing, and then clearly, distinctly, the air splitting with the roar of a lion. A lion.

It took me a while to readjust, remembering which way was Joyce, and which way back. As the restless lion quietened down, I reminded myself that theologically, theologically speaking, it was watertight. The Church of England didn't insist on the resurrection of the body. The souls were long gone, or, if you preferred, had never been. It was just stones and bones and mud. Only ordinary people got scared, spooked out. They didn't have the hardness of heart of the educated, which the educated like me called enlightenment.

I slowly made my way closer to James and Nora, climbing

the steps to their narrow terrace, reaching out blindly and fumbling forward until I was right on top of them. I carefully laid down my tools, and checked the lettering on their broad recumbent stone, like Braille. I crawled my way round it, then back again, before quietly emptying the canvas kit-bag, and turning it inside-out just as Rifka had shown me. I spread the bag flat next to the stone, edge to edge, to catch chips of mortar and any disturbed earth. More mammal noises, rising into the night, but I was learning to ignore them. I cleared a devotional bunch of wild daisies on to the kit-bag, and a homage scrawled in eye-shadow which was utter nonsense. Steadying myself in a kneeling position, I was reaching forward with my chisel when I noticed two additional names on the stone. I sat back on my heels. Then I traced the names with my fingers. *George Joyce (Trieste 27 VII 1903 – Konstanz 12 VI 1970). Anna Osterwalder Joyce (München 8 III 1917 – Konstanz 17 VI 1993).*

Joyce had had children, who had children. Had they? There was space on the stone for more. Several more. Had the grandchildren had children? James Jesus Joyce spent his final afternoons, in the last days of 1940, walking the concrete promenades of the Zürichsee, hand in hand with his grandson Stephen. For God's sake, I scolded myself, it's James Joyce with a pint of stout and his spider-dance and small round specs. It's not even anyone scary.

A blinding light exploded inches from my face. A click. A torch, an electric torch clicked on, inches away, the enflamed bulb beaming straight into my flaring, blinded eyes. I was unsighted and stupefied, eyes trapped open, a rabbit, and then my heart overgulped and my eyelids were useless and I keeled over backwards.

When I came to, seconds later, I found myself enfolded in

the strong and consoling arms of a muscular adult wearing a vest. 'Shhh,' he said, rocking me gently. *'Schlaf, Chindli, schlaf, der Vater huetet d'Schaf.'* He was stroking my cheek, with the utmost kindness and concern. *'Mein Name ist Harald.'* He placed a consoling kiss on my pale and clammy brow. *'Wie heisst-du, mein Liebling?'*

I disentangled myself, elbowing him away, shaking my head, hissing into the quietness that I had no prejudice, really, and in fact a quarter of my professional colleagues were commonly estimated to be gay, but personally I wasn't, and had mentally slept with thousands of women, honestly I had.

I clashed the tools back inside the kit-bag, and crawled and scurried away between the gravestones, the pursuing torch-beam stretching and scrambling my shadow. Other torches came on all around me, tracking me, narrow searchlights darting and probing through the cemetery's spaces and stones.

'Halt! Komm zurück! Lass uns miteinander sprechen! Einfach nur sprechen!'

Breathless, confused, I vaulted the wall of the Fluntern cemetery, Zurich's premier gay cruising ground. Landing, I lost my footing and crumpled to the pavement. I pushed myself up again, limping and stumbling towards the van, not deluding myself that only the scuffle of gay lust had kept me from the bones of James Jesus Joyce. Physically I just couldn't have done it. I knew that now. I wasn't up to it, and it was never going to happen, but it wasn't entirely my fault.

It was Joyce's fault. James Joyce, whose outright eminence went unsung, buried abroad without honour, his daughter insane, his son abandoned, his understandable books dimly misunderstood. He wasn't like Thomas à Becket, the incurable show-off. He wasn't the furious Davy, who still had

103

so much to prove. James Joyce could live without a come-back.

By the ancient logic of relics, in which the bones themselves had personality and power, it therefore couldn't happen. The bones had resisted, conspired, insisted on staying where they were, wrapped safely in the black earth with Nora, endlessly entertained by the flitter and skim of men and heaven above. Joyce didn't want to come back. He'd said all he had to say.

My hands shook on the steering wheel as I turned left and right, following each floodlit and lime-green sign to the auto-route. I'm not gay, I told myself, I'm perfectly normal. I'm just an Anglican deacon in a Swiss cemetery in the middle of the night with a spade and James Jesus Joyce. Or I was a failure: it had nothing to do with Joyce, and the fault and the fear were mine, all mine. When it came down to it, my hands and knees and ear to the ground, pressing down, pushing down, getting beneath the surface, concentrating, listening, getting right down and grounded to hear the infinitesimal rumour, when I was actually called on to chip and dig, I was nothing but my own dad, more Dad than Mum, that endless argument coming out in his favour, which I'd never thought was fair.

This was something Dad would never have done. Never.

Please God, make Mum right, and let me amount to more than that. Being my father's son, and nothing more, was a long way short of the distinguished ideal I had of myself. I'd always wanted to *be* someone, to be *someone*. I wanted to be different, my own self-made man.

Dad was dead. He would not be back in a minute. He was unable to help. At last, after thirty-four years, I was free to do anything I wanted. Helena was arriving tomorrow. Not tomorrow, later today, at a quarter past ten in the morning. I had absolutely no idea what it was I wanted.

I saw Céligny signposted off the autoroute. I indicated, took the slip-road, and started to climb. To avoid ending up a poor copy of Dad, to have any hope, I needed consciously at all times to will myself to be more and other than I was. Joyce had been a blip, an anomaly, but there was nothing to worry about. Dad was dead, Joyce was dead. They were *all* dead.

There was no need to worry.

In the village of Céligny, I parked in the church car-park. Carrying my tools, I stumbled past the new cemetery and along the grassy track to the old one, where the high rusting gates were chained and padlocked. My breath was silver in sudden moonlight. Hanging the kit-bag over my shoulder, I climbed up and over.

Richard Burton was three stones along to the left. I brushed away some loose gravel, and called to mind everything Rifka had taught me. I started slowly, with the chisel. I knelt, and found the angles, and chiselled. And discovered it was no different from excavating Mr Woo, or Een So. When it came to the crowbar, I dismissed any last doubts by consoling myself that famous movie actors, preserved for all eternity on film, unchanged by death, must always have imagined a performing afterlife. Living, they'd wanted whatever was the opposite of being in the dark, dead and buried. It was a bit late now to be expecting peace and quiet.

Richard Burton was easy. I'd done the practice, I'd put in the time, and his blocks of clay-heavy mud lifted tidily into Dad's faded kit-bag. I then replaced the stone, confident that no one but Rifka would ever have guessed. I applied the finishing seal of mixed cement and filler, and as I did so, I confirmed at long last my sure exclusion from a world overwatched by the English God; cheerful, amiably distant, Lord of all mildness, and Lord of all calm.

It felt like a curtain rising, or a crust breaking. It was like falling through a safety-net, my whole life until now the progress, sometimes willed, sometimes resisted, towards this inevitable breakthrough.

What *harm* would it do?

I didn't believe in a watchful God. I didn't believe, if I did this, that I'd burn forever in the eternal fires of hell. Sorry, Dad. I think Mum was right.

Burton's Leg

'Believer who does not believe,
Munificent and mean
Trustless and trusting, insecure,
How will you get you clean?'

T. H. White, *Vodka Poem to Richard Burton*

I woke up a new man, feeling seventy-five million dollars. In cash. In the bank. In Geneva.

If I could have chosen freely from Moholy's catalogue (if I was Moholy, or one of his customers), I'd have chosen Richard Burton. I'd seen him first in *Desert Rats*, at a time when I was seeing all the films featuring James Mason. Meaning the real James Mason, the film actor, who in *Desert Rats* plays Rommel. Richard Burton was born Richard Jenkins, but he rejected his natural father and his natural father's name. Given a free choice, I too would have taken a Burton for my father, like Burton did, and Richard Burton was really something.

I jumped out of bed, checked my watch, ran my fingers over the pockmarks in my cheeks, then sprinted on the spot, a flurry of paces from a tireless wing-forward. And then I jogged to the bathroom. After my late night in the two cemeteries, I'd slept in, and it was only an hour and a half until Helena arrived at the airport. My nerves had vanished. I was actively looking forward to it.

I was feeling good. Better. I admired myself in the mirror and puffed out my chest. Maybe a little better even than that.

In the kitchen, I circled Dad's kit-bag, upright on the linoleum. I supposed I ought to hide it. I bent at the knees and prepared to lift, a simple task for a man of vigour such as myself. However, I soon discovered that Swiss earth and the remains of Richard Burton were surprisingly heavy. I squatted down with my elbows on my knees, confronting the bag, contemplating it. Then I unclipped the strap at the top, loosened the bunched canvas, and peeked inside. I felt around with my fingertips, and with my thumb and forefinger I carefully pinched out a bone. It was covered in mud. I pushed most of it off with the flat of my free hand, and recognised the bone as a tibia, or fibula. It was Richard Burton's leg-bone.

Washing it off at the sink, turning it from end to end, I was soon thinking that without the mud the bone was surprisingly light, inconsequential. I left it to drain with the plates and saucepans. Then I closed up the kit-bag, hauled it through to the bedroom, and bumped it to the back of the closet.

I went hunting for breakfast. This meant the kitchen again, and a search through all the cabinets and cupboards until I found the Chaplain's sherry. It was a sensible precaution to take, I thought, because Richard Burton's real father was a drunk. He was also a miner, a man, but Burton always had grander ambitions. From the valley he escaped to the grammar school, then to Oxford, then Stratford and the Old Vic. And on to Hollywood, where as the popular star of many blockbusters it would take only a small step to enter the public affections, earn a knighthood, and inherit from Olivier the crown at the National Theatre, which he'd lead in triumph to the twenty-first century.

Nothing could stop him but the drink, rendering him fluent and incapable for days on end, vulnerable to poetry and bad behaviour and blackouts. Burton had a horror of blacking out, which he entirely forgot when under the influence. And then he'd black out.

I'd intended to pour the sherry away, but instead slid it to the back of the counter, confident I was man enough to resist. Then I went back into the open cupboards, looking for food and sellotape.

In Cointrin International Airport, about ten miles north of Geneva, the information announcements are preceded by an electronic chime identical to the first five notes of 'How Much Is That Doggy in the Window?' Twice already, after an airport announcement, I'd sung the second five notes, and both times it had made me laugh. The loudspeakers went *How Much Is That Dog*—, and I can't have been alone in the airport instinctive with my —*gy in the Window*. I loved being abroad. It gave me an advantage. Abroad, I was part of the world. At home, I was part of the scenery.

I'd left Moholy's van skewed diagonally at Setting Down Only. I was in that kind of mood. Burton's leg-bone was now sellotaped along the inside of my own lower leg, and Richard Burton was the famously handsome unstoppable, bunching the impressive muscles in his shoulders, setting the jaw in his magnificent head.

The boy had come from nowhere. Or not from nowhere, but the village of Pontrhydyfen, the twelfth of thirteen children, flinging his grapple-hook at the moon. He conquered Stratford, and the West End, and Los Angeles. He made the impossible possible. He had seventy-five million pounds in Swiss bank accounts and was married to the most beautiful woman in the world, not once, but twice.

'Don't be daft, boyo. It doesn't happen.'

'You just watch me.'

Looking for International Arrivals, I turned and whacked my knee against an abandoned trolley. I chomped my lower lip and grabbed my leg, hopping a semi-circle and grimacing. My top front teeth were showing, in the process of not, just about, saying Fuck, or something worse, like *Ach Fie!* or *Mocchhyn Du!*

Who was I trying to fool? It was an act, I knew it was, but it was also my contemporary and changing character, part of what it meant to be living and breathing now. I was a deacon adrift, waiting for Helena in Geneva airport, but that was never all. Richard Burton was a Welsh valley boyo but also a Commander of the British Empire. He was a lover of lyric poetry, but also a hard bastard when the ball was buried at a ruck. He was a ladies' man, but with a weakness for the costume and posture of celibates (*Becket* (1964), *Night of the Iguana* (1964), *The Sandpiper* (1965), *Exorcist II – The Heretic* (1977), and *Absolution* (1979)).

It was fine being an impostor, or an actor, as long as you gave it everything. I shouldn't *worry* so much. I could marry. Helena could have my children. And if it didn't work out, I could marry someone else.

She'd probably be expecting a present. I had no flowers, no chocolates, but I didn't care. I was a Richard Burton of the twenty-first century, and Richard Burton was a Casanova of the twentieth century, and Casanova, and so on. I was an international swordsman, and Helena was at the Arrivals gate. I could see her. She was looking the other way, wearing a green puffa and a dark bobble-hat, jeans, her bag at her feet beside her boots, and from this distance she seemed almost vulnerable.

She turned and saw me. And she smiled. Life was almost worth living again. If I wasn't mistaken, she paused just for a second, falling in love afresh, I thought, with my wide-apart blue-green eyes, the ravaged face with its sculpted bones, my romantically wasted skin. As she felt for the handles of her bag, I flashed her a rare and winning smile.

Courage, man. She's right there, lounging at the edge of the pool with her famously violet eyes. All you have to do is *talk*. Open your mouth. Talk. This is your moment, your time. This is the instant which makes all the difference. This is your fatal Cleopatra.

I took a deep breath, looking down from my full five feet and ten inches and also one extra half-an-inch, though I felt much taller. We were now as close as we could come without embracing, or stepping back. There was Helena, dark hair escaping the edges of the hat, blue almost violet eyes, dark eyebrows, almost a smile, and observably the same Helena who in the night, and in the dark morning, no matter how hard I tried to banish her from my mind, still had the power of ambush. And there was I, Jay Mason, pocked, devious and in trouble. I smiled a great deal, and then wrapped her in my arms.

She responded stiffly, pushing me away.

'I warn you, Jay. I'm not very happy with the way you've been acting.'

111

'You look lavish.'

'Don't. I've put on half a stone.'

'You are a dark unyielding largesse. You are Aberystwyth beach at sunset.'

'And you're full of crap.'

'Okay. You look a bit chubby.'

'That's better.'

'Your cheeks are a bit puffy, like a hamster.'

'But don't overdo it.'

I went to hug her again, and this time she was softer, less rigid.

'Thanks for calling,' she said, a minor concession.

'Hey. I was always going to call. How was the flight? You must be exhausted.'

'Actually, I am.'

'You probably want a shower.'

'Actually, I do.'

Richard Burton was an expert on women. He was the lover of Sybil Williams and Susan Hunt and Elizabeth Taylor and Sally Hay, and a thousand others he didn't even bother to marry. He enjoyed the elegance of women, their humour, their brave promises, their suicide attempts, their decent gestures, their utter deceit, their lap-dogs, their unshakeable loyalty, and their million-dollar necklaces.

We were mostly silent driving back to the city in the van.

Helena was mostly silent. I told her about the weather, suddenly more dramatic than usual, metallic clouds dragging storms from the mountains, cut only by the sunshine of angels. I pointed out the world-famous water-jet, which today was on, each free-falling drop in the morning sunshine making a rainbow, all the way down. I pointed out Mont

Blanc in the distance, and the Protestant Cathedral. 'Geneva's a wonderful city,' I said. 'You're going to like it.'

'It's not a holiday.'

In which case, I impressed on Helena my good fortune to have been sent to a one-time city of God, home to the United Nations and the International Red Cross, and headquarters to 420 other equally worthy non-governmental organisations. As one of Europe's leading centres of social progress, it was a city of humanity and enlightenment where supplicants still arrived in search of divine intervention. Geneva was the world's capital of good intentions, and a unique island of goodness.

'So why are so many of the shops closed?'

'Ah, that,' I said. 'You're right. It's not the best week ever for shopping.'

Even though it was only Monday, many of the shops had already shut. There was a large-scale popular protest planned for the weekend and, following lurid tales of imminent violence broadcast on television, Geneva was slowly closing down. To reassure the city's resident army of diplomats and bankers, the local political leaders had promised zero tolerance, with riot squads drafted in from other cantons, and emergency paramilitaries on standby over the border, in France. The Palace of Nations, in fact the entire United Nations complex, would be enclosed behind a sectioned fence made of steel barriers more than two metres high.

It was hard to imagine. Until now, the only two policemen I'd seen in the city, not counting VIP escorts and helicopters, were in a stopped patrol car, questioning an attractive woman student on suspicion of bicycling without a licence.

But I wasn't much concerned with the state of the world. With poetry, yes. And yes, with the exquisite predicament of love.

113

'If Geneva really is the capital of good intentions,' Helena mused, 'then the large-scale popular protest might be expected to succeed.'

While Helena was in the shower, I tidied away some clothes, then threw open the windows. The women in white coats were still hard at it in the windows of the packing-plant opposite. Several buildings to the right, on my side of the street but one balcony further up, there was a canary in a cage who liked to sing. One of its favourite songs was an imitation of a car alarm.

In the living-room, I killed time by browsing the low-rise cityscapes made on the bookcase by left-behind Bibles and thick biographies. Like the Chaplain, and probably the Chaplain before that, I'd already skipped through the indexes of the biographies looking for the secret which explained the greatness of Franz Liszt, or Lenin, or George Eliot. It turned out, discouragingly, never to have been their stay in this particular city. It was always their family background, and their upbringing, and the combination of a lucky circumstance with some indefinable, inimitable gift.

I pulled out the I-Ching, the Chinese Book of Changes. We'd consulted it once at theology college, and back then it had warned Helena to be careful of ambitious plans, which were likely to be misunderstood.

We hadn't believed a word of it. In the bedroom, I checked Burton was well hidden, and took out one of my cardigans, the blue or the black. Helena was still in the bathroom, but I waited patiently, sitting outside the door, and she eventually came out in a billow of steam and the humid smell of soaps. It was very similar to the aromatic feelgood smell of relics, rubbed in the appropriate way. It was lavender and strawberry, and flora allegoria.

She was wearing a towel, tucked up under her reddish arms. Her dark hair was flat on her head, and her cheeks were glowing. I did look briefly at her dimpled knees, and the shining bones of her shins. And I did glance in passing at the softer muscle of her calf, and the fading ink-pricks where she'd recently shaved.

But primarily, I was waiting there to offer her the cardigan.

Helena smiled. 'You know. Sometimes I actually believe you're nice.'

'Just being professional.'

'In that case, stop looking at my throat.'

'Your neck, actually.'

'Just don't.'

She took the cardigan, and leant back against the door-frame as she found the front and undid the buttons. One of her buttocks flattened against the edge of the door, and I wanted very much to make love to her, because that was the meaning of life.

'Close your eyes,' she said.

'Why?'

'I'm going to take off the towel and put on the cardigan.'

'So why do I have to close my eyes?'

'Privacy.'

'I've seen you naked hundreds of times.'

'Just do it.'

I closed my eyes. She was moving very close in front of me. I heard the towel fall, and she must have known that, and she could easily have changed in the bathroom.

'You can look again now.'

I opened my eyes and she was standing naked, arms out wide. 'Yaah!'

She laughed, and shrugged into the cardigan, turning and quickly buttoning it while I was still spluttering, looking everywhere. By which time it was too late, and she was all buttoned up, the lambswool reaching just below her buttocks.

'We need to talk,' she said, and padded barefoot through to the living-room. The sleeves of the cardigan reached the palms of her hands, and her curled fingers stretched the sleeves a little further, her arms straight, cocking her wrists so that her knuckles pointed upwards. She went over to the window, and tried out the view.

'I haven't much appreciated your behaviour.'

'I've not been well.'

'I've heard that. When you didn't come back with the Chaplain, I was worried. You ought to have made an effort.'

'Let's get married.'

'For God's sake, Jay.' Helena turned round and let go of the sleeves. She crossed her arms. 'It's about time you started taking this seriously.'

She was pretending to be angry and unavailable, but I wasn't so easily deterred. I knew that women changed their minds, because at Helena's age Elizabeth Taylor was married for the fourth and positively final time and irreversibly in love with Eddie Fisher, who sat in vigil by her hospital bed as she survived a vicious mystery illness, during which clinically she died, on four separate occasions.

Eddie Fisher was the husband one before Burton.

'Do you fancy going out? See the sights?'

'I want to sleep. I'm tired, Jay, very often. I'm having a baby. We are. You're having a baby. Things have to change.'

'Why? We can muddle through, like we always used to. If

you didn't keep saying that things had to change, I might never have panicked. *Why* does anything have to change?'

'Well,' Helena said. She curled into the armchair and drew her legs up beneath her, pulling the cardigan tight over her knees. 'Money, for a start. How are we going to survive?'

'Let's not talk about money.'

'Yes, let's. Let's talk about money.'

Starting off poor, in the rags stage of the story to richness, Burton's immediate prospects in Pontrhydyfen involved twelve hours a day up to his thighs in a two-foot seam of coal. Every terrace in the village was a casebook of crippled and tuberculose lungs, malnutrition, despair and unnecessary death. Poverty was waiting, always waiting, and the only remedy was money.

It was no accident that in his sober years Burton was resolute in his escape from 2 Dan-y-Bont to 73 Caradoc Street, and then away from Pontrhydyfen altogether, to 6 Connaught Street, Port Talbot, and to Exeter College, Oxford, and 24 Lyndhurst Road, Hampstead, to the house he called Pays de Galles in Céligny, Switzerland, before the ultimate film-star safety of Casa Kimberley, at Puerto Vallerta in Mexico.

Money offered salvation. It also sourced his extravagance and downfall, the folly of the Krupp diamond and a purple Rolls and 150 Welshmen on a jolly to the London Dorchester. Burton wanted the miner boyos to see the distance he'd travelled, and to show them his own paid-for heaven. But at the beginning it was simpler than that. He was getting married to Sybil Williams from higher up the valley, who may or may not have been pregnant, and money was an absolute essential. Otherwise, like Burton's mother, who was very special and not like other boys' mothers, Sybil might die from puerperal fever at the age of forty-nine, and that was seriously no way to live. Really, it wasn't.

I sorted out the bed, and left Helena to sleep. Then I phoned Rifka on her mobile. I wasn't in a church kind of mood, so I arranged to meet her at the Colombo.

At the Colombo, nothing was as popular as cricket, and for one-day internationals Mr Dharmasena removed the window so that Sri Lankans could watch from the pavement. But whatever the sport, the television was always on, and today the British Lions were starting their New Zealand tour with a soft midweeker against a backward North Island province.

Apart from a table of hungover Australians, I was the only customer, and Mr Dharmasena himself offered me free drinks, as a thank-you for yesterday's service in the church. I fancied a Guinness, and said so, but by the time he'd brought it over I'd changed my mind. I had to be serious. I had to avoid the pitfalls which led to a second child in a Devereux care-home, so blasted by her father's chronic absenteeism that the only words she ever spoke were 'Rich! Rich!', as if always calling Burton back from his own self-destruction.

Rifka arrived just as the game kicked off, and sober and silent we watched the first few minutes. The Lions, with only three Welshmen, were soon ten points down to a Waikato side that Mervyn Davies (on his own, man) could have mesmerised with his eyes closed and just back home from the mine. It was a disgrace, and well before the second try I was picking out the Welsh boys in the pack and thinking: 'that could have been me'. In front of 30,000 people in the Waikato Stadium, that could have been me.

I turned away from the screen and asked the waitress for a Rivella, and then another one for Rifka. It was a drink I'd discovered in Switzerland, made from extracts of milk. It was extremely unalcoholic.

'Now,' Rifka said. 'What is it that couldn't wait?'

I shifted my chair closer towards her, and hoped for some intercession from Burton's leg. She moved her chair closer to mine, which was, by lucky coincidence, exactly as I'd hoped. I wasn't beyond flirting with Rifka. Even if Helena was my Cleopatra, Rifka could still be one of my other willing co-stars, Claire Bloom or Sophia Loren.

'There's something bothering you, isn't there? Do you want to talk about it?'

'No,' I said, but Burton was always a talker. He claimed to have talked out all the novels he wanted to write, before he actually wrote them. He couldn't help himself. I pushed the untouched Guinness a little further away, and wrapped my hands round my brown bottle of Rivella. 'I need money.'

'Not a problem. Dig up James Joyce.'

I reached under the table, pulled up my trouser-leg, and put out my shin where Rifka could see it. Then I let the trouser drop, and went back to my bottle. Rifka looked at me curiously, as if I'd done something very strange, and I wasn't having that.

'*What*?'

'Nothing. I just didn't know that James Joyce had an interest in the rugby.'

'It's not Joyce. It's someone else. I want to know how much Moholy will pay.'

'Depends who it is.'

'That,' I said, 'is Mr Richard Burton.'

Her face fell. Burton wasn't good enough. In 1948, more than half a lifetime ago at the age of fifteen, Richard Burton had been selected to trial for Welsh Schools. It was the finest

119

moment of his childhood. They put him in the Possibles, not the Probables, and he didn't make it. His whole life, that was the pattern, and there was always the problem of getting so close, being so nearly there, and then failing, and falling short. I reached under the table, and with a wince I wrenched free the sellotape. I put Burton's leg-bone on the table.

With total poise, and only one brief glance at the Australians, Rifka fetched a newspaper from a rack, brought it back, and dropped it casually over the bone. She sat down again. 'Not that there's anything wrong with Richard Burton,' she said.

'No, you're right.' Under the newspaper he seemed so small, when once he'd been a big man, an open-side flanker from the Valleys. 'He wasted his talents. He was a genius, but flawed.'

'But there are bones in Moholy's catalogue worth a significant amount more. More difficult people. More famous ones.'

'I know that.'

'I mean Burton's interesting, but he's not top of the range. He's not James Joyce.'

It was the second half, and an Englishman was stretchered off. The Lions started a revival inspired by replacements and Celtic verve, that compulsive mix of foolery and hardiness. In fact, the fleet Welsh backs were breathing fire.

I asked Rifka if she'd ever consider working with me on someone more important than Burton. We could collaborate, help each other. We could co-operate. All I wanted was a leg-up, at the beginning of my body-snatching career. Everyone needed a hand, at the beginning, and Burton had stood on the shoulders of his mentor Philip Burton, and after that the playwright Emlyn Williams, and then John Gielgud. Without the help of others greater than himself, Burton would have stayed a no one.

'Me and you. We'll go halves. Who's worth the most?'

'I've stopped, Jay. I've given it up. And Moholy doesn't want just anybody, not any more. I told you. He has someone specific in mind.'

'I need help,' I said, hanging my head.

'Yes, probably. But not from me. Ask your girlfriend. See if you can corrupt her.'

'As if. She's worse than I am.'

It took several moments for my slow brain to stop, turn, and wonder how exactly Rifka knew about Helena. But by then Rifka was already on her feet, throwing some coins on the table.

'James Joyce,' she said. 'After that, once you get yourself started, that's the only income you'll ever need.'

An Irishman missed a penalty in extra time, gifting the game to the lean New Zealanders. I was in a café and bar, licensed for beers and wines and spirits, and overcome by an increasingly familiar restlessness. I left before it developed into a thirst.

Out in the street, I tried to think exclusively about Helena, but it was noon in the daylight of Geneva, and lunch-time for women and girls. I had the bone rolled up in Rifka's newspaper, and I carried it through the streets like a baton. There were millions of them, and every woman on her lunch-break a potential lover for the Richard Burtons of this world, assuming there must be many, seeing as there was one.

Small breasts, I liked, and big hips. While not neglecting buttocks and bare backs. Legs, when visible, brought to mind the truly amazing amount of sex I'd never had, with thousands of women I'd never meet, and all of it discreet and brilliant. Come on, Rich, with that protester over there wearing a vest and cut-off jeans, intercede on my behalf.

121

I'd wasted so much time, and here in Geneva the ebb of life was measured by clocks on every corner, and on every building, and clocks in the parks constructed from flowers. On every street the time wasted in a city of talks and interminable waiting was displayed behind bullet-proof glass, and in every luxury shop the honest watches told exactly the same time. One second more than before, and one second more than before. Time was passing, and then I'd die. The watches and clocks were everywhere. Remember you will die.

The only place in Geneva to escape this precision engineering was the heart of the Parc des Bastions, on a bench facing the Reformer's Wall. I double-checked in every direction that I wasn't overlooked by a clock, and then sat down in the sunshine with the newspaper across my knees. The centre of the Reformer's Wall, 100 metres long, was dominated by an immense statue of John Calvin, who disapproved strongly of the cult of personality. Bible in hand, Calvin was chief among a sculpted pantheon of Reformation heroes, ten metres high, many times as large as life, stylised and stony-faced, offering a generalised censure of anything I might care to contemplate.

The girls who came to skate. They were students, or squatters from the Boulevard des Philosophes, wearing cropped T-shirts with *Bread Not Bombs*, and *Battle of Seattle*, and *Barbie Sucks Cocks in Hell*. And as they dipped and swung their hips and shoulders, inventing circuits of zeros and eights, I thought, frankly, is there any young woman you wouldn't? And why not? And for that matter, why not the Guinness in the Colombo?

The Jenkins family, from the early days when Burton was still a Jenkins, would go at least twice every Sunday to Bethel, one of three chapels in the village of Pontrhydyfen. And then, when everyone else had gone home, the Jenkinses would stay behind to clean the floor. Richard despised the harshness of the Welsh Baptist soap, but back home at Dan-y-Bont he'd entertain the family at tea-time by repeating the sermon of the day. Already, in the proud melancholy of his youth, Burton could echo in his minor-key voice the wide variety of Thou Shalt Nots.

No games. Richard Burton at scrums, waiting for a back-row to creep round the blind side, then Boom!

No theatre. That first opening night in the West End, stealing the show from Gielgud, just in the way he used a broom.

No smoking. Behind the Co-op, from the age of eight. No drinking. While singing *Camelot* with Julie Andrews on Broadway, a bottle of vodka for the matinee and another for the adults in the evening. No fornicating. From the earliest days with Stanley Baxter in Streatham's Palais de Danse, with Irish nurses, usherettes, shopgirls, actresses and sweet little kickers from the chorus. Sex with Ophelia coming back from Stratford, in his car as big as a boat. No fighting. After a gallon of beer and a day-return to the Arms Park, essential brawls in London, with Londoners (*why? Because they're there, bach*). No poetry. Except plainstyle, which was emphatically not the preferred style of the young Burton as he bounced from pub to Soho pub in a living proclamation of *The Green Fuse That Drives the Flower*.

Richard Burton was guilty of all the sins responsible for the ruination of mankind and the degradation of the soul, and at the age of thirty-five, next year, he was condemned by name in *L'Osservatore della Domenica*, the weekly newspaper of the Vatican City.

But that was next year. For now, Burton still had a painful memory of the facial pustules and boils sent as frequent cautions from God, so fierce and long-lived he gave each of them names. Rhyd ap Llewelyn, and a hot resilient carbuncle on his neck, known to its friends as R. S. Thomas.

The pockmarks would stay with Burton all his life, as reminders of the many things he did that he shouldn't, that he knew he shouldn't, but that anyway he did. For how else was he supposed to cope? He'd taken on too much, or the wrong struggle, and had always to grapple with the several lives he conducted at once, knowing anyway he was going to die. So why bother about the boils? Why not return, with added insolence, the condescending stare of Calvin?

I jumped up, throwing away the newspaper, brandishing Burton's leg-bone open to the naked eye.

No one noticed. I flourished and shook it. No one. I held it like a detached umbrella handle, then balanced it on the end of my finger like a stick for the spinning of plates. Then like a swagger-stick. I jammed it between my teeth. Nobody cared. I laughed out loud, and ran in the direction of the flat, the leg-bone tucked under one arm like a rugby ball. I side-stepped a man in a suit, and utterly bamboozled another, throwing an outrageous dummy to a flying winger *who wasn't even there.*

Helena was so unhappy, so unhappy and strong. I'd made her very unhappy, but that I was going to fix. An amendment was in order for today's schedule of music. In place of our Anglican and earthbound arrangements of the Nunc Dimittis, we would now be singing an extra hymn, Guide Me O Thou Great Redeemer, to the tune of Cwm Rhondda, blasting directly skywards and with added descant on the second bread of heaven. Money was no object. We were going all the way to Casa Kimberley, all the way to the moon.

*

For the bones of famous people, Switzerland is the centre of the universe. They are the country's greatest natural resource, where Europe comes to die.

At Fluntern in Zurich, for example, only two stones down from Joyce, almost his neighbour, was the Italian Nobel prize-winner Elias Canetti (1905–1994). On the way to Kilchberg and Thomas Mann (1875–1955), the bone tourist could divert to Küssnacht on the Zürichsee, for the psychiatrist and analyst Carl Gustav Jung (1875–1961). *Called or not called*, was Jung's chosen inscription, *God will be present*. As with Davy, the grave looked quite undisturbed, despite the knee-bone in clingfilm in my kitchen cupboard.

The celebrity dead were a rich seam which ran right through the country, from Zermatt to the Ticino border, where for bones the village of Ronco could be highly recommended, not least for Paulette Goddard (1914–1990) and Erich Maria Remarque (1898–1970). And at the end of the day, as dusk fell, there might still be time for Herman Hesse (1877–1962), on the sunlit slopes of Montagnola.

I drove Helena out along the lake. After several hours' sleep, she was more like her old self, though her old self in a rotten mood. She sat hunched inside the seat-belt in her puffa, staring across the flat black water.

I said: 'We should never have split up. It was a mistake.'

'Not now, Jay.'

'People make mistakes. And they get back together. It happens all the time.'

'You've changed,' she said. 'Geneva's made you all disjointed. All get up and go.'

'I'm getting my act together.'

'Oh yes? And where does that leave us?'

'I want to show you something.'

Our first stop was Corsier-sur-Vevey, across the lake from Evian where blue and white mountains rose sharply against the pink label of the mid-afternoon sky. The small Corsier cemetery was a little miracle, a treasure-trove, and we walked along each row of stones, sometimes stopping, then moving on.

'What exactly is this in aid of?'

'Look. Queen Ena of Spain.'

After Ludovic Lazarus Zamenhof, inventor of Esperanto, after Oona and Charlie Chaplin, we were ambushed by James Mason (*1909–84 Never say in grief you are sorry he is gone, rather say in thankfulness you are grateful that he was*). It was the gloomy English film-actor, of course it was, but my stomach still hollowed, thinking only of myself.

'I hate it when that happens,' Helena said, stopping at James Mason with her arms crossed. 'That always spooks me out.'

Her family name was Byczynski. Helena Byczynski, from Eastbourne in Sussex. I admired the curve of her dark eyelashes, the twitch at the corner of her mouth. She even had a sense of humour, and this was the beginning of a great, great love story, Burton and Taylor, Mason and Byczynski. Helena would teach me how to live, and wasn't that the point of getting together, with anyone? With Helena I'd have the courage to outbid Onassis, buy the world's biggest diamond, live on a yacht, write a book, meet as equals with Coward and Bacall and the Duchess of Windsor, or I supposed their modern-day equivalents.

I looked closely at James Mason's grave. This business wasn't as straightforward as Moholy seemed to think. And Rifka knew that. It was trickier than a technical problem to be solved with practice and the right tools. It was essential to be emotionally prepared, defended. You had to have the attitude, the brash and the danger. Women loved the danger.

We drove the short distance to the quiet village of Tolochenaz, in the hills above the lakeside town of Morges. I parked the van at the Audrey Hepburn Pavilion, a new building which housed a small museum dedicated to the memory of the actress. The clouds had cracked apart, and this was a beautiful country, green and blue, with snow in the distance in the mountainous upper air.

Audrey Hepburn was buried alone, further up the hillside. As we climbed the winding path, I really wanted to believe, in agreement with the museum in the Pavilion, that some people were stars, kissed on the cheek by God. It could happen to anyone, born with some extra quality not inherited or learnt, but given, like rake-thin Audrey with her radiant smile, the princess of wish-fulfilment in a white Givenchy gown.

We stood either side of Hepburn's isolated grave. Some of us were special, with special missions in life. I mentioned to Helena, in a casual kind of way, in this quiet and un-frequented place, looking down at the most simple of stones, that in the whole world there could hardly be an easier way to make serious money than by digging up the famous dead.

Especially in a country like Switzerland, where there were many famous dead people, and hardly any police.

'You can't dig up Audrey Hepburn,' Helena said.

I was expecting her to say that. 'Nobody would ever know.'

'She's a woman. She's suffered enough.'

Besides, it would be scandalous. Audrey was everyone's favourite plot: I am a princess. *But nobody knows it.* She was an angel with a twenty-inch waist, elegant to her December end and so frail and wide-eyed at the death that she liked to be brought to this very same hillside, where the feathering of her breath in the mountain air reminded her that she was still alive. Hers wasn't a story which could end happily in Moholy's catalogue, followed by a sideboard in a secretive magnate's study.

'That's for mere mortals,' Helena said, 'for dead white males.'

'Sorry?'

'Some of those others we saw. I wouldn't have minded digging *them* up.'

'Really?'

Helena winced, and sat down on Hepburn's flat recumbent. With her feet on the grass beside it, she loosened the laces of her boots.

'I'm knackered,' she said. 'Definitely not the woman I once was. Where's that bread?'

We'd stopped for some bread and salami in the village, and we ate it on Audrey Hepburn. Helena cross-legged, me with my legs out in front, feet in the grass. All around us were the first purple crocuses of spring, though Helena said they weren't crocuses, they were bulbecottes, or some such. I was hoping for further small-talk about dead people. There was no one about, apart from us, and we'd also been alone in Corsier. It wasn't as if anyone actually cared.

'Well, why not?' she said, pushing me off the stone with her feet. She spread out her puffa, and lay back with her hands behind her head. 'The faith is disappearing, isn't it?' She bit into an apple and looked up at high-flying clouds banked like cliffs, England in the sky.

'Yes,' I said, 'I suppose it is.'

'It is in Geneva. First the churches go, then the graveyards. Graveyards can't last. It's a land issue.'

'Not a life-after-death issue?'

'Be serious.'

Helena saw it how it was, to an ordinary person not in thrall to outmoded notions of good and evil. Land was increasingly precious, and the less we believed in life after death, the more likely it was that cemeteries would be some of the first land we thought of claiming back. Like here, and in Corsier-sur-Vevey.

'Alpine meadows, sunshine, big white jagged mountains. It's a perfect location for executive villas.'

'It's a kind of recycling,' I said. 'Isn't it?'

'Oh, sure. There's nothing ghoulish about it. In the least.'

Helena stood up, and flattened down the thighs of her jeans. She heeled off her walking-boots, and watched the ripple of her toes in their white cotton socks. Then she peeled off the socks, and walked in delicate circles over the wind-dried grass, pointing her toes, her feet flattening into one ordained footprint after another.

'Spot on,' she said, 'and to placate the dead, should that be necessary, some of the proceeds from each white male can go to a decent cause. Something relevant.'

Right. She was so right. Some of the money from Humphry Davy, for example, we'd give to research into bronchitis and emphysema, to the continuing benefit of mine victims. The bones of Joyce would pay for English reading and writing lessons at the camp for refugees. Charlie Chaplin would fund an Alpine tour for the Sunshine Variety Club. Sweet Audrey. Even Audrey, if it ever came to that, wouldn't mind (the angel) if the sale of her bones supported orphaned children in those blasted outposts of the earth she liked to visit as United Nations special ambassador for peace.

'Theologically,' Helena said, 'it's watertight.'

She was concentrating on picking a small purple flower with her toes. At the third attempt she made it, and limping, favouring the foot with the flower, she brought it over. She lifted it towards me, and I took the flower of the mountain as she loomed above me, the sudden sun behind her head in a spreading corona of light, and I had to shade my eyes.

'You mean theoretically,' I corrected her, having also thought it through. But I knew what she meant. It was acceptable to dig up dead people. She was my Elizabeth Taylor, who could match me in my danger. We were the desperate duo, life-long partners in crime.

She knelt down in front of me and took the collar of my shirt in her fists. 'Jay, don't go weird on me.'

'What?'

'Don't talk about digging up dead celebrities.'

'Theoretically, the money earned could improve the lives of the living. You said so yourself.'

'It's body-snatching. It's barbaric.'

'Well,' I said, putting my hands round her back and pulling her towards me, hugging her close and tight so she couldn't see my face. 'I didn't actually mean it, of course I didn't.' Her small clenched fists were still on my neck, a hard and unyielding obstruction between us. 'As if I actually meant it. That would be ludicrous. Barmy. No one in their right mind would even consider it.'

No, they wouldn't. And why should I be different from anyone else?

The more drinks I drunk or drank, the more my left eyelid lowered. And I developed a nervous twitch in my cheek. We were sitting in a restaurant somewhere near the lake, Helena and I, the two of us back in the city and celebrating the fact that I was going to have a baby with the most beautiful woman in the world. Who'd come to find me. And also the fact that I was in my right mind, the same as everyone else, with no intention whatsoever of digging for the dead.

Any more of the dead.

I ordered another half-litre of Swiss white wine, filled my tiny Swiss wine glass, drank it, then filled it again. This was vengeful drinking, as if sobriety had let me down. It was a mistake ever to have flinched from cigarettes, excessive alcohol, and casual sex. In exchange for restraint, I'd been hoping for greater brain-power, the better to assess my own place in a universe full of extraordinary stories about the infinite variety and watchfulness of gods. I now deserved a lapse, because the gods were always having lapses the other way, when I understood practically nothing.

I refilled my glass, and drank, and waited for the miracle. No faith or intelligence was required. Only swallowing, a brief period of standing by, and then all the benefits of a clean and economical escape from the self.

It was commonly agreed that Richard Burton was a genius who failed, but that was a nonsense. Either you were, or you weren't. In every area of his life, except perhaps when he was sitting quietly in his Céligny library with a book, no, especially then, Burton was someone who was consistently making and reinventing himself. The strain was intolerable, and one more Bloody Mary, one more bottle of vodka, might always banish the fear that the essential Burton was somehow inadequate.

I felt an increasing remorse for bringing him back, but knew of an age-old remedy for feelings such as these. With the base of my glass I traced some curves on the table, and gradually the miracle began to happen. The past was

131

forgettable. Now and in the future, all things on earth were possible.

It wasn't just the wine. We'd been somewhere for aperitifs, and then somewhere else for more aperitifs. It was a mild evening in Geneva, and we sat outside at pavement tables where I acted suave and self-contained, which for me was odd, but then I wondered what it actually meant to act oddly. Every life, from one angle or another, was acting oddly, and tonight I was just another poser on the pavement with a drink. And then we went somewhere else for aperitifs, and because there was no Miner's Arms where swarthy men in flat caps burst into spontaneous renditions of Sosban Fach, I decided on the Blackout Club, in the Paquis.

I coughed, and walked Helena to the bar (just the one, just a quick pick-me-up), and ordered a sherry, on ice. We turned to have a good look at the bar's representative sample of Geneva's party people, middle-aged diplomats and Lithuanian women in states of undress between seventeen and thirty. The men were in suits, or catalogue casual, and in one corner some lucky Arabs, insensible to the restraints of Calvin, were thoroughly enjoying themselves. The girls from the cold Baltic preened and shimmied. They had all the right triangles.

At the restaurant, over a pink linen tablecloth, I was charming. I recited some poetry from my standard repertoire (*All the world's a stage*, I think it was that). Then my party piece *to be or not to be*, but backwards.

Helena had already heard it. I'd forgotten that. At first, she hardly drank at all. In the old days, I seemed to remember, she used to like her drink, especially when dressed up, as she was tonight. She was in black, but gloriously, like a widow after murdering her husband. Her new dress started (or ended) just below her shoulders and finished (or began again, going up again) just above her knees. It peaked at the hips and bust, not unlike a similar dress, in blue, on a blonde girl sitting behind Helena and to the right. I made eyes at her, but let's be fair. She was making eyes at me too, and it seemed highly unlikely that after Helena there would ever be any more women, or even any more wives. I drank another glass of wine, and alleluia the miracle again, get set for the marriage of the century.

I was sitting forward, elbows on the table, chin on the backs of my hands. Helena swatted away my arm so my chin nearly banged my plate.

'I think you've had enough,' she said. 'Let's go home.'

Big girls with small breasts. Small girls with big breasts. Big girls with small breasts. Small girls with big breasts. I found myself travelling in a large object commonly known as a bus.

Inside the flat, Helena said she was bushed. I think that's what she said, so I sat down on the edge of the double bed, and bounced up and down.

'Go sleep on a chair,' Helena said.

'I'm so glad you came. I love you.'

'Look, Jay. I'm not going to sleep with you. You're drunk.'

She didn't mean it. We'd slept together hundreds of times, and I was a good lover, and imaginative in bed. I often imagined other women.

She was now saying something else, but I don't think I was listening. As she spoke, I leant back on my hands and let the drink increase my awareness of detail: the down on her earlobe, the single bitten nail on the index finger of her right hand, the sunspots on her neck. It was a kind of preparation, and if not, then a kind of replacement.

'Come here,' she said, holding out her arms. 'Just come here.'

I stood and stepped between her welcoming arms, and she held me, and I thought she might be crying. I held her tight, as close as I could, a body-to-body crush in which I lost myself, forgetting who I was. Yes, that was love, I remembered now. Forgetting who I was. I wanted to hear her breath. I turned my head, wanting the little weather of her breath on my cheek, my neck, and although Helena had a very lovely back and spine, my hands found themselves somehow round towards the front of her strapping black dress.

'James.'

What now?

'I mean it. Go and sleep in the armchair.'

'Let's get married.'

'You're dreaming. Sleep it off.'

I went to hold her again, but she poked me in the ribs. 'Actually,' I corrected her, but not nearly quick enough to sound sober, 'I'm fantasising.'

'What's the difference?'

'More details.'

She pushed me away, and looked at me with love, or perhaps pity. 'Jay, you should try and *mean* the things you say.'

'I'm a good catch. You could do a lot worse.'

And not just once, but in one mistaken marriage after another, with the very rich but violent heir to the Hilton hotel chain, and a senator in decline many years her senior, and an opportunist builder of bungalows. Oh yes, I had her now.

'Good night, Jay,' she said, resting her hands on my chest, gently pushing me from the room. 'Sleep well.'

I waited outside the door, thinking it would suddenly open and she'd pull me in. But the door didn't open. I went into the kitchen, and poured a very small sherry into one of the mugs. Down the hatch. I poured myself another, slightly larger, and officially considered it my first.

Then I carried it through to the living-room, not the mug, but the bottle, and balanced on the arm of the armchair. Genuinely, for most of the day, I'd been determined not to drink. But up on the hillside above Morges, Helena had reminded me what I was. I was no one out of the ordinary, and there would be no body-snatching, and no salvation. So I had a drink, because I couldn't see the harm, and at this rate, drinking from the bottle all day and every day, I still wouldn't kill myself for another twenty-six years.

So I'd had a drink, to help me forget, I forget what, and now I was astonishingly drunk, except after a while it wasn't astonishing any more, just a fact of existence. I was drunk, and the miracle needed constant refreshing to help me conceive of all the contented and fulfilled people I never was. And sometimes, even if just in snatches, to believe I could become them.

All I wanted was Helena, a house near a stream in the shadow of mountains, and lots of little Byczynski–Masons laughing and gambolling in a water-meadow. With occasional trips to the city for the company of younger and prettier women. And then Helena again. In my cups, I could imagine every detail, and therefore concluded it must be possible.

From my haughty position on the arm of the chair, I pulled off the cushions and tumbled them to the floor. I ought to sleep, but it wasn't in Burton's nature to give up so easily. I had another nip from the bottle, not prepared to settle for Possible not Probable, a lightweight at wing-forward, with the wrong type of bones to make my presence felt.

Burton was an avid reader who failed as a writer (he wasn't James Joyce), but still he went on writing. He was an ambitious lover who failed as a husband, three times, and then he married again. He was a natural actor and heir to Olivier with a blighted future in TV specials in the limited States of America, but he never stepped back from his craft. He was a family man who failed to protect his family, his brother the granite Ifor falling down drunk after a family binge in Céligny's Café de la Gare, and paralysed for life. But still Burton sent twice-yearly cheques and Taylor's old dresses and plane-tickets and cars to cousins and nephews and nieces in the valleys.

He never gave in, not even to the ancestral pull of vague Welsh melancholy, the hiraeth for the green hills of an idealised home. He fought that like everything else, and by the end he could be found shuffling round Geneva in white shoes and a red turtleneck, frail and crooked and beaten, his arms withered, his bones gnarled and jarred by rugby at the pitheads, his body thinned and weakened by the fastness of life, abused and brittle, the spent valley boyo a regrettable feature in the bars of international hotels, but still reciting poetry, an obvious success, drinking, still acting, failing.

He left unsolved the conundrum of how best to live.

When still a boy, his elder and beloved sister Cis, who did most of the work of bringing him up, used to ask him why he couldn't be happy. He was the strongest and smartest of all the Pontrhydyfen boys, and still he wasn't happy. The young boy Burton would tap and tap his fetching head.

'Too much of this, Cis. Too much of this.'

He thought too much, and at the end, in the free-fall of his self-destruction, this was his most frequent thought: there must be more to life than putting on make-up and pulling on tights and replicating the frustration of others.

Acting was not a serious vocation. It was a light and flippant thing to have grown old while going through life disguised. To have lifted up, week after week, other people's words in the echoes of old beliefs, knowing that this play-acting would be the main business of life, in the slender hope that acting itself was a kind of discovery, with its own kind of truth.

I wanted to be someone else, anyone else.

The drink wasn't working. That was the worst of the failures. Richard Burton never gave up, not even at the bottom of his three daily bottles of vodka, with crystals of alcohol forming on his spine. And yet, despite his dedication to the drink, he remained himself, always the small boy from the Baptist Chapel, hauled back from greatness by the niggard claims of conscience.

Thou Shalt Not.

What had held us back, as he'd held back all men of fire and passion for many centuries, was John Calvin. If it hadn't been for him (no games, no theatre, no drinking), the great Burton and others like us, the strong and the brave, we were the ones who'd have inherited the earth.

I decided to dig up John Calvin. It made perfect sense to me. He deserved it, and that would get me clean.

One for the road, and then I gathered up tools, humming over and over Land of My Fathers. Just inside the doorway, I drained the bottle, Jay Mason Minor the adrift and exiled deacon, the rationalist, the son of his vicar father and mummy's favourite. And even now, still now, at the age of thirty-four, also this wild Welsh boy shining out with greatness. It was another of my lost lives, unled, not lived.

My ancestors would have known me well as I stumbled outside into the darkness, deep in drink, and back to the man's work of mining.

Jung's Knee

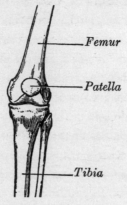

Femur

Patella

Tibia

'It was only after I had reached the central point in my
thinking and in my researches, namely the concept of the self,
that I found my way back to the world.'

Carl Gustav Jung, Commentary on *The Secret of the
Golden Flower*

The next morning I was woken by Helena padding out of the
bathroom, the cistern refilling. I rolled on to my back: I was
on the woodblock floor of the living-room, my neck stiff and
my shoulder sore to the bone. From the kitchen, I heard a
stifled gasp, then Helena in the doorway hands on hips. She
was wearing my blue-black cardigan as a dressing-gown, the
wool at the end of the sleeves bunched between her fingers.
She took a step forward, and kicked me hard on the sole of
the foot.

'Ouch.'

'What the fuck is that?'

'What?'

'You know what.'

I did a single sit-up, to get myself sitting up, and immediately wished I hadn't. After my second successive late night I felt terrible, tongue dry, bones aching, head splitting in a serrated line through my bleeding right eye to my nostril. Relics were supposed to heal, as in miracles, but secular remains plainly couldn't be trusted. I stood up and shuffled to the kitchen for gallons of water.

And in the middle of the floor, splayed open to reveal a muddle of dirt and bones, a brown plastic bin-liner. Black for waste. Brown for recycling. It was the new skeleton I'd dug up last night.

'I can't believe you did this,' Helena said. 'This is sick. You seriously need help.'

'I'm not. I don't.'

'Put them back. Right now. Wherever they came from, put them straight back.'

'Helena, just.'

'What?'

'Just be quiet for a moment.'

I was an idiot to have left the bin-liner out in the open. I didn't remember leaving it there. I didn't remember coming back from the cemetery. All I could remember: I didn't know who it was.

It was supposed to have been John Calvin. And last night, this too I remembered, there had been many incontestable reasons for choosing John Calvin. Revenge was one. Money another. In the catalogue, Calvin was at the top end of the price range, up there with Constantine and Karl Marx. These were the big three in the spiritual history of the West.

At the time, completely plastered, I was confident it'd be a breeze. Calvin was nearly 500 years dead. He had no close relations to offend or traumatise. In his own lifetime, he'd placed no value on burial, or his own bones, so the man himself couldn't have cared less. After 500 years, it would be more like digging up Elizabeth Taylor's Snowflake (*1973–1979 My Darling Most Precious*). And Calvin was only round the corner, so I didn't even have to drive.

The weather had been perfect, the half-moon in a patchy sky enough to outline the stones and, further on, the sharp angles of the mechanical digger. With a fresh wind rustling the trees and muffling abrupt noises, I vaulted the low wall in a single fearless bound, and stalked lightly across the grass to Calvin's corner. You can do it, I told myself. I was hoping, even now, without a recent drink, or a clutch of agreeable girlfriends, or a yacht with yapping dogs on, that I was actually Richard Burton, rugged and dauntless, the Major Smith of *Where Eagles Dare*. I was counting on the continuation of miracles.

It took me a little while to locate Calvin's headstone, which was the size of a shoebox and marked only *J.C.* Following Rifka's advice, I immediately went to work on the seal of the recumbent. I'd expected it to be more difficult, after 500 years, but I soon had the mortar away and the stone quietly sliding. I applied my skills with an absolute drunken concentration that allowed me to do one thing very well. I wouldn't have been able to talk at the same time, for example, or care about anyone coming.

Using the trowel, digging, I expected the old bones to have risen close to the surface. I sank the trowel at least three feet, even a little further, then probed even deeper with the crowbar. There were no bones, no remnants of anything. The grave was full of nothing but mud. John Calvin wasn't there.

I was feeling stubborn, a pig-headed and self-willed Celt, and I'd come to the cemetery for relics. I had the attitude and the skills and the tools. I closed up Calvin, and started in my tenacious way on the next grave along. Or maybe not the next one, but the next after that. Anyway, it was quite close by, and it wasn't easy, but after all the effort and the drink I refused to leave the cemetery without some celebrity bones.

I soon had them out and into the bin-liner. The earth went back in, the stone back on. And for the second time that night, just as I had with Calvin, I brushed the stone clean and tidied the edges and applied my home-made paste to the join, replacing the mortar I'd earlier chipped away.

The details were a blank. No matter how hard I tried, I genuinely couldn't remember who I'd taken in place of the absent Calvin. I had no memory of the stone, or any dates, no names in my head. I remembered that John Calvin wasn't there, but the rest was impenetrable, a haze, a blackness.

'Am I supposed to be impressed?'

'I was drunk.'

'So why drink so much?'

'I don't know. Cry for help?'

'Yesterday was a very strange day, Jay, but this is worse. Much worse. I didn't realise how far it had gone. Jay.'

'What?'

'Listen to me. Why are you being so odd?'

'I guess I'm just an odd kind of person.'

'You didn't use to be, not like this. Not odd. Inconsistent, maybe.'

'Then I'm an inconsistent kind of person.'

'So cold.'

'I'm a cold person.'

'You're not yourself.'

'So who am I, then?'

'Frankly, Jamie, you're being an arsehole. And you're making an idiot of yourself. Look at this. Just look at it.'

She gestured at the upright lump of the bin-bag as if she was going to slap it, and then kick it. In the end, she just walked around it, the sleeves of the cardigan gripped tightly in her hands. 'You're a fucking mess, James Mason. You need help.'

'I know,' I said, suddenly falling in on myself. 'I know I've not been myself. I *am* a fucking mess.'

'There's more, isn't there? Tell me the worst. Tell me everything.'

I put down my third glass of water and went through to the bedroom, which smelled warmly of Helena in the morning. I opened the closet, and brushed aside my various shirts and cardigans to pull out Dad's heavy kit-bag, now damp through the canvas in patches.

'Oh no.'

It was open. Helena peered in, over the top. 'And who the fuck is that?'

'That,' I said, feeling very awkward, and even embarrassed by my lowly taste in the famous, 'is Mr Richard Burton.'

'Who?'

'The actor. Burton and Taylor. Liz and Dick.'

'Oh God, oh no. What else?'

'That's it.'

'Why? What on earth possessed you? And does anyone else know? You've got to sort yourself out, Jay, because this is frankly unbelievable. When we talked about it yesterday, I assumed you were joking. What the hell were you thinking of?'

'It seemed like a good idea. Harmless. And for the money.

You know. Because it's the information age, and real things command a premium. I thought it was a kind of materialism, in keeping with the times, but taken to a higher level.'

'For God's sake, Jay, feel the difference. They're not just another commodity.'

'Aren't they? People buy them. They pay handsomely. Apparently it's a buoyant market, and the future of the antiquities industry.'

'But it's still not right, is it?'

Of course not. Obviously it wasn't. I'd been overwhelmed by a fantasy of my own making, a deluded Welshman living the hero of one of the old Welsh stories, in which only the Welsh were hard and grand and heroic. The attempt to live like Richard Burton was absurd, as if I had the same failings, the same appetites, and girls rolling over me like wheels.

'Either the bones go, or I do,' Helena said.

She'd started to fold her clothes on to the bed, and I suddenly most urgently needed her to stay. The bones go, the bones. I did not want to speak with the dead. I wanted to stay on good terms, in a sane and acceptable manner, with the living.

'The bones,' I said. 'I'll get rid of the bones. God's honour.'

'Today.'

'Out. Gone. Never to be seen again.'

I could chuck them with the rubbish. Only Rifka knew about Burton, and she hadn't been all that interested. And no one but Helena had seen the unknown bones from the cemetery of kings. It ought to be easy. However, even after disposing of the bones, there was still the problem of Moholy.

As far as Joseph Moholy was concerned, I'd now had two fine nights in which to fetch Joyce. I'd kept the van, so presumably I was taking advantage of the favourable conditions. I had some explaining to do. From Rifka, I already knew that Burton was inadequate as a replacement for Joyce. However, I also had Jung's knee-cap, up in the kitchen cabinet. I couldn't actually remember seeing Jung's name in Moholy's catalogue of bones (*Switzerland*, Volume One) but I was confident he'd outscore the disappointing and unreliable Burton in almost every category.

If I offered Jung's knee in the place of Joyce, I could return the van at the same time, and so discharge my obligations. Admittedly, this would leave me back at square one, but it showed the extent of my recent failings that square one looked like progress.

I fetched Jung's knee down from the cupboard in the kitchen, still wrapped in its safety clingfilm, not realising that Helena had followed me.

'And what's *that*?'

'It's nothing. Jung's knee.'

'Jesus Christ. Another one.'

'It's only his *knee*. I'll get rid of this first, then I'll come back for the others. Don't be angry. I'm going to make it right.'

I dressed in a hurry, kissed Helena on the cheek, and left the flat without checking a mirror. It was a while now since I'd stopped enjoying my reflection, and I knew anyway from photographs that I was rarely how I looked in mirrors.

It was raining. I sat behind the wheel of the van watching each raindrop splitting on the windscreen like a dice coming up five. It was metric rain, methodically swept aside by the wipers, throwing more fives, again to be swept away. I bet on fives. I won. Must be a lucky kind of guy. Fives. Fives again.

If only I'd waited, been less impatient, I'd have made fewer mistakes. One more day and last night's digging would have been rained off, like cricket. I sat there in the early-morning gloom, going nowhere, with the wipers wiping away the rain, and wondered how I'd managed to get it quite so wrong. I watched a large black aerosol-can skipping across the road. It was made of foam-rubber and branded in white cut-out letters, *Consume, Be Silent, Die*, and it bobbed past my windows and away towards town. Right. Like everybody, I knew that reform was needed, in fact it was always in the back of my mind, but first I had to see to myself.

I should start with the clothes. Bending to get behind the wheel, I'd noticed what I was actually wearing. Should have looked in the mirror. In my haste to end all connection with relics, I'd managed to put on one red sock and one yellow, the Chaplain's judo trousers, and a blue and white striped pyjama top I'd mistaken for a shirt. I looked like a lunatic.

Helena was spot-on. I was a fucking mess, and I needed help. Fearing for my own sanity, thinking I probably needed to see somebody, I placed Jung's knee-cap on the passenger seat beside me, and pulled out into the ambient traffic of Geneva. As I set off for Moholy's gallery in the Rue de la Croix d'Or, I was the most scared I'd ever been of breaking up, of cracking apart. I blamed it on my age, and loneliness, and Geneva. And the fact that from a standing start I'd now twice brought back a body from the dead. This had to stop. I was far from home and my distance from cake-bakes and other anchors was sending me doolally.

Giving way to one of the day's first trams on the Rue de Candolle, I glanced down at Jung's knee-cap in clingfilm on the passenger seat. The precaution of the plastic wrapping was a madness in itself.

A car behind beeped me. I was as mentally solid as the next

man. I hastily unwrapped the white shell of Jung's knee from its clingfilm, and moved on, Carl Gustav Jung skittish and free on the seat beside me, a person of undoubted distinction, raised in the European provinces and son of a Protestant pastor.

That was more like it. He was someone I could relate to, even if, two years ago at the age of thirty-two, he was already Oberarzt in a white coat and high collar at the Burghölzli clinic, second-in-command to Bleuler, and a pioneer of meaningful associations between words, objects, memories, names, institutions, the Red Cross, Switzerland, cheese, holes, ground, mine, bones, gold, and questions, questions, questions.

Jung took special responsibility for those poor deranged souls whose every belief and action was an expression and search for the self, the destination always the same, only the journey which changed. Any path could be the one path, the direct route to self-realisation, but for those who ended up at the Burghölzli, stone-silent or raving, the true path most probably wasn't the one they'd taken.

The analyst in Jung still found that interesting, in fact life-errors were always interesting, but they did make driving conditions difficult.

- If I am understanding you correctly, Herr Mason, you are entertaining a Middle Aged belief of human relics haffing some mysterious power? Hein?
- I never said that.
- You are sinking proximity to dominant bones can be modifying behaviour?
- I'd like to believe in life after death.

Carl Gustav Jung had eight uncles who were also parsons, on both sides of the family, and like all children from religious households he grew up with the dragback that what people actually thought and believed was of some significance. Later, as stepfather of Psychology, he encouraged everyone to tell their own intimate story, which could then be analysed to explain them.

- The vays you are being since coming in Genf is telling me you are haffing a problem.
- I have no problem.
- I sink Herr Mason you do.
- I don't.
- So.
- I don't.
- (And the voices?)
- (What voices?)
- Do not be vorrying. It is alles quite normal.
- I'm very glad you think so.

Jung rejected Freud's mechanistic approach to identity, and speculated on the collective unconscious. This allowed everyone access to the same pool of mythical archetypes, bringing us one and all together. We are all everybody. What one person was, everyone could be, which made it more plausible, just as a random example, that a single moment of intense suffering somewhere in the Middle East, say 2000 years ago, could be a valuable lesson to us all.

For the individual, becoming a complete human being was a matter of integrating all the different possibilities. The individuation process, or *Menschwerdung*, created the spiritual *Übermensch*.

I thought of Becket's brain spilled across the flagstones of Canterbury Cathedral, Davy doped and alone in his Geneva hotel room, and Burton crawling in his vomit, public as a dog in the lobby of the high-class Dorchester. I wasn't convinced that a spiritual *Übermensch* was what I really aspired to be.

Jung also spoke to the dead.

As a young man, moustache still in patches, he was introduced to séances by his mother's side of the family, the Preiswerks. In the family darkness, Jung was enthralled when his cousin Hélène took on a second personality named Ivènes. She then became her own grandfather, the Reverend Samuel Preiswerk, reproducing his precise tone of voice before passing through many other incarnations scattered through the centuries. She was Seeress of Prevorst and the Countess of Thierfelsenberg, she was Madame de Velours, and she suffered a Christian martyrdom under Nero in Rome.

In 1916, as a non-combatant in neutral Switzerland, Jung reconsidered the collective unconscious, and renamed it the land of the dead. The two terms were interchangeable, as were other phrases in Jung's vocabulary of analytical psychology. 'Splinter personalities' or 'complexes' were the same as spirits, which were so common a presence in human experience that they accounted for the astonishing range of behaviour open to each and every one of us. The interplay of the ego with alternate complexes (or, in other words, the influence of spirits) was what made each human personality dynamic and unique.

From this time on, the spirits themselves increasingly chose to speak through Jung's patients, and his particular talent lay in believing whatever his patients believed, in the living dead and synchronicity and secret orders of invincible Teutonic knights (who kept tight the secret of the Grail). I am Napoleon. I am an American heiress and I am deeply unhappy. I am the Messiah. The secret of Jung's compassion was that in everybody else, whatever their story, he saw himself.

These spirits talked to Jung at length, in a detail scarcely believable, as if genuinely they were people and beings from other times. One possible explanation was life after death. Another was *cryptomnesia*.

Secretly, we know everything.

At that, I had to laugh. Alone in the car, not being mad, driving to Moholy's gallery with Jung's knee-cap on the seat beside me, I had to say that I felt I knew very little, if anything at all. Nothing, in fact.

   – *Secretly*.

   – You're bonkers, aren't you?

   – I am never using that word. My personality sometimes is disorientated. It is normal. I haff never been denying it.

In his research into the phenomenology of the self, Jung discovered he was quite a phenomenon. He sometimes believed he was Jesus. Christ was his culture hero, the psychological image of wholeness. He was the ultimate and unspotted archetype of the self, unique and occurring only once in time. Or perhaps twice. Switzerland could be the new Eden, where the four rivers meet, and Jung a selected vessel of grace for the conveying of certain revelations which would enrich the lives of the ordinary. There was no great mystery to it. Jesus was a Pisces, according to Jung, and not a Capricorn, which was quite clearly the hidden clue to his character.

Jesus wasn't Jung's only madness. He spent hours training a dachshund to whimper in the presence of demons. He walked in his garden talking with Philemon, an invisible spirit. He kept a loaded pistol next to his bed, and swore he'd blow his brains out if ever he felt he'd entirely lost his mind. How sane was that? And in that state, with the pistol cocked at his bedside, how could the second-best doctor at the Zurich Burghölzli ever hope to help? Jung could be paranoid, and fly into fits of rage, ranting like one of his patients in need of the standard restraints, pads and chains, electrotherapy and opiates, and as a last resort a good therapeutic wrapping in a clammy wet bedsheet.

There, that ought to dampen the spirits.

I was still in the van, and still driving, but I was a long way from Moholy's gallery. I'd ended up somewhere out by the airport, or maybe not. I was utterly lost. I saw a sign to CERN, and another to France, and one which simply said East. I opted for Centre-Ville, driving back in past a refugee camp, the United Nations, and Geneva's Museum of Human Atrocity. I considered paying it a quick visit, looking at what was possible and going quietly mad, but on Tuesdays the museum was closed.

I drove past a barracks, the headquarters of several multinational corporations, and many walled consulates. It was a city I hardly recognised, of secrets and contra- dictions, of much spying, like a psychoanalyst's view of the brain.

Without knowing quite how, I ended up in front of the Church of All Saints. I bumped the van on to the kerb, and sat for a while doing nothing. At least I knew where I was. I had the padded steering wheel firmly in my hands at ten to two, and I started softly to bump my forehead against twelve, frightening myself, as if I were somehow possessed.

Get a grip. Get a hold of yourself.

Jung would have concluded that I'd driven to the church for an obscure purpose, but Jung was dead and the relic business was nonsense. I needed to put it behind me, and sever all connections. I went into the church for the circle of purple silk which had once wrapped Becket. Get rid of *everything*. The emptiness of the church made it cold, and unwelcoming, and I didn't want to linger. I opened the safe and pulled out the silk from beneath the unused wafers, the body of Christ, hold you in eternal life.

On my way back out, I stopped at the bags of jumble. I couldn't go to Moholy's looking like this, and in the bottom of the second bag I remembered an old grey suit. It was several sizes too stout, and also too long. I tried to fill it out, feeling heavy and Germanic on a comforting diet of sausages and dense brown bread.

Back in the van, flopping about in the suit, I kept Jung unwrapped. I was feeling a little unhinged, and needed all the help I could get.

In the window of his gallery in the Rue de la Croix d'Or, Joseph Moholy the seller of legitimate antiquities had a fist-sized statue of Tlazolteotl, eater of filth and goddess of unbridled sexuality, in the act of childbirth. And Napoleon's pinnacled hat.

I left the van on the kerb and pushed through the doorway, activating an old-fashioned bell, perhaps even antique. A suited boy sitting behind the sales desk stood up and politely asked me to wait. He said Mr Moholy had been expecting me, and went through a screen at the back.

I'd rearranged the suit, rolling up the sleeves and turning up the trouser-legs, and if it still looked unusual it could plausibly be a fashion. This time, I'd concentrated on the correct and most direct route to Moholy's, and altogether I'd regained a measure of control. My earlier behaviour I dismissed as the natural consequence of a huge hangover and not enough sleep, two nights in succession. As for my mood-swings, everyone behaved like this, and people changed and adapted all the time. It was a common pattern, and this was what it meant to be me, to be alive. I wasn't ill, and Mum had never been ill, either.

I was fine.

After the energy of relics, I was frankly disappointed by the still lifes of the artefacts and art objects in Moholy's gallery. I sensed that they were important, of course they were, but in a secondary and slightly unsatisfactory way, as if none of them was quite important enough. It was as if these objects were stepping stones to relics, and relics in turn were suggestions of something else, the one thing everyone was actually looking for, and for which all other remains of the dead were just substitutes, or shadows.

Moholy came in, without the boy. He was wearing holiday clothes, a beige suit and a shirt in sea-blue linen, open by a single button at the neck. He made a point of shaking hands, his grip firm, his palm much drier and cooler than my own.

'And how's my friend James?'

'I'm fine, thanks. A bit on the tired side.'

'I meant James Jesus Joyce.'

I'd almost forgotten. Joyce seemed such a long time ago. 'I've done better than that,' I said, holding out the knee-bone, wrapped now in Becket's beige silk. 'I have a valuable extract of Carl Gustav Jung.'

Moholy was cautious, and didn't immediately reach out for the bone. Nor did he visibly betray any excitement. 'That's most interesting,' he said, holding himself back.

'Carl Gustav Jung, the world-famous thinker and psychologist.'

'Yes, yes. I know who he is, thanks. It's just that this wasn't what I was expecting. And with Jung, in particular, there are certain problems. As far as his relics are concerned, he presents a specific level of difficulty.'

'How so?'

'He was cremated.'

My heart glided from my ribcage, not touching the sides. 'That can't be right. He has a gravestone, in Küssnacht. I've seen it.'

'He was definitely cremated. They buried the urn.'

'Are you sure?'

'Positive. It's the kind of thing I always check when adding to the catalogue. Where did you get the bone?'

For the first time since our afternoon with Liz Taylor's dogs, I remembered that Rifka had mentioned it was probably a fake. Probably, she'd said. Or that there was something doubtful about it. I couldn't remember.

Moholy reached out his hand, took the knee-cap and the silk cloth, and examined both more closely at his desk.

'It's Jung,' I insisted. 'It *is* Jung. I know it is.'

I was surprised by my own certainty, but it had to be Jung. I'd sat in the car while it analysed me, and gave me false directions. It had encouraged me to examine my inner uncertainties, and engage fully with my recent disintegration. Only Jung could have done that.

'Perhaps he left instructions with one of his juniors,' I suggested hopefully, 'one of his disciples. Maybe he authorised a mock cremation while keeping back at least some of his body-parts for another purpose.'

It didn't seem impossible. Jung had started his career as a doctor, a junior assistant specialising in anatomy, and he had no latent sentiment for corpses. Not even his own.

'Yes,' Moholy said. 'I like your reasoning. Go on.'

Strangely, I noticed he was now showing more interest in the circle of purple silk than he was in the bone.

'I don't know what that purpose would actually be,' I said.

'But obviously something important. Some kind of secret, maybe, which Jung thought was worth protecting. Then the bones left behind become the key to the secret. The fake cremation would certainly confuse anyone in pursuit of whatever it was he wanted to hide.'

I hardly knew what I was saying. Either the knee-bone *did* belong to Jung, and I had a rare sensitivity to the well-recorded phenomenon of relics. Or it didn't, and I was mad as a rat with a gold tooth.

'Do I seem like a person of sound mind?'

'It is widely accepted that Jung was cremated.'

'But the knee-cap. What about the *effect*?'

I was pleading. I wanted desperately to know if I was the only one, the only person since medieval times so intensely sensitive to relics. Jung too had considered himself unique, a religious prophet with extraordinary powers who alone could do what he did. In his opinion, there was no one quite like him.

'That *would* be a bit mad, wouldn't it?' Moholy said, turning the circle of silk thoughtfully in his hands. Inspecting one side then the other. 'To think you were unlike anyone else. That would truly be close to madness.'

'Yes,' I agreed, 'it would. What exactly are you saying?'

'You're not the only one. I get it too.'

'Thank you. Thank God for that. I was beginning to think there was something wrong with me. I've been acting like I'm everybody.'

'Don't you worry,' Moholy said. 'What you've been feeling is quite normal. It happens to everyone.'

'So we're not mad?'

'That's normal, too. At some stage, everyone alive thinks they're mad. Even me.'

154

'But this could still be Jung's knee, right?'

He picked up the circular cloth by two fingers, letting it hang like a flag, turning it under the broad flood of light from an antique desk-lamp. 'Try and think more laterally. Jung was also an adept of mandalas.'

He twisted the lamp to point diagonally upwards, and held the circular cloth so that the light picked out the lines woven inside it, each corner of the square touching the circumference, and then the smaller rectangles blocked inside the square. 'To my mind,' Moholy said, 'the pattern on this cloth looks not unlike a mandala.'

He laid it flat on the leather inlay of his desk-top, and flipped the lamp-light back down. 'Buddhists use them as an aid to meditation. What a mantra is to the ear, a mandala is to the eye.' He turned the cloth by small degrees through a full circle, each time moving his head to get the advantage of different perspectives. 'It's a kind of cryptogram depicting the state of the self. Where did you find this?'

'It was in the church. With Becket.'

'It's not that old,' Moholy said. 'I wonder why it was used to wrap up Becket?'

'Maybe it has some connection with Jung.'

'Not maybe,' Moholy said. 'Definitely.'

Jung's fascination with the mandala came at a time in his life, ten years from now, when he needed to recover from non-combatism and expressive sausage-dogs and the cocked revolver on the bedside table. All over Europe, then as now, civilisation and Christianity were in crisis, our mental state and outlook restless, nervous, confused. Our religion seemed stale, our politics tired, and we looked elsewhere to replenish our grounds for hope.

There was a brighter future to be had in exchanging our

poisonous individualism for the Indian concept of *atmen*. Our notions of God the Creator and of human beings living single lives could be replaced by cosmic law and a cycle of rebirths. We were not living unique lives, but just one turn in an ongoing cycle of birth and birth again. It was a solace I could repeat to myself like a mantra. 'I am not my own man. Thankfully, I am not.'

The mandala was a diagram of this new self, a symbol of order which Jung's patients were encouraged to draw during periods of psychic recovery. The protective outer circle and the strict inner square bound and subdued the lawless powers roaming the psychological darkness, which within each mandala the patients could depict as they liked. In fully washable crayon. Jung had understood that with the self there is no linear development, only a kind of circum-ambulation.

'Basically,' Moholy said, laying it flat on the desk, 'it's a map.'

Jung used to draw his own personal mandala on a daily basis, a mental hygiene as regular as cleaning his teeth. It was the map of his personality, which was always changing, and also the whole Universe, one and the same.

'That's not the type of map I had in mind,' Moholy said, reaching into his desk-drawer for a black-handled magnifying glass. 'I think this is a geographical map. Look at these marks.'

We both crouched low over the table. At one level, I knew this was barmy, but Jung had made his great discoveries by believing whatever mad people believed, and, under magnification, Moholy was sure he could see several tiny holes in the cloth, like pin-pricks, each one in the centre of a small embroidered rectangle. He fetched a second desk-lamp, with a green shade. There was just the suggestion, at various points on the cloth, of the curve of different-sized circles, as if the holes had been made by the point of a compass.

'Now that,' Moholy said, 'would truly be interesting. But what does it actually map?'

'Maybe it's just a cloth.'

Moholy revolved the circle of silk a half-turn, then another quarter. 'Something round, I imagine.'

'Or something square.'

'You know, this could be just the missing piece I've been looking for. The silk was with Becket. I knew there was something important about Becket. Maybe this was it. There must be some sort of connection between our Swiss relics and this particular piece of material. Watch this.'

Moholy took off his jacket and pushed up his shirtsleeves, then rummaged through the desk before securing them with red elastic bands. He also brought out a yellow retractable tape-measure, and very carefully measured the width of the knee-cap I was claiming as Jung. He noted the measurement, then put the bone aside. If the mandala was a map, as Moholy was suggesting, or a puzzle, then Jung's knee-cap could be some kind of indicator, or arrow. Moholy's hands went inside the drawer again, and brought out a brass compass with points on each extended arm. Taking care, he positioned the compass precisely on the cloth.

The large square sewn inside the circle, he'd decided, could represent the square surface area of a cemetery, not unlike Geneva's Cimetière des Rois.

'You've been there, haven't you?'

'I have.'

'And it's square.'

'It is.'

The hand-embroidered rectangles inside the square corresponded to the location of selected graves in the cemetery, and this particular mandala was the kind of map in which X marked the spot. Except there was no obvious X. The indicators, the arrows which would reveal X, had something to do with Becket and Jung, and perhaps other bones Moholy already owned.

Becket would have particular significance, as it was his toe which was found wrapped inside the mandala. Jung's kneecap was also involved, as the mandala pointed back to Jung as clearly as a signature.

Both of these bones had a unique length, or reach. Once Moholy had noted that measurement, he used it as the diameter of a circle he could describe with his compass. Starting at the entrance of the Cimetière des Rois, just as an example, and taking the measurement of the first bone, say Becket's toe, a circle could be drawn whose diameter was determined by this specific relic of Becket.

The Geneva graves weren't in regular rows, a neatness rarely permitted except to the military, in wartime. The circumference of the circle determined by Becket's toe would therefore run through the exact centre of only one other grave. This second grave wasn't yet X, not yet the location of the secret. It was simply the centre of a second circle, its diameter measured according to the length of another specified bone from that particular grave. The circumference of this next circle would also run through the centre of only one further grave. And so on.

It was like history. The correct sequence of bones, from the right people in the right order (and only one order would do), would eventually lead to X, the secret of how to live, that unique solution which fuelled the obsession of scholars. To collectors of relics, as to priests, to scientists and bar-room philosophers and analytical psychologists, it was always tempting to seek every answer in a single glorious revelation.

'Jung's knee-cap must be close to the last bone,' Moholy said, his eyes at the level of the table as he swung round the compass. 'It must be so. If Jung designed the map, as a puzzle of his own invention, he'd also make damn sure he was the most important piece. That's the way he was.'

Moholy twisted one final stiff-legged stride with the compass, and then sat back, eyebrows raised. 'Ah. Yes. That would make sense.'

I took a closer look, and saw that the further point of the compass was stabbed directly into an embroidered rectangle at the top left-hand corner of the square woven inside the mandala.

'Quite masterly,' Moholy said, 'I think I see it. Yes, I definitely see it now. How ingenious.'

'What is? What can you see?'

'Forget about James Joyce. I've changed my mind. Forget Joyce completely. I want you to have a go at John Calvin.'

If earlier I'd thought I was off my trolley, now I knew it for certain. It was one thing to give credence to the power of relics, and to follow Jung's defiant example of believing the unbelievable, but my already stretched credulity had reached its outer limits.

'Why?' I asked, paranoid and desperate for electro-therapy. I simply couldn't allow myself to go along with this madness – where were the pads and chains, the sopping bedsheets? 'Just tell me why. Why bother with different people? You only need one body. I can get you one body. Not a problem. Maybe I can get you two, which is all you'll ever need. You already have the confidence of your clients. Let

159

them choose whoever they want from the catalogue, and then give them some bones. Any bones. It doesn't matter. Buy a skeleton from Pakistan, or steal one from a teaching hospital. You see what I'm saying? The clients won't know the difference. All bones look alike. *Everyone's the same.*'

Moholy was running his finger through some objects in a leather trinket box on the corner of the desk: some buttons, an ivory crucifix, a chipped blue scarab. He picked out a small metal key, and used it to point at me.

'James, you've got a lot to learn.'

He turned and inserted the key into a mirror behind the desk, which was actually (and now obviously) a medicine cabinet. I'd probably avoided looking too closely, until now, because of the mirror.

'It's not the bones,' he said. 'It's what the bones *do.*'

Inside the cabinet, on mirror-backed shelves, there were two rows of clear glass jars, with silver tops and plain white labels hand-scripted in Indian ink. The labels had a simple elegance: just the name, black on white, in copper-plate. *Sir Humphry Davy* was in a jar on the top row at the left. At the bottom on the right, the label said *Jean Piaget*. Each clear bottle was full of round white pills, like ordinary aspirin.

'*Now* do you understand?'

No matter how small the relic, the grace of the whole body remained intact. Each pill needed only the tiniest fraction of bone-dust to be sold on in the best of faith. 'Oh yes,' Moholy said. 'We're pretty busy with the pestle and mortar.'

He closed and locked the cabinet. 'Switzerland's only the start. If the business continues to grow, we can look to expand into Père Lachaise, Kensal Green, Glasnevin. The world of the dead is, frankly, our oyster.'

I excavated my ear with my little finger, and found the

results unappealing. 'You don't think it's wrong to dig up dead people?'

'Don't be absurd. Hardly anyone believes it makes any difference. We're providing a service, saving a few of the more culturally significant bones while we actually can.'

'From what?'

'The future. Time itself. And next on the list it's Calvin. Can I count on your help?'

It was like being invited to Vienna by Freud. I was scared of going, and anxious about seeming ignorant, but I wasn't prepared to fall behind in what might possibly become one of the great modern movements of the brand-new century. Still, I had to be persuaded.

'You're a nobody,' Moholy said. 'Is that what you want? For the rest of your life?'

I still didn't answer.

'Don't forget I own your apartment. I could change the locks. Then where would you go?'

'To the cemetery,' I said. 'I'll go to the cemetery. I'll get you John Calvin.'

'As soon as you can, please. As soon as it stops raining. And James?'

'Yes?'

'Take Jung with you. He's giving me a headache.'

He spun the flat knee-cap across the table, and I caught it in my flapping hands. 'Thanks.'

'Don't mention it. You look like you could use him.'

I left the van at the gallery and walked home with Jung between my palms, touching him to my chest and sometimes to my forehead, like an Eastern beggar pleading for alms. What had I done now?

On Plainpalais, scarecrows had been planted in rows across the urban expanse of gravel. Farmers with big red hands leant on staffs and ate sandwiches and watched the office girls go by. It was therefore only natural that the Swiss interior ministry had called up coachloads of police in full military anti-riot gear, including protective plastic shields and helmets and shin-guards. The large black aerosol took a drink from a flask.

The police coaches blocked my road home, so I made a detour via the Pont du Mont Blanc. The drizzle here was snow in the mountains, which soon melted, making the green Rhone run icy and fast beneath the low city bridge. I stood at the rail, looking downstream at the poplar trees of the Île Rousseau, and made a layman's analysis of Moholy. His parents had fled to Geneva from Budapest in '56. According to Rifka, Moholy could provide a convincing eye-witness account of an only child living in a one-room flat with his mother, owning nothing, having nothing.

'Now he has everything,' Rifka had said, 'money and culture, yet the world still diminishes. It shrinks to a tiny disc of fulfilled desire. Perfect, but very small.'

'But perfect.'

'But small.'

'I don't feel sorry for him.'

'No,' Rifka said, 'not many people do. It takes a particular openness of mind. He's very lonely. His attention wanders, usually between suicide and religion.'

Moholy was lucky and not happy. He had everything most people wanted, and yet still he wasn't happy. He'd come from Hungary with nothing, and he knew it was wrong to be lucky and unhappy, and knowing it to be wrong felt like the beginning of spiritual awareness. There was something else, always something more, and that's what he was trying to find.

Back at the flat, as soon as I opened the door, I knew that she'd gone. Her case, everything. She'd left a message on the table, and it basically said she'd gone. It also said she didn't understand me, and that even though she still believed I was essentially a decent person, I was acting out of character.

At first, I took it quite positively. According to Jung, sexual freedom could have great therapeutic value, in direct proportion to the attractiveness of his female patients, his fragile and willing *Jungfrauen*. Now was perhaps an appropriate moment for me to accept the impossibility of monogamy as a route to self-realisation, and recall that every Sunday Jung invited his longest-standing mistress, Toni Wolff, to a dinner cooked by his wife. That was more like it. That was the way to do it.

And anyway, honestly, Helena was totally impossible. She had such high expectations, such unrealistic standards. I was already at theology college when we met. She should have realised the weirdness she was getting involved with. It wasn't my fault. Or rather, what I meant, there was an unbridgeable psychological disparity between women and men

I stood for a while, head empty. I ran a bath, but forgot to put the plug in. I listened to an electric fly on the window, off more often than on. I fell apart. And all my previous falling apart suddenly looked like a strategic retreat. This was the wheels coming off, and not just the wheels. I was coming apart in bits, bit then bit then bit. I was having a breakdown, a real, certifiable, Burghölzli-strength, italicised *gefühls-betonter Vorstellungskomplex*.

I crawled into the bed which Helena had left only that

morning, and I curled up in my oversized suit beneath the duvet, my head completely covered, Jung between my palms between my knees. I regressed. I went looking for Mum. I fled a cruel world which denied me understanding. And I was by no means the most difficult of her children to understand.

By 1908, a year ago already, not yet reconciled to his father's death, Jung called a halt. He stopped, and went to live in his boathouse on the shores of Lake Zurich, where inside himself he could find no more urgent ambition than the building of miniature villages from pebbles.

So that was alright then. Insomnia, stomach trouble and a continuous sense of being possessed by spirits reduced him to a state of withdrawal. His search for *Selbst* was tearing him apart, and he dreamed deep caves full of broken bones and mummified crusaders; dead, yet somehow not quite dead.

And very soon, because I wasn't experienced in severe emotional distress, nor heavy drinking nor late nights in cemeteries, I fell asleep. As an adolescent, whenever I felt confused and depressed, and a little mad with the teenage, this was how I'd attempt to solve my problems. There was something honest about adolescence, probably its confusion. Any other response seemed a sham.

I dreamed a journey. I didn't have much choice. Moholy had threatened to throw me out, so I phoned for an air-ticket, grabbed my toothbrush and a spare cardigan, and made my excuses to the church committee. It was an unplanned journey, and, even though nobody knew I was coming, there was a pulpit on the shuttle-bus, and I thought: life's a bit like that.

At the airport, I tapped Jung's knee-cap between my fingers and my wrist, making the mystical sound of a half-castanet clacking. I blithely approached the metal detector, handed over my keys and coins and Swiss-army penknife, and walked calmly on, bones hidden all through my body, while the X-ray machine showed up my superficial toothpaste. *How Much Is That Dog?*

I flew easyJet to the Land of the Dead, and the hostess smiled down at me, checking my seat-belt and back-rest.

– This is all connected with your dad, isn't it?

– I don't think it is.

– Digging up bones. Resurrecting the Dead. Surely.

And I accepted her pillow of additional comfort, which fell unreachably to the floor. Half asleep, turning in my economy seat, head at changing angles against the plastic window, I shuffled images of stones and gods and bones and earth.

Was it really a goldmine?

It was a journey.

Over the Channel, the view was eternal sunshine on a sea of cloud. This would explain why so many ex-airline pilots joined the clergy. It was like being blinded by angels, by the personality of God. The clouds evaporated at the coast, and between England's edge and London I counted the swimming-pools, always a welcome surprise. I looked out for them far below, chemical blue between lucky gardens and golf-courses.

– You're not a lucky man, are you, James?'

The smiling hostess was back, carrying a tray interleaved with individual packets of cashews. I liked cashew nuts.

– It changed when I started trying to be good.

– You were a bastard to your dad, you know.

– He was a bastard to Mum.

– I wonder. I wonder if he was.

– I tried to make it up to him, at the end. I wanted to do the right thing.

– I know. I know all about that.

Something had gone desperately wrong with the ticketing. I arrived at Heathrow, which wasn't my destination. I had no visa for England, no passport, and the scandal was: they let me in.

I walked straight in, looking dreadful from lack of sleep, obvious in my clerical collar, carrying two bin-bags of assorted bones. I knew the secret. They let me in because I was a recognisable English type: over-educated, disorientated, ineffectual. I had the patterned background of my many years at choir-school, and a character battered by an education ideal for a career on another planet. Such as nineteenth-century India.

They waved me in. They said: Come on in, James, we know your weak-kneed choir-school sort, and have nothing to fear from the likes of you. Welcome.

Customs waved me through, and that wasn't what I wanted.

But then it was the journey itself which mattered. The plane on its own was far too easy, so I took a cross-Channel passenger ferry from Heathrow Terminal 2, and on the observation deck, as the ferry pulled away, the plane and the boat seemed like an over-insistence on the old-fashioned notion that England was separate from everywhere else. And further away than you'd think. I stood with the rail in my stomach, gazing at the air traffic control tower, the wheeling gulls, and God on the sea in rays.

The sea-air smelled of chip-fat, and tonight's on-board band, Twice as Nice, looped through speakers from deck to deck. *Life is an Ocean*, they sang.

Well maybe it was, I thought, and maybe it wasn't.

And You Are a Boat.

Secretly, I knew everything.

It looked pretty rough out there. I went inside, and the guts of these boats were floating malls. It cheered me to see so many youngsters not falling for it. They weren't buying a thing, not cinema tickets or self-service burger meals, not magazines, or soft toys, not even premium lemonade with a single figure percentage of real organic lemons. There was a change going on, an awakening, a kind of reformation. They were putting up a fight to be themselves on the journey of life, and they even ignored the bells and whistles of the arcade games, except Manx Racer, because that was a lot of fun.

I claimed my complimentary P & O blanket, and kept walking until I found a seat by the window. If I was lucky, I'd get some sleep, but with the ship's engines rumbling through my stomach I often woke up in rambling thoughts of Rifka.

You're sitting on a goldmine.

Fee-fi-fo-fum, I smell the blood of an Englishman,
Something something something dead,
I'll grind his bones to make my bread.

Through scratched perspex the brown sea wallowed nauseous to horrible under a sullen morning sky. I could make out dirty white cliffs. I stretched, folded my blanket, then took a blustery walk on deck, where the wind had the tang of sea-salt and seaweed and horsedung. Twice as Nice were still in the speakers.

You Are, uh, Like a Hurricane.

Well maybe I am, I thought, maybe I am. *You Go, uh, Around and Around.*

At the relevant announcement, I rejoined my vehicle, and after nudging it down the ramp and following All Directions, I parked it in the staff car-park of Westminster Abbey, with my clerical collar clearly visible on the dash. By the time the on-duty deacons made up their minds (*Does he have the right? Should we clamp him? Yes. No. Yes and no.*) I could easily have taken a helicopter to wherever it was I was going. Or maybe I couldn't.

I could take a limousine, though that was absurd, because helicopters and limousines were reserved for the special and distinguished. Dream what you know: I started to run. The wings of my suit jacket flapped out behind me, my coloured socks flashing at each upward stride. Out of breath, fading, where was it I was straining so very hard to go?

To heaven. Obviously. Always to heaven.

Joseph Moholy or Mason Senior was blocking the way, the two-in-one of them sitting behind a table wearing a tight overcoat at least a size too small, the sleeves stopping well short of bony, hairy wrists. I couldn't resist asking, 'Why is your coat so small?'

'It's not our coat.'

From across the table, Dad bumped his shoulders and shot his cuffs, the sleeves barely reaching midway from his elbow.

'It's an experiment, but it isn't working yet. It's a celebrity coat, but at the moment I just feel stupid.'

'I think it might be working. I'm sorry, Dad, but I gotta go.'

'Give me a hug, then.' He held out his fleshless fingers, his all-bone wrists. 'Give me a final final kiss.'

'No.'

My step-through Honda was on its stand, engine already puttering. I made a long, cold, cross-country journey in tight-lipped, ear-plugged silence. While I should have been watching the indicators of container lorries, I cursed Dad and Moholy for their parting words, following me along the hedge-enclosed ribbons of B-roads.

'Be yourself!'

Such useless advice that I had to laugh as I stood there on the verge of the road, the wind coming up behind me, parting the hair at the back of my head, the cold wind on the white line of my scalp. I had my thumb out, waiting for the next kind person to offer me a lift.

I lay awake for some time, warm and safe in the darkness beneath the duvet. Why, I was wondering, on life's grand journey, was I the one redirected through Geneva? I had godless contemporaries in their thirties living freely and making fortunes in London, with no care for tomorrow. And here I was, penniless and celibate in the non-place of Switzerland, with a disturbing sense of fate.

On the verge, the road stretching far in both directions, nothing on either horizon.

As a sermon, it was rubbish: life wasn't like that. Hitching wasn't anything even close. Get back on your bike. Or better, buy a car. Decide where you want to go, and go there.

I flipped myself out of bed, and went to re-read Helena's note. She needed space, and time to think. She'd gone to a hotel, and left the number. I could call her tomorrow, she said, but only if I was ready to pull myself together. I was tempted to call straight away. First, though, I had to pull myself together.

I let the suit drop off me, leaving it crumpled on the floor. Then I stood in the bathtub, and showered myself clean in water so hot I had to keep moving and scrubbing. Recently, I'd scarcely been in one piece. If it went on like this I was going to break apart, and I couldn't accept that this dis-integration was what it meant to be ageing and alive, until I reached a hundred. My weakness and inconsistency was a cause for shame, my life an embarrassing series of postures.

'I am. I am a weak and selfish man.'

No more breakdowns: I had to take a chance on being myself. I had to stand on my own two feet. Otherwise I could see it stretching out indefinitely, not knowing what I thought, or who I loved, or what was worth protecting. The time had come to stop skimming along the surface of things. I was what I was, and that was all, and all there was.

I turned off the shower, and stepped out of the tub. I didn't bother to dry myself, or dress. I went into the kitchen and poured a glass of sherry, but I didn't drink it, because that wasn't the kind of person I was. I took it into the bathroom, left it on the shelf at the back of the sink. I fetched a white candle left over from the Basilica, and my father's unsafe safety-razor. Then I sat for a quiet moment with Jung's knee, cross-legged on the damp floor of the flickering and candle-lit bathroom.

The psychiatric ethic, its objective as popularised by Jung and others, had never sounded overly demanding. Admit to yourself what you're like and what you want. Go on, sit at Papa Jung's knee and admit it.

   – I'm like you, Carl. I'm just like you are. You were.

   – And vot are you vonting?

   – The same as you wanted.

The Old Wise Man of eighty-five, Grand Master of Freemasons, Fellow of the Royal Society, with his own boathouse and choice of mistresses and nineteen galloping grandchildren.

No, that was no good. Jung wasn't interceding, he was *interfering*. Inside my head, there was always someone waiting, a kind of conspiracy in which a collusion of Masonic Knights Templar had planted a psychic trail of mandala, bones, something phenomenal. I was prepared to lose all this relativity and race memory in favour of an existential self. That would be fine. That's what I want, and not all that other stuff. I just want to be me.

I went to the kitchen for a roll of clingfilm, and, threatening Jung's knee with that hard plastic baton, I gave him one last chance. Despite all the guff and madness, Jung had still been capable of the purest insights. Analysing displaced persons from the Western Front, he noted that the closer people were to the really big issues the calmer they became. He also watched and waited for the deranged to cheat at Patience, a reliable sign of recovery. And despite the collective unconscious, despite the land of the dead, he encouraged the one whole man.

I saw, in the final analysis, that I'd been in fragments, in bits. I was fighting many concurrent battles, and parts of myself were scattered over a broad field, each one wrestling with a different impulse or instinct, a different idea of who I was. It sometimes led me to act in ways that were fundamentally out of character, like Carl Gustav Jung, with his cyclothymic personality in manic–depressive psychosis.

Only it was simpler than that. I was acting like an arsehole because Dad was dead and Helena needed a decision. That's right, I was in denial. And most probably alienated from my inner self.

I scratched at the silver roll of clingfilm, eventually snagging the edge. I unrolled yards of it and bandaged Jung's knee over and over, in layer after plastic layer, so many times that the ball with Jung at its centre began to look like ice. Which I put in a plastic box.

Back in the bathroom, by the light of the candle, I unscrewed the razor and took out the blade. I dipped the blade in the sherry, and while I held it there, I at last looked in the mirror. I hadn't changed, and my face was asking the same old questions. What do you think you're doing? Who do you think you are? How many years do you think you have?

No more sweeping aside and starting from scratch. I could not change between one personality and another at will, and I had to tackle this vacillation head on. Put simply, I'd had enough of not being me, and was about to opt out of the crush of the collective unconscious. As I took the razor-blade from the sherry and shook it dry, Jung's influence was already fading. Across my history, in his bold Gothic hand: *Erlassen.* Discharged.

I was going to perform an individual act, on my own body, without mythical dimensions. It was all my own idea, mine, the brainchild of Jay James Mason Minor, who wasn't suggestible to variant personalities and pieces of old bone. He had his own life and his own memories, and his own deep desires. He had his own body, and couldn't be conquered so easily.

I didn't think.

Jay Mason Minor's Thigh

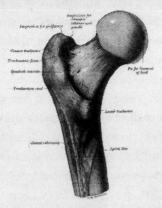

'I have said that the soul is not more than the body,
And I have said that the body is not more than the soul,
And nothing, not God, is greater to one than one's self is.'

Walt Whitman, *Song of Myself*

Ow. Ow ow. Ow.

It hurt. It hurt a lot. I hadn't been expecting it to hurt so much.

By the next morning, with the help of only three white butterfly stitches, the wound had stopped bleeding. I squinted at the brown blood on my pillow, the duvet up to my chin as I listened to the building's early-morning noises, including salsa, doorbells, and somewhere below a stop–start screaming-fit. It hurt, and I probably deserved that. But I was also very pleased with myself.

James Mason Minor, Jay. There *is* something different about you. Even if you're not sure exactly what it is.

I swung myself out of bed, wincing a little as I went to make tea. I reached for my ear, and then thought better of it, and went instead to check in the mirror. It didn't look too bad, almost unnoticeable, and the rest of my face was still mine, the same face that reflected every single day, the one which was always there and therefore the least interesting of faces, hardly worth describing.

I thank thee Lord that I am not as other men are.

I thought back to the last time I'd felt genuinely myself. Childhood didn't really count, but after that there must have been anchors, true memories always with me of an unchangeable person fixed and knowable as Jay Mason Minor.

I remembered thinking, all by myself, that I'd never die. But everyone thinks that.

Before Mum left, I'd wanted to be everyone. After, I didn't want to think about it. I escaped to University, and making the right noises I took advantage of the new modular system to study for a degree in Plantagenet Britain with History of Science with Genealogy with Film Studies and Analytical Psychology. I specialised in a little learning as a dangerous thing, and drifted like Moses blissful and ignorant in his basket, occasionally bumping the banks of the river. Mum had always predicted something grander, Moses with outstretched arms high and peerless on the mountain. She wrote to me often. From her tanned exile in Spain, gradually moving south, she urged me to aim for something more than my father, in all the obvious categories: women, action, money. Conflict, obstacle, resolution.

I tried my best for her, but I had girlfriends who wouldn't co-operate. They were merciless opponents, like Norse gods, finding no good in any of my actions. It was as if they were always waiting for me to do something wrong, which they then put aside for later, not in a closet but a scabbard.

When they left me, I was heartbroken. And when my timing was out, and I was the one who did the leaving, then I was also heartbroken.

Until then, I'd never been afraid of growing older, assuming there lay in store for me some particular greatness. But at twenty-five, running out of girlfriends and modules, I went back home. For half of every week I helped in the diocese, saving redundant churches. We climbed ladders, and painted and plastered and grouted, but without much success. The churches turned out to be redundant.

Mum wrote furious letters, asking me what the hell I thought I was playing at. I wrote back to say that, deserted by the gods, I was mostly playing at Patience, which wasn't a great game to play, deserted by the gods. She said come over, I said I was busy, and on sunny days just had to stay inside and watch the TV news. I was discovering something insubstantial in just being me, and, without the bracing example of others, I sank back into the swamp, or at least stayed in bed, with no idea of what I was actually for. All the bones dissolved from my body. I collapsed, in the tradition of centuries of over-thoughtful Anglicans, into human blancmange. I had no core. No pips. I had no nuts, no cojones. No backbone. I read many novels with indomitable heroes, and then went back to bed.

Was that me? Was that all I was? One day, while Dad was out in the parish helping the helpless, I opened a bottle of Christmas sherry, drank too much of it, and ended up in his wardrobe. I took out one of his vicar outfits, his costumes, and held the hanger appraisingly under my chin. I shifted my weight from one leg to the other, listening with compassion to direct experience of suffering, jumping my eyebrows at the offer, yes *rather*, of just the one more delicate triangle of egg-and-cress sandwich.

– Mmmm, quite delicious, thank you so much.

It was a simple black cassock, in polyester. I pulled it over my head, and found a mirror. It fitted me better than I'd have guessed, but my teeth were too good to be convincing. A few years of obligatory cake-bakes would soon see them off, and I'd looked a lot worse, especially at solstice. As I preened myself in Dad's mirror, I made drunken self-pity into a kind of compassion. I needed to look after number one, and, along with the uniform, church perks included rent-free accommodation and a licence to preach. Not forgetting the bonus superpower, granted directly by the Almighty, of absolving my fellow pagans and ex-girlfriends from sin.

It felt like a vocation: I had no idea what I wanted, in itself a strong qualification for the Anglican Church. We were both in decline, obvious to everyone, and joining the losing side was a true English instinct. We were a perfect match.

Dad was appalled. 'Don't do this to me.'

'I thought you'd be glad.'

'Don't you understand *anything*?'

Resigned, philosophical, practising my vocation, I said: 'I am the sheep of the family.'

Dad had expected more intelligence, especially after my exhaustive education. Instead, his own son was about to repeat the family mistake, doing what his dad did, somehow failing to see that a career in the Church was a life lost, like a death in battle: admirable, maybe, but also slightly dim, outdated, and a calamity which happened only to other people.

'Your mother isn't going to like this one little bit.'

'I'm not getting any younger,' I said. 'I need a career. And I know how this one works.'

'You don't even believe in God.'

I shrugged. 'I might change for the better.'

My brother Tom thought me inspired. I could pick my spot. In all its history, the Church intake had never been of such hopelessly low quality. Now was therefore a better time than ever to climb straight to the top, pushing the good and timid aside on the ascent to an enviable bishop's palace, and a forgiving red bench in the House of Lords. With a cute strategy and a little luck, I could dodge the provincial day-centres and the disabled children, starting as pastor to an exquisite private school, then chaplain to the England cricket team, travelling in all humility during the English winter to the balconies of the MCG.

'Don't be absurd,' Mum said, in a special and very rare telephone call. 'You just can't. I'd never speak to you again.'

'She's right, you know,' Dad added. 'It's absurd. You can't ape a life in Christ. And you can't just walk in. That's not how it works.'

I had a fairly good idea of how it worked. I padded my letter of application with weakness: I was indecisive and didn't know what I wanted, not even convinced by my own sense of vocation. It was exactly what they wanted to hear. I suggested I might incorrectly have heard the call, compensating for my mother's sudden absence. In any case, even if I'd misheard, theology college would give me an opportunity to reflect, among like-minded seekers, on just who I was, and who I wanted to be.

At interview, they asked me what I was really looking for. I was twenty-seven years old, and finally proving that I was my own man by opposing everyone's wishes.

I said: the same as everyone's really looking for.

'Which is what?'

'I don't really know.'

I was offered a place for one year, in the first instance, at a theology college in a Victorian mansion which had once been the County Lunatic Asylum. It was isolated, at the top of a hill, and as a compulsory part of the curriculum it had impressive views of the weather, breaking and changing over the three-way channels of a motorway. The windows were many but small, hardly wide enough to squeeze through on a black February day. It was also an amazing place for magpies, and, in magpies, sorrow statistically outdid joy by about two to one.

On the day I arrived, the first thing I saw was a single magpie, strutting across the lawn towards me. I saluted. I spat. And briefly made good the difference.

There was no immediate evidence of a shortage in recruits to the English Church. On the paths between wings of the building, under clouds which often looked like rain, there was a bustle and hum about the shared thrill of operating at the limits of socially acceptable behaviour. The college attracted the stubborn, and the lonely, the clinically nostalgic, and rebels seduced by the challenging discovery that wanting to be good felt rebellious. Everyone was ex-something, ex-airline pilots and ex-fast-food operatives, ex-husbands and wives. I was an ex-pagan, an ex-long-term student, and an ex-church-renovator, and I felt at home among all these ex men and women, SAS officers and divorced Montessori teachers who in pursuit of a primitive self had recently slept every night for a month in a coffin. In the middle of a copsey roundabout. Somewhere off the M6.

What united us wasn't conformity, or even faith. It was courage.

Of course, at any of the nation's fourteen Anglican theology colleges, at any given time, in among all the Jesus-freaks and heavenly rebels, there were also trainee ordinands full of sanity, joy and hard-won tranquillity.

I was never attracted to any of these people.

The work was tougher than I'd expected, and despite the exemplary heroics of the Bible, more than a quarter of the year dropped out. I buckled down, potted my apologetics, swallowed my doctrine, and at the end of the first year, as a reward for good behaviour, they allowed me back for another.

At the beginning of the second year, at last learning to be honest with myself, I had to admit that something strange was happening which I found unnerving. Whenever I set out in search of God, however reluctantly, I always found him, because God was always there. He was like everything displayed in an art gallery is always art, even *Break Glass in Case of Fire*, because that's the way we prepare ourselves to look at it.

He was everywhere. In the daily weather, in my own miraculous existence, in the shapely legs and round buttocks of Helena Byczynski, a twenty-five-year-old new arrival in what was now the year below me.

Whenever I caught sight of her (or the weather, or the miracle of my own existence), all my pretensions and silly little hopes drained away. I was suddenly prepared to renounce everything, my ambition and my distinctness, all that foolishness.

It was a spiritual awakening.

It was a warning I was losing my grip, loneliness an unfair opportunity for God. It had to be resisted along with grief, fatigue, failure and surprise moments of natural beauty, like windless winter mornings, or sudden storms in summer after dark. The secret was to keep a clear head. Identify which of these impostors was leading me astray. Then take appropriate action, so as not to lose my grip, and not to spiritually awaken.

I took up cricket. In the spring, in the absence of other volunteers, Helena Byczynski was elected captain of the college cricket club. Women were encouraged to join, and, abandoning the Anglican tradition of a slow afternoon at mid-on, Helena promised everyone a bat and a bowl. The college suffered some horrendous defeats, and I loved every minute of it. I did sometimes worry that I was turning into Dad, but in fact I was playing because I liked it, and I discovered that God was in the game of cricket, too.

Helena hated my earrings. She told me I was trying to be something I wasn't. I took them out, first one a week, then more quickly than that. On her cheekbones she wore gold-flecked moisturiser, and sometimes, in shorts or a skirt, she taunted me with flashes of the backs of her knees. The more time we spent together, the nastier we became, each of us wanting the other to know that our relationship went beyond the purely professional. It wasn't pity, or duty, or Christian fellow-feeling. It wasn't out of niceness that we loitered after classes, hoping from detailed inspection of the time-table that the other might chance to happen by.

In the refectory, she'd hold my eye while crushing the spine and skull of a wasp beneath the rim of her side-plate. I'd question her choice of make-up, or judgement on the Book of Daniel, as our conversations adopted a homely shape, usually disagreements in which Helena turned out to be right. She reminded me of Alice, my first real girlfriend, and in her school days Helena had also stood as a sidesperson. She'd never entirely lost the taste for its strangeness, and after a few post-University years working abroad, and then for a care charity, she'd wanted to be less conformist. These days, and even more so than when we were teenagers, Church was definitely not the done thing to do.

The first time we slept together, I asked her if she'd ever prayed about sex.

'Never needed to,' she said, rolling away from me, falling into sleep.

I lay there with my unringed ear crushed on my arm, enthralled by the back of her head. I already believed there was nothing we wouldn't do together, nowhere we wouldn't go. Helena was everything I'd been waiting for, though not very patiently, and at last, falling in love, I was stunned by its selfishness. It made me feel alive, and glad of what I was, because it had led to this. It was self-discovery, and it was exhilarating: I'd never felt more like myself. I felt frightened, I felt blessed.

At that time, through one summer and into the next, I could almost believe, almost, that I was Jay Mason, neither more nor less, a unique thought in the providential mind of God.

Alone in Geneva, far from home and prying eyes, I could basically be anyone I liked, at any hour of the day. But I didn't want to be alone and anyone, and I needed to be taken by the hand. I pulled a chair to the phone, and called Helena at the hotel. I was a suggestible person, an impressionable one, but there was nothing wrong with being influenced. As long as I picked the right people. While waiting for Reception to put me through, I kept reaching up to my ear, reminding myself who I was. Each time I touched it, it stung like crazy.

Helena needed persuading that we ought to meet. She kept asking if it was worth it, and whether I'd disposed of the bones. Have you decided to be normal? I told her I'd decided to be myself.

'Promise me you won't dig up any more bones. This is the most basic of things, Jay. You have to promise.'

'I promise.'

'Cross your heart.'

'It's crossed.'

After that, I sensed I was winning. She was still shocked by the bones, but did concede that it wasn't as if I'd hurt or killed anybody. She agreed, eventually, to see me, though she didn't want to rush it. She suggested we try and do something normal, like normal people do.

'Fine,' I said. 'Or at least, whatever's normal for people like us.'

'Jay. Stop it now.'

I didn't want to be difficult, but I had to be sure I was the kind of person who'd make a normal kind of apology by inviting her out to lunch. Was that really me? Or was it just what people did in films? Is that what made it normal? The Beau Rivage. On the terrace. She'd be impressed by the quality of tablecloth, and the panoramic view of the lake. But it didn't feel like me. McDonald's, then, but I hated McDonald's. What *did* I like?

I was the kind of person who'd invite her out to lunch, but still be aware of the cost. At the same time, I'd want it to be somewhere original. I therefore asked her out to lunch at the Hôtel du Paix, a hotel-training school near the Palace of Nations. For twelve o'clock, as soon as it opened, because it was never too early to make amends.

*

As myself, I felt clumsy and vulnerable. Especially as I was the day's very first customer in the training restaurant of the Hôtel du Paix. It had taken me most of the morning to get ready, mixing and matching clothes from the closet, never entirely convinced I'd found my own true look. Between each combination, I stood at the window checking the rain, because in weather like this, not even Moholy could expect me to fetch John Calvin. It was like a sign, a minor concession from the heavens.

Eventually, instead of a sweater, I decided on two shirts, one on top of the other. I could button them without risking contact with my ear. Apart from that, I didn't want my appearance to matter. My clothes said nothing about me. As for the problem of my recent wound, which actually didn't look too bad, I solved that with the Chaplain's Burberry scarf. The ear ached, but the cut from the razor-blade had dried beneath the stitches in a clean black line. I wound the scarf twice round my neck, as if I had a sore throat, and it was broad enough and therefore high enough to cover the day-old damage.

In the empty restaurant, one of my legs was twitching the underside of the table. I changed tables. My back was now in the angle of the corner furthest from the door, but it didn't seem to help. The scarf made me self-conscious. A plain one would have been better, in a dark or neutral colour, and I worried that Helena had changed her mind. She'd correctly sensed that I was not my own man. Even my leg had a life of its own.

I watched the trainee waiters as they stretched and dipped to lay the tables. They wore black waistcoats and starched white aprons as far as their feet, their deft movements reflected in the polished mirrors of the spacious room, all wood counters and brass rails and old-world excellence, except for the napkins and tablecloths, which were paper, ready for trainee mistakes. Lunch at the Hôtel du Paix was offered at a discount, because everything from the kitchen to the final table-side flambé was always an experiment, and therefore usually wonderful.

Helena was there in the doorway. Needlessly, I raised my hand, but a waiter was already beside her, bringing his heels together and elegantly taking her coat, her green outdoors puffa. He handed it to a colleague, and then escorted her to the table. He pulled out a chair, but an older man in a dark suit appeared behind him, whispering in his ear.

'Not yet,' he was saying. 'You must always give a lady and her host the opportunity to embrace.'

It was a continental thing. Helena waited, the chair was offered again, and she sat. She was so self-possessed. It was one of the things I loved about her. I saw now that she was dressed for travelling, for flying, in an old polo-shirt loose outside her jeans.

'I tried to leave yesterday,' she said, resetting the cutlery, 'but I couldn't get a ticket.'

'Fate,' I said.

'Overbooking. Everyone's getting out before the weekend protest.'

She shook out her hair, then crumpled it with her fingers, and I instantly regretted all the time we'd ever spent apart. I'd been so lonely without her, so lost.

'What happened to your ear?'

'Nothing.'

Damn. The scarf must have slipped down. This wasn't how I'd planned it. I unwound the scarf and bunched it in my fists, in my lap. A waiter came, and after a brief struggle, took it away. Helena leant forward over the table, looking right past my face at my ear, giving all her attention to my injury.

'I'm sorry about yesterday,' I said. 'I'm sorry about the bones. Everything's wrong. I love you.'

I reached into the top pocket of my outer shirt for Moholy's golden locket, which I placed with some solemnity flat on the paper tablecloth, keeping it covered with my palm. I pushed it into the centre of the table, slewing aside an ashtray and a small vase, which wobbled, alerting a waiter. Helena put it to one side. The waiter removed it.

The twitch in my thigh was in full fast-forward as I ceremoniously raised my hand. The locket's gold chain lay coiled to one side, like a model anchor-chain, on deck.

'Don't *give* me things,' Helena said. 'Just tell me.'

'Some things I find difficult to say.'

Obviously, or it would never have come to this, not if I could say it straight. 'It's for you. It opens. There's a catch on the top.'

Helena put the tip of her index finger on the coiled chain, and dragged the locket towards her across the table-top. She picked it up and held it in one hand, like a cigarette lighter, with her thumb on the catch. She needed both thumbs. She sprang it open. Stared inside, her eyes wide and unblinking. Then closed it again, and blinked. She glanced over her shoulder, but the restaurant was empty. Then over the other shoulder. She lowered her head, the closed locket in both clutched hands.

'What,' she whispered, looking up, 'is that?'

'I love you.'

The language of love was surprisingly uniform, with most people loyal to the well-worn formulas. This could make love seem banal, almost collective. My own gesture had

185

more character than that. It was evidence of my unique devotion. I was offering Helena a real bit of the real me, and there were no substitutes, no stand-ins. And it was all my own idea.

'They have no known practical function,' I said. 'It's like a piercing.'

'Is it?'

'Well, no, actually. It hurts a bit more than that.'

I flinched my fingers up towards my ear, as if about to make the sign of the sound of money, or magic the appearance of a silver dollar, which in fact, on this particular occasion, didn't magically appear.

'Don't leave,' I said. 'I need you. I love you.'

There were tears in her eyes, and she was suddenly up and moving, hauling her chair round next to mine, causing several student waiters to leap attentively, arrive too late, fluster, then melt away. She grabbed both my hands, and crushed them in hers, lifting them up close in front of her lips.

'Now,' she said, definitely tearful, squeezing my fists as hard as she physically could, '*now* I'm worried about you, you dolt. What the hell were you thinking?'

'It's symbolic.'

'You've cut off your earlobe. Your own earlobe, Jay. You've cut it off and given it to me. This is not good. Completely not a good way to do things.'

Strangely, in the rush of emotional blood to my head, the blood pulsed and throbbed with particular insistence through the absence of my earlobe, as if the blood there was circulating through air in an invisible loop, making brief contact with the outside world, then coming back again, returning with a slight chill to my heart. What had I done?

I suddenly wanted to cry. 'I love you.'

'And I love you back, you great lummox. Always have. Why else would I be here? It's not for fun. Not for the scenic tour of Switzerland's quaintest cemeteries. I cannot conceive of life without you. If you're deciding otherwise, it's a wrong decision, and I'm not accepting it. In fact, you're always making wrong decisions, but at least you're decisive. You really do try, don't you, Jay? You genuinely want to know what it's all about. That's not as common as you might think.'

'I'm a deacon. You're not even a believer.'

'That doesn't mean I stopped loving you. In fact I loved you more. You weren't satisfied with boy meets girl. You had the courage to attempt a different story, man and God, fruit and forbidden trees, all our woe.'

'What a dummy.'

'Well, you got it wrong. But at least you're brave. Looking for salvation in accountancy is also wrong, but it isn't even brave.'

By now we had our hands joined more comfortably, resting on the table, and I'd managed to recover some composure. 'What else?'

'What else what?'

'What else do you like about me?'

'Well, since you're asking, you can be genuinely altruistic, you really empathise. When you want to.'

Was I? Did I? I failed to contain a smile. We were having a minor disagreement in which Helena turned out to be right, just like the old days. She was also being so very nice to me, and not as a remnant of her interrupted professional training. Recognisably, she was saving me. And that had always been the pattern, whenever I'd allowed myself to be saved.

She sat back, and with both thumbs sprang open the locket for another look.

'My first earlobe,' she said. 'My first lobe. I've never been given a lobe before.'

'They're completely senseless,' I said, fingering the one which was still there. 'Serve no purpose whatsoever.'

'Well, thanks a bunch. Next time give me something you actually need. Like a finger, maybe, or a whole hand.'

'Except for earrings,' I said. 'Earlobes are good for that, and you never liked my earrings.'

'I know. I saved you then as well.'

'You did. God I've been lucky.'

'So are we going to give it a go?'

'Yes. I think we should.'

'You're sure?'

'No posing, no posturing. I'm sure.'

'I'm still pregnant, you know. It's not a future which is going away.'

'I know. I know that. It's just there were so many different ways I could see it going. I was worried I wasn't up to it. I overreacted.'

'I think you probably did. And your dad and all that. Can't have helped.'

'No. I'm sorry.'

I'd lost sight of what I wanted, and what I wanted defined who I was. I wanted a happy ending, I realised that now. This was the real me. This was my chance at a happy ending.

'But the bones, Jay. That was off the wall. Did you manage to get rid of the bones?'

At the Hôtel du Paix, the waiters were so perfectly trained in discretion that they'd delayed bringing us a menu. I raised my hand, and someone was with us before I could even think of clicking my fingers. Although I never clicked my fingers, and that wasn't what I was thinking.

In Lent of her second year, Helena packed it in. There was so much to learn: the apologetics, the ascetic theology, the biblical studies, the Church history. It was both too much and not enough. However deeply we explored the doctrine, the liturgy, the moral theology and the Old and New Testaments, it was never entirely convincing, so why not skip the reading and leap straight to the faith and feeling?

We feel it to be true. We just do.

The Anglican God was such an implausible mix of infinite power and diffidence. And at that time the Church itself was like the opposite of miracles. Every month brought some new and unimaginable calamity, making organised religion seem inadequate, and stupid. The Commissioners were incompetent, the clergy adulterous, the liturgy infinitely flexible. The once virile Anglican tradition, which Mason Senior would have recognised, was gradually being enfeebled, the priesthood reduced to a roadshow of religious disc-jockeys, sunny intermediaries between the laity and the heavenly music. This one's for all you kids out there. Whoo whoo.

Helena wanted reform. Change was necessary, but not in the slow gradations commended by the Synod. She wanted a second reformation, a revolution. In the meantime, she dropped out of college and went to the aid of refugees in Calais. It wasn't that she disbelieved in prayer, but she preferred to plan, and to help. It seemed fairer. She dared me to follow, but I dodged the great rolling ball of her love, rolling on, hideously impressive. I told myself that by staying I was standing alone and strong, and that other things before now must have gone very wrong to make me ready for God. I couldn't now afford for this to go wrong too.

Come the summer, I signed a declaration that I wasn't in debt, and presented myself for ordination as a deacon. Of the family, only Tom attended the ceremony. 'Congratulations,' he said. 'Nice one, mate.'

Helena was also there, supporting me, loving me, and the certainty and scope of her love made my own feelings seem small and skittish. To be worthy of her, I had to amount to more than a straight biography of the narrow life I'd lived. This dim perception, that I could be more than myself, was the starting point for any belief I possessed, in God, in love, in Helena. There was something more. There had to be.

The Diocesan Director of Ordinands suggested I try for a curacy in one of England's many Urban Priority Areas, where young deacons with energy were always in high demand. I organised nine months on a mission station in Zambia, and stayed almost twice that long.

To the African natives, I meant no harm. The villagers believed on their mothers' lives in a man-eating creature from the bush, the fearsome Sasabonsam. I offered them an Anglican spirituality not entirely decided about crusts on or crusts off. Without the brisker appeal of mass stadium marriages, or group suicides to a Messiah hidden behind a meteor, my personal mission attracted little attention, and I never knowingly baptised a single Christian.

For weeks at a time I didn't write to Helena, or phone her. Maybe, I don't know, not being nice to her was my way of saying I loved her. To everyone else, I wrote and phoned and was nice. To Mum, I sent funny character sketches, and cartoons of vicars boiling in pots. She told me I was wasting my life. To Dad, I sent herbal remedies, and carvings of eccentric Olukun, the Benin spirit of the sea, with mudfish legs and a lizard in each hand. For Tom, I compiled graphs of how little money the local farmers and craftsmen earned in a year, and made bar-charts of the disparity between costs of African labour and margins of Western profit.

Gratifyingly to everyone, except perhaps the Zambians, in its own way Zambia was awful, though my memories had since softened significantly, brown boys running and a glowing reference from the Archbishop of Lusaka, who liked to win at backgammon.

Back in England, Helena was now working for an organisation which monitored the connection between government aid packages and arms deals. I went to meet her parents, Mr and Mrs Byczynski in Eastbourne, who were disappointed in me but didn't know how to object. It was as confusing as if Helena had brought home a poet, and awkward for educated people to be openly ashamed. However, a fully ordained vicar earned a stipend of fifteen thousand a year, and no one could raise a family on that.

I remained a deacon, and attached myself to a provincial cathedral. They found me titbits around the Close. Whenever I was asked to provide emergency cover for some exhausted rector, I'd preach bitter sermons on selfishness, yes I mean you, because beneath outward differences which blind us, but which to God are barely noticeable, God discerns the same pride, the same vanity, the same petty and complacent preoccupation with the self. We were all as bad as each other.

The Cathedral Press published my *Commentary on Seneca's De Clementia*, of which I was overly proud, and which counted for nothing. I taught a course at the University. I blessed some newly-weds who'd broken a mirror. I exorcised a brewery which repeatedly failed its health and safety inspection. And in the remotest English countryside, I investigated the theft of altarware from unattended country churches. There was never any great mystery. The churches were unattended.

I was avoiding so many things at once, I didn't know where to turn. I wrote an application to the MCC, but they replied to the Bishop, who smartly reminded me of the priority of our Urban Priority Areas.

'I know just the place,' he said. 'I know exactly where your presence will best be felt.'

The Diocese sent me to shadow Dad in his new inner-city parish for a day and a half in the middle of a working week. I was appalled. Dad was seeing every day what most of us only see at intervals. Death and disappointment. Indifference. Despair.

He'd aged terribly. As proof that he'd made no youthful pact with the devil, Dad had every male-pattern loss, hair gone or greyed, a stoop, and a hard little paunch over his plain black belt. He'd stopped wearing his collar, and distrusted his safety-razor. He also had four different churches in four different wards, too much for a healthy man, twenty years younger. And he wasn't a healthy man.

He was seriously ill. Cancerous cells had been discovered in his blood, and when out walking he often had to stand very still, resting. He'd concentrate on something inside, trying to speed it up, or slow it down. He'd close his eyes, locating each of his vital inner organs, checking them over, willing them back into shape. And when he opened his eyes again, the whites would shine like glazed porcelain, glittering and brittle, sick.

His GP suggested Dad apply to a private hospital for an

urgent operation on his bladder. On a Church stipend. Failing that, he ought to insist on some help in the parish.

I did think about it. I did. I squared my shoulders, trying to settle on myself the necessary qualities to cope with social reality. Some basic level-headedness, for example. Reliability would have come in useful, as would a quietly confident twinkle. Perhaps, if I had it in me, a certain understated authority.

I said no. Definitely not. It simply wasn't me.

They sent me anyway, and in Dad's horrific parish I was more than ever an impostor, a priest-impersonator. My own short life seemed such a meagre thing to hold up as an example. Do what I do. Be like me. How could that help? Was that all I had to offer?

I over-adapted, and launched myself zealously at all the parish's problems. I raised money, supervised initiatives, then raised more money, which I spent on microwave-ovens and reclining chairs and other material comforts for Dad's loyal congregation of ageing ladies. Unfashionably, I was an evangelist to the old, who were more in need, I thought, because they had less time to make up their minds. In their oversized dark glasses, for the shingles, the old ladies accepted my meals on wheels inscrutable and all-knowing, like ancient rock-and-rollers.

I paid for their hair-appointments, and their notelets with matching envelopes, and vet's fees for their cats.

On Sundays the men of the congregation, in RAF-coloured coats, sat separately and so self-possessed they seemed Chinese. I followed them back to the pub, and had satellite installed in the C of E retirement home, for the cricket. I was a roaring success, and good-humoured, endlessly patient, I wondered if this was finally me, or just my belated version of Dad.

None of my local achievements seemed to please him. He only brightened on the weekends of Helena's visits, when he'd force himself upstairs to make us up a double bed. He'd joke with Helena that he was bang up to date, and he knew how it was. These days young women did everything, even feminists, and not before marriage but instead of it.

'I know,' Helena said, the two of them always laughing, 'it's all quite dreadful.'

When she left on Sunday nights, she'd tell him not to stand up, and reach over the back of his chair to kiss him on the baldness of his head. And by Tuesday, Dad's health would have dipped again, and I'd intensify my efforts, seeking out novel ways to involve myself in the community. I helped the Lions club with their triathlon. I accompanied the scout-cubs to defend their ladders while window-cleaning the Estates. I swam 1500 metres for Shelter, even though I couldn't swim.

A jocular local police sergeant, bored with catching vandals who spray-painted their own names in bus-shelters, found it amusing to ask Jay Mason Minor, the stand-in vicar, if he'd like to take part in an identity parade. I accepted. It was a service I could provide to the community, and there was money involved.

Every month or so, I therefore changed out of my vestments into caps, coats, hats, jackets, whatever was this year's in-thing with the nation's house-breakers. The local force was then royally entertained whenever the confused victim of a break-in would stammeringly pick out the vicar.

'There,' the fat sergeant would say, rocking back on his copper's flat heels, convinced that this false identification proved something very important about life's big questions. He never said exactly what that was. And before long, the parish being such a hideous old English place, there was always another parade. The natives were beyond saving, and the line-ups were for robberies from the guide-dog box, a vandalised allotment, and the gradual theft from local churches of all furnishings of any potential value.

Instead of the urgent operation he needed, Dad had the same operation six months later on the NHS. Tubed up in bed after three days of oxygen and post-operative hallucinations, Dad reached out for the hand of his second son, an insubstantial presence at the bedside. His recovery took longer than predicted, but as soon as he could sit up unassisted, the nurses helped him, still in his pyjamas, to a taxi.

Back at the vicarage, Dad used to sit in his dressing-gown with his chin on his chest, hands clenched on his paunch, staring at his son in vestments. He looked like death. Physically he was a ruin, his face more bone than blood, his inexact hands rattling the spoon in his mug of hot water whenever he went to drink.

I tried to cheer him up.

'Tell me honestly,' I said, spreading out my arms, showing myself off before midweek Communion. 'Do I look like a vicar?'

'You're dressed like one.'

'If I ever start looking like a vicar, shoot me.'

'Really?'

'Well, just tell me.'

'Son?'

'Dad?'

'You don't look like a vicar.'

Neither of us smiled. 'What's the problem, Dad?'

'They say that the person who's been stealing from the churches disguises himself as a vicar.'

'Yes, I've heard that.'

'How can you afford Sky for the old codgers?'

'Dad, you're not well.'

I replaced his glucose drip, and knew that he needed a nurse, at more than forty pounds a morning. During the night of the 7th Sunday after Trinity, a communion cup was stolen from the church closest to the vicarage. Dad had been at the bedroom window, taking some air. He claimed to have seen the thief leaving the building.

'Did you get a good look at him?'

'Not really. He was dressed like a vicar.'

The police treated the old man gently. He was frail and ordained, and couldn't be expected to talk much sense. Within a week, I was called to the station. Either side of me, facing the floor-to-ceiling mirror, the usual suspects, but this time in black clerical shirts and tight white dog-collars. Numbers One and Six looked ill at ease but harmless, like curates fresh from college. Five, a nail-biter with a tattooed head, kept running a finger inside the band of his collar, and was anxious to be elsewhere. Two and Four, on either side of me, even dressed as vicars looked villainous and bad to the bone.

I was desperate. I knew that Dad was behind the mirror making his choice, and I wanted to be picked out as the only suspect who could plausibly pass for a vicar. In the endless questioning and interrogation of who I was, I wanted to know if this, after all, was the answer.

The sergeant was beside himself. He thought this was fantastic. He stroked his fried-breakfast belly and chuckled with delight as he walked slowly from One through Six. He wiped away a tear, then laid a hand on my shoulder.

'Not today, son,' he said. 'Apparently you're nothing like him.'

'None of you,' Dad grumbled, shaking his head as I pushed his wheelchair back to the car. 'Not one of you looked plausibly like a vicar.'

'Thanks,' I eventually said, as I sorted out the ramps. 'Thanks, Dad. I owe you one. I think.'

At the end, he liked to sit sideways in the driver's seat of his car, the door swung open, his feet trembling on the pale tarmac of the vicarage driveway. He wanted to go somewhere, to do something, but he didn't know where or what. He used to hunch forward with his shoulders high and his hands crushed in prayer between his thighs, shivering and shaking, an old man dwindling in flesh and blood.

He needed another operation, this time on a kidney, but by then his spirit had gone, no longer earth-bound by the love of living.

It was my turn at the family funeral. Tom's contribution, fresh in from a diamond merger in Johannesburg, was to wonder whether it really had to be in a church.

'For God's sake, Tom, he was a vicar. All his life that's what he was.'

'Yes, but he's dead now, and isn't it more important what *we* feel?'

'We're having it in church.'

Helena was kinder. And even Mum came, back from Spain in her bright summer clothes.

'A cremation would have been quicker,' Tom hissed. 'And cheaper.'

'Tom, for God's sake.'

'You're such a fraud, Jamie. You don't believe a word of it. And he knew that, too. It was you who probably killed him.'

The Suffragan Bishop was there, and a single archdeacon. I stood beside Dad's lacquered coffin, not in the pulpit but on the step, and even then, and only a deacon, I understood that it wasn't a whodunnit. I wasn't there to investigate, or take revenge, nor to work out why.

I knew that, and I ignored that. I acted the rogue cop, incensed but logical, on a personal quest to find out who and why and where to lay the blame.

'The bad carpets,' I said, pausing for effect. 'The bullock doses of tannin. The lack of recognition. The pathetic waste of a heroic stance gone unnoticed. The minimal salary, and the complacency of the conformist and sickly bishops.'

In my bitter and considered opinion, Mason Senior had died for the Church of England as surely as Thomas à Becket, the top of his skull sliced clean off with a broadsword, with such force that on its follow-through the sword itself had shattered on the flagstones of the cathedral floor. Hugh of Hornsea had then planted his foot on Becket's neck, poked the point of his sword into the open wound, and scattered about the blood and brains.

I left a long silence, in which there was much coughing and shoe-shuffling. I could have gone on, but tears frightened me, and I was about to cry, and I wasn't ready for the rogue cop's subsequent voyage of self-discovery. I fell back on the comfort of the Burial Service. The confidence, the bluff.

We should not have you ignorant, brethren, concerning those who are asleep.

Within days, a letter arrived from the Bishop. He suggested in writing that I take a break, some time to reflect. He knew of an interesting short-term opportunity abroad, in Geneva. It was still a few months off, but he encouraged me in the strongest terms to apply.

The longer I thought about it, the more the idea appealed to me. Geneva would be an escape during which to reflect, and make a fresh start, where my familiar self would be hidden from anyone who knew me, especially if they wore summer clothes and thought I deserved better, or had violet eyes and were determined to love me. It was maybe my last chance to see who it was possible to become, before it was too late, before I was left with nothing but Jay Mason Minor, not through accumulation, but default.

The night of the funeral Helena encouraged me to prove, as she'd always argued, that I was a believer in life. And not in condoms. That was four months ago, almost to the day.

The bones. In the flat I still had the bones. All things considered, Helena accepted the news philosophically, unshockable after the earlobe. It took us the rest of the meal to agree on what to do with them, and we were now walking off our experimental pudding between the Hôtel du Paix and the Cimetière des Rois. Helena had the locket round her neck, underneath her clothes, just as I'd always intended.

'It's heavy,' she said, 'and it bounces. But I think I'll get used to it.'

The cemetery was a joint idea. My own first impulse, now that we were back together again, had been to leave the city, the country and every problem of my own making behind. After all, it was a mess. I had uncertain status in an apartment I didn't own, which I was sharing with skeletons. Richard Burton was in the closet. Someone else was in the kitchen, and I didn't even know who it was.

I genuinely couldn't remember who it was I'd dug up the night before last. As Richard Burton, it was impossible to over-exaggerate my drunkenness. Calvin's grave had definitely been empty, I remembered that clearly, but the rest of the information was gone. I just couldn't remember.

'We could go to the police,' Helena suggested, before I reminded her that I was the one who'd done the digging. And also that we'd agreed, I thought, about this being a rare but genuine instance of a crime without victims. It was nothing but old bones.

'Richard Burton's old bones,' Helena said. 'Burton's not a problem. We say sorry and put him back. Honest mistake. All we have to do is find out the identity of the other one, and then do the same. It'll be a new experience for you. Actually resolving a problem, seeing it through to the end, instead of running away.'

'You think we have to?'

'Then we can move on. You'll see. In the long run it makes life easier. And it'll do you some good.'

Helena didn't believe that in one afternoon I could have learnt to open graves, remove the bones and then replace the stone. Or at least I could, and obviously had. But it was unbelievable that I could have done it without leaving any incriminating evidence.

So off to the cemetery it was.

It had stopped raining, though the weather had yet to make up its mind, the sun still smothered behind a flat puzzle of cloud, in which from edge to edge the challenge was the gradual shadings between white and grey. It might still rain again, and I hoped it would. As long as the showers kept coming, Moholy had no choice but to wait for Calvin.

A helicopter chopped by, tracking foreign dignitaries between luxury hotels, and we walked for some distance along the United Nations perimeter-fence, erected to keep the powerful safe from the people. The city had begun to itch and fidget as the young and discontented steadily arrived. Even though the main protest rallies weren't scheduled until the

200

weekend, it was worth coming early. Later in the week, stricter controls were expected at the borders, and every available room in the city would be taken.

Nobody knew what the protesters were planning. Nobody was even sure what they wanted, apart from change, and perhaps that's all they ever wanted to say. Wherever they came from, and whatever their specialist interests, they all had reform in common. They didn't believe the world had to stay the way it was, even if none of them had quite fixed, at least not yet, on a readily workable alternative.

The challenge to this demonstration, like every other, was the news. Without publicity, all the effort and organisation and the cycling from Southampton finished as an early-evening one-minute montage, contrasting the dignity of mounted police with a pretty Czech anarchist, sitting on her boyfriend's shoulders, advancing popular freedom by taking off her top.

How could they make this one new? They'd be up to the usual pranks, blockading and banner-hanging, and cementing volunteer Germans to parking meters. Apparently a French group called Farmageddon would be transplanting corn across the entrance to the UN, hoping for some digital pictures of crushed wheat beneath the alloy wheels of diplomats.

But they'd done this before.

Every protest needed its one memorable event. Something entirely original, and also sensational.

'Like a crucifixion,' Helena suggested. 'Same principle.'

'Though not a crucifixion,' I hoped, 'not an actual one.'

'Obviously not. Not an actual one, no. But something like it.'

Without that, it was just thousands of young people brave

enough to oppose the unchecked licence of a powerful media and business elite, again, and again seeing their claims for change ignored.

Already, several days before the protest, there were smaller, special-interest demonstrations. And inside the cemetery of kings, in with the small yellow digger and the amateur shrines glinting and flapping with letters and plasticked flowers, about twenty people were standing in a circle holding hands. Like many other single-issue organisations (Stop the War, Actors Against Aids) this group inside the cemetery was taking advantage of the larger protest to publicise its own concerns. Three policemen, a pair of photographers, and a TV camera looked on as cultural loyalists from Buenos Aires continued their campaign for the repatriation of the body of Jorge Luis Borges. On his headstone, over the insensible Old Norse inscriptions, they'd taped angry open letters (*Jorge Ven a Casa!*), and sheets from lined yellow jotters: *Maestro, You Belong in Buenos Aires.*

They did this about once a year, and traditionally it was a good-natured occasion, but from our point of view it was a disaster. Any trace I might have left in the grass was now trampled and lost. Also, the Cuban heels of a Borges protester were sinking slowly into the grass right next to Calvin's plot, which Helena had expressly wanted to investigate.

Ignoring the enthusiasms of Argentina, we acted the innocents and peered scholastically at Calvin's headstone, with its simple inscription *J.C.* It looked completely untouched. There were no scratch-marks on the raised recumbent, and the white pebbles between stone and grass were neat and tidy, only an inconclusive handful spilling over. That was how it was supposed to look, both before and after. This was the benefit of practice, and Elizabeth Taylor's dogs.

'I bet you didn't even try.'

'I did.'

'Calvin's still down there.'

'He's not. I swear. I looked, and he isn't there.'

'So where is he then?'

'I haven't the faintest idea.'

Apart from the Borges direction, which was impassable, we had a close look at all the graves within a reasonable distance of Calvin. I might have tried any one of them, though I'd probably have chosen one of those nearest. Calvin wasn't in a row, not even approximately, and there were several graves which could qualify. Some of them had candles in jam-jars, and letters in tattered homage. Many of them didn't.

I closed off my nostrils between fist and thumb, opened, exhaled. I bumped a central knuckle down the kinked bone of my nose, walked a little, and stopped at François Simon, star of early French cinema, who for acting purposes had taken the name of his son, Michel. His son Michel was now also a film-actor, and used the screen name François. It was an intriguing equation, time turned upside down, but there was no incriminating mark or scratch anywhere on François Simon's stone.

'Come on, Jay. You must have more of an idea than that. Who was it?'

'I really don't know. I was drunker than I thought possible.'

'But you must have looked,' Helena said, 'surely? How could you not have looked?'

'It wasn't that I didn't look. It's just that I can't remember.'

'Was it someone famous?'

'This is Geneva. Switzerland. They're all famous.'

Left and right of Calvin, behind and in front of him, with no obvious trace of recent disturbance, most of the other stones belonged to Mr and Mrs Smiths, who neither of us had ever heard of.

'And that's the skeleton you have in the closet?'

'No. That's Richard Burton.'

'I mean in the bin-bag in the kitchen. You know what I mean.'

'I can't say. I shouldn't think it's a nobody, a Mr Smith.'

'But definitely not John Calvin?'

'Definitely not. Absolutely categorically one hundred per cent not.'

By this time, one of the policemen overseeing the lively Argentines was watching us suspiciously. After walking once more past the nearest graves, we prudently headed for the exit.

'Great work,' Helena said. 'It could be anybody.'

I didn't appreciate her sarcasm. If nothing else, at least I'd confirmed my talent for digging up the dead, discreetly, as if their stones had never been disturbed.

'The bones themselves should tell us,' Helena decided. She wasn't a quitter. If she was, we wouldn't still be together, and it was Helena who'd hurried us back to the flat. In the kitchen she unzipped her puffa, and peered into the bulky brown bin-bag. 'Yes, well. Maybe the bones can tell us something. But probably only after we've cleaned them up.'

At first, I planned to take half the bones and wash them in the bathroom, while Helena did the other half in the sink. Then she decided this was unfair on Burton, who apart from his leg-bone was still encased in mud in the kit-bag at the back of the closet. So she started on Burton at the sink.

And I grabbed Mr X in two hands and swung him through to the bathroom, lifting him into the shower. It was easiest to join him, and I sat naked for a long time beneath the steaming water, cleaning off one bone after another with a nail-brush. I didn't hurry. I took my time, spitting out the streams of water which sometimes found out my mouth.

There wasn't any flesh, as such. However, I did discover some dark and surprising flitters of matter, like scraps of black web, which hung about the joints and disconnected vertebrae. It was like flesh without substance, the blackest earth. It was human moss.

I put each clean bone on the bathmat, and after pulling on some jogging pants I rolled up the bones and carried them through to the living-room. In the kitchen, Helena was finishing off Burton, holding his skull under water until it stopped bubbling and drowned. The rest of him was already in the drainer, and I looked for evidence of his influence on Helena, something unexpected, like say a bottle of sherry down from the cupboard. But either relics didn't work on women, or I had a particular gift, because even from this distance I could feel a suggestion of Burton's intercession as my eyes were drawn down the back of Helena's polo-shirt to the exquisite curve of her buttocks, and her hips sliding East West East.

She turned round, and snibbed her hair behind her ear with soapsudsy fingers.

'For heaven's sake,' she said.

She turned back and shook the water from between Burton's ears. 'Don't even think about it.'

'What?'

'You can scrap that idea right now. These bones have no special powers. They're just bones. They have no discernible influence.'

Taking care to keep the two skeletons apart, we dried them off in the living-room, sitting cross-legged on the floor and using opposite corners of the same large towel.

'What about this black stuff?' Helena asked.

'It's pretty stubborn. I couldn't get it off.'

Helena took Burton, all clean now and wrapped in towels, back to the closet. I kicked aside the rug, and laid out the other set of bones according to size on the grained yellow wood of the floor.

Scrubbed and buffed, they'd come up a porous colour between yellow and grey, with various intermediate shades of brown. The mouth had no teeth, we noticed now, and the skull was bulbous at the forehead, but still it was un-mistakably the intense skeletal face of a homo sapiens, an actual human person.

It didn't scare either of us. It wasn't a dead body; it was older than that, and old bones were deceptively lightweight, and out in the open there was a palpable thingness about them. They were just *things*. Helena picked up an arm-bone. She smelled it, then put it back.

'Nothing. No effect whatsoever.'

'On you.'

'It's in the past, Jay. That little phase is over. You are never going to wake up and find yourself a completely different person. You are what you are.'

'And what's that?'

'Suggestible, mainly. Now let's see who we've got.'

Helena sat on the front edge of the armchair and bumped it forward to look directly down on the bones, her hands flat between her thighs. After a long time, weighing the bones very carefully in the balance, she said: 'It could be anybody.'

'Don't be daft. I wouldn't have dug up just anybody. It wouldn't make sense.'

'There must be clues. We should be able to figure it out.'

'How?'

206

For the next hour and a half, we worked at reassembling a human skeleton, mixing, matching, making the shape. On all fours on the woodblock floor, we circled the bones like insects, and gradually, the human skeleton began to defeat us. Chips and sticks of bone were left spare, probably from the feet or the tricky fingers, or the hollow section of spine backed up from pelvis to skull. We couldn't make it all fit.

The bones, in our provisional arrangement, were running. Flat out, glancing behind, jaw dropped open, eye-sockets wide and aghast.

It wasn't very big. And all the teeth were missing. I went to check in the shower, and poked through what was left of the mud in the bin-bag, but I didn't find any teeth. Back with the bones, I stared hard at what we actually had.

'Stop,' I said. 'I think I've got it.'

'Who?'

'Charlie Chaplin. Look at him.'

Without any discussion, our first instinct had been to assemble the makeshift skeleton in full flight, like Charlie in a Keystone caper, scarpering from a livid fat flatfoot. Now why would we have done that?

'Durr,' Helena said, tapping the side of her head with a finger. 'Chaplin's in Vevey, not Geneva. Try again.'

'It's quite small,' I said lamely. 'Maybe that's important.'

'You're right. It isn't very big.'

'But celebrities are famously smaller than they look.'

'Or maybe not. There might be pieces missing. He might be bigger than he looks.'

Helena was back on her knees, rethinking the legs, bringing the feet down flat, heel to heel. The bony arms she assembled close against the body, with the skull now straight on so that its empty eye-sockets looked directly upwards, its jaw still open and awe-struck. Helena closed its mouth. It now looked stubborn, jaw set, determined not to reveal any secrets.

'Let's be honest,' Helena said. 'This isn't working.'

'No.'

'And we'd only make the situation worse if we put the bones back in the wrong grave.'

'Probably,' I said. 'Though we could always just chuck them.'

'Show some respect. I have a better idea.'

During her night alone at the hotel, and then again when she'd been rubbing and scrubbing at Burton, Helena had seen the truth that bones were just things, inanimate objects. They weren't a unique point of contact between man and God. And they definitely weren't people. Of course, she herself would never personally have dug anyone up, but seeing as we already had these bones, and they were already up, who would we actually be hurting if we decided to make the most of them?

'Don't think about the bones,' Helena said. 'Briefly, just for a moment or two, think about the money.'

'We're going to be a family,' I agreed. 'We'll be needing some money.'

'Even more so than usual. Just to get us a start in life.'

'For the future.' (And our baby, and my life as Jay Mason Minor at last finding its own unique shape.)

'*Our* life,' Helena insisted, '*our* life taking shape. We can't rebury this skeleton for the simple reason that we don't know who it is. Now think back to everything Moholy's ever said. Is there any way we can exchange these bones for a decent amount of money?'

I went over to the window and looked out. It was dark now, but the cloud was higher, a solid all-night block rebounding the glare of Geneva's street-lights. From the terraced lawns of his villa, strolling down to the lakeside, Moholy would be assessing the same overcast sky, the prospect of rain forever delaying the promised resurrection of Calvin.

If only the moon would break through, and the clouds crack apart like vertebrae.

Calvin's Hip

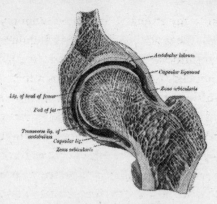

'The imitation of the saints will be useful in shaping life, if we learn from them sobriety, chastity, love, patience, temperance, contempt of the world, and other virtues.'

John Calvin, *Commentary on Romans 4:23*

Helena was asleep on the side of the bed nearest the window, breathing deeply and evenly. Personally, watching the pale violin of her back, I was thinking I like this very much, but still I couldn't sleep. The moonlight was taunting me, a thin silver line between the curtains. This and the ache at my earlobe and almost everything else was making me anxious.

I slipped quietly out of bed, and padded through to the living-room, wanting to make certain that no phantom power lingered in the bones of the dead. In the curtainless window, a three-quarter moon was high and bright, flouting the absence of cloud. The ghostly light picked out our skeleton, rigid on its back, arms stiffly by its sides. I lay down next to it, close but not touching, like a new and considerate lover. And then I waited for its energy to make itself known. Come, now.

Nothing.

I turned on to my stomach, hands between my legs, cheek crushed against the woodblock floor, and squinted side-on at our amateur solution to the human puzzle. A rib was actually a forearm, I noticed. And that finger was a toe.

If I just shuffle that rib. If I give a little more space to the elbow. I had a sudden flurry of ideas for radical new solutions, and I was soon on my knees making the changes, all of which ended in failure. I put the bones back how they'd been before, with only minor adjustments, still some way from all the bones in all the right places, making the best connections. I tinkered a little at the edges, made superficial alterations, always aiming at the perfect skeleton as a kind of universal answer, a summary of the entire universe.

And once I had the bones true, some time soon I hoped, then between the flat rack of ribs I'd project a veined heart the size of a small fist, a garnet-coloured thing, blinking, beating. I'd join its clutched rhythm by arteries like plastic tubing to other major organs, to lungs creasing and billowing, to a liver trembling, to a curved palette of lamb-of-God kidneys. Then skin, going over twice at the elbows and knees, the slack sexual organs, adding hair on the legs and the backs of the hands, leaving clear the rising and falling chest.

Finally, most delicately, the face, the mouth, the tender eyelids, the eyes. Blue. Blue-green. I stopped at the face, concentrating, using the contours of the bones as a guide, eager to make it right.

It was a thin face, about thirty-four, thirty-five at the most, a troubled face under darkish hair swept upwards in uncombed handfuls. The forehead was broad but the chin a little spent, the nose long and pointed from the pinch of three generations of vexed clerical fingers.

And I grimaced, gritted my teeth, and softly banged my clever forehead against the hard wooden floor. No, no, no. I was doing it again, always the same thing. That was me, I was describing myself, Jay Mason Minor, a selfish and unremarkable man of God.

It was no one special, with no special powers. We could do what we liked with it.

The next morning, I'd already cleaned out the shower by the time Helena came through from the bedroom, rubbing her eyes and yawning, wearing the stretched Jesus T-shirt I kept for jogging. I was now sweeping up in the living-room, where mud had dried in footprints across the woodblocks. It was a bright morning. The weather had held, and early sunlight flooded the room.

Helena stretched out her arms, frowned, then rearranged the skeleton in a stern, no-nonsense manner, bony hands on chipped hips, head slightly to one side, a foot raised and ready to stamp its Calvinist reproach on any suggestion of frivolity. The foot had a few pieces missing, undermining the effect.

'Why not?' she asked, admiring her work, checking it from different angles.

'Why not what?'

'You did actually dig up John Calvin. You blanked out. Why *wouldn't* it be Calvin?'

'Because his bones weren't in the grave marked *J.C.*, where they should have been.'

'You were very drunk. Admit it, those bones could be anybody.'

'I'm not disagreeing. The bones could be anybody.'

'Ergo therefore hence. They could be the grim John Calvin.'

After nearly 500 years underground, if anyone was to believe it was Calvin, they'd have to concede that the skeleton was wearing well. The cleaned-up bones looked surprisingly modern, but we couldn't claim to be experts. We had no knowledge of how bones were supposed to age. They were the famously undecaying part. A bone is a bone is a bone.

'Except for the teeth,' I said. Would anyone know if Calvin still had his teeth?

'You'd expect bad teeth, five hundred years ago.'

'Would you? I think these bones look newer than that.'

Though now we looked more closely, new and old hardly seemed like useful terms. Bones in bogs from the Iron Age were found in better shape than these, younger, as good as new. It depended on the composition of the soil, and other inexact factors, such as the godliness of the soul. We might be looking at the miracle of pure living, its very own preservative.

'If we can't tell it's not Calvin,' Helena said, 'then neither can Joseph Moholy.'

'I knew you were going to say that.'

'We pretend it's Calvin, and sell it to Moholy as Calvin. He'll never know. The fact is, we're all the same beneath the skin. All bones look alike.'

'He wants John Calvin. He was fairly decided about that.'

'Joyce, Calvin, what's the difference?'

'If he ever finds out, I shouldn't imagine he'll be thrilled.'

'How will he tell?'

'The effect.'

'Sorry?'

'The intercession of the relic. That's what keeps him interested. The effect the relics have. If the bones fail to make his clients think and act like John Calvin, Moholy will know we've sold him a fake.'

'Back to the real world, Jay. They're just bones, *things*. They can't intercede, whatever his customers may like to imagine. They have no effect.'

'In your opinion, which is irrelevant. As is mine. All that counts is Moholy's opinion, and he expects his relics to intercede.'

'You're moving into strange territory here.'

I wondered where it could get any stranger. 'Let's not pretend it's John Calvin,' I said. 'I don't think we'll get away with it.'

I told Helena everything I could remember about Moholy's gallery, with Jung's knee and the silk cloth and the compass, and Moholy's abrupt change of mind from Joyce to Calvin. To Moholy, Calvin was more important than just another relic. He was a significant waymark on Jung's map. It wasn't clear, but Calvin was either a vital indicator along the way, or he was actually the end, the aim, the objective answer to everything.

'In which case,' Helena said, 'even more reason to deliver. It's the jackpot.'

'What about the Iraqi salesman?'

'Don't be such a fatalist. We'll be fine.'

Helena went to the bookcase, and picked out the I-Ching. She then stepped astride the stern assembly of Calvin, feet firmly planted either side of his hips. She licked one of her fingers.

'Page one,' she read. '*To ask a question of the oracle, you will need yarrow stalks, coins, or in the oldest tradition for the most authentic reading, bones*. And bones,' she said, looking up brightly, 'we got.'

With the I-Ching open around one thumb, she selected three bones with obvious sides, deciding on the shins and a cracked section of pelvis. 'Ready to roll,' she said. 'You go first.'

'Is it wrong to dig up dead people?'

'That's not in question,' Helena said.

'Ask that question first.'

The I-Ching was a sophisticated version of cleromancy, reading significance into patterns of bones scattered from a shaman's bag. Helena was now down on her knees, weight forward on her elbows as she rolled the bones, consulted the book, then rolled again. She did this six times, while I recorded each result on the back of an envelope. According to the lie of the bones, the I-Ching was unambiguous in its response. *Not necessarily*. Yes and no. It was the same wise advice I recognised from the Church of England.

Helena sat back on her heels, and clicked the end of the pencil between her teeth. Now for the bigger question, of much greater relevance.

'Should we carry on regardless?'

The bones rolled and stopped, trapping permutations from the air, ravelling the ancient hazard that everything was connected, and the world hid endless readable meanings. The I-Ching's final decision was that we had no choice but to carry on regardless, in this and all other matters.

'Well,' Helena said, 'there you have it.'

There was something inevitable about what happened next. Thinking it through, I condensed all the possibilities into one single option. Either do something, or do nothing. That was the on/off switch, the most basic of human choices.

If I did nothing, it seemed likely that I'd regress to wherever I'd been before, somewhere shy of square one, disintegrating as a person. Doing nothing was a surrender, a kind of torpor, which I'd always instinctively understood was a danger to my state of health. It was the duty of all good Christians, I reminded myself, to serve some useful purpose.

I dismantled the skeleton and gathered up the bones, tumbling them in handfuls into the blue plastic sports-bag I'd salvaged from the jumble at the church. Helena hovered around me, though we still hadn't agreed on any definite plan of action. Think of the baby, we were both thinking, think of the money.

'For God's sake,' Helena said, 'it's either this or living like clergy, always scrabbling for cash. Is that really what God wants?'

I checked the weather, and dressed while accepting I didn't really know what God wanted. I had no idea what he had in store for me. Except, it ought to be said, the weather was fine and holding, and despite all my idiocy and cruelty, Helena had found and saved me, and had recently risen from my bed. Maybe I was just lucky.

By accident, it turned out I was wearing black, all black. Honestly, I hadn't even looked. I'd randomly picked out my black church shoes and my black trousers, and my black polo-shirt and my bobbly black cardigan. So John Calvin was known to dress in black, but coincidence was just one of those things. The future was not already written.

My breakdown had not been inevitable, nor destined. More likely, it was the devil's work made light for idle hands. If I'd been working as hard as God intended his ministers to work, none of this would have happened. It was the result of laziness, and a refusal to act when actions defined us. It wasn't as if not knowing which way to turn had marked me out as special. Self-doubt and conflicting impulses were universal, but they weren't the way to get things done.

In fact, I had to snap out of it. It was such a waste. I had to put myself to work, not necessarily paid employment, but the diligent and productive use of whatever talents and resources I had.

And in Geneva, this Friday morning, my major resource was bones. Don't just sit there. Get up and go. With the assistance of an inbred work ethic, Helena's idea quickly developed into a project. I would deliver the anonymous bones in the blue plastic sports-bag to Joseph Moholy. I would offer them as John Calvin, and Moholy would reward me handsomely, and Helena would be in my bed tonight like last night, and also tomorrow night, and the night after that. We would, as it happened, live happily ever after. I could see the destined future quite clearly, including the more immediate future of what to do next.

'Have you made up your mind?' Helena asked. 'What is it we're going to do?'

'I'll phone Moholy.'

And that's exactly what I did. I phoned Moholy, and between us we shared the excitement of being so amazingly fortunate with the weather. Fate must be with us. The conditions had been perfect. And yes, I'd managed to do what he asked.

Moholy was euphoric. He wanted to send Rifka to pick me up right away, but I countered with a better idea, one I'd prepared in advance. After considering what Calvin himself would have wanted, Moholy's rich villa seemed inappropriate, as did the gallery. We set a time to meet at the church.

Even cancelling his other appointments, Moholy couldn't be there before ten.

I fetched my black zip-up jacket, and the bag of bones, and headed for the door. Helena was still undressed, in the Jesus T-shirt and looking bemused. 'Where are you going? It's much too early.'

I said I didn't want to leave anything to chance.

'What will be will be, Jay.'

Except I didn't believe that. John Calvin would have believed it, or something like it, but I wasn't John Calvin. I didn't have John Calvin's bones. In fact, all we had in common was a thorough disdain for the history and influence of relics.

That morning, for the first time since I'd arrived from England, I was disappointed by the city of Geneva. The sky was cloudless but the sun hazed, as if fighting its way through the warm wind crawling off the lake like a gas. This was the dreaded Föhn, which had evaporated last night's cloud.

Apart from sapping the will, the Föhn made distant objects seem closer. Or so the Chaplain had once told me, Mont Blanc near enough to touch, its summit like Napoleon in bed (is what he said), with his hat on and the sheets pulled up to his nose (if that was the way I chose to see it). It was one way of seeing it, and today the mountains did seem alarmingly close, almost ominous, a disturbing debris of the Flood, the consequence of one among many of man's grave dis-obediences. Which was another way.

Helena was right, and I was hours early, so I took an indirect route. All in black, carrying my bank robber's bag, I felt self-conscious, as if it was obvious I was about to do a bad and terrible thing. I bought a ticket for the passenger ferry, to Eaux-Vives, hoping for fresher air out on the lake, and I sat in the stern watching the spread and fizz of the wake, breaking green and white like beer-bottles.

Cities, like people, could change on a daily basis. Geneva's most famous landmark, the 450-foot water-jet in the sheltered V of the lake, was off. It simply wasn't there, leaving unmasked the grand façades and garish rooftop acronyms of the city's 500 banks, fat on the wealth of human wickedness. Geneva was a great idea unlived, an ideal city sunk in corruption, a local economy financed by the life's work of dictators and pimps and assassins, of non-executive directors and emergency ministers for defence. The quiet of the city was the still outside of the can of worms. It was the calm of the rock, under which countless crawly things creep.

The Clerical Appointments Board, at my interview, had suggested that the city of Geneva might be the saving of a man like me.

'It's only a few weeks, but you'll be perfect. You're already half a Calvinist as it is.'

'I'm an Anglican, as are we all.'

'Yes, indeed. But you don't really enjoy it, do you, James?'

'Who does?'

'Learn something from Geneva, James, before it's too late. Reflect a little. Grow as a person.'

And so on. I wondered now in what way exactly they'd thought I was a Calvinist. They must have said that for a reason. In what way, exactly?

John Calvin had a vision of Geneva as a holy city, a new Jerusalem offering a tangible image of the presence and providence of God. It would stand at the crossroads of the human adventure, a pivotal centre negotiating the problems of the planet. The idea survived the man, and Geneva persisted in modelling itself as the capital of civilisation. From headquarters in Geneva, for example, the League of Nations would supposedly ensure peace on earth for a thousand years.

Instead, it had been superseded by the limp United Nations, and the ineffective High Commission for Refugees, and the vicious World Intellectual Property Organisation. Calvin's treasured Geneva was in decline, a favourite site for the stalling of treaty negotiations, for peace not to break out, for hope punctured, for disappointment.

And to be perfectly honest, it wasn't even all that clean.

I checked my watch. Once, in the reformed Christian city of Geneva, strangers could tell the time by the regularity of religious devotions. Now, Genevans and tourists owned luxury watches and clocks. So what was I planning to do? Herd the watch-wearing population into the Champs du Bourreau, and have them all burnt?

I was not Calvin. I didn't want to be Calvin. There was no imperative to go go go. There was plenty of time to get to the church, and I should just slow down, stop, remind myself that relics, and especially pretend ones like the bones in my bag, had no supernatural powers.

At the entrance to the Jardin des Anglais, on the south side of the lake, there was a precision Swiss timepiece made from flowers: a clock-face of geraniums and pansies in a sloping grass bank. The gardens themselves were a walkable pattern of lawn and tended flower-bed, and deliberately resisting the influence of Calvin, I bought myself an ice-cream. A red-flecked red ice-cream from the Mövenpick kiosk, open again after the long winter, and not just two scoops, but three.

With little regard for the urgency of doing good, I found a bench beside the bandstand which faced a sculpted fountain depicting all of the big four seasons. Around the fountain, lounging on their rucksacks, youngsters here for the protest shared bread and hunks of cheese. They were like flashes of colour and hope, so much more colourful and hopeful than the city itself, and they deserved to be indulged. My tolerance, I suspected, wouldn't last long. At the very latest, by the time I reached All Saints, I'd have to be acting securely in character. If this was going to work, I had to locate my inner Calvin.

I fed some crumbs from the bottom of my waffled cone to sparrows, jumping two-footed back and forth like wind-up toys. More young people arrived, many of them women, all with breasts and interesting buttocks. The world was rude and suggestive, and that was the way I liked it.

Since Helena had brought me back to my senses, I was less likely to make the mistake of supposing a Calvinist thought turned me into Calvin. I had Calvin in me, just as I had Becket and Davy and the others. They were all in there somewhere, but this time I planned to stay in control. I patted the plastic sports-bag on my lap. I was about to deliver bones to Joseph Moholy. If I was going to convince him that they were once John Calvin, the great reformer of Geneva, I'd have to act like Calvin, as if I were under the influence.

I finished my ice-cream, and reached into my pocket for a paper handkerchief. I shook one out, and dabbed at the corners of my mouth. I wiped off my fingers, then jammed the used tissue between the slats of the bench, looked at it ('Litter-bug and sinner,' said John), picked it out and returned it to my pocket.

Consciously making an effort to act like Calvin, in this day and age, what would I actually be like? A girl sat next to me, a dusty cyclist in an expressive T-shirt. *Love Me Love My Bike*. She started unlacing her boot, and most probably these self-styled freedom fighters saw John Calvin as an established enemy of freedom. They'd be wrong, or at least partly wrong. At the beginning, especially then, Calvin was better than that.

Against the bandstand, I now saw the layers of mountain-bikes D-locked together, with soft panniers and motorcycle helmets weighing heavily on the back wheels. Some of the protesters looked normal, others didn't. They were a mixture of fluffies and spikies, though in agreement about shoes. They all wore boots.

The girl next to me was now relacing hers, and in the spirit of community I asked her if she was looking forward to the weekend. She was very friendly, and happily answered all my questions, explaining that her particular group were a mixture of Danish, Dutch, English and Americans. They were planning, as their contribution to the protest against the evident inequalities in world capitalism, some carefully choreographed cycling. Some of them were anarchists. She thought that most of them were probably atheists.

I dared to ask, as the sun shifted through the trees, scattering sparkles across the fountain, what was actually so wrong with the world.

'The good suffer and the evil prosper.'

'In Geneva?'

'Especially in Geneva. It's a favourite location for the headquarters of multinationals. It's where Calvin wrote the rules, and where the conditions for inequality were perfected.'

'Thank you,' I said, 'thank you very much. Most informative.'

She was mistaken about Calvin. He was a fearless progressive, and had boldly rebelled against corrupt institutions and unjust authority. His steely northern core was our Protestant inheritance, and, atheists though they might be, these protesters were northern Protestant atheists. Whatever religion they'd rejected, they'd inherited to some degree the Protestant revolution. It was as inescapable as the industrial version, and no one could live as if it hadn't ever happened.

The faith itself might be eroding, but the structures and values remained. To save the planet, there were legions of new Calvinists prepared to persevere and make sacrifices and dedicate themselves diligently to the cause. Even their battle-cry was a version of Calvin's work ethic: something must be done. The Protestants of yesterday were the protesters of today, when it was only resistance which kept spiritual issues visible to the eyes of the people.

The Appointments Committee had been quite correct, and in many ways I was already a Calvinist. I was in sympathy with the protesters, and full of respect for John Calvin himself. After routing the established Church he was initially famed for his tolerance and wisdom. He decreed that sins only counted after the age of twenty. It was as sensible a theological reform as I'd ever heard. He laughed at fortune-telling, and advised men of seventy not to marry women of twenty-five, and dismissed a minister who insisted that anyone who'd died before the Reformation was damned.

In his pamphlet *An Admonition Concerning Relics*, John Calvin correctly pointed out that all bones looked the same. Therefore nobody could be confident of the saint they were actually venerating (*or, it may be, the bones of a dog, or a horse, or an ass*). High expectations led to disappointment, he warned. Don't set yourself up to fall flat on your face. It was all eminently wise, and John Calvin had been much maligned, usually by libertines and Catholic historians, for the obvious common sense of opposing cakes before sandwiches, tele-vision before breakfast.

It could go unnoticed that standing alone, heroic against abuses of power, he'd presided over an unlikely outbreak of

223

goodness. Cardinals in purple with full heads of hair were too busy noticing with a smirk that Calvin meant Baldhead. They underestimated his ability to change, and to act out of character. He arrived in Geneva a shy and minor cleric, humble and meek except in defence of the honour of God. As it turned out, as long as Calvin lived, God's honour nearly always needed defending.

In the early days, though no one dared say it, and he wouldn't have wanted to hear it, John Calvin reminded his Geneva citizenry of Jesus.

I looked at my watch again, and there were things to be done. This was my last chance to back out, and even though I already knew the outcome, that did nothing to lessen the struggle. Inside myself I could locate a certain sternness, and a capacity to believe myself special. They weren't Calvin's best qualities, but if I was special, if I was chosen, then it hardly mattered because nothing could go against me.

Calvinism faced the facts. Some people were chosen, and some were not. Life was unfair. From what I'd seen, and from what I'd read, that was what life was most like.

I wanted so much to be among the lucky ones. I'd always wanted to be divinely elected, someone who could get away with anything, and still end up in heaven. That's what at last I was finding out, if I was among the chosen. I was thirty-four years old. I was privileged and English and still hadn't suffered, not really. I had a tenacious and loving girlfriend, and a baby on the way, and a solid gene-memory of linseed and glorious flashes through extra cover. How much luckier could anyone get?

I stood up, and brushed crumbs of waffled cone from the blackness of my clothes, using the predestination of Calvinism as a source of self-belief. It was like Zen for the colder climates, inspiring unmatchable courage. You can do it. If it's predestined, as Calvin claimed, it's already done.

In the vestry I robed up in a simple black cassock, thinking myself back into Geneva's glorious past. I felt pale, stick-thin, though also determined and more than a match for Joseph Moholy.

It was risky, but too late to change my mind. I did wonder if I could have gone any other way, and been somewhere else, doing other things. I was perhaps living out the wrong destiny, one which belonged to a different type of person, but at my age it seemed ridiculous not yet to have settled on who I was, still waiting for the breaking of the first morning, the singing of the first bird.

This is where I found myself on the journey. And for me, however it may have been for anyone else, the most convincing sermon for the journey of life was always hitching. This wasn't necessarily the best place to be. Or even where I actually wanted to be. But it was where I was. I had doubts, of course I did, but I repressed them, and then made repression a virtue.

I went to the sink, and vigorously scrubbed my hands. Given a free choice, I'd have preferred to be almost anywhere else. I felt a bit ill, but then so did John Calvin, more often than not. Responsibility made him sick, physically sick, giving him sporadic one-sided headaches. Big decisions brought on anxiety attacks. As did insufficient sleep. He suffered a malady of the trachea which made him spit blood while sermonising, and he was often laid up with an internal abscess, wicked intestinal influenza, and haemorrhoids. He bled from a thousand wounds, but found comfort in the well-established Calvinist principle of doing what he didn't want to do. If he was chosen, it would all work out. If he wasn't, then he was bad and benighted and doomed forever to failure.

Calvin kept it going for the twenty-one years he ruled in Geneva, his health ruined by ferocious discipline and a stern internal world impervious to temptation and relief. Surely I could do it for an hour or so. Anyone could.

I was still nail-brushing my knuckles when someone opened the main door and briefly let in the traffic. I scurried out, shaking my hands, but it was only Helena.

'What? You didn't think I'd desert you? What's wrong?'

She'd stopped me short, because I didn't know if Calvin ought to be seen with a woman, not this early in the morning. And especially not a pregnant one.

'I brought tea, to keep everyone civil.'

She carried her plastic shopping-bag into the vestry, and emptied it beside the sink. There was a thermos flask, several tea-bags, three mugs, and, I saw with horror, a packet of chocolate biscuits.

'For God's sake,' I said. 'Hide the biscuits.'

'Excellent,' she said, dropping them back in the bag. She appeared to be amused, 'John.'

'Not funny.'

'Very good.'

'Thank you.'

I still had a nagging feeling that something was wrong, but convinced myself it couldn't be Helena. Three years ago, John Calvin had married the widow Idelette de Bure, who already had two children of her own. By my age, he was trying for more, and there were three babies, perhaps four, who died at birth. In a few years' time, as a widower, Calvin's only serious dispute with Geneva's English community would involve an attempted abduction of his five-month-old godson. The boy's mother, Lady Dorothy Stafford, disputed Calvin's urgent assurances that the child's father, on his death-bed, had willed it so. The episode made Calvin look weak and foolish, human.

It made me more confident of my impersonation, but still I sensed something amiss.

'You'll be fine,' Helena said, reaching up to touch my cheek. I flinched away. 'Perfect. And don't ever smile.'

'There's still something wrong.'

'Maybe it's the emptiness,' Helena suggested, looking round the church, hands on hips. 'Shall I put out some chairs?'

'Definitely not. He can stand.'

And Helena had to do what I said, because even though I was famously kind to women I was a man, and unlike any woman on the sixteenth-century earth I'd started University in Paris at the age of twelve. I therefore knew almost everything, including Latin, Greek, Hebrew and the importance of correcting the punctuation and spelling in other people's editions of Seneca's *De Clementia*. I knew what was right and wrong, and was suddenly struck by what was wrong.

'We need a congregation.'

'Just like that.'

'We need some people.'

'Are you sure?'

'Trust me. It's a Protestant thing. The minister carries out the wishes of the congregation, and when Moholy arrives I want you to ask for a sermon.'

Helena looked at me closely, checking the whites of my eyes. 'You don't think you're overdoing this?'

'Really,' I said. 'With relics it's all or nothing.'

227

'Alright. I'll see what I can do. But you're beginning to make me nervous.'

Helena went back out into the noise of Geneva, and I made good use of my time alone by rubbing my hands raw on a towel. During his years in Geneva, Calvin had preached 4000 sermons. My own talent for preaching was limited, because there was nothing simple I wanted to say. However, one more short one ought to be possible.

Sooner than I'd expected, Helena was back in the church with six or seven people, not dissimilar to those I'd seen earlier at the fountain. They were girls with slightly alarming eyes, and pale bearded men, with a disillusioned curl to the lip.

'I had to make a deal,' Helena said.

'Tell me later.'

'You may not like it.'

'Maybe not. But that man at the back is Joseph Moholy.'

I lifted my chin, clean red hands lightly clasped at about the level of my chest, and welcomed Moholy to the front of the church. Rifka was with him, and I suddenly realised I'd missed her. She looked so sensible, and kind, and it was as if I could always be certain, without taking any special trouble, that she'd be on my side and protect me from coming to harm. I had no idea why this should be.

Against my express wishes, Helena was bringing a chair from the vestry. Noted, marked down, recorded for later judgement by the Consistorial Court of Discipline. Moholy showed some interest in the various youngsters, leaning nonchalantly against the walls or sitting cross-legged at the back. Some of them had brought in boxes and bags, and even bicycles.

'Get rid of these people.'

Clever, I thought. Very clever. It was already a test, the first stage in Moholy's authentication of the bones. I didn't hurry. I was increasingly confident of my Calvin.

'No,' I said. 'The doors of the church remain always open. The people of Geneva are welcome.'

'Says who?'

'These people are not anarchists. There's no cause for alarm. They're cyclists.'

'Jesus was on the side of the needy,' Rifka said, as if to Moholy, then looking to me for confirmation. 'Isn't that right?'

I was grateful to her, understanding that she wanted to help, even if I didn't see exactly how. Or why. Unexpectedly, I had a flashed memory of how easily Calvin's stone had moved and slid. Underneath, the earth had been loose, and quick to work, as if someone had already been in there, and broken it up quite recently.

I had a new, unexpected thought: *I wasn't the first.*

And at that moment, looking closely into Rifka's wide and innocent eyes, I had the strong conviction that Moholy didn't know this, *but that Rifka did.* Her innocence was an act. It was a form of mockery. She *knew* I couldn't be Calvin, because somehow she already knew I didn't have Calvin's bones. So why hadn't she told Moholy?

John Calvin the chaste minister of God had once come home to find his sister having sex with a trusted colleague. He was incensed when his mentor, Guillaume Farel, aged sixty-nine, married a much younger woman. Betrayals and disappointments happened, all the time, to everyone. If Rifka had tricked me, after getting me involved in the first place, I'd call her to account. And then by God I'd burn her.

Moholy had something else to say, but thought better of it. He nodded, hitched up his elegant trousers, and sat down on the single chair which Helena had provided. She'd positioned it in the centre of the black and white aisle, level with the absent front row of pews, and Rifka stood beside and slightly behind him.

Out of habit, as I took my place on the step, I sought inspiration from the church itself, and found myself uplifted to see it so empty and undecorated, even unfurnished. Yet with a decent congregation, too, of the unwashed. For everyone's benefit, as I began, I made a rhetorical point of saying I'd be brief. It was purely rhetorical. Calvin was rarely brief, and in the nineteenth century the pastor in charge of the Bibliothèque de Genève, when disposing of the manuscripts of Calvin's sermons, had offered them for sale by weight. They were all on the same subject, sin, and John Calvin was mostly against it.

I started by asking a universally relevant question. 'How many among you have been looking for Jesus?'

Moholy was paying close attention. In his chair at the front he sat with arms and legs crossed, indulging me with his patience. At the same time, his eyes were unwavering, missing nothing, his head quite still as he listened carefully. It was all part of the test. We'd have to be careful, Calvin and I. We'd have to be very severe indeed.

I was vigilant against any taint of humour. I conscripted all of Calvin's favourite words, and then assembled them for battle. On the one side, there was pollution, pure filth, impurity, defilement, befoulment, spatter, stains, infinite depravity, ordure, stench, and stink. On the other, as well as confidence and sure salvation, there was reform, rebirth, restoration, restitution, renewal, and even revolution.

Follow in the footsteps of the lives of the saints, I advised. Act like Job, like Daniel, like Jeremiah. Emulate the Apostles, or anyone more and greater than you are. Aspire to the *imitatio Christi*. Stretch to your full potential. And then you will truly be followers of Jesus.

I was aware of the door opening and closing on the traffic, like an ear unblocking, then blocking again. It was one of the surly young men, leaving. He wasn't going to stay and be insulted like this, addressed like a Christian, but by then I'd pretty much finished. I bowed stiffly, by nature a shy and scholarly man, and meekly withdrew to the vestry. Helena followed me in, and after checking the door was properly shut, she hugged me. I didn't respond, my arms tensed chastely at my sides.

'Brilliant,' she said. 'Fantastic. You're such a star.'

I reached into the mugs and took out a tea-bag, leaving two between three.

'Not yet,' I said. 'In a minute. Let's just see if it worked.'

'He looked pleased. He didn't look doubtful, anyway. And he never took his eyes from your face, not once.'

'I'll take the bones. You bring the tea.'

Secretly, under the surface, I was delighted with my sermon. I too had noticed Moholy's apparent satisfaction. It had gone more smoothly than I'd anticipated, and we were going to get away with it. Calvin wanted to be back. There was so much sin in the world, in need of correction.

Moholy was still in his chair as I handed him a mug of tea, and offered him sugar. 'One lump? Or none at all?'

And then I introduced him to Helena. At first he seemed confused, as if he'd never heard of Idelette de Bure. 'She knows everything,' I said. 'I couldn't have done it on my own.'

'Everything?'

He must have known, surely, that John Calvin was in favour of marriage for priests. It was one of his chief disagreements with the Catholics. Marriage was an evident improvement on feigned chastity, and syphilis, and Moholy should have known that. I offered him the blue plastic sports-bag. He carefully put down his mug, and then balanced the bag on his knees. He coughed into his hand, and unzipped the bag a few inches, widening the gap with his fingers and peering inside.

'It's all there,' Helena said.

I shushed her, and borrowed a stern expression from the Reformer's Wall. At the sound of Helena's voice, Moholy let the gap in the bag close up, though he didn't rezip it. I suddenly wondered how I'd ever thought that Helena wouldn't be a problem.

'Is this girl special to you?'

I think I blushed. Everyone was waiting, and this was not an innocent question. Moholy was probing, making up his mind, as if there was significant and decisive information he suspected me of somehow withholding. Unfortunately, I didn't know what that information was.

'Is she more special to you than anyone else?'

And now I sensed that Helena was also interested in my answer, perhaps even more so than Moholy. And she wasn't expecting me to reply in character. She wanted an honest answer, and she wanted the world to know.

'Come on, Jay. The man asked you a question.'

'We cleaned him up,' I said, but this wasn't the important and decisive information that anyone wanted. 'He's all there, in the bag. John Calvin.'

I felt my face under scrutiny from every angle, as if everyone was searching for a confession, a betrayal. 'In your sermon,' Moholy said, 'you kept talking about Jesus. Why was that?'

'It's not unusual. Jesus is a big subject for us Christians.'

'Mr Moholy asked you if I was special.'

'Yes,' Moholy said. 'Let's go back to that one. Are you in love with this woman?'

'I really don't see the connection. It's not relevant.'

'You be careful,' Helena said. 'It's very relevant.'

'Have you and this woman had sexual relations?'

'None of your business.'

'Why not?' Helena interrupted. 'Why are you so ashamed to admit it? Yes, yes we have. And we do love each other. Very much. And I am very special to him, and he is very special to me.'

I looked at individual tiles on the floor of the aisle, one and then another, because Helena had ruined everything. She was very special to me. We loved each other very much. We did have sexual relations.

It seemed unlikely now that I'd ever live up to Calvin.

'I'm sorry,' Moholy said. 'Sorry for you both.'

'We're also having a baby,' Helena added defiantly.

'Are you? How very, very disappointing.'

Moholy unzipped the bag fully, and pulled out the first bone which came to hand, a cracked section of hip I thought, treating it with none of the veneration he usually reserved for relics. 'There's something not quite right here. Between the villa and the church I stopped at the cemetery. Calvin's grave hardly looks disturbed at all.'

'That's how it's supposed to look,' Rifka said helpfully. 'Jay has a gift for it.'

'Money,' I said. I could feel the situation slipping away, and in all my guises I was terrified of losing control. 'I've delivered John Calvin. Let's discuss the money.'

However convincing I may have been up to this point, I was now unmistakably Calvin. John Calvin had always been attentive to money. It was Calvin who'd decided, to the enduring benefit of Geneva and its banks, that lending money at interest was no longer usury. In fact, against the advice of that dusty user's guide to good living, the Bible, money-lending could be actively encouraged, as long as the loan imposed no oppression or hardship. Geneva grew rich on loans to Louis XIV the Sun King, who at Versailles was building expansive man-made lakes at the cost of several men's lives a day. Some people were chosen, and some were not. Life was unfair.

Moholy was knocking the hip-bone repeatedly into his palm. I'd never seen him so tight-lipped. 'This is wrong,' he said. 'There's something very wrong here.'

Rifka took the blue plastic sports-bag off his knees, and after looking round for a good place to put it, just dropped it on the floor. Moholy stood up.

'I'm taking this bone with me, to have it tested. Think about that. And then perhaps, when I have the results, we should have this conversation again, starting from the beginning. It might even have a less predictable ending.'

He walked briskly towards the door of the church, his steel-tapped heels clacking along the aisle. Rifka followed him, leaving the bag behind like an insult.

'Wait,' I said, taking a few steps after them. 'Come back. What's the problem?'

Moholy turned on his heel, as if he meant to skip back and slap me. His head was trembling, and he had to bite his lip. 'I think you're aware of what I'm looking for. By now, you must be. If you'd found it, we would not be here speaking like this. *As you well know*.'

He opened the door, letting in the traffic, and by the time it swung shut both he and Rifka had gone.

'Oh damn it,' Helena said. She kicked the leg of the chair, making it skitter round at an angle. 'I knew it. I knew this was going to happen.'

'Then maybe you should have said something a little earlier.'

She walked to the wall with her head in her hands. 'It was a bad and stupid idea. Stupid and foolish. But you wouldn't listen, would you?'

'My Calvin must have been rubbish.'

'It wasn't. It was actually pretty convincing.'

'Though not to Moholy.'

'God, this is such a fuck-up. Such a simple idea to earn some serious money, and we've completely botched it.'

'I botched it.'

'Maybe that was the problem,' Helena said. 'Your Calvin was *too* good. And it turns out Moholy isn't a total nutcase. I didn't know that before, but he wasn't how I pictured him. Whatever he lets his clients think, that man I just met isn't a believer in relics.'

'He is. We talked about it.'

'Oh grow up. And listen. He never expects relics to have any influence. That's a sales pitch. In which case, he must have thought it was *you* who was half insane, and acting like a lunatic. Once he worked out you were acting Calvin, he concluded we must be up to something.'

'Maybe,' I said. 'Although there is another possibility.'

I planted my fingers on the top of my head, as if physically I had to hold my racing thoughts inside. 'Moholy believes in relics. Bear with me. Moholy was expecting Calvin. Calvin hated relics, thought relics were a nonsense, and a waste of time. Perhaps I should have acted *indifference*.'

'Oh God,' Helena's hands went to her mouth. Then she

squatted on her heels, bouncing gently up and down. 'We never thought of that. It's *Calvin* who wasn't a believer. In the role of Calvin, you therefore wouldn't have let the relics have any effect. I'm such a bloody fool.'

'No, *I'm* a fool. I should never have believed I could carry it off.'

I was not chosen, not special. I had no plated destiny out there waiting, nor any of the perception or presence of the truly great. I wrenched at my black cassock, yanking it over my head, badly snagging my ear. God that hurt. I dashed the cassock to the ground, not Calvin, and with no desire to be Calvin. I expected far less of myself.

'I've had enough,' I said, scooping the sports-bag off the floor. My underneath clothes were dark, nondescript, a uniform of defeat. I was not any kind of messiah, in any given sphere of human achievement. 'This whole scene is definitely not me. Whoever this is, I'm putting him back.'

Mr Smith's Back

'In a good country virtues wouldn't be necessary. Everybody
could be quite ordinary, middling, and for all I care, cowards.'

Bertolt Brecht, *Mother Courage*

Even in Geneva's Cimetière des Rois, only a third of the
graves were amateur shrines. More likely than not, our
unnamed bones didn't belong to anyone famous, but instead
to one of Switzerland's majority of Mr and Mrs Smiths,
ordinary men and women who lived their fears and dreams in
private, their weakness and envy, their failure. There was
something dreadful and unforgiving about digging up the
bones of someone unknown.

The bones, even though the plastic sports-bag was now
zipped tight as we crossed the city, had made no discernible
impression. It wasn't John Calvin, or anyone special; it was a
Mr Smith, a Helena Byczynski, a Jay Mason Minor. That
night in the cemetery, drunk as I was and in a fearful hurry,

it would have been easier even for Richard Burton feeling wild and dangerous to pick out a Mr Smith. No pesky sauerkraut jars and candles. And later, no keen-eyed fanatics to seize on the slightest mistake.

The bones in the bag were a nobody, any old Mr or Mrs Smith, and there was a vacancy under the stone of Calvin. I was going to put them back, in broad daylight if I had to, because I was also a Mr Smith, a loyal member of the same family, and no one would blink an eye.

As I walked in anger ever further from the church, clutching the blue sports-bag to my chest, Helena struggled to keep up. She kept telling me not to panic, and that it wasn't the end of the world. We didn't even know what kind of test Moholy was planning for the bone. There was still hope. Which was easy for her to say because the fact of the matter, as far as I was concerned, was this: for women, the discovery of Mrs Smithness had always been less of a disaster. She frowned at that, meaning as a thinker I was inferior in every imaginable way. I assumed she was probably right.

In Geneva, I'd taken hold of my destiny. It hadn't worked out. Or it had, but I was destined to be a nobody. I was Mr Smith, not even Major Smith from *Where Eagles Dare*. I wasn't even convincing as plain John Calvin.

The failure of my Calvin bothered me. Moholy had definitely been looking for some specific reaction to the bones, but not *my* reaction, or not the Calvin reaction. Perhaps I shouldn't have simplified, and insisted instead on Calvin's secret doubts and essential confusion. I'd offered an unfair portrait, not the whole man, and Moholy was consistently more subtle than I'd anticipated.

We stopped at the flat for my digging tools, and there was no particular trick to it, nothing special to record or report. I

238

was no longer convinced that the world had something to tell me, was sending me messages, signals, warnings. Instead, this was the first day of my relinquished life. I was giving up, my nothingness increasingly apparent to me.

In the manner of Mr Smith, whose obscurity is always an injustice, I was very angry. On the way to the cemetery, we had to push past some protesters urgent on mobile phones, all engaged in the identical pursuit of feeling extraordinary. But not everybody could be extraordinary, because who would that leave to be ordinary? They were getting in my way, and I resented their presumption that anything would ever change. Who did they think they were? I knew as well as anybody what was wrong (the weak and innocent suffer, the rich and manipulative flourish, simple), but I wasn't the kind of person who could expect to make a difference.

Consume, stay silent. If they weren't careful, the protesters would destroy the few small pleasures we had. Die. Shopping wasn't much, and television had its faults, but both were better than nothing.

Thankfully, the cemetery was quiet, an annexe of the city separate from today's advance sparring between protesters and police. It was empty, only the small yellow digger on its rubber caterpillar tracks jolting awkwardly left and right, pursuing its endless business.

We cut directly across the grass to Calvin's corner. I threw down the tools and the bag of bones, rolled up my sleeves, and was about to get cracking when Helena pulled me back, yelling something I couldn't hear over the creaking digger scrushing the gravel of a nearby path.

'Wait till the digger's gone!'

'What?'

'Wait!' she said, shouting louder. 'Let me check something!'

She knelt down beside Calvin, and clawed away a few of the white pebbles bordering the grave's edge. She was looking for the join, the seam. She wanted to satisfy herself that I'd at least been man enough to make an actual attempt on John Calvin. She dabbed her fingers along the bottom edge of his recumbent stone.

'A-ha,' she held up the pad of her index finger, for both of us to see. It was now an undercoat colour, like paint on a battleship. 'You actually did it.'

'Of course I did.'

'What? You'll have to speak up!'

The digger had jerked right then left. We both turned to see where it was headed, and watched it rattle and shudder directly towards us. It stopped at the edge of the path closest to Calvin, its poised bucket only metres away, raised and shaking. The driver was wearing ear-protectors attached to an orange hard hat, and dark glasses. He had a black fleece zipped to his chin. There was something familiar about him.

It was Rifka. She hooked her sunglasses on to the end of her nose, and looked out over the top. Then she cut the engine, flipped off the hard hat, and jumped down from the cab. Her glasses fell off, but she caught them as they fell, and slipped them into her fleece.

'People.'

'What are you doing here?'

She greeted us both with a smile, as if nothing could be more ordinary than the three of us here, like this. She hadn't changed. There was something amused in her eyes, but her natural authority now seemed more pronounced, unmissable.

'If you could both just stand aside for a moment, I'm about to dig for Calvin.'

'Good one,' I said, but even though Rifka was still smiling, and standing there relaxed and not aggressive in any way, I knew she wasn't joking.

'Moholy's decision. About ten minutes after we left the church. You made him all twitchy.'

'We noticed.'

'And now this. He wants Calvin, the real Calvin, and quickly. Even though a mechanical excavator isn't normally our style.'

'You could have refused.'

'Moholy isn't always a very nice man. If he was, he wouldn't always get what he wants.'

Rifka unzipped her fleece and reached into the top pocket of her shirt, bringing out her pills. She shook some out into her cupped hand, and slapped them into her mouth. She chewed before swallowing.

'Those pills,' I said. 'Rifka, what are those pills?'

'They thin the blood. Now. I'd like to stay and chat, but Moholy's in a hurry. I don't want to be rude, but I ought to be getting on.'

'You can't,' Helena said. 'Not with the digger. What about discretion?'

'He doesn't care any more. It's suddenly more important than that.'

'Someone might come.'

'Who? The police are busy with protesters. And in cemeteries mechanical diggers work every day of the week, except Sundays.'

'What about *Calvin*?'

'John? He wouldn't have minded. He never wanted to be buried here in the first place.'

'We know that,' Helena said. 'That's not what I mean. You can't dig him up because we've got him here in this bag.

Moholy obviously wasn't happy. So we were planning to put him back. However, if you really want Calvin that badly, you can just have him. Give her the bag, Jay.'

It was a nice try, and more evidence of the Helena who never surrendered, but it didn't work. I held out the bag, but Rifka barely glanced at it.

'Well, you're right about one thing,' she said. 'Moholy definitely wasn't happy. After the church he went straight to the University lab. There's a technician there who boosts his salary by carrying out Carbon-14 tests for cautious antiquities dealers. He'll have preliminary results by tea-time.'

'So why are you here?'

'Moholy knows it isn't Calvin. And let's not be childish here. It isn't, is it? So then Moholy decided if he wanted something doing, he'd better do it himself.'

'Or through you. Why you, Rifka? Why do you always do what he says?'

I was still thinking about the pills in her top pocket, beginning to understand why I'd never worked her out. She could be anybody. 'You do this by choice, don't you? You're not scared in the least. If it's not the money, and you're not frightened of what he might do to you, then what's really in those pills? Who *are* you?'

'I'm one of God's many children. Who just happens to have an aversion to John Calvin. Always disliked him, from the day he arrived in Geneva. He had his chance to make this city astonishing, but John could be very wrong-headed, especially about relics. We both know how wrong he was about relics, don't we, Jay? He should have known better, especially at the beginning, and I don't feel any particular sympathy for the sour-faced kill-joy he let himself become. Now, if you'll excuse me.'

242

'Wait,' I said, though with no real idea of how to stop her as she vaulted back up into the digger's cab. She paused, her fingers already closed on the ignition key. 'How did you get the keys to that thing?'

'I asked the driver.'

'And he just handed them over?'

'I asked him nicely.'

'And where did you learn to operate heavy machinery?'

'I don't know. I just seem to get the hang of things.'

She fired up the engine, which coughed a crab of black smoke from the upright exhaust. She put her dark glasses back on, and the hard hat, settling the ear protectors. Then she bumped the digger off the path and on to the grass, its scratched bucket nodding at the end of its jointed hydraulic arm. We stepped back, looking left and right, sure that someone would come. The digger lurched and twitched to within feet of Calvin's stone, sliding one final turn on the grass to bring the clawed bucket directly above it, poised and trembling.

I shouted up at Rifka that the other method was better, there was no need for this, but she couldn't hear a thing above the mechanical racket. I was still shouting as Helena tugged me by the elbow, the two of us backing away between François Simon and a couple of nobodies, back past the self-important vault of Sir Humphry Davy.

The steel bucket of the mechanical digger pitched down on to Calvin's stone, bouncing the front curve of the caterpillar tracks off the grass. It lifted, and pitched again, and this time the stone cracked. At the third attempt, the stone smashed, and the bucket broke clean through. This was no place for Mr Smith. Someone would come, and there'd be trouble. Mr Smith would get the blame. Let Rifka sort it out, if she was so special.

We turned and jogged away, and round the first corner we heard another bang, and then another. Then we collided with a march against third-world debt, which carried us back towards the cemetery, before veering sharply away towards the city. As ordinary, law-abiding citizens, quite conformist and therefore non-believers in God, we wondered where on earth we could look for refuge, or any kind of sanctuary.

Mr Smith had no cathedrals, no palaces, no castles with invincible hidden keeps. Frequently, he was barged off the pavements. The public places still open to him, still his, were the library and the park. In Geneva, the libraries and parks would be closed until this particular movement for popular reform had passed on by. We couldn't go back to the church. Moholy would find us there, and ordinary people no longer found sanctuary in church. They went shopping. They consumed, they were silent, they died.

We put our heads round the red door of a Pizza Hut, but so much plastic deadened our spirits like it did the bones. It becalmed and smothered us. The more forceful of our Mr Smith emotions were embarrassed to show themselves, and hunkered down.

The only sanctuary open to us, when everything else failed, was each other. I suddenly loved Helena very much. We kept moving, arm in arm, often glancing behind as I conceded that I'd never now amount to a man in any way remarkable. Surrounded by banks, I felt encouraged to stop, to save, to bank whatever adventures I'd already had and return gratefully, humbly, as curate to Morton in the Marsh, where in the out-of-town supermarket without my collar not one of the Christmas regulars would quite be able to place me.

We eventually came up short against the United Nations

anti-protester perimeter. It was a chain-link fence two metres high which closed off the Palace of Nations and all its public parkland, including the lakeside frontage, in case anti-capitalist anarchists planned to attack by boat. Only policemen and diplomats were allowed inside the fence, and also journalists, to ensure their safety, even though the sense of being safe was never truly what was going on. That wasn't what was truthfully happening to Mr Smith, which was never accurately reported.

On the safe side of the fence there were soldiers carrying machine-guns which at a thousand yards could kill 250 people in a minute. We were about two feet away. A national serviceman shouted at us, and waved us off, because any unauthorised approach to the fencing was classified as a provocative act.

Keep your head down. Consume, stay silent, die. It didn't seem such a bad strategy.

On the opposite side of the road was the grandly stepped entrance to the Museum of Human Atrocity. It remained open to the public, all year round, all week long, except Tuesdays. It was usually empty. Even rebranded, as the Red Cross International Museum, it had never sounded like a fun attraction for all the family.

The attendants were so pleased to see us they forgot to check our zipped blue bag for bombs. They ushered us straight in, and down some metal stairs to a large air-conditioned room divided into several separate boxes, each offering a full audio-visual experience of flood, earthquake, famine.

It was always the ordinary people who suffered.

There was a life-size reproduction of a concrete cell, three metres by two, which somewhere in Liberia had once

245

contained seventeen political prisoners. The floor was printed with seventeen pairs of different-coloured footprints, making it more footprint than floor, the crowd of missing bodies echoing to soundscape recreations of tortures, garrottes, mutilations.

It was a permanent exhibition of bad luck. Along the outside walls, a simple line at eye-level traced the dates of wars and natural disasters that had killed at least 100,000 Mr Smiths: 100,000 was the number needed to qualify for memorial. At first, the line was only occasionally interrupted, cut with lethal volcanoes and plagues. In the modern era, disasters mobbed year after year, the line of the times heavily stacked with man against man, and many more than 100,000 dead.

In the next room there was a cinema screen, a row of metal benches and, in floor-to-ceiling perspex blocks, the original Geneva Convention catalogues of five million World War One prisoners. The screen was showing a looped sequence of stills from the Battle of Solferino, in 1859, paying special attention to amputation before the age of anaesthetic. And also, fortunately, before the age of colour.

Helena went to fetch coffee from a vending machine she'd spotted in the corridor. I sat on a middle bench facing the catalogues, my back to the screen, but reflected in the perspex I saw the stills become moving pictures, war becoming mobile in the spoked iron wheels of artillery. There was film of black and white explosions, though also, again fortunately, before the age of sound.

'You were right,' Helena said, handing me a doubled-up plastic cup. She blew across the top of her own and sat opposite me, facing the screen. 'Moholy must be very angry. Why did we never think he'd test them?'

'I even prepared him for it,' I said, remembering the time I'd suggested his clients couldn't tell the difference between one bone and another. God. No wonder he was being careful. He must have been expecting me to test out my theory, but on him. 'He was already suspicious when he arrived at the church. He was always on his guard.'

'There's something I still don't understand,' Helena said. 'He hasn't had the results of the carbon tests. But he sent Rifka anyway straight to the cemetery.'

'Makes sense. If our bones weren't Calvin, then Calvin still had to be where he'd always been, under the ground. He assumed we'd never even tried.'

'Okay, so our bones weren't Calvin, let's face it. But before the test results, how could he be so *sure*?'

'I wish I knew,' I said. 'My Calvin impersonation might have been limited, I admit that. But it wasn't completely useless.'

'Rifka in the digger was fairly extreme,' Helena said thoughtfully, sipping the top off her coffee. 'What's he going to be like when he finds out Calvin isn't there?'

We both looked bleakly at each other, our paper cups in both hands. Then Helena glanced over my shoulder at the Imperial Japanese in full military assault on China. At least here we were safe.

'I should never have got involved in the first place,' I said. 'Utter lunacy.'

'Don't be too hard on yourself. It was a very promising idea.'

'Yes. But for a different type of person.'

Someone special and singular, with virtues and qualities I could only ever approximate. I couldn't do what distinguished people did because I wasn't distinguished, and the

247

characteristics which made great men great overwhelmed a man of ordinary merit, like me, a Mr Mason Smith.

I suddenly felt embarrassed to be thirty-four, an under-employed deacon and self-imposed exile. I was embarrassed by my everyman fears and ambitions, which after thirty-four years had made me nothing but a beacon of embarrassment, the English disease and enemy of all achievement. In retreat, as Mr Smith, I discovered a resilient nostalgia for Anglican safety and reticence. If we escaped this situation unscathed, I swore to devote the rest of my professional life to summer fêtes and donkey sanctuaries, and other fail-safe institutions the God of England was known to favour. I'd lose myself in a forgotten parish in the dales. It would be something, and more than most people: the *Reverend* Smith.

An American Marine Mr Smith attacked a bunker of German Wehrmacht Mr Smiths with a flame-thrower. We all flinched.

We needed some kind of miracle, and I lifted the bag on to the bench beside me, pulling open the broad-gauge zip. Relics inspired miracles; it was a fact of religious history. I therefore reached into the bag for a hollow fragment of bone, a vertebra about the size of a boy-scout's toggle. It had a hole in the middle for the vital spinal fluid, and from almost every perspective it could be turned and blurred to make a face. It wasn't a charm: I was too knowing for that. But I closed my fingers on it anyway. However scattered, however small, the grace of relics remained intact.

'Me too,' Helena said, holding out her hand. I gave her the clavicle, and it was light, so light, such a lightweight angle of bone. She pressed it against her forehead.

Nothing.

We swapped bones, but no special attributes rubbed off,

248

nor any evidence of that wistful odour of sanctity which lifted the lowest spirits. Quite the opposite. We felt disappointed, drained, ordinary. Embarrassed to be in possession of a bag of bones with no obvious qualities.

Which didn't necessarily mean that relics had no power.

Just that the bones of a Mr Smith had this particular influence. I asked Helena if she felt in any way changed.

'I feel a bit silly.'

'A bit sheepish?'

'Exactly.'

At the mercy of events, passive, buffeted, buildings on the screen crumbled for no apparent reason around Iraqi and Afghan Smiths. We hunched our shoulders, sipped at our drinks, and withdrew into a smaller version of the people we wanted to be. Our ingrained sense of our own Smithness would not go away, no matter how hard we tried, no matter what we did. We were ordinary people, with the standard Smith-issue bones.

We allowed ourselves to become dispirited, and the result of this disarmament was a cynical bloom of egalitarianism: everyone was the same, the great and the good buried beneath the earth the same as we Mr Smiths. Those who tried to stand out were guilty, along with pride and arrogance, of hypocrisy. They knew they were no different from us, because we all ended up alike. Bones. All the same bones.

'Even special people aren't very special,' Helena said, persuading me it was so. 'Whenever they die, a neighbour or close friend can always be found to say that they were just like everyone else.'

'They kept themselves to themselves,' I said, nodding in agreement, looking at Helena over the rim of my cup. 'He was just so *ordinary*.'

'So down-to-earth. She used to work on her roses, like the rest of us. She was a person like any other. Not at all a star.'

I pictured Noël Coward, of Switzerland, in the last years, meeting David Niven, of Switzerland, in the last years. This was in the show-tent at the Circus Knie, at the height of its winter season in Geneva. They meet, heavily overcoated, in seats two or three rows back, both men at an advanced age and leaning forward on sticks, wattled chins on the backs of hands, gummily chewing at the best plastic teeth that millionaires can buy.

'How are you, Noël?'

'How are *you*, David?'

'It's my legs, Noëllie, my legs.'

'It's my hip, Davie, my hip.'

And Mr Smith from the row behind, unnoticed until now, pushes his unmemorable head between theirs, and he says, because it's the same for everybody, 'Personally I get it from my back. Oh, my back, my back.'

Finishing her coffee, Helena made nasty observations about people who thought they were special. And I couldn't agree more. Pretentious. Idiots. We rediscovered the small, hard, surviving mind of Mr and Mrs Smith.

Thomas à Becket, lying brainless on uneven flagstones in his own blood, was found to be wearing a hair-shirt alive with worms and wingless insects. They were squirming and twisting towards his injuries, the surviving monks said, like ravenous black vermin.

'Right,' I said. 'And for what? Look at the hopelessness of the Anglican Church today.'

Richard Burton crawling on all fours to the lifts at the Dorchester, howling and retching up his guts. How special was that? The carpets in his yacht the *Kalizma* were changed every ninety days, humming with the stain and stink of Taylor's yapping lapdogs, the most beautiful woman in the world an ever-expanding harridan and scold.

Even Audrey Hepburn, too saintly to be raised from the dead, was a fake, a total phoney. She was born, the most famously English of actresses, as Edda van Heemstra Hepburn-Ruston, and during her early days as a dancer in London the virgin princess abandoned an unplanned baby. The discarded mite was raised secretly in middle America, by a fellow trouper with no professional future. Not after that, anyway. Hepburn constantly checked and regulated this parallel but unlived life. She made sure it never interfered in any way with her fabulous career in the movies.

'Thanks,' Helena said.

'Not a problem.'

As an ordinary man, believing only in ordinary men, I had greater need of a God. Mr Smith needed a God, desperately, more desperately than other men. I sat forward and fingered my warm skull, the bones of my eye-sockets, and prayed for God to exist, if that was feasible. And if he did exist, for him not to be ridiculous, or embittered. As usual, whenever I tried to pray, the voice of ambition taunted me that I'd once wanted to be someone special. That I'd never prayed for anything else, and this was still what I was praying for now. If there was a God, somewhere up or down, it reflected well on His creation. It reflected well on me, because I was one of His. It made me special, and, if not that, then whatever else was worth believing?

Part of the excitement and incentive for my contact with relics was the feeling that it made me distinct. I'd just wanted to say, in the history of everything, I AM HERE. There was no harm in trying.

In the history of English literature, in temporary possession of the actual bones of the real James Joyce, I'd have staked my place on the map. This is the place, *my* place, next to the relics of Joyce. Picking over the remains of John Calvin, arranging him however I pleased, I was saying I AM HERE, on the still-changing chart of the Protestant Reformation. This was *the* John Calvin, stern and dressed in black, who'd caused so much of the trouble. I am here, in the History of the World, in the flesh, planting my flag among the great and the dead, who previously seemed so distant.

And if not Calvin, then here I am, in the history of the English saints, of electro-chemistry, of womanising and drinking, of psychoanalysis. I AM HERE. This is the place. I took some part.

The bones of Mr Smith were a nothing place, in central middle of nowhere, flying no flags. It was where we'd always belonged, because as history repeated itself at the Battle of Solferino (40,000 Mr Smiths, wounded and suffering and all unnumbed), neither of us was feeling very singular, nor very brave. We knew what was coming, what was always coming, and we and our unborn baby could not withstand events, flame-throwers and tortures and garrottes. All we could hope for was luck, and an instinct that it was better to bend than to break. Heroes were charlatans, and heroic gestures offensive to those of us who'd learnt to bend.

Neither of us aspired to invading China. We just wanted to go home, our love the only way we'd ever be special. We'd go back to the flat, pack up and travel to somewhere forgetful, wherever it was that everyone else went, never to be heard from again. Accepting defeat, there'd be no more pushing ourselves forward, insisting I Am Here. We'd be there, anywhere, it didn't matter where. Scared of the dark, we were also scared of the light.

In the flat, I'd leave a note for Moholy saying sorry. I'd contact Lambeth Palace, to regret my ordination, because a man like me had no obvious future in the Church. I was not a reverend but a Mr, through and through, and nothing more ambitious than that. I'd stop looking for spiritual answers, and Helena and I would marry. In the photographs we'd bride and groom, both going nowhere, but at least going there together. We'd set up a quiet little business, covering costs by supplying a steady demand among the young in love for the growing cult of love-lobes. Young lovers would exchange their earlobes as evidence of undying devotion. There was nothing gruesome about it: these were gifts freely offered between consenting adults. Earlobes had no known physical function, no operative value. Under anaesthetic, the removal of an earlobe, hygienically stitched, would cause only momentary discomfort, comparable to a piercing, or a tattoo. We'd provide a full service in our shop with parlour, though nobody would be served while under the influence.

The basic cut-and-stitch business would be supplemented with a mail-order line of lobe-lockets, in a choice of precious metals, some with small glass windows. Each exclusive locket-design would be offered as a matching pair, with a high-carat chain of adjustable length to wear the earlobe of the loved one as close as possible to the heart. We might invent a formal ritual of exchange, and a money-spinning little book of earlobe dos (*wear this locket always, as evidence of the sincerity of your love*) and don'ts (*try this at home*). With a little luck, and the absence of world events, we'd live anonymously ever after in the flat above the shop.

And like all Mr Smiths in the English tradition, we'd try to look on the bright side. Mustn't grumble.

That was it, the future for the family Smith, with our children the little Smiths an acceptable excuse for all those things we never did.

Helena moved across from her metal bench to mine, and squeezed my shoulder. Her eyes weren't violet, they were blue. 'You're not worried?'

'No more than usual.'

'I mean that Moholy will catch up with us.'

I thought about it, then shook my head. It seemed presumptuous to think that Moholy would make the effort. It was too extreme, and not the kind of thing which happened to ordinary people, like us. We wouldn't be worth it.

I locked the door of the flat from the inside, then went back to check it was locked. I threw the keys to Helena as I passed the sitting-room. I stood still, then took two steps back. Rifka was in the armchair, hands in pockets, fleece zipped to her chin. She shrugged. Then she winked. Moholy came out of the bedroom. He smelled of drink.

'Come in,' Moholy said, 'come on in.'

He beckoned us into the sitting-room, and kicked Rifka's feet. Rifka stood up. Moholy took over the chair, sitting forward with fingers steepled, trembling, his neat and compact body highly strung. 'Been anywhere nice?'

Rifka still had mud from the cemetery on her jeans. She'd taken off her trainers, which was thoughtful of her. But she hadn't left them by the door, to warn us, which wasn't. They were underneath the window. She went into the kitchen in her socks, and noisily searched through the cupboards. Moholy held up his hands.

'No complaints, please,' he said. 'None of this is yours. You have nothing. You *are* nothing. Sit on the floor. On the floor, I think I said. That's right, side by side, facing this way. Thank you. To be honest, I'm not expecting a great deal of trouble.'

'We don't want to cause any,' I agreed.

'Frightened?'

'Of course we are,' Helena said. 'Who wouldn't be?'

'Sit down. You *are* frightened, aren't you?'

'Jesus,' she said, 'is it really that surprising?'

Moholy thought about it, working a little muscle in his jaw. 'Yes, actually it is. I think you know why I'm here.'

Since leaving All Saints earlier that day, and after sending Rifka to the cemetery, Moholy had been waiting with some impatience to hear from his man at the lab.

'I now have the results,' he said.

'I think I can explain.'

'It's not Calvin. Conclusively not. The initial test-forecast shows someone nearly contemporary. Male. No distinguishing bone characteristics. A little overweight, possibly. Otherwise healthy.'

'Not that healthy,' Helena pointed out.

'Where's my John Calvin?'

Moholy had already gone through the flat, and at the back of the closet he'd found an almost complete Richard Burton. After performing his own personal tests, which included a couple of slugs of sherry from the kitchen, he knew that these bones were not those he most badly wanted.

I held the blue sports-bag up in front of me, like an apology. 'These are the only bones we have. Honestly. And you've already had them tested. You know these bones aren't Calvin.'

'They're not, no,' Moholy said, coming over and snatching the bag away from me. With some distaste, he held it out at arm's length, and then dropped it. It landed and stuck. 'These are nobody. Tell me where you've hidden John Calvin.'

'Ask Rifka,' Helena said. 'She was in the cemetery, not us.'

After smashing Calvin's 500-year-old recumbent stone, Rifka had used the digger to haul out the earth, deeper and deeper. All that came out was earth.

'Imagine my surprise when she phoned to tell me,' Moholy said, kicking the sports-bag hard against the wall. I flinched, but it was bones, not a corpse.

'You offered me bones, and said they were Calvin. They weren't. Yet Calvin wasn't in his grave. It looks bad, I think you'll agree. I tell Rifka that can't be right, and ask her to check again. A little later, she rings me back saying she's found paste round the seam of Calvin's vault. Recent paste, which isn't even dry. Someone has already been there, someone very skilful and discreet, as if they'd already practised on someone else. I pay a visit to my own flat, and find Richard Burton. I realise someone's been practising, without my knowledge. I'm disappointed in you, James. I was quite prepared, it turns out wrongly, to trust a man of the cloth. Now, I want John Calvin, wherever you may have hidden him. Somehow, and to be honest I don't know how, you've understood his true value, which inspired your foolhardy attempt to deceive me with inferior bones. As if I wouldn't be able to tell the difference.'

'We're just ordinary people,' I said. 'We're in a long way over our heads.'

'It's not what you think,' Helena added. 'Pick another body. Any body. We've got Richard Burton. We can get you someone else.'

'I don't want anyone else. I want John Calvin.'

'He wasn't there,' I said. 'He never wanted to be buried in Geneva, and his followers must have obeyed him. They secretly buried him somewhere else.'

'Don't be obtuse. That's a fanciful story which nobody even half intelligent has ever believed. Everyone wants to be remembered.'

'Not John Calvin.'

'Even John Calvin. I want his bones. And you must have worked out why. Otherwise you wouldn't be trying so hard to steal him away from me.'

'Honestly,' Helena said. 'We know nothing. Why is John Calvin so suddenly exceptional?'

Moholy looked at us both in turn, his sharp fingers pressing hard between his furrowed eyebrows.

'He isn't,' Moholy eventually said, exhaling, relaxing his shoulders, shaking out his hands. 'And you know that. And I know you know, because you've already seen inside his grave. I want the skeleton you found buried under John Calvin's stone. I want the bones of Jesus Christ, the man.'

The bones of Jesus are the great lost relics of history. They are the missing paragon of all other relics, and a model of the unique objective which shapes a collector's dreams, dreaming of his own pre-eminence among collectors. They are the Secret, the Grail, the Philosopher's Stone. Or would be, if they existed.

On the third day, Jesus rose again in accordance with the Scriptures; he ascended into heaven and is seated at the right hand of the Father.

If this is so, then it follows as an article of faith that he left nothing behind, except perhaps those dubious secondary relics religiously treasured for more than two millennia. If he didn't ascend into heaven, if he was not the son of God but in fact another Mr Smith, one more among the rest of us, then he must have left behind his bones.

'I doubt,' Moholy said, 'if in today's changed world, to large numbers of people, a disproof of the ascension would come as a vast surprise.'

The past could change. Virgin birth and resurrection were increasingly seen as symbolic events, even by Christian theologians. Nobody was special. Nobody went straight to heaven. Moholy and other professional collectors had keenly followed the debate, and then thought it through: if Jesus didn't ascend, son of God or not, there were other qualities he might also share with the mortal Mr Smith. His earthly flesh would rot, his bones would stubbornly endure.

Where then were the bones of Jesus Christ?

For 2000 years until now, but especially during the Middle Ages, the last great heyday of relics, this question would have been a blatant heresy, punishable by drowning, burning, hanging and drawing and quartering. Inevitably, in such inauspicious days for questions, the bones of Jesus became a secret too perilous to tell.

'This was always my objective,' Moholy said. 'Nothing else but this. All I ever wanted, even as a boy in the churches of Budapest, was to have and to hold the bones of Jesus.'

'Of course,' Helena said, nodding. 'You could name your price.'

'Please. I'm not a philistine.'

'But I'm right, aren't I?' she pressed him. 'They'd be the most valuable of all relics, wouldn't they?'

'You limited little person. They'd have the most *power*.'

The historical Jesus went missing in Jerusalem on the day

of his execution. That was the place and time at which ambitious collectors therefore began their quest. The event itself was diligently recorded by Josephus, the Jewish historian, and also by Tacitus, a Roman, and between them they provide enough contemporary evidence for even the most sceptical to accept an actual crucifixion of a real Jesus, with those vague yet familiar characteristics, in about the right place at about the right time.

It's immediately after the crucifixion that details become scarce.

After Jesus died on the cross, he may have been buried. The reality for every other crucified Mr Smith, in Palestine in about AD 30, was a ritual humbling to a status so low that all rights to dignified burial were refused. Soldiers stood guard until Mr Smith died on the cross, then abandoned him for a short time to the crows. As a penultimate indignity, and the final discharge of their responsibilities, the soldiers then hauled Mr Smith down and dumped his corpse in a trench. At night-fall, the dogs came.

By Easter Sunday, after running away on the Friday, those who cared about Jesus wouldn't have known where to find him. Those who knew, the soldiers, couldn't care less.

'So even if Jesus didn't ascend into heaven,' Helena protested, 'his bones were lost at the start. What's the point of looking for them now?'

'Because maybe Jesus didn't die on the cross.'

If a routine crucifixion was going too slowly, the Romans would break Mr Smith's legs, then cut him down and bury him alive.

'It's not *my* idea,' Moholy said, defensively spreading his hands. 'It says so in the Bible. Now have a look at this.'

He fetched the bag of bones from the corner where he'd

kicked it. He unzipped the bag and upended it, clattering the body of bones to the hard wooden floor. The smaller ones scattered like buttons. Moholy picked out the long thigh bones, then the bones of the lower leg Helena had used for the I-Ching. 'Look,' he said. 'Unbroken. No evidence of fracture. I thought you might have broken them yourselves, to make me believe it was Jesus.'

Actually, I'd wanted him to believe it was Calvin, which at least explained why my Calvin impersonation, which both Helena and I thought rather accomplished, hadn't convinced him. Moholy had been expecting me to do Jesus, however that was done.

'Then I realised you'd be cleverer than that,' Moholy said. 'You'd have known I'd already worked out that Jesus didn't need his legs broken.'

'And why was that?'

'Because he was poisoned.'

The vinegar on the sponge. And when his side was stabbed to check he was dead, blood flowed. The Roman soldiers were ignorant, thinking Jesus must be dead because he didn't flinch.

'The Jews were smarter than the Romans,' Rifka said, coming back from the kitchen. Like Helena and me, maybe out of solidarity, she sat on the floor, but out of the way and under the window, next to her muddy shoes. 'The Jews knew that if Jesus was dead, there wouldn't have been any bleeding.'

He was hauled down from the cross, hands in tatters and head lolling, buried alive in the famous tomb with the stone sealing its entrance. On the third day, he was gone. Either he'd risen from the dead, or at some stage during a three-day period, which gave ample time for planning and preparation, he'd been moved in secret by Simon Magus and others among the disciples. Hidden away in a nearby cave, Jesus was then fed a purgative of up to one hundred pounds of myrrh and aloe.

'It's all there,' Moholy said. 'In the Bible.'

'Quite a mouthful,' Rifka said dryly. 'That's lots of aloe. I wouldn't recommend it.'

Jesus was nursed, nourished, slowly brought back to life.

The sightings of the resurrected Jesus, as recorded in the Gospels and Acts of the Apostles, insisted on his physical reality, eating and drinking. His literal survival was further supported by the registered birth of his two little sons.

'And one daughter,' Rifka added. 'Sweet little Phoebe, who later married Paul, Paul of the road to Damascus, letter-writing Paul.'

There was also the less joyful record of his divorce from Mary Magdalene, and his subsequent remarriage. 'To Lydia,' Rifka said helpfully, 'a female bishop from Philippi. Quieter than Mary. Less to report.'

All of which suggested a type of survival. An obscure and messy survival, silently endured, largely unknown. A standard Mr Smith existence, in which the virgin birth was explainable. The miracles. The Resurrection. All of it could be explained away. Jesus did not die on the cross. He was married and middle-aged with children, he was divorced and old and crippled. There were no special people marked out by the heavens for greatness, not even Jesus the son of God.

The last time Jesus was seen in public, as recorded in Corinthians, he came as an apparition to Paul. Paul was in Rome at the time, and that would have been in AD 64, when Jesus was feeling his age.

'So he died in Rome,' I suggested, beginning to see the

connections Moholy was trying to make. And considering I was effectively his captive, with a folk memory of the fate of the Iraqi antiquities dealer, I was prepared to suspend some if not all of my disbelief. 'In Rome the relic trade would already have been active, and that's why his bones could well have survived.'

'No, no, no. It's never as simple as that. You'd know as much if you'd taken an interest for as long as I have.'

'First he has to get to Rome,' Helena said. 'How did he do that?'

'Easy. With Peter and John of Zebedee, hidden below decks in the ship carrying their Christian mission from Jerusalem to Patmos. After a brief stay in Philippi, they were joined by Paul at Corinth, and Paul led them on to Ephesus before a final journey to Rome the capital of the world, the new Jerusalem.'

'Hold on a minute,' Helena said, 'if he was alive, why didn't he just come out into the open and reveal himself, as the second coming everyone wanted?'

'Because Paul was a political realist. He kept postponing the second coming. The legend of the Ascension was spreading, and the more it took hold, the less Jesus felt able to deal with the pressure of being Jesus. And then suddenly it was too late.'

In July of AD 64, the year of the final recorded sighting of Jesus, Rome burned. The Emperor Nero, accused of fiddling, needed a scapegoat. He decided (um, eenie, meenie, minie, mo) on the Christians. The leaders Peter and Paul were hunted down and murdered, martyred. Miraculously, items of their clothing and various bones were immediately saved as relics, despite the testimony of Tacitus who describes Christians at that time being strapped into the skins of wild beasts, and torn to nothing by dogs. Others were crucified, and set alight at dusk to save fuel on street-lamps for the benighted citizens of Rome.

'It was terrible,' Rifka said. 'Just terrible.'

'But if Jesus escaped being eaten by dogs,' Moholy went on, 'and he wasn't crucified a second time and used as a street-lamp, there's no reason to think that some astute Christian survivor wouldn't have cherished that tired old man, his bones dwindled by nothing more violent than regret and old age. I've spent many years working on what happened next, and I can tell you as a fact, without the aid of carbon-dating, that the bones of Jesus did not end up in your tacky blue sports-bag. Look.'

He picked up a bone from the floor, any bone, but long enough to hold between his fists. Flexing it over his knee, he silently counted to three, then abruptly snapped it in half. He then ground one of the jagged ends into the other, setting our teeth on edge. He stamped on other bones, any bones, then stood on top of others, rocking backwards and forwards. An elbow cracked, and then a vertebra. Moholy was too heavy a burden for Mr Smith's back, and a popped shard of bone scooted beneath the chair.

'See? I can be so cruel. The bones of Jesus would be just like these ones, to look at. But they'd also have the effect of making me a better person than I am. And I can tell you, I'm not feeling *good*. The relics of Jesus are out there, and those are the bones I want.'

'And you're sure they're out there?' Helena was braver than I was. Always had been. 'Millions of people would say they weren't.'

'Do you believe in the Resurrection?'

'I don't know.'

'Do you believe that Jesus was sucked up into heaven? Do

you? Leaving behind only his vials of blood and his milk teeth and the Holy Navel and the Holy Prepuce. Is that what you believe? The *carne vera sancta*. Is that really all that's left to us?'

After Rome, as the Church began to establish itself around stories of resurrection and ascension, the Jesus bones needed to be hidden. Perhaps, at the beginning, no one thought it would last for long. It was only a temporary measure, until sense prevailed. But, every year, the bones of Jesus became a greater heresy and danger, and the organised Church was as eager to find them as anyone. The good men protecting Jesus therefore had to devise increasingly angular and intricate codes, which when deciphered revealed the various secret resting places of these most holy of relics. Many an occult text is in fact a narrative and map of the secret travels of Jesus.

'Other people know more about this first stage than I do,' Moholy said. 'But it lasted well into the Middle Ages. My own detailed interest is in the period when the story starts all over, in 1538, right here in Geneva.'

Several years into his private collection of relics, not long after the acquisition of Isaac Newton's treasured cranium, Joseph Moholy experienced a moment of outright revelation. For some time, he'd been aware of the observable influence of relics. Thinking logically, he made a conjecture that the bones of Jesus should therefore have left a trace of their influence in history, in the few places in the world at any one time where people were acting well. Why in one place and not another? Because certain people, in certain places, had briefly been swayed by the bones of Jesus.

Moholy tracked the sixth-century emergence of the prophet Muhammad, and the moral improvement which spread back to Europe in defiance of its hateful crusades. He lost the trail in the dark of the Dark Ages, but found it again in the open improbability of the Italian Renaissance. Quickly followed by the robust improvements of the Reformation. And then: nothing. The Enlightenment had been a step backwards, justifying industrialisation, industrialising war. It was not a tendency full of love, full of Jesus.

Since the Reformation, there had been no great movement for goodness, only isolated instances of resistance to what we accepted as our natural depravity. These were small steps, which often faltered. In the last hundred years, all we'd managed were feeble global attempts at living well, like the United Nations and the World Council of Churches, most of them based in Geneva. It was like a bulb flickering, almost but never quite shedding light.

I thought back to my first impressions of Geneva, the world's graveyard of good intentions.

'This is where the trail went cold,' Moholy said, 'with John Calvin in Geneva in the 1540s. There is no doubt in my mind,' he went on, 'considering the authority and detail of his early teaching, that John Calvin had come into possession of the bones of Christ.'

The single most important Protestant reform was Calvin's insistence that everyone had a personal relationship with God. Just like Jesus. The idea seemed to have come from nowhere. It was certainly a shock to the Catholic hierarchy. Calvin persevered. He opened the city-gates of Geneva to refugees from all across Europe. He fed the poor. He arranged for the healing of the sick.

At that time, as a capital of dissent, Geneva attracted all Europe's dissidents and heretics: Gnostics, Hermeticists, Jansenists. Full of hope, in the fever of reform, one of these

265

seemingly marginal groups had decided that at last the time was right, after 1500 years, to make public the primary relics of Jesus. It was the resurrection of the body, the second coming, though not in the way the faithful were expecting.

'In that case,' Helena asked, 'why did Calvin write his pamphlet against relics, making them into objects of ridicule?'

'John Calvin was a very brave man,' Moholy said. 'Very brave. But it was too hard, even for him.'

The bones made him the extraordinary man he was. In less than ten years a minor French cleric, by nature scholarly and withdrawn, had created a miracle city of God. He was a foreigner, and not even properly ordained. It was an achievement so unlikely that some people, both friends and enemies, suspected supernatural assistance. They were right. Calvin had the bones.

He found it exhausting, a daily struggle, all that power and the constant obligation to be good. Despite his miracle recovery from many illnesses, being Jesus wasn't all that easy, or comfortable. Far easier to hide the bones away, take the credit for reform, and start lending money at interest. At heart, John Calvin was also Mr Smith. He crumbled under the pressure of being different, special, and eventually, resentful of the overwhelming influence of Jesus, he attacked all relics to hide the frustrating truth that none of his success was his, his destiny not his, that alone without help he was nothing.

'It worked out better than he could ever have hoped,' Rifka said, apparently as familiar with the story as Moholy. 'Calvin's spiteful posturing against relics meant that for a long time Geneva was the last place on earth anyone would have looked for Jesus.'

Calvin and his immediate Swiss circle were the new guardians of the secret. The influence of Jesus was irrepressible and compelling, but still they hid him away. They were frightened of the possibilities, of power to the people, and what all of us might one day become, every Mr Smith a Jesus.

'Hold on a minute,' Helena said. 'If they're so powerful, and Calvin hid them in Geneva, wouldn't the city itself have seen some benefit, however faintly?'

'Quite right. There'd be a trace, like radioactivity, a low hum of goodness beneath the surface. How about this: since 1538, Switzerland hasn't been involved in a single war. Think about that. This tiny medallion of land has survived untouched for half a millennium between the most rapacious nation-states in history. Meanwhile, Jean-Jacques Rousseau was born in Geneva, of all places, but ridiculed for believing that men were naturally good. Later, the Red Cross was founded, to grow and flourish, soon followed by the United Nations. None of this is coincidence. My parents were good Hungarian people expelled from Budapest with nothing. Homeless and hungry, their immediate instinct was to aim for Switzerland. Jesus is here. The whole world knows it. That's why nations come to Geneva seeking peace. Think about it.'

'Amazing,' Helena said. For some time, we'd both been following Moholy without blinking, a captive audience as he paced back and forth, explaining the world and everything in it.

'I am *this* close,' he said, turning side on, holding out his finger and thumb with a space in between about as narrow as a toe-bone. 'And you two are the only remaining obstacle.'

Threatened with understated pain, with imaginable agony, and with no gods to answer my prayers for rescue, my instinct was to copy all the desperadoes I'd ever seen pleading. In moments of crisis, that was all I had: what other people did, what other people had always done.

'We're not an obstacle,' I said. 'We'll do anything we can to help.'

'You were first to open the grave.'

'It was empty. I swear. I had no idea about Jesus.'

'Of course you did. Only a half-wit could have missed it. That's where Calvin arranged to hide the bones. Don't you see? There were always rumours, right from the start, that Calvin's body wasn't there. But if John Calvin was buried somewhere else, then who was under that unassuming little stone of his in Geneva? He said he didn't want a stone, and in Geneva his word was literally law. What was the real reason for erecting a stone against his stated wishes?'

Moholy was sweating. He was exciting himself, and had to shake some air between the buttons of his shirt.

'Remember how the headstone's marked? No dates. No place of birth. Just J.C. *J.C.* The most obvious clue was there all the time. I can't believe no one else has ever seen it. Jung saw it. It's so obvious even *you* saw it. You stole the bones. You are the new owners of Jesus.'

From the corner of my eye, I saw Helena swallow. We glanced at each other, then immediately looked away, awed by this bravura display of twisted thinking.

'If we did have them—' Helena said. She coughed, and had to start again. 'Sorry. If we did have them, why would we hide them?'

'To keep them for yourselves. Out of your own ambition. Or to sell to someone else. You'd find plenty of buyers.'

'That would be a betrayal,' Helena said, thinking fast. 'Trickery, deceit, and a disloyalty to you personally. We'd have to lie without even thinking about it. Which would be unforgivable.'

'Exactly,' Moholy said, narrowing his eyes. 'And quite frankly, no matter how much I admire you both for your resourcefulness, I'm not of a mind to forgive you.'

'But if we had the bones of Jesus, we couldn't do any of this, could we? We couldn't possibly lie to you.'

'Right,' Rifka said, nodding at Helena's evident wisdom. 'She has a very good point there. If they've hidden the bones but are under the influence, they simply couldn't do it. The deceit of it would be beyond them.'

Moholy stopped and looked thoughtful. Frustrated, but still thoughtful. He checked us both over. 'I have to admit that right at the moment neither of you exactly reminds me of Jesus. You're frightened, both of you, and a little pathetic.'

'We are,' I said, abject and mortal, Mr Smith and no big deal. 'We're so pathetic. We're nothing at all like Jesus. We really don't have his bones.'

'Which could just mean you don't have the bones *here*.'

'Not here. Not anywhere. Promise. Cross my heart.'

'Jay, be quiet,' Rifka said. 'You're testing everyone's patience. And if I were you, I wouldn't risk doing that.'

'Tell them why,' Moholy said. 'Tell them what they're up against.'

With a certain weariness, Rifka explained that Moholy had a fresh batch of pills from the crushed bones of Suleiman the Magnificent, Sultan of the Ottoman Empire in all its heartless pomp. In many ways, Suleiman was the most enlightened of sultans, famous for his wisdom and aesthetic taste, and even a sense of humour. However, he showed no mercy to those who betrayed him, most notoriously after the conquest of Baghdad.

'Have pity on us,' I said, appealing to Moholy's better nature. 'I know you have it in you to show pity.'

'Perhaps,' Moholy said. 'Perhaps I do. But I'm not so sure about Suleiman. I must say I feel quite nasty. Not nice at all. Give me the Jesus bones, which I know you have. And then pray their effect is positive.'

'We don't have them. Really. We haven't found Jesus.'

In a rage, Moholy seized another bone and broke it over his knee. He used one jagged brown end to jab at us with emphasis. 'Let's go through this again. *You* had the mandala map. *You* had Jung's knee. *You* were first into Calvin's grave, and *you* fobbed me off with some crappy worthless skeleton, because, as you once ludicrously suggested, all bones look the same. All bones are not the same. *You* know that.'

'Some time ago,' Rifka added, inspecting the cuffs of her fleece, 'Mr Moholy was cheated by our agent from Iraq. You may have heard.'

'Please,' I said, 'I beg of you.'

'One morning, before dawn, the poor man had his fingers securely taped to a city tram-line.'

'And in Geneva,' Moholy continued, with some force, 'the trams run on time.'

'Please, don't,' I said, shuffling forward on my knees. 'I'll do anything, anything.'

'Too late,' Moholy said, before reconsidering just for a second. Perhaps this was Suleiman's famous wisdom, a stutter of reluctance before the vengeance. 'You know,' he said, 'I might just believe you when you say the bones aren't here. If they were, you wouldn't be so defeated. Of the two of you, the girl seems much more together. She can fetch the bones from wherever you've hidden them.' He glanced at his watch. 'But for you, James, the adventure is over. Rifka knows what to do.'

Moholy looked into my face, and he laughed. 'God. You're such a little nobody I almost feel sorry for you.'

From his pocket he pulled out a bottle of pills, shaking them next to his ear, then tapping one into his hand. Then another. And another. He checked the label. From where I was I couldn't read it, but the label made Moholy smile. Briefly.

'Take these,' he said. 'A little test. They're not Suleiman the Great.'

He knelt down and popped them into my mouth, one by one. I tried to swallow them. I'd said I'd do anything to save myself, and I would. It took a while for the last pill to go down, so Moholy took my cheeks between his fingers, and pushed and pulled until it did.

'Cheer up,' he said, slapping me twice on the jaw-bone. 'Try and see the funny side.'

Chaplin's Shoulder

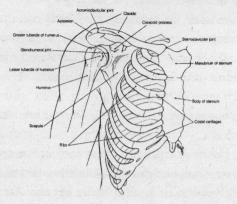

'Inevitably one is led to the conclusion that Chaplin does not exist, or, at least, that a cohesive unity known as "Chaplin" never appears fully at any one time. It could be held that this applies to all of us, that no one is the same at seven o'clock in the morning as at seven o'clock at night.'
Raoul Sobel and David Francis, *Chaplin: Genesis of a Clown*

I felt smaller, flat-footed. I couldn't put it into words, but I felt somehow diminished. Though also, at the same time, strangely unvanquished.

It was just before dawn, darkness leaking conviction, and I was lying flat on my back on a hard public road, the heels of my shoes butting the kerb. My hands were straight out above my head in the gesture of surrender, the knuckles of each ring finger stuck fast with duct-tape to the stainless steel of the nearside tram-track. I'd been lying in this position, though not always so calmly, for several hours.

According to Rifka, this was Moholy's way of expressing displeasure. He'd examine a map of Geneva's tram network and, while it was still dark, have his enemy's fingers duct-taped over the silver indent of the track, usually about ten metres beyond a right-angle bend. In Geneva, in the silence of early morning, the first punctual tram of the day could be heard from quite some distance. It would zing the overhead cables, thrum then rumble through the hard steel tracks, tremble into my knuckles, through my wrist, along my arm, my bones conducting the vibration to my shoulder and jaw, knowing all along what was coming.

Ahead of blind corners, as a precaution, the tram-drivers rang an electric bell like the end of lessons at school.

Fortunately, because Suleiman the Magnificent wasn't all bad, Rifka had taped me half-way along a straight. The tram-driver might be awake enough to see me. If he was, he might even have time to stop.

Rifka had already been walking away, even as I tried to call out, but my throat was dry with fright and I couldn't manage the words. I wanted to know who was in the pills Moholy had forced on me, and, even though no sound came from my mouth, Rifka had turned and soon understood what I wanted.

'No idea,' she'd said, 'but wait until sunrise. Whoever it was, you're about to find out if he was lucky.'

I lay there trapped, hands taped above my head, looking for signs in the sky of a new day dawning. I was impressed by the quiet. Like the solid citizens of Zurich, the Genevans valued their sleep, and even though it was Saturday and the first official day of an international anti-everything demonstration, the streets were still deserted. In fact, sleeping late on Saturday mornings was one of the many endangered liberties which justified the struggle.

Using my stomach muscles, I raised my legs, keeping them straight until they made a right angle with my body. Then I tilted them back further, my spine rolling up from the road-surface as my feet made a line with my shoulders, and still further, over my head, feeling with the tips of my shoes for the tarmac beyond the outer tram-track. I scraped my head under my shoulders, grazing my remaining earlobe. I was now on my knees, facing the palms of my hands, elbows out, fingers pointing back towards me. I felt like a floppy dog, or a water mammal.

The flat strip of duct-tape was wider than my fingers, and the edges and ends seamlessly affixed either side of the steel track. There was nowhere I could start biting, or tugging with my teeth, and from this position I could get no leverage on my single fingers by pulling with my arms. I tried twisting and turning. I had a go at chewing through my own wrist. I even almost shouted for help, but a floppy dog, a water mammal, I couldn't endure the indignity.

I did a forward roll, and finished back where I'd started, hands in surrender above my head, heels against the kerb. Still no sign of the dawn.

Moholy was teaching me a lesson, and I was no fool: flat on my back I was learning my station. I was also learning the amazing adhesiveness of industrial duct-tape. And finally, down but never quite out, I discovered my astounding talent for the day-dream. Helena's baby was only the start. After this one, we'd have two or three more, four or five. We'd have eight children, three boys and five girls. By then of course we'd be married, the traditional salvation of a ladies' man like myself, who found himself unexpectedly compromised.

Our children would all be darlings, naturally, occupying

the top floor with Pinnie their nanny, though I'd be delighted to see them at dinner, on those evenings I wasn't engaged.

Helena would be the happiest wife in the world. All I asked was that she change her name and renounce any life she might have of her own. She could spend her time checking the household accounts, planning the rose garden, and preparing gourmet feasts for the cook's day off, thus leaving me free to think intricate thoughts of astonishing depth.

In return, I'd find gainful employment at a higher annual salary than the President of the United States, though I wouldn't let it change me. My tastes would remain simple: our own Swiss home, a potted palm, tiger rugs, a den panelled with fake Oriental weapons, and oil paintings of Arabs detonating their flintlocks from the saddles of piebald ponies. As far as possible, I'd do my bit to spread the wealth of nations to the littler people, whom I had once been among, and would gladly address their socialist movements in the lapses between yachting with my equals.

I was flat on my back, arms outstretched, two fingers taped securely to a tram-line in Geneva. I was staring up at the blackness of the universe, and smiling. Cretin. If my hands had been free, I'd have slapped myself about the cheeks. I'd have knocked myself out with a single punch. Instead, I banged the back of my head twice against the road, then looked left and right. No one. My eyes and mouth shrivelled. I was going to cry, but then my eyebrows regrouped, clenching into manly resolve.

Keep a grip on reality. For the sake of your fingers, little man, for sanity.

Realistically, in the real not the dream-world, don't get married. It significantly decreases the risk of divorce. And without divorce, there could be no ex-wife to upset fastidious dinner-companions by flinging mud at the picture windows. Having children was asking for trouble. Open your eyes. The girls were anorexic and stayed out late, or travelled Europe in a camper van with gypsies and the Cirque Imaginaire. The boys were just biding their time, before writing vicious memoirs and auctioning my pyjamas.

As for spreading the wealth of the world, that was always fine in principle, though with the obvious exemption of all 200 million US dollars of whatever was rightly mine, kept safe and somewhere pleasant without taxes, like Switzerland. Be realistic: be a capitalist reactionary. There was no purpose or beauty in life, but at least there were amethyst pinkie rings, and custom-made lavender automobiles, and loyal Japanese domestics.

The sky above, beyond the delicate grid of electric cables, was definitely a shade lighter. I sensed the first hint of a silver ribbon, and then the shadows of broken clouds slowly rippling into early-morning scoops of raspberry and grey. In the curtains of an apartment window, the abrupt fly-killing blue of television. Maybe all Moholy's victims saw the same thing, exactly that, just before Geneva's first tram. Or felt this particular softness in the weather, like a concession, or this warm wind, well travelled, or this ringing in their ears, or this uncontrollable twitch in their straight but trembling legs.

Not my life, but all my stupid ambitions flashed before my eyes, versions of me in many different guises, and every ambition just the urge to change, to be different, other than Jay James Mason Minor, the person I actually was.

Vibrations skittered down the tracks. Then a rhythmic tapping, and turning my head to the left, along the converging parallel lines, I sighted Rifka walking towards me. She was banging the rail with a stick. She was concentrating each of her steps on my single tram-line, like an acrobat on a tight-rope, each footfall in line with the last, but banging and scratching the rail with a bamboo cane.

'Dring-dring,' she said. 'How much do I sound like a train?'

She knelt beside me, opened a saw-blade from her pen-knife, and jagged it roughly through the tape. I glanced behind her for the early tram. 'Not today,' Rifka said. 'All public services suspended for the duration of the protest.'

I stood up slowly, flexing my fingers and easing the ache from my back. I brushed some dust off the knees of my trousers. Then, with a straight arm and a closed fist, I swung hard at Rifka's head, aiming a decisive clout. She ducked, and I turned a complete circle, finishing where I'd started. I swung with the other hand, missed again, and lost my balance. As I fell over, something jarred hard against my leg. It was Mr Smith's useless shoulder-bone, still in my pocket, the shape of an undersized boomerang. I sat up and hurled it away.

Just my luck. It came spinning back, clocking me on the forehead, knocking me straight back down again.

'Don't blame me,' Rifka said. 'This was all Moholy's idea. He knew there weren't any trams.'

I was speechless.

'He's a very unhappy man, very lonely.'

I raised my expressive eyebrows, then took my cheeks between my fingers and forcibly pushed and pulled, like Moholy had. I was absolutely furious.

'Forget about the pills. Joseph likes his little mind-games. Now come on. Helena's at the cemetery. She needs your help.'

I glanced up at the brightening sky, and still sitting in the road I crossed my arms. I wasn't going anywhere. As far as I was concerned, Rifka was Joseph Moholy's stooge. She'd taped me to the tram-lines. And all that time ago it was Rifka who'd introduced me to Elizabeth Taylor's dogs. If it wasn't for her, I'd never have ended up like this, in trousers too baggy for me, in jackets too tight for me, always in somebody else's shoes.

'Helena needs you,' Rifka said. 'Moholy wants Jesus by the end of the day. He's obsessed.'

The cemetery, of course. More digging, more hope, more failure. I was opting out, with a mite of dignity still intact, a Mason one rank up (at least one, maybe two) from a Smith. I stood up, I squared my shoulders and raised my chin, looking slowly about me for the uphill road which led to the lovely sunset.

'Yes, the cemetery,' Rifka repeated, snagging my collar with the crook of her bamboo cane, and yanking me off-balance in the opposite direction, so that I rapidly had to steady the hat I wasn't actually wearing. I let my legs buckle, making her catch me under the arms. She dragged me, the heels of my shoes scraping the road. I crossed my arms. She dropped me, and I jumped back up, spinning my fists.

'For God's sake, Jay, trust me. Just follow me.'

I looked her in the eye, and gradually, ashamed of themselves, my fists stopped spinning. By small stages they opened again into hands, and found themselves patting my clothes for pockets, desperate for somewhere to hide. I then became engrossed in the point of my shoe, turning all by itself left and right on the gummed and speckled pavement.

'Talk to me,' Rifka said, 'I'm trying to help you.'

But to be honest, I didn't feel much like talking. Everyone had been making fun of me, and I wanted my mum, I wanted my mummy, who wasn't like any of the other boys'

278

mummies. She used to call me Little Man, and cut me waistcoats from her old vaudeville costumes. She sometimes threw crockery, or went up to people in the street and punched them for no reason, or handed them lumps of coal.

I'd never done enough for her. I realised that now, ragged in Geneva, after a sleepless night in the streets. I resolved to do better, and now that Dad was gone I could settle her close by in a Santa Monica cottage, with a friendly couple to keep house, a full-time nurse companion, and a self-replenishing stock of henna for the lustre of her silver hair.

'Hey! Ho!'

Rifka was clicking her fingers in my face, and my head jerked up and I blinked wildly. She pushed me in the chest, and I toppled backwards on my flattened heels. I dropped off the kerb, and fell again, hard on my backside.

'Listen to me,' Rifka said, following me down to the road, kneeling over me, her wide face with its broken nose the only face in the world.

'Look at me. Do you trust me?'

Her grey eyes, still scuffed with brown, were now very close, and filling my field of vision. Right from the beginning, I'd always trusted her. I had no idea why.

'Listen to me. Jesus wasn't in Calvin's grave. You know that. You opened it up, and there was nothing there. Moholy has therefore set you an impossible task. Either you need a miracle, or you and Helena need to work out a plan. Now, I don't know what that plan will be, but I'll help you as much as I can. Why? Because I feel sorry for you almost as much as I do for Moholy. Now come on. Follow me.'

For reasons I didn't yet understand, I believed her when she said she wanted to help. I stood up and dusted myself off, picked up Rifka's discarded cane, and flexed it a few times. I checked I'd suffered no bodily damage by splaying my feet and bouncing at the knees. Then I sniffed the air and, in my own good time, gestured Rifka to lead the way.

It wasn't long into daylight, but I soon noticed we weren't the only people that morning heading towards the cemetery. And all of us on foot. There were no buses running, and no trams. There were no taxis, and only a few parked cars. Like everyone else, we walked freely in the middle of the road, enjoying the early air off the lake, and the simple everyday sight-gag of Geneva's pelican crossings. The red man was Swiss, patiently waiting his pedestrian turn. But the green man, when his time came to cross, was manic, with swinging arms and pumping legs, racing for the other side.

Except today, with no traffic, there was no reason to run. We didn't take the shortest route. Instead, like fish, our growing crowd flicked left and right, out-thinking riot vans and road-blocks, those at the front excited on mobiles, converging us with others blocked and rebounded from different directions.

It was somewhere near the Rue de Coutance that we saw our first young woman in a black leotard, with sewn-on fluorescent bones. I assumed I'd been overdoing it, and pretended she wasn't there. On Plainpalais, over the inverted concrete arcs of the skate-park, I glimpsed someone dragging what looked like a supple and bouncing rubber skeleton. At the head of our group, I now noticed as we surged down Rue de la Muse, we were proudly flying the skull and crossbones.

'It was on the television,' Rifka said. 'It was in all the papers.'

It was a front-page sensation, the brazen theft from the Cimetière des Rois of Geneva's acclaimed John Calvin. For the first time in nearly 500 years, Calvin was world-wide news, his grave desecrated in broad daylight by the bucket of a mechanical digger. In the absence of witnesses, there were pages of after-the-event pictures, reports, commentary. It was the exact opposite of Moholy's stated intention to keep the project secret, and the press had no educated sense of proportion, no theological perspective. They were calling it an outrage against the safety of the dead. All cemeteries everywhere could soon need protection, fencing, night-patrols with dogs. In fact, this was bad, very bad, almost as bad as the last time.

In the cold winter of 1977, on Christmas Day, the tramp and millionaire Sir Charles Spencer Chaplin had died from complications. He was buried near his Swiss home the Manoir du Ban in the cemetery of Corsier-sur-Vevey, with views overlooking the lake. Two months later, in the early hours of 2 March, as the year's thaw was just beginning, his diminutive oak coffin was disinterred by two Eastern European refugees, Roman Wardas and Gantcho Ganev.

Wardas was Polish, tall and agile, a natural leader to the slower and rounder Bulgarian, Gantcho. After an evening's drinking, the two men decided that Oona Chaplin, Charlie's recent widow, could be expected to pay handsomely for the safe return of her famous husband's remains. They stumbled out to the graveyard, and encouraged each other to dream. The heavy and affable Gantcho visualised a people's republic in which everyone was genuinely free. Wardas pictured a fully equipped garage and body-shop. He'd already priced it, and the latest pits and hoists required a ransom not far short of 600,000 Swiss francs.

It didn't seem extortionate.

On the night of the crime, jittery Gantcho forgot the torch.

As a punishment, Wardas made him do the digging. They squabbled, then bickered, but both men fell silent at the sight of the actual coffin. It was the size of it. They'd forgotten that Chaplin had shrunk to the age of eighty-eight, and from a start of only five foot three. Roman Wardas couldn't help laughing: he pulled the coffin out, and lifted it high above his head. He balanced it on one flat hand, the other behind his back, dipping and cavorting like a waiter in *Modern Times*. Something inside the coffin lurched, tipping it from Roman's grip. It dived point first on to Gantcho's foot.

Then their stolen van wouldn't start. Roman took a look under the bonnet, and scalded his hands on the radiator cap. Stumbling backwards, snorting, he jogged the bonnet prop, and the bonnet slammed bang on Gantcho's fingers.

In the village of Corsier, the coffin clamped between their forearms, they realised they'd locked themselves out of their flat. They therefore carried Charlie to a nearby wheat-field, and with the sun already rising they reburied him, not very deeply, in the nearest corner.

The next day the cemetery was discovered in such a mess that news of the macabre theft spread quickly across the globe, in a dizzying series of spinning front pages. Roman and Gantcho took cover in the nearby city of Lausanne, waiting for their fingers to heal before telephoning Oona, only to discover that theirs was at least the fifteenth call claiming a ransom. Oona needed to know which of the claimants genuinely had the body.

Roman and Gantcho went back to the field, in the dead of night, to take a flash photograph of Charlie's coffin to send as evidence. They started digging. The spade broke. Walking backwards with the camera, to get the coffin into focus, Gantcho fell in a ditch. Two days later, in the developed photos, Roman's cap was clearly visible on the ground at the edge of the frame.

At three o'clock the next morning, by moonlight, in the increasingly trampled corner of the field, Roman yet again uncovered the tiny coffin. He prised open the lid, and flinched. Charlie's lips had withered, uncovering his teeth in an evil rigid grin. Roman kept clear of Chaplin's eyeline as he pulled tentatively at a patent leather and spatted ankle-boot, which came away in his hands. The foot was still inside. Grimacing, turning his head away and looking from the corner of his eye, Roman tried to pinch out a single bone from the many small bones in the weakness of the human ankle. It was too horrible. He respectfully, though approximately, replaced the boot and the spat.

He called Gantcho over. Think of the perfect republic, he said, in which all people are genuinely free. Gantcho closed his eyes and plunged his hand into the coffin. He came back up with a bone from the shoulder. While Gantcho reburied the coffin, Roman wiped off the shoulder-bone on the hunched back of his partner's jacket, sniffed it, rubbed it off again, then sealed it in an envelope addressed to Oona, with a note already inside.

Give us the money, or your husband will. Just give us the money.

Roman and Gantcho then bombarded Oona with calls from a Lausanne public phone. They dropped their ransom from 600,000 francs to 250,000, in only enough time for police to trace the line. It had been seventy-six days since they'd first lifted Charlie from the cemetery in Corsier-sur-Vevey.

On 17 May 1978, they made their final call from the traced public phone, which was now under all-day surveillance.

283

Looking out for the cap in the photograph supplied by the developers, armed with information from the landlord of the flat, and fingerprints from the broken-down van, police identified two Eastern European mechanics named Roman Wardas and Gantcho Ganev. After a botched raid on the phonebox, there then followed a lengthy chase involving truncheons and whistles, and some tricky business in and out and up and down with an open window and an escalator. Finally, both men were restrained and arrested, and thrown into the back of a van.

They pleaded guilty, but swore in court caps in hand on their mothers' hearts that they'd acted out of character. They couldn't explain themselves, and had no idea what had ever possessed them.

More than twenty years later, for Calvin not Chaplin, the protesters seemed only too happy to take the blame. Attitudes had changed, and they were actively volunteering. Someone smart had already constructed an instant website (www.johncalvinsbody.org) to drip-feed suggestions to the gerbil press. It started with rumours, followed by denials, until it was all but certain.

Latest: Angry Protesters Resurrect John Calvin.

There was even the possibility, offered globally by the website as an exclusive, that tomorrow, as a climax to the weekend of protest, the skeleton of John Calvin would be hanged from a window in the UN International enclave. And then burnt. And then the ashes scattered in the lobbies of Geneva's banks.

In one of many online interviews, johncalvinsbody.org agreed that yes, the newspapers were right, a stunt like this must have taken an enormous amount of organisation and planning. *Why Calvin?* It was the will of the people. It was Mr Smith with attitude, the revenge of the little man against the work ethic, and tightened belts, and the joyless accumulation of capital. It was an impudent *better had* after 500 years of one-way *better not*. They even invented a name, the Calvinistas, for anyone who supported their action.

Calvin's bones were the compelling media event that every protest needed. The story had everything. There were sinister masterminds, historical perspectives, human interest and, in natural light on Saturday morning as the sun climbed higher, a massive photo-opportunity involving hundreds of protesters arriving at the cemetery either carrying or dressed as skeletons.

Geneva was suddenly full of them, including real bones wired up from toe to skull, riding with big toothy grins on the shoulders of supportive medical students. There were soft-toy skeletons, and plastic skeletons, and skeleton rave masks which glowed in the dark. There were life-size cardboard cutout skeletons from children's bumper books of the human body. The protesters were claiming that every single skeleton was Calvin, and photographs featuring bones and baffled police were already pasted on web-pages across the world.

The skull and crossbones was everywhere, as a flag, as a bandanna, on hats. It was roughly cut from cloth of all colours and patterns, and sewn into clothes, or the scarves pulled up to hide the faces of the reticent. Everyone was a pirate, just for the day, a convert to the little man's ancient battle against authority, in which backsides needed kicking, ears tweaking and noses snubbing. Toes needed to be trod upon, and beards needed twisting.

I saw uniformed police take wild swings with batons, and chase after bones which looked authentic. The more portly constables stood sweating and panting on corners, scratching their foreheads, tilting back their uniform caps.

The cemetery itself had been cordoned off, a plastic police-tape backed by a chain of officers on the cemetery side of the wall. Only journalists were allowed inside, and the international press took photographs from behind the police, looking for exciting angles on a body-snatched Protestant Reformer.

On the street side of the wall, there was whistling and a growing chant: '*We've* got John Calvin. *We've* got John Calvin.' The protesters bobbed their various skeletons up and down, and a bony girl in a skeleton suit jumped on to the flat-topped wall, and did a spiny contemporary dance.

Helena was up near the front, stretching to see over the police and into the cemetery, a solid and indifferent mass of people keeping us apart. I felt my shoulders drop, the victim of some terrible, unknowable injustice. It wasn't *fair*. But I couldn't be swayed by that. I quickly perked up, rubbed my hands together, and gave a little hop. I shaped my hands for a dive, and lowered my head. Then I wrinkled my nose, and tunnelled straight through. Or not quite straight, actually in several circles, intermittently bobbing up my head to check my position, before diving again and finally popping up only inches behind her.

She seemed so much taller than me, but that couldn't be right. Inspired by a huge surge of sentimental affection, I wanted to weep for joy, but I couldn't. I stood behind Helena and strained and grimaced, but no tears came.

Unscripted, she turned round, and I scratched the back of my head.

'Jay!'

She yelled out my name above the whistles and chants, and

the press-pack baying for poses. She clasped me to her bosom, lifting me off my feet, then dropped me and grabbed at my hands, fumbling for all ten of my remarkably intact fingers.

'How?' She was still having to shout. 'How did you get yourself free?'

She clasped me again to her bosom, swinging me this way and that, and I had to steady my hat.

It was quite clear that the Cimetière des Rois wouldn't be providing us with any more bones, not today. We'd need to think of something else. As we nudged our way out, escaping the growing crush at the front, I inadvertently stepped on the toes of the minister from the American church. Even ravaged and unfrocked as I was, I think he almost recognised me. I flicked my eyebrows and thumbed my nose. I think he was probably mistaken. To confirm him in this impression, and in the absence of mallets and pies, I zipped behind him and administered a kick to the rear, before dropping to my knees and crawling away, through an otherwise impassable thicket of boots.

When I found my feet again, at the outside edge of the growing crowd for Calvin (*We've* got John Calvin. *We've* got John Calvin), I'd lost all sight of Helena. And Rifka had simply vanished. The numbers, the popularity of the protest, made it almost impossible to locate individuals. I made several false pursuits in one and all directions. Then I saw Helena, waving both arms at me from the forecourt of the fire-station. I waved back, and had just set off towards her when I was caught up by a surge of gardeners, streaming in the opposite direction. I dodged my head between bobbing rakes and hoes, as her wave slowly faltered.

They put me down again at the Place Neuve, by the central

statue of General Dufour. On any normal day, the equestrian statue was surrounded by constant traffic, with seven roads large and small converging on the one besieged square. Today, between the gates of the Parc des Bastions on one side and the columns of the Victoria Hall on the other, the roads were being relaid as lawn. This was the French group who'd been intending to plant wheat at the entrance to the United Nations, but who'd found the security overwhelming, with paramilitaries under orders to prevent popular disruption at all costs. And this time, because they couldn't get any wheat, they had grass.

Even here, in the morning sunshine, there was a squad of riot police under the ramparts of the Old Town, at the junction with the Avenue Corraterie. A riot sergeant stepped forward towards some shoeless Basques juggling spangly batons. He told them they weren't allowed on the grass.

'This isn't grass,' they said, looking down. 'It's road.'

'You're not allowed.'

At which point, all the philosophical young people decided to sit down. At first they sat on the pavement and traffic islands, then increasingly on the turfed road itself, and then, for one intrepid skeleton, up on the horse behind General Dufour. The horse was wearing an orange eye-patch, and a pink and blue bandanna sporting the skull and bones.

I looked everywhere for Helena, my hand shading my eyes, stepping forward and back, narrowly missing the upturned tines of several unattended rakes. She was nowhere to be seen, and among all these people I wondered how I'd ever be able to find her. Then I remembered we were supposed to be looking for Jesus. There was an obvious place to start.

*

The church floor was coloured with clusters of yellow and green Karrimats, rumpled sleeping bags; there was the lingering smell of living human bodies. This was the deal Helena had made with the protesters. In return for sitting through my sermon as Calvin, they could set up camp in the empty spaces of the Church of All Saints, although today they were up and already out, reforming the Western world. And like the good Calvinistas they were, they'd been busy.

Either side of the aisle was a scatter of unfinished banners (*Capitalism Kills the Plan*; *Bread Not*), and placards painted with blood-stained pound and dollar signs. I stopped to be impressed by two stacks of flat yellow life-jackets, of the inflatable type in demand on aeroplanes. Then my gaze travelled over bags of pink fright wigs, some papier-mâché cartoon bombs, and many paper sacks soft with the petals of flowers.

'Nearly finished.'

There was a young boy sitting barefoot on the stairs to the pulpit, sewing skulls and bones of many colours on to three-pointed hats in black.

'No hurry,' I said, but he was already collecting up his work, and humming his way past me to the door. As it closed behind him, the whistles and klaxons of the protest blurred, became distant, like the horns and halloos of sabs at shire-hunts in merry old England.

There was no sign of Helena, or Rifka, but I couldn't think where else they'd go to look for Jesus. From inside the door-way, I sized up the long strip of polished aisle. It was like one side of a convincing argument. Black tile connected with black, and white with white, each deftly touching at the corner, but that didn't make the aisle all black, or all white. I took off my shoes. With a short run-up, I slid as far as I could in my socks.

289

Then I carried my shoes into the vestry, using my other hand to hold up my trousers, which had a new habit of accordioning towards the ankle. I closed the vestry door, and turned the head-and-shoulders mirror the right way round. Yes, just as I thought.

My head and shoulders were blessed with the look. I looked funny. Vicars were funny, and they had funny clothes, with their tunics and dalmatics, their chasubles and pallium with pins. In Europe, men of God were small and funny, relicts of another age in black and white, religion a frivolous pursuit compared, say, to factory work on the one hand, and on the other to accumulating as much money as humanly possible in a single show-biz lifetime.

Still clutching my trousers, I found a fresh collar in the laundry and slipped it one-handed into the ragged clerical shirt I was still wearing from yesterday. Then, for the benefit of the mirror, I grabbed my throat with both hands, thumbs pointing forward and fingers at the back, and squeezed until my face went red and my eyes popped out. My trousers fell down.

Take yourself seriously. Leave the trousers: they can't fall any further. I settled my neck with a twist and a grimace. Then I jutted my head forward, getting into my own face. I checked the whites of my eyes (yellow), my gums (one shade of red short of bleeding), and asked myself what, exactly, was holding me back. Maybe it was the teeth. It was my Anglican teeth, a delicate shade of sweet sherry, stained forever by biscuits and crystallised fudge at the fête.

I should have been more conformist, like the rest of them, and happy to act the buffoon. I stepped out of the wreckage of my trousers, and crossed my hands demurely to each opposite shoulder of my clerical shirt. In my socks, I skated slowly but elegantly into the church, past the altar, and then backwards past the altar, then forwards again, enjoying the lightness of the draught on my bare white shanks. I slid with some élan to a halt, and faced my imaginary flock.

As acting Chaplin of the Church of All Saints in Geneva, I opened out my arms, and mimed a sermon. With silent insistence, I preached the slapstick of the times. Nothing seemed quite right or in its proper place. Modern life was like a fisherman trawling the harvest, a farmer ploughing for fish. I paused for breath, and to mop my glowing brow. Anyone in pursuit of purpose and meaning was setting themselves up to fall flat on their face.

There was someone coming, the soundtrack of civil disobedience starting and then stopping with the heavy wooden door. Unfortunately, I was still flat on my face, where in my mime I'd fallen. I tried to scramble up, but my socks slipped and slid away, and I fell again. I did, though, manage to compose myself. Unlike Charlie (unlike Roman and Gantcho, comic mechanics), I could still bring myself under control, count steadily to a measured ten, and refuse the decline from comic to worse.

Helena stood quite still beneath the western window. I started breathing again, slowly, and counted off the black and white tiles, all of them thankfully in order, one black, then one white, as far as Helena's feet. I stood up very carefully, and raised my hand in greeting just as the bareness of my legs encouraged me to reconsider. A little tongue-tied, I held up my fingers, requesting five. Then I turned and skated with dignity towards the altar, straightening my non-sliding leg in a rapid one-footed turn to the vestry.

I slammed the door behind me, blocking it with a couple of bicycles. I didn't want Helena to see me like this. I'd promised to stop living through other people, and I wasn't sufficiently myself to face her. It was quite involuntary. It was the pills, it had to be, there was no other explanation, or none for which I could find the appropriate words.

The least she expected, since we'd agreed to make our life together, was a consistent and recognisable Jay Mason, deacon. I therefore pulled and scratched at the package of returned laundry, thinking that if I dressed the part, then the rest might follow. I piled all the clerical vestments over my head, one after the other, including two server's cassocks, a set of six choir surplices, an alb, and a Geneva-style pulpit robe in wash-and-wear polyester. I finished with my dad's thick red festival chasuble, like an over-stuffed cushion.

She was banging on the door. I had everything in place except one final embroidered stole, green and gold like a belt of achievement from an exotic martial art.

I wrapped it once round my extended waist, knotting it clumpily at the front. Moving side-on to the barricaded door, left shoulder forward, I adopted the stance, knees flexed, back straight, a very plump cushion prepared for combat.

Come on, then.

I bounced a little, my head and neck rigid with Eastern intent. Come on, Joseph Moholy, I'll give you Jesus. Defying the bulk of the robes, I pulled my left elbow into my body, just so, and raised the other hand, deceptively limp and close behind my ear. I bounced again, poised to strike.

The door banged open, toppling the pair of bicycles.

I narrowed my eyes, maintaining the stance. 'Hai!'

Helena stood there in the doorway, hands on hips. She clenched her jaw, which made her chin tremble, then stepped over the bicycles and into range. Without even the customary bow of respect, she launched a cowardly attack, cutting and slicing with stiff hands, chopping at my shoulders and head. I covered up and lost all martial shape as she gradually forced my retreat, over the bicycles, out of the vestry, as far as the edge of the altar. She finally subdued my spirit by clamping my arms to my sides, then clutching my head to her neck.

'Jay, it's me. It's me. Feel me.'

She took my hands in her own, and the soft flesh and living blood of Helena easily outbid the dry residue of powdered bones in pills.

'I'm sorry.'

'You spoke,' she said.

'I really am sorry.'

'Are you alright?'

'I think he gave me Chaplin.'

'No, he didn't.'

'I'm sorry, but I think he did.'

'Jay. One, the pills don't work. Take that on board. Two, even if they did, Moholy can't have given you a dose of Charlie Chaplin. So be a bit more normal. Please.'

She sat close to me on the step as I unknotted the stole. Then I tried for the chasuble, but it beat me. I couldn't raise my arms high enough to pull it off, so Helena had to stand above me and help, tugging it over my head. And then again with the next vestment. And again, and so on. She repeatedly snagged my ear, which may not have been an accident.

'Moholy definitely doesn't have a Chaplin pill,' Helena said, doing her best to reassure me while ignoring my ows and ouches. 'I remember reading about it. Before Charlie's body was reburied, the entire family plot was embedded in steel and concrete. It was made impenetrable. Oona's decision.'

'Good thinking, Oona. Ow.'

Helena rested her hands on the top of my head, and by now I was back to a simple cotton alb over my clerical shirt and collar. 'So calm down, okay? We're in a tight spot. But it's going to be fine.' She gave my scalp a consoling scratch, keeping me safe in my senses.

'Probably the trauma of the tram-tracks. That's bound to mess up anyone's head. A little bit.'

She came down to my level and looked into my eyes, though only with medical intent, checking I was back to my old self, that I was all there. I told her about being rescued by Rifka, which had Helena baffled.

'Why would she do that? I thought she worked for Moholy.'

'She does. She could have left me.'

'There must be something in it for her.'

'Maybe she's secretly a good person, and just likes doing good things. She guessed you'd be there at the cemetery.'

'Bully for her,' Helena said. 'And not a difficult guess. Moholy wants more bones. The cemetery's the obvious place to find them.'

'Don't be mean,' I said. 'She saved me from the tram.'

'There was no tram.'

'They knew all the time there weren't any trams.'

Monsters, the both of them. For a moment Helena looked unusually stern, her mouth a thin line which started twitching, then lifting at the edges. She snorted. 'Oh lighten up, you silly man.'

'Well, I would,' I said, not finding it quite so funny, and keen to restore my dignity, 'if it wasn't for the small matter of Jesus. Which you seem to have completely forgotten.'

I flounced into the vestry to fetch my trousers, tying them tightly through the loops with a purple-tasselled cincture, which had fallen out with the laundry. I took off and discarded the alb.

'There is no Jesus,' Helena said, coming in after me. She was equally happy to argue in the vestry. 'At least agree with me on that.'

I shrugged. 'How would you ever know?'

'Well, not in Calvin's grave anyway. That's Moholy's private little fantasy.'

'Actually,' I said, 'I found him quite convincing. What he said about Switzerland. It's true that no other country in Europe has been so peaceful. Maybe the bones of Jesus *are* having an influence.'

'Listen to me, Jay. No more Chaplin, no more jokes, and listen very closely. In the last century, the Swiss army opened fire twice, once in 1918, and once in 1932. Both times, it shot at its own people. They're a bunch of clowns, with cuckoo clocks. *That's* why they haven't been at war.'

'So the influence is comic?'

'There is *no* influence, from *any* bones. Get that into your stupid stubborn head. The Swiss are never invaded because they safeguard the loot and spoil of whoever's actually fighting, even if it arrives in the form of gold fillings. It has nothing to do with Jesus. In fact, you might say, quite the opposite.'

'Try to imagine,' I said, 'just for a moment, that Moholy's right.'

'And Jesus is responsible for clean trains which run on time. Sure. Get to the point, Jay. Calvin's grave was empty, wasn't it?'

She stacked the bicycles against the wall, and checked they were steady. 'Jay. Calvin's grave.'

'It was empty. Definitely empty.'

295

I was remembering the condition of the soil, which had been loose and easy to work. It was as if somebody else had been in there before me. 'Maybe Moholy's story is true. J.C. in Geneva stands for Jesus Christ, not John Calvin. It was just that somebody else got to him first.'

'To who?'

'To Jesus.'

'Let's not think that,' Helena said. 'For sanity's sake. The grave was empty because the rumours about Calvin were accurate. He never wanted to be buried in Geneva with a headstone, and he wasn't. That's all there is to it. The grave was *always* empty, since fifteen-whatever. There were never any bones to be found.'

'In which case, what do we do now?'

Moholy was still expecting us to deliver the bones of Jesus by the end of the day. It was either that, or run and hide. So running and hiding it was, then. Run, dodge, dive into vacant doorways.

'Rifka,' Helena said. 'She must have been watching us. That's how she knew where I was. She's probably always watching. We can't run and hide.'

'You don't think so?'

'Someone's keeping an eye on us. I'm sure of it.'

'I feel that, too.'

'And then there's Suleiman the Magnificent. Where would we go? He has spies all over the known world.'

'Helena, don't.' I felt lost, and increasingly aggrieved. 'You said the pills didn't work. I thought you didn't believe in them?'

'I don't,' Helena said. 'And I hope you don't either. But all that matters is what Moholy believes, and among other things Moholy wants to believe in Jesus. There must be a way out of this. It can't be beyond us.'

Personally, I still hadn't dismissed the running and hiding option, but, failing that, I supposed it was always possible to believe in a providence which arranged for everything to turn out well. I certainly hoped so, because Jesus was a very big problem. Obviously, we couldn't deliver the actual Jesus.

'Let's just accept that from the start,' Helena said. 'There are no Jesus bones hanging about that we can gratefully put our hands on.'

Other bones were now out in the open all round the city, but the skeletons liberated from schools and labs were far too young. We still had Richard Burton back in the closet. And Jung's knee. I'd almost forgotten Jung's knee.

'Too recent, all of them,' Helena said, 'we can't pass them off as Jesus.'

'And we still have the other skeleton in the blue bag. The anonymous one.'

'Which is next to useless,' Helena said, 'as we've already discovered.'

Basically, we needed other bones.

'Moholy can't actually test for Jesus, can he?' I said, exploring a sudden aptitude for ingenious escapes. 'Carbon-14 dating only dates. It can't identify. He can discover the age of the bones, but not the identity.'

'Go on.'

'So if we had some two-thousand-year-old bones, they could safely stand in for Jesus, if that's what someone wanted to believe.'

'Brilliant. Only one problem. Where do you suggest we find a complete skeleton which is two thousand years old?'

'Okay. So there's a flaw in my theory. But try this. We can both *not* believe the Jesus story, *and* deliver the bones from Calvin's grave.'

'You've lost me. You said the grave was empty.'

'Exactly. It was. But Moholy doesn't know that, or doesn't want to believe it. We get him some bones the same age as Calvin.'

'I don't understand. Why?'

'When he tests them, Moholy will work out for himself that it must be Calvin, not Jesus. From the dates. He'll be disappointed, obviously, but he'll understand how it happened, which might just be enough to save us.'

'That is quite amazing.'

'Thank you.'

'But we still have the same problem. Where are we going to get a complete set of five-hundred-year-old bones?'

We stopped. We looked at each other. At the same time, we both said:

'*St Ursula*.'

I reached the Basilica of Our Lady without once tripping over a kerbstone, despite keeping a constant lookout for any sign of Rifka. I didn't collide with a fat policeman. I didn't fall down a manhole.

Helena was therefore right: I couldn't possibly be Charlie Chaplin.

As if to prove it, I was still wearing my priestly shirt and collar, and I'd double-locked my trousers with a strip of police-tape found in the road. I looked shabby, but not entirely lost, even with Dad's ex-army kit-bag slung over my shoulder. I'd been back to the flat for Richard Burton, to offer him in fair exchange for the bones of Ursula.

The Catholic Basilica, like the Anglican church, was unlocked. It was also empty, apart from a very tall nun with glasses who frightened me witless by gliding out quietly from behind a pillar. I lowered my head, out of respect for silent orders everywhere, and made the sign of the cross. Only I was half-way through before realising I didn't know how it went, so I bluffed the ending by touching my nose, then scratching the back of my neck. I hurried past the nun to the Lady Chapel, and the bones of British St Ursula.

St Ursula wasn't there. Senseless with panic, I flipped up the altar-cloth. She wasn't underneath. I checked and double-checked a nearby confessional, one side then the other, both the forgiven and the damned.

She was gone. And in her place was the leg-bone of St Clothilde of Geneva, safely returned from her tour of the Italian south. St Clothilde was the wrong period, neither AD 64 nor AD 1530. Her label said she'd died in 734, but at least she was closer to Jesus than the bones I had in the kit-bag. I decided to take her. I was just fumbling with the clasp on the gold reliquary when the nun floated in to join me. I spun round, hands innocently behind my back. She peered at me through her glasses while continuing to shift her rosary, and again overcome by panic I attempted to rectify my sign of the cross, this time starting with my temple, both shoulders, navel, hip, and finally the inside of my knee.

She smiled beatifically. And moved on.

I turned back to the ornate box, opened it, grabbed the leg-bone, dropped it, caught it. After a shuffle through the kit-bag, I replaced it with the leg-bone of Richard Burton. With St Clothilde safely on board, I hefted the kit-bag and scuffled out into the side-aisle. It was blocked between me and the exit by the smiling nun. Forehead, both shoulders, navel, hip, both elbows, knee and the instep of my lifted foot. I smiled as best I could, and then walked splay-footed and bandy-legged to the door, turning only once to see her staring after me. I doffed my imaginary hat, did a running one-footed turn, and banged through the spring-loaded door.

As planned, Helena was waiting outside, and she wasn't impressed. We had a single leg-bone, once of St Clothilde, not even approximately from an acceptable era. Moholy was expecting a whole body of bones. I let my shoulders drop, thinking wistfully of an idyllic domestic future in which a tricky bone would mean nothing more daunting than a plateful of tricky fish. In my mind there was grey sky above, and the white sun was shining, and I was sitting on a grey porch hugging my knees and coyly swinging my shoulders. I'd have no great ambition beyond a day's work, smelling the flowers, and Paulette Goddard in the role of Helena Byczynski stewing my boots for dinner.

I was no fool. I'd show her what I was made of. Using only ingenuity and my native wit, I'd shelter Helena from all of life's frustrations: I knew of somewhere *else* we'd find some plausible bones.

We waited until dark, after an afternoon spent quarrelling about the ethics of stealing a car. Helena correctly pointed out, more than once, that I wasn't being myself. Of course I wasn't; didn't she ever want to get anything done? I was still Chaplin: despite Oona's reinforced vault, Helena had forgotten the shoulder-bone pinched by Roman and Gantcho and sent to Oona as evidence. The police traded seized drugs, so why not bones? Moholy had obtained Chaplin's shoulder and made it into pills, several of which he'd forced on me with the result, among other surprises, that I'd climbed into an unlocked car in a quiet side-street. I then discovered that my amateur hot-wiring made nothing work but the radio.

It was gypsy violin, and I danced back and forth, making

Romany flurries with my hands, arching my feet, singing any old nonsense because the words were unimportant, le spinash or le busho, cigaretto toto bello.

'Stop it right now!' Helena shouted. 'The villa, you clown! We're supposed to be going to the villa.'

At that very moment, Rifka arrived in our deserted alley on a scooter. She kept the engine running, and planted both feet flat on the road.

'It's not stolen,' she said. 'It's borrowed. Now. Do you want to be helped, or don't you?'

'One moment,' I said.

Helena and I nervously put our heads together, and conferred. At one level, this was a gift from the gods. At another, it could be some sort of fiendish trick.

'Why should we trust her?' Helena asked, taking me aside.

'I don't know. But look at her. We do, don't we?'

Rifka smiled, calm, queen of coincidences, and shifted forward along the seat. Helena didn't think three people were allowed.

'Look at it like this,' I said. 'How else are we going to get there?'

Reluctantly, Helena climbed on to the scooter behind Rifka, which left me at the back, facing backwards, kit-bag of bones across my thighs and my knees tightly clamped around what was left of the back-end of the bike.

Rifka steered us expertly out of the city, the scooter heavy on its rear spindle, taking long curving detours around road-blocks and sit-ins. We were heading for Moholy's villa. As an idea, it was impetuous, hazardous, seemingly impossible, like a plan in a comedy destined to work out well.

We ran out of petrol on the dual carriageway, a few hundred metres short of the lay-by and bus-stop. Still wary of

Rifka, Helena suggested we wait here until it was fully dark, but when we climbed over the crash-barriers, and slid down to the lakeside shingle, Rifka came with us. We watched her skim stones across the lake, so smoothly they seemed to end up floating, and never actually sinking. Helena wasn't convinced.

'Think of it as part of the trick,' I said. 'Moholy wants us to have the bones of Jesus.'

'You therefore have to act with total confidence,' Rifka said over her shoulder, before skimming another effortless stone, 'with God on your side.'

'Let me get this straight,' Helena said, pointedly ignoring Rifka and lowering her voice. 'I'm supposed just to walk in.'

'Ring the bell. Moholy opens the door, and invites you inside. He's dying to know about Jesus. Somehow, as you go in, the door gets left slightly open, or on the latch.'

'Very scientific.'

'I'm not being scientific. And you'll have Rifka with you, as back-up.'

'Go through it one more time.'

Jesus had no fear. Rifka was right about that. Helena would therefore tell Moholy that I'd escaped the tram-lines by the grace of God. After collecting the bones from their hiding-place, a secret I'd kept to myself, I'd been delayed by the demonstration. I couldn't help it: I'd become personally involved, just as Jesus would have done. However, when the main events and rallies of the day were over, I'd deliver Jesus to Moholy as promised. I was a man of my word, who couldn't lie. I was surely on my way over, even as Helena spoke, any moment now I'd be at the villa with Jesus.

'And then I arrive,' I said, 'hopefully with the bones.'

'I won't ever actually say they're the bones of Jesus,'

302

Helena said. 'Just the bones we found in Calvin's grave.'

'Good thinking. Because when he tests them to the 1500s, then all of the above also applies to Calvin.'

'And what about Rifka?'

'I don't think we have a choice. If she'd wanted, she could already have ruined everything, several times over. I don't know why, but she hasn't. Let's hope for the best. Perhaps she genuinely wants to help.'

About half an hour later, in the full dark of night, all three of us were crouching behind a bush in Moholy's garden, looking through foliage at the windows of his huge down-stairs salon, its indoor light radiating yellow over the crushed white gravel of the drive. From the kit-bag, I offered Helena a fragment of Burton, as an aid to feeling urbane and socially at ease.

'Thanks, Jay, but no. I prefer to stay as myself.'

She stood up, rubbed her hands down her jeans, then was crunching over the gravel towards the door of the house, as determined and fearless as Jesus. Rifka followed just behind, like a disciple. It was nicely done. Helena reached the step. She rang the bell. Moholy came to the door. He invited them inside. The door closed firmly behind them.

They were supposed to leave the door open. That was vital to the plan.

Remembering my graveyard training, I crept back to the gates over the quiet grass, and crossed over where the gravel gave way to tarmac. I was now on the house side of the drive, where a line of white-painted rocks marked the border between lawn and gravel. I weighed a rock in my hand, and crept silently to the corner of the house. The silver Mercedes was parked beyond the doorway. I took careful aim, threw the rock at it, and missed.

Nobody came from the house to investigate.

I threw a bigger rock, which clanged noisily off the bonnet. No one came out. I picked up the biggest rock I could find, marched noisily over the gravel, lifted it in both hands above my head, and smashed it down into the windscreen, which blanched and crumpled.

Rifka came out as I was composing myself, brushing dust and grass from my shoulders. She looked at the car windscreen, and frowned.

'It's nothing,' she said, calling the news back into the house. 'Kids, probably.'

When she went back in, she left the double door slightly open. Right second time.

After a decent pause, I ducked inside the warmth of the house, and sidled past the open doorway of the salon, where some distance away Moholy was making drinks. With the kit-bag over my shoulder, I launched myself up the stairs three at a time, reached the first stone landing, veered left, jumped for the second flight, missed my footing, fell flat on my front, and bumped several steps back down again.

Damn that Charlie Chaplin.

I scrambled back up to the second landing, but someone was already on the lower flight of stairs, and coming up behind me.

'What noise?' I heard Helena say. She must have followed the others out into the hall. 'I didn't hear a thing.'

'There was definitely something. Rifka, go and look.'

The door to the first long room, Moholy's store-room, was locked. The only light on the landing came from a standard lamp in an alcove, and I turned it off, stepped into the alcove, and hid myself behind it. There must have been another switch downstairs. Someone turned the light back on again. I turned it off, on, with me underneath it, off again, on again. I reached under the shade, my shirtsleeve over my fingers, and unscrewed the bulb. It was hot, and my sleeve slipped, and I tried to juggle the bulb but it scorched my fingers and I flipped it over the banisters. It smashed somewhere far below. Peeking down, out from the darkness, I saw Moholy in the gawp of light from the salon's open doorway.

By now Rifka had felt her way up to the second landing, level with where I was hiding.

'It's nothing,' she said, looking sharply at me and making a murderous face. 'Just a blown bulb.'

'Don't be ridiculous,' Moholy said. Rifka had her finger over her pursed lips, and was holding up a key. She unlocked the door into the store-room, and pushed me through before closing it again behind me. I just had time to hear Moholy start up the stairs, and it sounded like Helena was coming with him.

The store-room was dark, and my heart was scudding. I couldn't risk the lights, so I blundered half-sighted past tea-chests and alien imported gods, groping towards oblongs of grey which I hoped were the uncurtained windows. I touched a pot-bellied black boy, and then another one, and so on, until I reached the end of the room. I found the door. I turned the handle, and it opened.

As I clicked it shut behind me, the lights came on in the room I'd just left. I needed a place to hide. Skirting the central podium, I started opening the cupboards beneath the display cabinets, but most of them were filled with bubble-wrap and boxes and resealable plastic bags. In one, there was a massy mortar and pestle. Apart from a few files, the cupboard in the furthest corner was empty. I pulled out the shelf and climbed inside, praying I was small enough to fit. Remarkably I was,

305

but only just, my arms squeezed tight and my cheek crushed hard against the pentangular wickerwork of the door.

On came the light, low-level to protect the relics, almost romantic.

'You're overreacting,' Helena protested. 'Light bulbs often explode on their own.'

'No they don't.'

'Rifka said it was nothing.'

'Rifka's gone strange on me. She's not the same Rifka she used to be.'

And also she must have stayed out on the landing, because I saw only two pairs of feet circle the pedestal in a clockwise direction. Slow, then stopping, like a couple of pensioners testing the air.

'Someone's in here,' Moholy said, his feet moving slightly apart. 'I can feel it. There's someone in here.'

'It's the relics,' Helena said quickly. 'Like when you showed them to Jay. There are loads of people in here, and they really *do* have presence, just as you always said.'

'No. I can really feel there's someone in here.'

'That's what I mean. Everyone feels it in the end. It's Van Gogh. And Byron. You know you can feel them. You can. I can. Everyone can.'

I heard him sniffing again. 'Well,' he said, 'you may be right.'

Helena was leading him out of the room, her feet beside his, slightly behind, as if guiding him gently by the elbow. He stopped once more, then turned off the light and closed the door behind him. I counted to ten, then spilled out from my cupboard. I reset my jaw with both hands, and rubbed at the side of my face, imprinted now with pentagons.

Then I went through the display cabinets, whispering softly

306

to the dead, cupping my hand to my ear. The dead weren't answering. I had to turn on the light, and read them each by their labels.

The way I did it was to assemble a body on the floor, bone by bone, in the shape of Jesus standing, or perhaps delivering a parable, getting the feet and legs right, and then the pelvis and trunk and the arms. From my detailed rebuilding of the bones in the apartment, I could now make a reasonable attempt at a human being. It didn't matter if a few odd bones were missing: Jesus was ancient and uncertain, but the basics had to be right, and the dates. I quickly hit trouble with the dates.

Moholy simply didn't have enough bones from the early sixteenth century, which when tested could conceivably pass for Calvin. After Suleiman's jaw and da Vinci's arm, the dates became ever more approximate, depending on what type of bone I needed next. Body-building was still a tricky business, and there weren't nearly enough ribs, and no patellas at all. One foot in particular was very stubborn.

Marco Polo's heel found its way in there, and of course Jung's knee-cap, which I'd brought along in the kit-bag. I recruited Sir Humphry Davy's foot-bone, and Thomas à Becket's toe. And each time I took a bone from Moholy's collection, I replaced it with its equivalent from the kit-bag, and the bones of Richard Burton. As I worked out the combinations, I sometimes scratched my head with Michelangelo's finger. Until finally, looking down at the skeleton, the finger-bone to my chin, I found myself tolerably satisfied with my construction of a compound body. It wasn't perfect, but it was acceptable. If Moholy only took one bone for testing, as he did last time, there was a decent enough chance, given providence and the existence of God (and perhaps a strong hint from Rifka), that he'd select a bone sufficiently close to Calvin's era.

I broke up the body, and fed the bones into the kit-bag, which of course was now empty. After double-checking I'd made all the replacements, I hefted the bag on to my shoulder, and turned off the light. I crossed the store-room, treading infallibly between the tea-chests, and the door at the other end was open. I went down the first section of stairs, turned on the landing, and swiftly descended the rest. I touched the front door, opened it, stepped outside, closed the door as quietly as I could, turned round, and then rang the bell.

The door opened again, and as I placed the kit-bag at Moholy's feet, I felt entirely and unnaturally fearless.

'Look,' Helena said. 'Just like I was telling you. It's Jay. And he's brought the promised bones.'

Moholy himself lifted the bag into the salon. Everything was turning out well. I wasn't a sad little fellow, a universal victim. That wasn't the proper Charlie, untouchable behind a protective film, a mover and shaker welcome among millionaires and royalty, winner of the Handel Medallion, the Stockholm Peace Prize, and an Order of Public Instruction. In all due modesty he accepted every honour, including a knighthood of the British Empire. The tomming and foolery was simply a screen. It was a way to get what he wanted.

'Would you like to sit down?' Moholy asked, his face suddenly close to mine, looking concerned.

'Yes, I would,' I said, realising I did feel somewhat faint. 'Very much. That is most kind of you.'

I went from a chair to the floor to a chaise-longue, testing them for comfort. I lay along a settee, my feet raised on cushions. I was sure that Moholy and the ladies would understand. It had been a very wearying day.

Jesus Christ's Neck

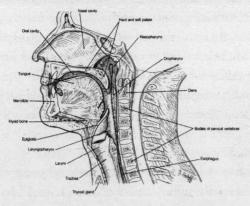

'It is no longer I who live, but Christ lives in me.'

Galatians 2:20

Only an hour or so into daylight on Sunday, the Lord's special day, and Joseph Moholy thought he was Jesus because we were all in a very small and fragile boat, on a very large and dangerous lake, but with no visible sign of a storm.

It was misty and achingly cold, even though Helena and I had brought the duvets from the house. The two of us were facing forward in the middle of the boat with our knees together and arms tightly crossed, and both of us were shivering. Rifka in the back seemed more comfortable, but she had the steering to keep her busy, and maybe even some heat from the busily puttering outboard.

'Where are we actually going?' Helena asked, her teeth chattering.

'To find hungry and sick people,' Moholy said, not looking

round from the prow. This morning's transfigured Joseph Moholy was nothing like my previous vision of Jesus, as a Mr Smith of mortal flesh on bone, ragged and forgotten amid the splendour of ancient Rome. I was now seeing a different Jesus, with infinite ambition, a driven force for good.

I'd woken up lying on my side, facing the glossy back of a settee in Moholy's vast living-room. A duvet, someone had found me a duvet. I closed my eyes, and turned over on to my other side. I wriggled and shifted but couldn't get comfortable. I opened my eyes. Moholy's face was inches from my own.

'Jesus fuck!'

I clutched my heart and lay on my back, and the ceiling seemed abysmally high. I glanced across, and Moholy was still there, cross-legged on the floor and wrapped in a blanket, his chin cupped gnomically in his hands. Then he was up, flinging off the blanket, already dressed in a collarless shirt outside baggy Indian-style trousers, and all-action sandals with Velcro straps. He hadn't shaved, and his stubble was thick enough to look like the shadow of a beard, making his face seem longer.

'Where's Helena?'

'She slept upstairs. I've already woken her. She's with Rifka in the kitchen.'

'What happened?'

'You fell asleep. You must have been exhausted.'

'On the settee?'

'You had us all worried. I slept beside you, on the floor, just in case.'

'That was kind of you. Thanks.'

'And I wanted to apologise. For the pills, and the tramlines. Sorry about that. It wasn't very nice of me.'

'Well, no, it wasn't.'

'You're sure you're alright?'

I pushed myself up into a sitting position, then checked my upper lip for the toothbrush moustache which wasn't there, and which had never been there. I was still in my clothes. Very tentatively, I swung one foot to the floor, then two, and stood up with my arms out, testing my balance on one leg and then the other. I didn't trip, slip or stumble.

'It seems to have worn off,' I said, discreetly moving my lobeless ear against the top of my shoulder. It was still sore, but less so. It was also a reassuring reminder of the real me, and I guessed always would be, now and for ever. 'No permanent damage.'

'Excellent,' Moholy said. 'Because we've been waiting for you for ages.'

In the big modern kitchen, Rifka was doing something at the stainless-steel range. Helena was leaning back against a metal counter, with her arms crossed. She looked wary, but surprisingly rested. I met her eye, and a twitch from her eyebrow instantly reminded me of the many events of yesterday.

Ah. Yes. I remembered we ought to be leaving. As soon as humanly possible. I therefore coughed into my hand and thanked Moholy for letting us stay the night. Helena didn't move.

'It looks like we're staying,' she said.

'Does it?'

'For the testing of the bones.'

Moholy would be sending a bone to his man at the lab, but we already knew that. I still had to ask Rifka to persuade him to pick out the jaw-bone, once of Suleiman the Magnificent, or perhaps the finger or an arm-bone. The resulting date close to the 1540s would persuade Moholy that the skeleton had to be Calvin. He could work out the rest for himself. However, I didn't see why Helena and I should have to wait for the results. We'd done as much as we could.

'You don't understand,' Helena said. 'It's a Sunday.'

'So?'

'Everything's closed. The University, the lab, everything.'

'Not to worry, though,' Moholy said, full of cheerful vigour, and all the joys of existence. 'There's more than one way to test a relic.'

'I'm sure there is,' I said. 'But we still have to be going.'

'You'll be staying,' Moholy said. 'And we'll be testing it together. In the true Christian spirit, I've decided we should all share in the one body.'

From his pocket, he took out a small bundle wrapped in Becket's purple circle of silk. Balancing it on the palm of his hand, he flicked away the edges to reveal three almost equal sections of neck-bone, presumably from the body I'd delivered last night as Jesus.

'I've deliberately selected small pieces,' Moholy said. 'We need to be mobile. We've got a busy day ahead of us.'

He held out the bones in the handkerchief. 'Go on, take one. Give the relic a chance to prove itself, in its own unique way.'

Moholy was wearing something odd and angular under the looseness of his shirt. As he stretched forward to offer us the bones, I saw it was a leather tool-belt, with various bones slotted into the hoops intended for hammers and chisels and bradawls. This wasn't a fair test: Moholy was way ahead of us.

'Thanks anyway,' I said, holding up my hand. 'I think I'll pass.'

'No, really,' Helena said, surprising me, picking out her

own section of neck-bone, like a chocolate from a box. She frowned hard at me, like a kick under the table. 'I really think you should.'

'Of course, if the test fails,' Moholy said, his morning brightness suddenly fading in lustre, 'and if I am unable to act well, I shall hold the two of you personally responsible. For my humiliation.'

'Ah yes,' I said, 'I think I see.'

Helena's eyes flicked up to heaven, as if reminding God that one day, whenever He had the time, it would be interesting to discover just how far a person had to travel to reach the limits of my stupidity.

'And if the bones work?'

'Well, all will be forgiven, obviously.'

I selected my sample of neck from the cloth.

'It can't hurt, can it?' Rifka said, taking the last piece. She closed one eye, and looked at me with the other through the hollow core of the neck-bone of Jesus. 'Why shouldn't we try to be good?'

Because one year ago, or perhaps in a couple of years' time, depending on the reliability of historical sources, Jesus was being nailed in public to a large wooden cross. That's what happens to the good guys, and it was quickly becoming clear that Moholy's Jesus wasn't a rabbinical Hasid, in the peaceful tradition of Hanina ben Dosa or Honi the Circle Drawer, wise miracle-workers with privileged access to the power of God. He was earthier than that, bonier. He was the raw factual Jesus of history, and not the tinkered Christ of Christianity. He wasn't serene, divine, detached. He was the pre-Easter Jesus, impatient, a rebel and man of action exhorting the villagers of Galilee to resist the Romans and their pampered client kings.

'Right then,' Moholy said. 'I hope we can agree that we're men of the people.'

Nailed through his palms and feet as an example to others, with so much more to come: the spear in the side and the broken legs and the crows and the dogs, buried alive, for crimes of public disorder. Moholy needed slowing down, and clever Helena insisted on breakfast. Coffee, some rolls she'd spied in the bread-bin. Moholy could hardly refuse, because the gospel Jesus stops to eat with just about everyone. He did hesitate, but only briefly, and then his better nature prevailed.

'Go ahead,' he said. 'Whatever you want.'

I liked to think, when it came to stalling and holding Moholy back, that I made an important contribution. 'Any unsalted butter?'

Rifka found some in the fridge.

And perhaps some marmalade. She found some in the cupboard.

Too easy. Lemon curd. In another cupboard. How did she do that?

'Tinned pilchards,' I suggested. What I really fancied for my breakfast, with a long day of goodness ahead of me, was a tin of oily pilchards.

'No problem,' Rifka said, 'cupboard under the sink.'

And of course when she tossed me the tin the last thing I wanted was pilchards. We put the fish and some uneaten rolls in Rifka's canvas bag. This was Helena's idea, and a sensible precaution against any far-fetched notions Moholy might be having that we'd eaten our final meal, a kind of last breakfast. We wanted to keep everything less ominous than that, less fatal.

'Lunch,' I explained, a little too loudly, handing the bag back to Rifka. Unfortunately, this also acted as a signal that we must be eager to leave. Moholy was already at the door from the kitchen to the garden, swinging it open.

'About time,' he said. 'Follow me.'

And we did. And fully intended to continue following, without hesitation, until the first opportunity to run away. Moholy stopped at an outhouse for some long-handled wire-cutters, then led us down the terraced lawns to his private jetty. Looking back at the villa, elegantly smudged by the dawn mist, it was tempting to run straight back up the dark green trails we'd made in the dew.

Like a prayer answered, the outboard motor on the small wooden boat wouldn't start.

'Let me have a go,' Rifka said. She pulled the cord, and it started first time in a rich blue cloud of two-stroke. She slowed it by the choke to an easy putter, and Moholy helped us on board. Wrapped in our duvets we faced forward as Rifka steered us away from land, into the mist lifting from the surface of glassy Lake Geneva.

In the boat I was cold, and I was also frightened. There were no bones of Jesus. Moholy's Jesus was a compound body I'd personally constructed from his upstairs collection of historical figures. They weren't even particularly virtuous. As a mix, they were neither all good nor all bad, but the full range of what was possible.

Jesus was Moholy's imagined triumph, a trophy beyond compare which made significant his empty and lonely existence. It was only now that I began to understand how lonely, and how empty. Moholy needed the bones of Jesus, more urgently than we'd realised, and our only chance of saving ourselves was to humour him. Now that he'd given us each a section of neck-bone, we had a vested interest in pretending the bones had influence.

We too would have to act like Jesus; he had us trapped in the necessity of goodness.

To convince him that we were carrying the holiest of relics, I pretended not to suffer. I even tried a form of meditation popular at theology college, in which the aim was to visualise an event in the life of Christ. Shivering, tucked up in a small open boat, all that came to mind was Jesus frightened. Jesus frightened in a small open boat. On a lake. I could do better than that. Jesus frightened in the desert, or in an overcrowded manger, cows snuffling at his new-born head. Jesus frightened by the rest of the day, every day, and the passing of time towards his immovable ordained death.

Jesus frightened as he moved west towards Rome, of his growing reputation as a Messiah ascended into heaven. Below decks, hiding from spies and atheists, how could he ever live up to that? Already at Patmos, he wanted to moderate the extravagance of his growing cult. He tried to talk to John of Zebedee, a visit which John exaggerated into a visitation, and the opening excesses of the Book of Revelation. It was getting out of control, even though Jesus personally explained his intentions and the implications of his thinking to Paul, and later Luke. Life and the best way to live wasn't as complicated as those two seemed to think.

'People, be good to each other.'

'Yes, fine,' Paul said. 'Now what about the details of the resurrection?'

'I am not the son of God.'

'We are all sons of God.'

'Yes, I know. I know that, Paul. But I am not the perfect example you want me to be.'

'But you *could* have been. Couldn't you?'

Jesus so frightened by the time he reached Philippi that he

ignored Paul's advice to stay hidden, and defiantly married the Hellenist Bishop Lydia, to remind his followers he was both human and fallible. Frightened the last time he was seen in Rome, in AD 64, ageing and feeble on the Appian Way, limping in the flame-light of Christians burning, his broken hands clamped in his armpits, thirty years since he was supposed to have died and risen and saved us from sin, and now with no imminent hope of salvation.

Jesus remembered simpler days, back in Galilee, when he and his brothers had confounded the powerful with no thought for policy, or replacement programmes. They'd just known instinctively that the world could be better than it was. He forgot how they knew that, but they weren't alone in their conviction that the rich were not obliged to be selfish. The powerful could be more considerate in their use of power. Jesus had never been any kind of monk, detaching himself from the world and believing it a virtue. He'd made his objections known.

Rifka cut the engine, and the boat drifted alongside an impressive chain-link fence, which emerged from the mist like a dappled trick of the light. On the other side was a sandy walkway in the grounds of the United Nations, which in times less fearful had been open to the public. We clutched the boat close to the fence while Moholy clipped an opening with the cutters.

'Is this a good idea?' Helena asked, huddled up in the middle of the boat. 'You're supposed to be a pacifist.'

'Never.'

Moholy was struggling with a stubborn link, but he persisted, and it gave with a snap. He was already prising the edges of the fence apart when Rifka stepped along the boat and tugged at his shirt, toppling him back on to his seat at the front.

'Not yet,' Rifka said gently. 'You'll get yourself killed.'

Moholy gave her a strange look, but Rifka had already cast off the boat, and back in the stern she restarted the outboard. She steered us into clear water, and then turned through the mist towards the city. We came in past the machinery of the water-jet, which was off, and the marina where the slightest breeze rattled the masts and steel-sheets of the yachts. We sensed the closeness of the city before seeing it, and then the hillside Cathedral rising like a minor Turner from the fog. Moholy casually tossed the wire-cutters over the side, and we slid in to the base of the concrete dock usually reserved for day-trippers from Evian, and Thonon-les-Bains.

Rifka tied the boat to an iron ring in the wall, then jumped out on to the concrete steps leading up to the quay. Helena quickly followed, leaving the duvet behind and stamping her feet for warmth. Then it was my turn. I jumped level with Helena, then climbed a step or two above Rifka, to leave room for Moholy. We all waited, but Moholy didn't jump. Rifka held out her hand, as Moholy balanced himself against the roll of the boat. He licked his lips, and looked closely at the dark water lapping at the lowest dry step, another ghostly step blurred but visible below. Moholy could easily have taken Rifka's hand and stepped on up, but he seemed transfixed by the sight of the lower step, shifting under the lurch and retreat of the lake. He rubbed the back of his hand across his unshaven chin. His bottom lip reached up towards his nose. He steadied himself on the edge of the boat, took Rifka's hand, and then deliberately stepped straight down on to the submerged lower step.

The sole of his sandal, just for an instant, for a tiny moment, seemed to hesitate on the surface of the water.

Then it slapped straight through, and he sank.

'Let's go!' Moholy said, planting his dry foot two steps

further up, shaking free of Rifka's hand, and leaping past us up the rest of the steps several at a time. We caught up with him at the top, and stood there on the quay waiting for whatever occurred to him next.

'*What?*' he said. We were all looking at his one damp sandal, and the water of the lake draining across concrete in a single timid rivulet. 'Let's *go*.'

Further along the quay, there was a man dressed as a cruise-missile lying in the shelter of the Brunswick Monument. Two of his friends were cutting open the foam rubber of the costume, and examining one of his legs. He couldn't walk. The others hadn't actually been there, but they thought he'd been hit by a plastic bullet.

I watched Moholy closely. At no stage did he make any attempt to touch the injured man.

For some time afterwards, we gamely tracked the print of Moholy's one sandal, as the wetness and shape of the impression gradually faded along the grey Geneva roads and pavements. This early in the morning, demonstrators were easily outnumbered by police, solid in squads at the strategic ends of the streets. They were impervious behind their plastic shields and their plastic visors, their plastic knee-caps and inarticulate plastic knuckles, safeguarding the complacent and powerful from the vexed and powerless. There wasn't much doubt: we did need Jesus at this time.

As the sun finally broke through, at last dispersing the mist and haze from the lake, skeletons appeared everywhere, spontaneously, even more skeletons than we'd seen yesterday at the cemetery. This was now officially The Protest of Bones, as proclaimed on banners and hurriedly printed T-shirts. But the demonstration itself was everywhere at once, and nowhere. We couldn't find its heart.

At Place Neuve, we came across jugglers and cyclists, fire-eaters and violinists, and great masses of young people in all the brightest colours doing nothing much but sitting on the new-laid grass. The entire square, until yesterday thrumming with traffic, was like a park in summer, and along with the tom-toms and chatter was a heady sense of expectation. There was also the strong feeling that nobody knew what to do next.

We picked our way through a sit-in of youngsters, our hands held high to apologise, treading carefully in search of steps on solid earth. We joined them at the edge, sitting, doing nothing. Calvin would have disapproved, but Moholy looked on kindly, and we were taking our lead from him.

For the first time in twenty-four hours, I slipped out of my grubby collar, and stuffed it roughly in my pocket. I loosened the top buttons of my clerical shirt. I saw a T-shirt saying *Eat the Rich*, but then a more comradely one with *Jesus Saves Sights of Specific Scientific Interest*, which was in among a giggle of evangelist Americans. They all had day-glo badges, *WWJD, What Would Jesus Do?* There were so many different groups making up the protest, from the Red Brigade to the Christian Bicycle Alliance, that nobody knew how best to make their complaint.

Moholy, full of faith, confidence and optimism, all the best bits of religion, set off on a tour of the square to find out what was planned for the rest of the day. We admired his enthusiasm, but from afar, and while sharing the bread and pilchards. We offered a fish-roll to a Dane wearing a sky-blue bandanna with a yellow skull and bones. And he halved it with the skeleton-girl next to him, making this the feeding of the five. Several days ago, I might have mistaken the Danes for Smiths, but to Jesus there were no Mr Smiths, and in fact this was brother and sister Lars and Karen Knudsen from Silkeborg, who objected to Shell's disposal of North Sea oil platforms in the Scandinavian fjords, and who along with thousands of like-minded named and motivated protesters would carry on moving from city to city with ever brighter ideas until the world eventually changed.

By the time Moholy came back from his tour, we'd finished the food and there were no baskets of leftovers, not even for him. He'd somehow collected a small band of followers, though not the evangelists, and discovered that our earlier perception of the protest was correct. It had no focus. There were the skeletons, which were fine and highly mediatic, but they weren't actually doing much. And before dawn, some Italians in white overalls had liberated a thousand refugees of many nationalities from an enclosed camp on the southern outskirts of the city. This had created an unexpected problem. The refugees were now streaming into the city-centre, and, like everyone else, they were hungry. The city had closed up for the day, and nobody could find anything to eat.

With my tongue, I loosened a pilchard bone from between my teeth. I looked at Helena, who looked at Rifka, who looked at her fingernails. Interestingly, I thought, a police helicopter was hovering overhead.

'Geneva is full of food,' Moholy said. 'This is ridiculous.'

He'd found an objective, and there was nothing overly grand about the responsibility he now assumed. He was concerned with essentials, whether people had enough to eat, and he had an idea for solving the problem. A few of those he'd assembled together quietly murmured their approval. Moholy was offering leadership, and these people were desperate for leaders, hoping that this time, when they did emerge, they wouldn't be as fake as Ben and Jerry.

'We need to get organised,' Moholy said. 'We need a base of operations.'

Moholy gave a good impression of knowing what he was doing. He therefore quickly gathered a crowd, which increased as he led the way through embattled streets to the former Anglican Church of All Saints. 'It's my church,' Moholy said. 'I'll do as I like with it.'

It was a few minutes before eleven, and we were met at All Saints by an awkward stand-off. The protesters who'd been sleeping in the church, in return for attending my sermon as Calvin, had been using the tower as a lookout. In the last half-hour, a different congregation, the one which had assembled unbidden at the same time last Sunday, had once again arrived at the door. They would not be deterred from coming together, to think on spiritual things.

The protesters in the doorway were stubbornly keeping them out.

Led by Mr Oti and Mrs Meier, the Anglicans were refusing to leave.

Moholy came between them. Undeniably, there were those who already knew that Moholy owned the church. And there were others, mostly among the protesters, who were impressed by the following he'd collected between Place Neuve and here. But it was easy to rationalise, and lose sight of the facts. Later, there would be many different versions of events, but it was still a fact that this localised argument was swiftly resolved by the presence and self-assurance of Joseph Moholy.

He insisted that both congregations stay, and that Anglicans as well as protesters could contribute to the success of the second reformation.

Jesus, as always, was full of surprises. He asked me to lead a service. 'Just a short one,' he said. 'A few words to keep everyone happy, and then we'll change the world.'

The heavy door, as it always did, soon closed us into the soft brown bag of England, as quiet as mushrooms growing. Like last Sunday, and too many Sundays to remember before that, in the days of the former Chaplain, the church committee and the Sri Lankans and the other English-speaking regulars assembled in neat rows, but from the back, as if the pews were still in place. The protesters were less experienced. Some of them even came to the front.

Moholy nudged me, and I moved reluctantly forward towards the altar, feeling under-dressed and unsure of myself. I remembered the last time I was here, as Chaplin, but I resisted a slide along the aisle. Christianity couldn't be laughed away. It had to be taken seriously. In my country, on my continent, it represented the most persistent collective attempt to account for the human condition. For more than 2000 years, millions of people had used it to make sense of *everything*, and you couldn't just laugh that off.

Up on the step I turned. I lifted up my hands.

The protesters, arms crossed or hands in pockets. The loyal Anglicans, heads bowed. And Moholy in a chance beam of sunlight at the back, Helena on one side, Rifka on the other. Rifka popped a couple of pills. For the first time in my career in the Church, it was as if I were genuinely being held to account, an Anglican deacon in a position to preach to Jesus. With the added complication that Moholy believed he'd given me a Jesus-bone. In his eyes, I was a deacon *and* I was Jesus, and so was he. So what would the son of God preach to the son of God?

Keep it simple. Be yourself.

But no, that wasn't right. I was finding it difficult to grasp the personality of Jesus. He was so selfless. He was change-able, unpredictable, as an innate characteristic of sharing what it meant to be human. He could be anyone. He was a carpenter and King of the Jews, a peasant and heir to the royal line of David. He was a revolutionary, a prophet, a mystic, a teacher, a charismatic leader and a misguided clown. He was father and son, lamb and shepherd, and the shifts could be so sudden and radical that sometimes he wasn't recognised even by those who loved him most. Mary Magdalene once mistook him for a gardener. The disciples on the road to Emmaus talked with him for many hours before realising who he was.

Why not Moholy? Why not any of us? We could all be Jesus. Jesus could be us.

'Our Father,' I said, instantly becoming Jesus, as every one of us did every time we said this prayer, 'Our Father, who art in heaven.'

It was an impersonation, and always had been, and this sudden revelation filled me with joy. I reached out for everything I was certain of, a conclusion with which the Jesus in Moholy must surely agree, and the same revelation my father shared at the end of every Lent. Help the weak. Doubt the powerful.

'People, for God's sake, be good to each other.'

We had to keep coming back to this, as Jesus always did, because it was the truth.

I skipped the Eucharist, despite the reserves in the safe, the back-up box of a thousand hosts and the bottles of dark red Sanctifex. I wasn't prepared to wrestle with the issue of whether Jesus would eat himself. It was the kind of exquisite complication a professional theologian would love, but I wasn't that, so I jumped straight to the dismissal, and for superstitious reasons omitted the last words of the last line of my very brief service. It had always felt like bad luck to bring it to an end, a final full stop.

God *will show us the path of life; in his presence is*

And after a little doubtful murmuring, my small but loyal share of God's people agreeably finished it on my behalf: *Amen.*

That was it, that was all. Now it was Moholy's turn for his own version of Jesus, his impersonation, and the always vital task of feeding the hungry.

Moholy was true to his word. He had a plan. He stood at the front of the church, where until recently I had stood, and he offered leadership. His plan was simple.

To give the demonstration a focus, and a heart, we would enlist as many protesters as possible to tear down the nailed chipboard protecting the city's franchised fast-food restaurants. Damage to the properties themselves should be minimal. Among the demonstrators, there were hordes who'd already worked for these chains, in this and all the other countries of the world. That was one of the reasons they were here, protesting, dissatisfied with the way the planet was organised.

The franchise operations were identical everywhere, so the ex-employees would be familiar with the equipment and stocks. They knew how to break out the cold-store and turn up the music. They knew how the griddles worked, but after that their imaginations could run free, unfranchised. Come and get it: fast food, but not as the accountants would know it.

That was one aspect of the plan. But Moholy also had another, more specific objective, for which he'd need one wired skeleton, a real one, and a handful of courageous volunteers. While the main demonstration created a diversion at the entrance to the United Nations, this small group of volunteers would go by boat to a hole already cut in the perimeter fence. After entering the park of the Palace of Nations, they would infiltrate the World Intellectual Property Organisation, and hang the wired skeleton by the neck from a top-floor window, beside a large banner proclaiming the execution and death of Geneva's John Calvin.

Moholy didn't explain why or exactly how the parable was supposed to work. To some people, this didn't seem to matter, though it was also true that many others were unsure what to make of him. There were those who grinned smugly and walked off, shaking their heads, as if there was a better answer which was perfectly obvious and which they alone perceived, but which equally they had no intention of sharing, now or ever.

It had been the same the first time round. His own family thought Jesus insane. Others saw him as simply eccentric, and a tiny minority considered him a dangerous threat to the prevailing political system. But even if Jesus wasn't the son of God, he still had popular appeal as a reasonable first-century visionary, and it was on this understanding that many agreed to follow him.

Inspired, I was one of the first to leave the church, dashing out into the bright Swiss morning. Helena and I were going to help with the diversion at the UN, and already Moholy had his volunteers for the boat. He and Rifka would be in neither one place nor the other, but instead they'd be here, there and everywhere, ensuring that everything worked out well. It was so unexpectedly wonderful, I forgot that it ended unhappily.

On the road out to the Palace of Nations, we were able to

recruit any number of ex-short-order chefs who wanted, at last, to compose wild and unbudgeted combinations of their own unlimited invention. I found three Spanish girls who'd worked dunking fries through two years of their Masters on the Economics of Democracy. They were happy to lend a hand. In some of the franchises, people were already eating, and they'd made long tables out of the slabs of chipboard from the windows, overlaying the little bitterness of the standard plastic seating arrangements.

These transformations were evidence of divine justice, or the revenge of the exploited, or a sign that the police were simply tired of standing in the way of reforms the majority clearly wanted. As the day wore on, the police were softened by so much non-violence, by playful skeletons, and flower-petals, and a phalanx of protesters in inflated yellow life-jackets, for no obvious reason.

I slipped my crumpled collar back into place, finally beginning to understand. I wasn't Jesus. I *knew* my neck-bone wasn't Jesus, the primary resource of the Christian life, the pivot of Western history. But I did believe in Jesus, or at least the possibility of someone with a more solid grasp than the rest of us on the true patterns of existence. Whatever the disputed truth about his death, there remained the example of his life, and the one-time wonder of a Jesus of blood and bones. His kind of enlightenment was open to us all. He was a man. Act like him: no divine paternity required.

We ducked into an alley to avoid three speeding police vans. Moholy and Rifka were near by. They were always near by, and wherever they went there was a perceptible surge of energy. None of us claimed to have all the answers. We were more like heralds, delivering an urgent message which couldn't wait: there must be better ways to organise how we live now, before it ends in disaster. We were following in a long tradition of dissenting prophets, from Micaiah ben Imlah to Ezekiel to Jeremiah, Jonah and Amos, Elijah and Elisha. Come one, come all.

Come Joseph Moholy and the mysterious Rifka, and Helena Byczynski and me.

For years you look for Jesus, and nothing. Then several come along at once. In all my life I'd never seen Helena so radiant, as if channelling the goodness of all the causes she'd ever defended, making up for God's absence with her own commitment and energy. This might not have been the second coming, and He may not ever be coming, but it was a day of joy, and we could still believe in days like this.

At the Palace of Nations, and it was the middle of the afternoon before we reached the main entrance, the atmosphere suddenly changed.

In front of the two-metre-high fence, the human cordon was made up of soldiers, not police, and they were all very young, and carrying guns. Many of the protesters wore scratched motorcycle helmets, and the front rank stood less than a metre from the line of soldiers, while a loudspeaker in three languages advised us to disperse. It was a recording, not a person. Smoke and particles of tear-gas drifted in the wind.

Helena insisted on snaking through to the front. Someone going the other way handed her a flat box, and my heart gradually sank as I followed her ever closer to the fence.

There was no sign of Moholy, or Rifka. I felt strangely lost without them, and even as Helena smartly identified open channels through the packed crowd of bodies, I looked beneath our feet for lingering evidence of Moholy's one wet sandal. I couldn't believe that he'd abandon us now. For reassurance, I took out my fragment of neck-bone, and clenched it in my fist. Nothing happened. It didn't help. I dropped it, and didn't even look to see where it fell. I'd have to find another way to explain myself.

We were now only two or three heads from the front. Helena opened the flat box, and handed me several rolls of coloured cotton. They were miniature flags, wrapped round sticks of balsa, and it was as if everyone else had taken a step back. We could now see the hair in the nostrils of the para-militaries fronting the fence. They kept raising and lowering their guns, and making defensive gestures with their elbows. The loudspeaker went on and on behind them, advising us to disperse, getting on everyone's nerves.

Helena stepped forward and slotted a little red flag into the rifle-barrel of a national serviceman. It unrolled from its stick, *Bang!*

'Time to be good,' she said.

Being good was one of the ways to be different. Like the other times I'd acted with high hopes, I still wanted to distinguish myself. That would explain why I believed in Jesus. It had nothing to do with Moholy or pieces of bone. Knowing my own weakness, I needed to believe in people different from and better than myself, and before I knew it I was an ordained deacon in a religion founded on the greatness of a single individual. From the start, in even the strictest Christian households, for 2000 years, Jesus had been feeding and reinforcing and perhaps even creating our Western need for heroes. The history of Christianity was founded on our willingness to believe that some people were special. Meaning that I, too, could be special. If Him, why not me?

But, like him, I was also frightened.

I summoned the resolve of a Thomas à Becket, and pro-jected his exultation at witnessing what I was doing: the first deacon in 500 years to risk his life for the Church of England. It was stupid. So stupid and unnecessary. But that had never stopped Becket. Come on, Thomas. The chainmail is sweeping the aisles, they're thumping at the doors. You could bend. You could run. Moholy was out of his mind on Jesus, and this was the moment to run. Go on, run. Hide. This is suicidal.

I searched out all the Becketness I'd once ascribed to his cold and lifeless toe-bone. Becket was in *me*, not the bone, and I didn't have to be close to Becket the relic to have him intercede. The bone was just an excuse, an explanation.

I stepped forward, and placed a green flag in the barrel of a shaking rifle. It unrolled. *Pop!* The soldier frantically nudged me away with his elbow, but was scared of breaking ranks.

And just then, on the other side of the fence, a wired skeleton was tumbled from a mid-floor window of the World Intellectual Property Organisation. It was bouncing from the neck, its bobbing skull grinning insanely above the neat cream ruff of a noose. From the next window along, a banner unfurled. CALVIN IS DEAD. They'd only made it half-way up the building, but it was still impressive. The crowd on our side of the fence cheered and whooped.

The paramilitaries were now isolated, with subversives on both sides of them. I felt their sudden fear and, also, a sharp pain, the absence of Moholy. We were undefended against folly, and error. I should have worn a crash helmet.

On our side of the fence, from way back in the crowd, protesters were pushing forward, hoping to break through to the pioneering heroes on the other side. The soldiers pushed back. Helena was turned in the wrong direction, standing on her toes, craning her neck in search of Moholy.

At least one gun was raised. At least one serviceman lost his nerve.

And then they shot my Helena in the back.

She fell. And as she fell, the crowd by instinct sucked itself out, leaving her alone in a suddenly silent hole of road. I was too slow to catch her, and the side of her head rebounded horribly off the tarmac. Do something, man. Jesus. Just do something.

I shouted at her. She didn't respond. I was down on my knees. Pulse, breath, anything. Shout. In those first few seconds, I was already deep in my deepest resources, the surface closed over and expressionless, assessing the damage clinically like a Davy, with the information to hand, and hoping like Davy for positive scientific results. Helena was dying, was going to die. That was the entirety of my information. There may have been other factors which were also relevant, but just now I didn't know what they were, and perhaps they wouldn't become known for many centuries to come.

Pull yourself together.

Jung would have left no question unasked. Ask the dead, ask the living, but for God's sake, ask. Is there any other possible outcome? I picked Helena up in my arms, and I started to run. There must be some other outcome.

At first, I had no idea where I was going, except away from the fence and through crowds and back towards town. Helena's legs and arms and head were flopping heavily with each of my laboured paces, and it was true, in those first faltered steps, before I fully knew what I was doing or where I was going, that I had a moment of doubt, a wet blanket of Mr Smithness. Helena was dying, already dead in my arms. None of us were chosen people, not Helena, not Rifka, not even Moholy. We were never destined to get away with this, and all our efforts were vain. We were the same as everyone else.

But still I kept on running, running, because everyone else, too, could be like us, changing, adapting, one moment defeated as Mr Smith and the next blazing with faith as Richard Burton, physically invincible, rallying his indignant Possibles against all odds to one final effort.

Run, find Moholy, run.

I kept up a brutal pace by being severe on myself, knowing I deserved Helena dying in my arms because I'd never been sufficiently humble. I should have tried harder, and prayed more often, and been more grateful. It was a punishment for drinking and over-eating, for worrying, when I should have trusted without question my life and destiny to Calvin's awkward city of Geneva. I didn't dare check that Helena was still breathing, because what will be will be, and I found some comfort in that. Some.

Keep going. Be stubborn. Back to Becket. In moments of true need, rising to my full potential, I was everybody. I was Becket and Davy and Burton and Jung and Calvin. Added up, I too was almost Jesus.

Out of breath, stumbling, head weightless and starved of oxygen, I saw Moholy and Rifka at the closed and chained gates to the Parc des Bastions. There were improvised ladders either side of them, and protesters were swarming up and over, into the park. They all had skeletons, of all shapes and sizes, all types and materials, dragging them behind, throwing them on ahead.

Rifka saw me first. She turned Moholy towards me, and Moholy lifted up his arms. I laid Helena at his feet, and we all knelt. It was too late. Helena's face was white, and her head fell limply to one side. Moholy touched her neck, but it was too late. He leant down his head. He closed his eyes, and touched his unshaven cheek to the smooth coldness of her forehead.

And I couldn't help but notice, as he was doing this, that Helena's lifeless and half-opened fingers were taken up quietly by Rifka, and gently cradled in her compassionate and feminine hands.

While we built the pyre, the late sunshine turned the stonework of the Reformers' Monument a colour close to mustard. In the open spaces inside the park, facing the Reformers' Wall, this firelight vigil would be the final offering of the Protest of Bones to Geneva's gods of reform.

Now, as darkness fell, the ten-foot statues of Farel and Calvin, of Knox and Theodore de Bèze, shifted and flickered in the flame-light. *Post Tenebras Lux*, said the monument, Light Follows Darkness.

After the disturbance at the United Nations, the park had been isolated by a siege of police. Thousands of us sat silently on the grass, watching the ritual burning of the weekend's collected skeletons. In all their different materials, their different shapes and sizes, they fed the blaze of the pyre in the Parc des Bastions, the flames crackling like a memory of burning martyrs, like the sound of bodies breaking a thousand sticks. Television crews eager for footage panned out then zoomed in, each skeleton in flames like a Buddhist monk, about to topple. The real bones were gloriously stubborn, and solid in the flame-light like X-rays.

Helena hadn't been shot. Or she had been shot, then been healed by a miracle. I didn't know what to think. There was a spreading bruise on the side of her head where she'd hit the pavement, and she said her whole body hurt like hell.

'What about the baby?'

'Fine.'

'How do you know?'

'It's fine.'

She clutched her knees and went back to fire-watching, at liberty like everyone else to see in the flames pictures of the past, the future. Or nothing. Or swarms of early-evening insects, bouncing off the thermals.

We were sitting in a row, me and Helena, then Rifka and Moholy. Moholy had his feet stretched out towards the fire, and at least once today, the last time very recently, he must have found himself back at the lakeside. The synthetic sole of one of his sandals, as it dried, was gently steaming.

My Head

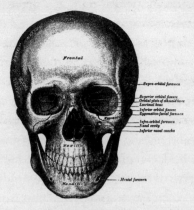

'Over an infinitely long span of time, all things happen to all men. As reward for his past and present virtues, every man merited every kindness – yet also every betrayal, as reward for his past and future iniquities.'

Jorge Luis Borges, *The Immortal*

In the city of Buenos Aires, in the Palermo district, there is a newish museum dedicated to the memory of Argentina's most celebrated writer, Jorge Luis Borges. It is in the Calle Anchorena, the setting of the young Georgie's childhood fantasies, and the museum takes the form of a house refurbished in the style of the home where Borges once lived, also in the Calle Anchorena. The original is a little further along the street, and a little further on again, about as far as a fanatic's stone throw, is another memorial, the slightly older Fundación Jorge Luis Borges, established in 1995 by the writer's widow, Maria Kodama. Although the museum and the foundation coexist as rivals, boasting their differences, neither institution displays a single original manuscript or letter. They own nothing of Borges's writing.

Between them, what they do have is a selection of photographs, and various ornaments and personal items once belonging to Borges the man. His favourite stick, for example, and some of his old man's sombre and portly suits. They have his desk, and the watch which he couldn't read but kept in his top pocket all the same, attached to his lapel with a chain. They have ticket stubs from his blindly optimistic trips to the cinema, and domestic objects of surprising intimacy, such as his double bridge of gleaming man-made teeth.

On hearing of the engagement of an old flame, unwelcome news to an elderly man some years past his prime, Borges had called in the dentist. For reasons which have remained unclear, the teeth he still had in his head were extracted. His replacement dentures were a perfect set, top and bottom.

I wrote my letter to the Museo, not the Fundación, out of respect for Borges's widow. I didn't want to upset anybody. Although it might seem incredible (I wrote, and it was a letter I savoured in the act of writing), the bones of Jorge Luis Borges, until recently buried in Geneva's Cimetière des Rois, had unexpectedly entered my possession. I gave a box number, in Geneva, to which the Museo could respond.

Several weeks had now passed since the climax of the Protest of Bones, and the city was still recovering. Some of Geneva's citizens, and not all of them pessimists, thought their city would never be the same again. The municipal authorities had been hard at work. They'd rapidly established, by a series of dating-tests at the University, that none of those bones which had survived the fire belonged now, or had ever belonged, to John Calvin. This included a comprehensive analysis of the skeleton so callously hung by the neck from the World Intellectual Property Organisation.

Unfortunately, Calvin's grave was still empty. Perhaps it had always been empty, as some commentators liked to suggest. In which case, various theories could be put forward about where the body actually was.

By common consent, the best guess was America. Calvin's bones would probably have made the crossing with a band of loyal long-ago pilgrims. East coast, to begin with, perhaps not far from Salem. As the years went by, Calvin was gradually moved inland, his bones making a full contribution to the fantastic early idealism of America's mid-west States. They had Europe's best people: the hard-working, the adventurous, the disaffected, all of whom believed they were chosen. They may have been mistaken, but they got a lot done. Still did, and it made sense for Calvin to continue seeing his future on the American side of the ocean, where ninety million people were personally in touch with the living Jesus.

The city and people of Geneva finally had to accept that in all probability their champion John Calvin would never be recovered. A replica stone, the size of a shoebox, was set in place over his repaired plot, and blessed by the Protestant Bishop. As consolation for the absence of Calvin, the Bishop claimed that an empty grave was an outcome in the history of the city which seemed predestined. It was precisely what Calvin himself would have wanted.

The day after the Bishop's blessing, the Cimetière des Rois was reopened to the public. By which time I'd been staring at the blue plastic sports-bag for nearly a fortnight. It contained our only remaining bones, and I'd resolved once more to establish who these bones might be. I'd then know the fairest way to dispose of them. To find out, I was dependent on

337

Helena's bright idea that the paste of cement-dust and filler should give it away. However undisturbed a stone might look, the self-made mortar I'd used as a sealant ought still to be soft. It remained my best hope of detecting the identity of the skeleton, and I was there, first thing in the morning, waiting at the gate, on the day the cemetery reopened.

For the sake of appearances, with several others who'd come to pay their respects, I stopped at Calvin's restored shoebox, and solemnly shook my head. Then, when everyone else had left, I went straight to the nearest graves, and began my investigations.

Closest to Calvin on his left was a Mrs Smith: *J'ai plus de souvenirs que si j'avais mille ans.* I knelt down and felt for the seam of the recumbent. The join was hard and rough, old, untouched. Not this one. There was a Mr Smith behind, and another in front, and several more from the family Smith in both directions to the side. None of them was secretly held together by mortar soft to the touch.

Not far away at all was Jorge Luis Borges, who at the end of his life could only see the colour yellow. *Jorge ven a casa.*

I felt round the base of his red granite recumbent, but the mortar was undeniably dry, and brittle with age. It wasn't Borges. I tried François Simon: the same. It was impossible to tell. I'd waited too long, and in the time that had passed since my night as Burton, the paste of cement-dust and filler had become as solid and uncommunicative as mortar in place for years.

But life must go on.

The bones in the blue plastic sports-bag, spurned by Moholy, were becoming an embarrassment. I didn't know where to put them, or rebury them with the appropriate respect and dignity. As the next best thing, and unquestionably an improvement on doing nothing, I decided they might as well be Borges. They could be Borges. He was in good health, well fed and almost contemporary, a close enough match to the results of Moholy's test, should anyone care to test him again. I let myself be persuaded. *Of course* it was Borges. I should have guessed. Otherwise why assemble this story? It was the influence; it was the bones.

In my letter to the Borges Museum, I was wary of making unfounded claims, but the jumble of bones as they crowded my desk-top did seem to emit a specifically Borgesian energy.

The goal that led him on was not impossible, though it was clearly supernatural: he wanted to dream a man. He wanted to dream him completely in painstaking detail, and impose him upon reality. The magical objective had come to fill his entire soul; if someone had asked him his own name, or inquired into any feature of his life until then, he would not have been able to answer.

The assistant director of the museum wrote back, deftly phrasing an uncommitted kind of curiosity. The people of Argentina, he wrote, were not unfamiliar with the ongoing lives of the dead. Evita, not the person but the corpse, had been kidnapped from a chapel of rest and secretly shipped to Milan. The hands of Juan Perón, Borges's favourite politician, had been amputated at the wrist, and ransomed.

For many years, as was public knowledge, the Museo Jorge Luis Borges had led an international campaign seeking the repatriation of a national and cultural treasure, namely the remains of Borges the writer. The recent violation of John Calvin, a close neighbour of Borges in Geneva's Cimetière des Rois, had only confirmed the widespread consensus that Borges would be better protected and appreciated in Buenos Aires, where he undoubtedly belonged.

Without explicitly declaring an interest, the governing body of the Museo managed to suggest they'd be grateful for indications of authenticity, price and import regulations.

I was not a dishonest or greedy man, and nor was Borges. I referred to Moholy's catalogue, and quoted the catalogue price. Except for a small bone of indeterminate function I was holding back as a keepsake, all I now had left, in front of me on the table in the kitchen, was the skull. The rest of the body I'd packed into various sizes of padded envelope, which over the course of the last month I'd posted in stages to the Calle Anchorena, where Borges used to live.

On the outside of each envelope, on the customs declaration, I'd written *Gift*, value *Nil*. In return for final payment, I now owed the Museo Borges the skull. I was going to miss it. I curved my hand flat across its dome, stroking it lightly from front to back. I felt no remorse: it wasn't Calvin. And if it *was* Borges, and it might as well have been him as anyone else, there were no children, and his wife he married late, and in unconvincing emotional circumstances. His mother, with whom he'd spent by far the greater and more intense part of his life, was long gone, and she wasn't anyway the type of woman to have cultivated an attachment to human remains. At the end, it was said, she'd pleaded with the maid to throw her out with the rubbish. And her last words, when they came: 'Fuck. Enough suffering.'

I picked up the skull by the face, cheekbones delicate between the pinch of my fingers. I lifted Borges level with my eyes, eye to eye, like a baby, fondly moving his toothless skull from side to side.

You're just like Calvin, Georgie, all head and no heart.

He was just like me. As a skull, he was just like anybody, not the great international writer wearing on his chest the ribbon of the Grand Cross of the Order of Bernardo O'Higgins, but the boy, aged twelve, shipped to Geneva as a cure for compulsive masturbation. His head was my head, all of us the same beneath the skin, with only one fact of importance to remember: *remember you will die*. So make the most of it, by living as many lives as you can. Or live one life as fully as possible. Do both. It amounts to the same thing.

I put him back down, and rested my chin on the table-top directly facing his. If nothing else, just for a moment, I AM HERE, like a tourist in the history of literature. In contact with the skull of Jorge Luis Borges, I can at least say, I AM HERE.

I am here.

I am.

I filled a shoebox with polystyrene chips, and, for added protection, considered some bubble-wrap. For the moment, I left the skull where it was, and went to check on Helena. She was lying in bed, reading a novel, almost fully recovered from whatever it was that had slammed her so hard in the back. As well as the bang on the side of her head, there was an almighty bruise between her shoulder-blades, which was still in the process of fading.

On that first Monday, immediately after the protest, we'd read on a website that the police had fired plastic bullets. There were witnesses, from in front of the Palace of Nations, who claimed they'd also fired real bullets, into the air. Not one newspaper carried either story.

Helena raised her hand without looking out from behind her book. Then that hand went back to fiddling with the chain of the locket, at about the point where it crossed the smooth ridge of her collarbone. I sat on the end of the bed, and watched a black bug move slowly along the spine of her book, so slowly and deliberately it was hard to imagine who it intended to bug. A tram went by. The man upstairs reset his samba record.

The flat was ours for as long as we liked (make yourselves at home, Moholy had said, invite your friends, your family, anyone you want), and for weeks now we'd slept in, ignoring the urgent e-mails and calls from the Appointments Committee and the Church Commissioners. Their letters we found useful as coasters, and for recording the predictions of the wise I-Ching.

Whenever we remembered to ask, the I-Ching suggested we should carry on regardless. Though I think even the I-Ching was secretly pleased, given the growing baby, that both of us had also found work. With her first week's wages, Helena bought me a watch, a Swiss one. She said it was to remind me of our baby (tick, tock, she said), but also because the public clock we saw most often, on the Norman-style tower of the Church of All Saints, had been deliberately stopped at the stroke of one. This was the time at which Moholy had first opened his exhibition of relics, one o'clock on Tuesday afternoon two weeks after the protest.

He wanted to get visitors into the right frame of mind, he said. It wasn't an experience bounded by time. At least not on the Swiss model. It wasn't so precisely engineered.

In the week after the demonstration, Moholy had moved his collection of relics out of the villa. As a form of rent for the flat, he'd consulted us freely on the labelling, and the layout of relics in the church. I suggested that anything connected with Byron ought not take the place of the altar, and that we avoid too prominent a display of those bones still supposedly buried.

The exhibition, a collection of ancient and modern relics,

was open every afternoon from Monday to Friday. It was a sensation, All Saints the perfect location for displaying bones at their glorious best. The church architecture allowed only certain sorts of movement, as if in this kind of space only certain ways of thinking were possible. It was exactly the slow, reflective approach that Moholy had always imagined, and the public loved it, even though, in truth, the relics were rarely as described on the labels. Richard Burton was standing in for many of the originals, but in a bravura performance the lost heir to Olivier tirelessly enacted audacious portrayals of the formerly great and good. Burton could be almost anybody, with an added roll of the r.

The visitors left enthused, often in high spirits, sometimes even thirsty.

Moholy publicly stated that all profits from the exhibition would be used for the promotion of good works. The relics were therefore fulfilling, without any question, their vaunted function for good. Moholy soon expanded the collection to include bones sourced from outside Switzerland, and the public kept on coming, avid for contact. They wanted to touch St Francis on the elbow, rub shoulders with the saints. They wanted to shake Herman Hesse by the hand. On Fridays, our most popular day, we filled the church with candles, and in the flicker of these most primitive units of light, the bones could say all or nothing.

Moholy stopped short of exhibiting the bones of Jesus. The public wasn't ready, not for that, not yet. He did keep at least one of the Jesus bones about his person at all times, ordering bespoke pockets sewn into the linings of his suits. He even slept with them, though sometimes the bones had the bed, and Moholy slept on the floor.

After his leadership success on the Sunday of the protest,

and then more consciously as days went by, and then weeks, Moholy deferred sending the Jesus bones to his man at the lab. There seemed little value in attempting to put a date on God, or the son of God. He was eternal. He didn't start or finish, and he couldn't be tested, at least not scientifically, not at the University lab. Moholy did have moments of doubt, as Jesus too must have had his doubts, but one thing or another would soon reassure him. His liking for canvas sandals, for example, or an unexpected taste for simple living.

Moholy invited United Nations supplicants of all kinds to use his villa in Geneva as a base, re-equipping the rooms once full of antiquities and relics as offices. His business profits, and now also the proceeds from the exhibition of relics, funded a revival of schemes recently abandoned by the Anglican church. He fed the homeless in Les Grottes, and rescued several Latvian hostesses from business bars in the Paquis. He was often featured in the local newspaper *Le Matin*, and also the less sceptical *Temps de Genève*.

'How does it feel?' a journalist asked.

'Fantastic. Like a whole new beginning.'

Moholy infuriated his fellow Genevans by consistently denouncing the city as the cradle of capitalism, a primitive belief system dependent on the most basic of human instincts (I want I want), a darkening of the truth about human nature which other beliefs attempted to enlighten. He used his growing profile to ridicule those who thought they had the answers, but at the same time he called upon the people of Geneva to rethink the way they lived their lives, and resist a system which was violent, unjust and evil.

And he should know. He'd been taking advantage of it for years.

He gathered followers around him, and gave some of them

special status, though they didn't always know what to do with it. He issued invitations, welcomes, challenges, summons. Geneva once again became a centre of pilgrimage for dissidents from around the world, and the city started to change in character, radicalising, probing at the Western world's epidemic discontent with self-interest. It was developing into a centre for genuine debate, which drew even the dinosaur United Nations into dialogue.

Moholy was disparaged by established protest-groups as bitterly as by the Genevan authorities. Who did he think he was? He took these attacks from both sides as evidence he must be doing something right. He was forceful, and convincing, and resigned to the probability that before too long something dreadful was likely to happen to him.

Occasionally, he almost had me persuaded. Maybe the bones, somehow, I don't know how, contained some tiny grain of Jesus. There were evenings, after we'd closed up the exhibition, when Moholy would sit rocking at the organ, his euphoria let loose. That was when I'd tell myself that of course he wasn't Jesus: he was having far too much fun. At top volume, he was a madman wanting to save the world, setting the swell and pedal to Trumpet and Bombard, and the fifty-six-note Great to Vox Humana.

I did sometimes wonder why I didn't tell him. But I wasn't all bad, or I hadn't the courage, I don't remember which. I convinced myself that the strength of his will to believe was in itself evidence of some divine presence. It was a miracle that the madness of Joseph Moholy could be channelled, through the example of Jesus, into wanting to do some good.

So it wasn't exactly the second coming, but Geneva at this time did often feel like the beating heart of a second Reformation, home to a fresh outbreak of goodness. Just like the first time round, everyone was a star, everyone's story equally important.

I did my bit. I wrote down everything that had happened. At the Church of All Saints, I sold tickets and was the English-speaking guide on guided tours. As a reward, on Sundays, Moholy gave me the freedom of the building. On Sundays, he said, I could do what I liked. I could clear away the relics. I could wear my dad's red chasuble. I could even preach.

I *always* preached.

Often starting with the text 1 Corinthians xv, *By the Grace of God I am what I am*. I was a pope in my own parish, with a vision of spiritual and personal freedom, spiced with the occasional experimental sermon. The Sri Lankans came, and we prayed for cricketers everywhere, though mostly in Sri Lanka. The church committee came, and other ex-English regulars, and even some stragglers from the protest. I brought in some extra chairs.

Between us, we explored the spiritual crisis in contemporary society, one of the few features of any society which was always contemporary. I then proselytised for Moholy's causes, a little sheepishly at first, but gradually with more boldness, proposing that the doorway to the fullness of life was the death of the self.

Mrs Meier and Mr Oti would look quizzical in the front row, sometimes frowning and shaking their heads to keep me honest. They convinced me that the Church hadn't slipped far enough from the spindle of public life to be a credible focus for a reforming counter-culture. However, in other ways they were always surprising me. As a congregation, they decided that All Saints on Sunday was now a non-conformist english church, without capitals. Its new creed rejected the belief that all God asked in return for the outrageous privilege of being born English (or close to it) was apathy, or embarrassment and cake-bakes. The middle class in the developed world at the beginning of the twenty-first century were chosen: we were lucky, and someone had to take that seriously.

The Church of England disowned us, but we'd expected that. The Anglican liturgy and creed, its word and sacrament, its conformity and sets of regulations, had none of them eased our human quest to recover Jesus. We therefore revenged ourselves on Anglicans everywhere by always remembering to pray for them.

And then I would preach, warnings mostly, against the defeatism of ever thinking the moment had come when you knew pretty much who you were, and all you were going to know. As if neither more living nor more reading would greatly alter the self. I was an advocate of the example of others. I gave thanks and praise for our identity with our fellow man, and commended change, and flickering with being. Be born again, I said, not just once, but again and again and again.

Don't, I said, just don't, don't ever just be yourself.

During the week, on those evenings we weren't necessarily best as ourselves, Helena and I would sometimes borrow relics from the exhibition. It was like paper–scissors–stone, depending on who each of us chose. There were red-hot connections (Byron and Greta Garbo) and icy stand-offs (St Francis and Evita). There were also some unexpected successes (Florence Nightingale and David Niven).

'I still don't understand it,' Helena said. We were lying in bed, at the end of another afternoon at the exhibition. We hadn't brought anyone back, but Borges's skull was still in the kitchen. I was reluctant to send it until certain the story had reached its end. It was getting dark outside, and Helena straightened a bare arm at the grey ceiling, closing one eye and sighting the dull lampshade in the V between her thumb and forefinger. 'It's not Jesus.'

'I know that.'

'We *know* it's not Jesus.'

At that moment, watching the spread of Helena's fingers between me and the ceiling, I was choosing to believe that we both went back before the creation, that in some form we'd always existed, part and particle of God, specks, sparks of God, connected to everything and everyone. I turned on to my side, and put my hand on her growing belly, and wondered if our baby would find me out.

'Moholy's Jesus is a mix and match,' Helena said. 'Just a muddle of bones cobbled together from his own collection. So what's going on? Why is he pretending to be Jesus?'

I flopped on to my back. Since the last time we'd talked about this, I'd thought of another solution. 'It could still be the bones,' I said. 'No, listen. Even if they never belonged to Jesus, Moholy could still be under the influence of the bones. Only the influence isn't Jesus.'

'But they're a mixture.'

'Right. They're a jumble of different people. But maybe the co-operative of bones, all working together, is more powerful than the sum of its parts. They're acting as Moholy's own personal communion of saints, and they make things possible for him just like mine did for me. You have yours, too, probably.'

'My what?'

'Your heroes. The people you'd like to emulate, even if you don't always admit to it. That's your communion of saints. Along with your family, who you can't escape, and your own fragment of uniqueness, that's what makes you what you are.'

'Not convinced,' Helena said. She picked up my hand and

put it back on her belly, covering it with both of her own. 'Try the other option, which is much more likely. Relics, holy or secular, singular or mixed up, have no power whatsoever to influence behaviour. They're inanimate. They're just things, old bones.'

'Visible, though. Touchable. They can act as reminders, meaning we don't have to learn everything in person.'

'You know what I mean.'

'They offer something to aim at, and then the big decision becomes simply who to choose. That's what Jesus is for, in case you were wondering.'

Helena reached up both her arms, hands flat facing the ceiling. I copied her. Between us, in our uncertain future, we had an outside chance of catching the ceiling when it fell. I hoped Helena was happy. In her view of the world, love, by definition, worked out. It was re-righting. If it was love, it couldn't be too much what she didn't want it to be. Otherwise it wouldn't be love.

In a joint decision, made by Helena, we'd decided to stay in Geneva. I'd wanted to postpone anything definite until I was sure of myself, but she said she wasn't going through that again. Since then, I'd been waiting to be tempted by the urgent appeal of a clean and sudden break. It hadn't happened, or at least, not very often. As for my worldly ambition, I could accept that the happiness I was suffering at Helena's hands might set me back by several years.

Helena rolled over towards me, her hands flat beneath her cheek.

'How often d'you think about Rifka?'

'All the time.'

'Did you see her postcard?'

She was in the Sinai. She'd gone back to visit her parents,

and to clear her head by camping in the hills. It wasn't a vacation, she said, and she couldn't say how long she'd be gone. She did, though, intend to come back. And that was a promise.

'Do you ever think what I sometimes think?'

'About what?'

'You know. Rifka.'

'I try not to.'

'What if Rifka was first to the prize?' Helena asked. 'Moholy was right all along, and Jesus was buried in Calvin's grave. Only Rifka worked it out for herself, before Moholy did, and she got there first. She was the one who found Jesus. Do you ever think that?'

'Rifka was fairly strange. I don't think Jesus would have smashed up Calvin with a digger.'

'I think he might well have done.'

'Don't,' I said. 'I don't want to think about that.'

I rolled off the bed and went back to the kitchen to parcel up Borges. I sat down at the table, but still I felt hesitant, delaying the packing of the skull by popping rows of bubble-wrap. Then I put down the plastic, and picked up the head-bone. I held Jorge Luis Borges firmly in both hands, and pressed his forehead hard against mine. I closed my eyes and stood up, his head against my head. The skull was cold. I moved it slowly side to side, and gradually it grew warmer. Write it down. Rolling the head-bone side to side, up and around, maintaining head to head contact at all times. And in my head, I think deep inside my head, writing. Keep writing it down. So that perhaps one day, yes one day, if you carry on regardless, you shall hear the word of the lord.

Acknowledgements

The K Blundell Trust, for welcome financial assistance while writing this book, and the Hawthornden Foundation for a productive retreat.

Tim Beard, Tom Guest, and James Russell, all of whom I should have thanked earlier and more often.

Stuart Williams and Zoe Waldie, for knowing what's what.

And Laurence, yet again, for her patience.